the FBI. [...] her suspense to feature strong psychological twists and a
from the University of [...] taken her into the minds
literature. She's a member of [...] ations and onto
Writers and Romance Writers of America. Visit Elizabeth graduated English
at www.elizabethheiter.com

Former naval intelligence officer and US Naval
Academy graduate **Geri Krotow** draws inspiration
from the global situations she's experienced. Geri loves
to hear from her readers. You can email her via her
website and blog, gerikrotow.com

Discover more at millsandboon.co.uk

K-9 COLD CASE

ELIZABETH HEITER

COLTON BULLSEYE

GERI KROTOW

MILLS & BOON

First Published in Great Britain 2021
by Mills & Boon, an imprint of HarperCollins*Publishers* Ltd
1 London Bridge Street, London, SE1 9GF

www.harpercollins.co.uk

HarperCollins*Publishers*
1st Floor, Watermarque Building,
Ringsend Road, Dublin 4, Ireland

K-9 Cold Case © 2021 Elizabeth Heiter
Colton Bullseye © 2021 Harlequin Books S.A.

Special thanks and acknowledgement are given to Geri Krotow for her contribution to *The Coltons of Grave Gulch* series.

ISBN: 978-0-263-28331-0

0321

MIX
Paper from
responsible sources
FSC™ C007454

This book is produced from independently certified FSC™ paper to ensure responsible forest management.

For more information visit: www.harpercollins.co.uk/green

Printed and bound in Spain
by CPI, Barcelona

K-9 COLD CASE

ELIZABETH HEITER

This book is for my husband, Andrew,
who gives me my own HEA every single day.

A special thanks to everyone at Mills & Boon for
helping me bring my K-9 Alaska series to life,
especially my editor, Denise Zaza, assistant editor
Connolly Bottum for managing all the details and
publicist Lisa Wray for sharing the stories with bloggers
and reviewers. My sister, Caroline Heiter, brought her
beta reading magic to this book, and my husband,
Andrew Gulli, kept me fed and working! A special
shout-out to my #BatSignal writer pals, especially
Tyler Anne Snell, Nichole Severn, Regan Black, Louise
Dawn and Janie Crouch, who brought motivation and
inspiration during virtual writing sessions.

Chapter One

You have to be the calm in their chaos.

Jax Diallo repeated the mantra in his head, the words he always reminded himself of when he was sent to the scene of a tragedy. Being an FBI Victim Specialist wasn't for the faint of heart.

As the FBI vehicle he was riding in slammed to a stop, Jax closed his eyes for a few seconds, tried to center himself. Tried to prepare to walk into the aftermath of a bomb.

"Let's go!" one of the Special Agents said, hopping out of the vehicle with his partner, two Evidence Response Technicians on their heels.

With the doors open, the bitter Alaskan wind penetrated the vehicle. So did the unnatural quiet of nature, as if all the animals had taken off. The silence was punctuated by staccato bursts of sobbing, from victims or family members still on the scene. Or maybe a first responder or law-enforcement officer who'd never seen anything like this.

In the distance a phone rang and rang, before going silent and then starting up again. A friend or family member searching for a loved one, desperately hoping for an answer to a call that would never be picked up.

"You ready, Patches?" Jax asked quietly.

His Labrador retriever stared up at him steadily, the soft brown eyes that always reassured victims also working their magic on Jax. She'd transitioned fast from a scared, abandoned puppy into one of the FBI's best therapy dogs. Right now she could read his mood as well as any victim's she'd been sent to help.

He gave her a reassuring pet, then climbed out of the SUV. Twenty feet ahead the beautiful greenery of a park was littered with the twisted metal skeleton of what had probably once been a park bench. Pieces of metal had blown into the street, and were still smoldering. Directly beside the park, a small freestanding building—maybe a bathroom—had collapsed, the front wall gaping open. Crumbled concrete, support beams and insulation spilled out of it. Around the edges of the park, one tree was pierced with a metal fragment, like a spear. Others were singed black and missing huge limbs.

As Jax got closer, he saw the detritus from first responders: abandoned needle covers, wrappers and blood-soaked gauze. The concrete walkway was stained a deep red.

The scent still lingered, too, burned metal and charred trees, and something worse underneath. A scent Jax recognized from too many other crime scenes.

The bomb had gone off just over an hour ago in the sleepy town of Luna, Alaska, on an otherwise peaceful Saturday morning. When it happened, Jax had been four hundred miles away, sipping his morning coffee on his back deck, with Patches asleep at his feet. Then his FBI phone had gone off and he'd grabbed his go bag and raced to the tiny nearby airfield, where a jumper plane was waiting.

The briefing on the plane had been short and information-light. A single bomb had detonated. At least six were dead and thirteen more injured. Right now the tiny Luna Police Department had no suspects, no obvious motive and no idea whether to expect more bombs.

Jax looked around the small park, with butterfly-shaped benches around the edges and a couple of trails leading into the woods. It wasn't an obvious spot to set off a bomb. There'd been no events here, except for an impromptu soccer game. All locals, no news coverage. If the bomber had a specific target, the park seemed like an odd place to go after them, because a bomb here was too likely to miss that person and take out others. If he hadn't been targeting a specific person, it still seemed like a strange choice, without the volume of spectators that mission-oriented bombers favored.

Not your job, Jax reminded himself. The agents would search for the perpetrator. He needed to help the victims and their families.

Kneeling down, he slipped special shoes onto Patches's feet that would protect her from bomb fragments and other sharp items in the rubble. Ideally, they'd stay out of the blast zone entirely, but that wasn't always possible. Then he stood, holding his arm out straight, directing her toward the park. "Come on, Patches."

She followed his direction, walking past the gawkers on the outskirts of the scene. She headed straight toward the woman sitting alone on one of the intact benches, with a vacant gaze and blood smearing her sweatshirt. When Patches reached the woman, she sat next to her, and the woman— girl, really, Jax decided as he reached her—seemed to refocus. She reached out a shaky hand to pet Patches, who scooted closer.

Ignoring the chaos behind him as the FBI agents and evidence specialists coordinated with Luna police, Jax knelt in front of the girl. He pegged her at nineteen. The shock in her eyes suggested she still hadn't processed what had happened. The grass stains on the knees of her pants suggested she might have been part of the soccer game. Or maybe she'd skidded to the ground from the force of the blast or in desperation to help someone she loved. There were a couple of bandages visible on her arms where she'd rolled up her sleeves, but nothing that would have caused the amount of blood on her shirt.

"I'm Jax Diallo," he said softly, not wanting to startle her. "I'm a Victim Specialist with the FBI."

Her gaze skipped to his, then back to Patches. She pet his dog faster, and Patches moved even closer, putting her head on the arm of the bench and making the girl smile.

"What can I do for you?" Jax asked. "Is there someone I can call? Do you need to get to the hospital to see someone?" He hoped the person whose blood coated her shirt wasn't in the morgue.

She glanced at him again, surprise and wariness in her eyes. "You're not going to ask me about what happened?"

"We can talk about that, too, if you want. I'm here for you. So is Patches."

Her gaze darted to his dog, at the mix of brown and black that had earned her the name, and smiled briefly.

"What's your name?"

"Akna." Her voice was croaky, quiet enough that he had to lean forward to make it out.

She'd inhaled smoke when the bomb went off. Or the blast was still impeding her ability to tell how loud she was speaking, even an hour later. Probably both.

"Akna, I'm a Victim Specialist. It's my job to help you and anyone else who needs me today or in the future. Right now that means getting you any resources you might want, or helping you contact someone."

She stared back at him, her gaze still slightly unfocused. But as she pet Patches, the fear and confusion on her face slowly started to fade.

Most people had no idea his job existed. But he was the lifeline between victims and their families and the Special Agents, who often didn't have the time or know-how to manage victims' many needs. Part of his role was to help victims navigate the criminal justice process, making it more likely they'd find the perpetrator and put that person behind bars. But the other part was simply helping victims get the resources they needed to move on with their lives.

"Akna, were you here alone?"

"Yeah." She shook her head. "No. Sort of."

"You were here for the soccer game?" he guessed.

"Yeah. We've got an online community board. Someone wanted to play." She shrugged, a fast jerk of her shoulders. "It was a nice day. I wanted some exercise." A strangled sob broke free. "How could this happen?"

"Is there someone you want me to call? To let them know you're okay? Or to pick you up?"

"I helped carry her over there," Akna said, gesturing vaguely toward the edge of the park. "I saw a couple of the players trying to lift her, carry her away from the rubble." Her voice picked up speed, picked up volume. "She was right by the building and big pieces of it fell on her. We thought it would be better. But—"

"She was a friend of yours?" Jax asked, keeping his voice calm, letting Patches do her own work as Akna continued to pet her, probably not even aware she was doing it.

Akna shook her head. "I didn't really know her. But she was on my team." Her eyes met Jax's and instantly filled with tears. "I think she was dead before we carried her over there."

"I'm sorry, Akna."

"Who would do this?"

"We don't know yet. But we're going to find out."

"We were just playing the game. I was running down the field, heading for the goal—it was supposed to be those trees." She pointed, her hand shaking uncontrollably. "No one thought to bring a net. And then...and then, there was this huge *boom*. It was so loud I could *feel* it. I don't remember falling, but then I was on the ground and people were screaming and then..." She sucked in a violent breath.

"Akna, you're okay," Jax said softly, in the same even tone he'd used with hundreds of victims. "You're okay. It's over."

"Akna!"

Akna leaped to her feet, making Patches stand, too. The tears she'd been persistently blinking back suddenly spilled over as she whispered, "Mom."

Then a woman with the same dark hair, the same deep-set eyes, rushed over, enveloping her in a tight hug. "I heard about the bomb. And I couldn't get a hold of you. Your phone kept going straight to voice mail."

"It broke," Akna sobbed. "I fell on it and it broke. And then I was trying to help Jenny and—"

"It's okay, it's okay," her mom soothed, smoothing back her daughter's hair. "I'll take you home."

"Akna," Jax said, holding out his card. "You call me if I can help you, okay? Anything at all. Anytime."

She took the card with a shaky hand, nodded.

Akna's mom looked at him questioningly, even as her gaze skimmed over his coat, emblazoned with *FBI.* "You're investigating the bombing?"

"I'm a Victim Specialist, not an investigator. I'm here for your daughter. If she saw anything that could help the investigation, she can talk to me. Or if she wants information about the status of the case. Or if she wants help finding someone to talk to about what happened today. The same goes for you, ma'am."

Surprise registered on the woman's face as she glanced at the card in Akna's hand, then back at him.

Akna swiped the tears off her face with the sleeve of her bloody sweatshirt, then whispered, "Thanks, Jax." Then she gave his dog a shaky smile. "Bye, Patches."

Woof!

Her happy bark made a handful of Luna police officers glance their way.

Akna let out a surprised laugh, then she left, her arm looped around her mom's waist.

Jax pulled out a notebook and jotted down the details Akna had mentioned, before tucking it back into his FBI jacket. Then he raised his arm to gesture toward the other group of civilians gathered at the edge of the park. "Let's go, Patches."

She headed toward them without pause, used to her role of calming people.

As he followed, snippets of their conversation drifted toward him.

"Why would anyone set off a bomb here?"

"...nothing here, man!"

Right now Jax needed to focus on the victims' immediate needs, on information he could gather to help them later and on the details that might matter in the investigation. But he had a background in psychology and he'd never quite been able to turn off the analytical side of his brain that sorted through why a person did the things they did. It had helped him back in his therapist days. As an FBI employee, it sometimes made him clash with the investigating agents.

But right now he couldn't stop wondering: What had a bomber been doing in this small park?

Jax had been to the sites of several bombs since he'd joined the FBI. Usually, they fell into two categories: big spectacles meant to cause widespread panic, or small explosives meant to kill a certain person. This didn't seem like either one.

This crime scene was different from anything he'd experienced. Even though knowing the motivation behind a crime didn't necessarily make it less scary, for Jax, it made it easier to comprehend. And usually, easier to comprehend meant a starting place for him, for the victims, even for the Special Agents in their investigation.

He squinted at the destruction in this once-beautiful

place and dread settled in his gut. Was the bomber finished or was he just getting started?

BEING POLICE CHIEF in a remote Alaskan town was supposed to be quiet. It was supposed to be simple.

Today Keara Hernandez had spent the day reassuring scared citizens that they were safe in Desparre, that the explosion in the town next to them was under investigation. That she'd have more information over the next few days, that it would be solved soon. She hoped her reassurances were true. But she'd been unable to get through to her colleagues in the Luna PD all day.

So now, instead of going home to rest, she was on her way down the mountain that separated Desparre from Luna. Getting to Luna was a two-hour venture if you went around the base of the mountain. Trekking up and then down the mountain again took half the time. In winter that trip could be dangerous. Right now, with May a few days away and the snow melted except in the highest parts of the mountain, it was much easier. But Keara felt every minute of the drive.

Her throat was sore after talking to more citizens in a day than she usually did in a week in her town full of recluses. Her shoulder ached from one of her regular calls, close to her own house. A belligerent drunk who liked to scream at his wife. At least once a week Keara was out there, talking him down and occasionally tossing him in a cell. Today he'd taken a run at her and she'd had to cuff him, bring him in the hard way.

She wanted to soak it off in a tub, relax in her quiet house, set apart from her neighbors by a few miles. She wanted to continue to live in the fantasy that a small town like Desparre would never face the same types of threats a big city like Houston saw.

The thought of her hometown made her chest tighten

and Keara pushed it out of her mind, punched down on the gas. This was a fluke. She'd lived in Desparre for six years and although bar fights and domestic violence weren't unusual, big, complex cases were few and far between. Other than the kidnapping case that had given Desparre way more attention than it had ever wanted five years ago— and a rehash six months ago when one of the kidnappers reappeared—Desparre and its neighbor Luna were places people came to stay below the radar. Not to set off bombs.

The idea made her shudder as she navigated off the mountain and toward downtown Luna, toward the quaint little park where she'd come more than once over the past six years. The first time she'd seen it, she'd thought what a fun place it would have been to take kids. Which was ir- relevant for her, since that part of her life had ended be- fore it ever got started. But right now she prayed the park hadn't been hosting one of their toddler play groups when the bomb had exploded.

The news had reported six dead and at least thirteen in- jured, but they hadn't offered many more details. The hospi- tal was keeping media out and police weren't talking, other than to say they were contacting next of kin and working with the FBI to investigate. And typical of the people who chose to live in this remote Alaskan area, the residents weren't interested in their own fifteen minutes of fame.

It had been twelve hours since the bomb went off, but Keara parked down the street, not wanting to get in the way of investigators if any were still on scene. As she hur- ried toward the site on foot, she pulled up the collar on her lined raincoat, wishing she'd opted for something heavier. The temperatures were already dropping into the thirties, the sun casting an array of pinks and oranges across the sky as it settled behind the trees.

Her footsteps slowed as the park came into view and the sharp scent of smoke invaded her nostrils. The front of the building housing the public restrooms was blown out, a metal bench shredded to pieces, the once-green field charred black in places. But it was the bloodstain splotches on the ground, on the benches, even on the side of the building, that made her stomach flip-flop. Made memories rush forward that she ruthlessly pushed down.

The area was cordoned off, but she didn't see any evidence markers, suggesting all the obvious evidence had already been bagged up and taken to the lab. There was likely more searching to do. Bomb fragments could fly a long distance, into the woods behind the park or buried under the rubble of the building.

Keara scanned the park, her gaze moving quickly over the civilians on the outskirts of the scene. She was looking for an officer who would give her straight information about the status of the case. All she saw was one Luna officer she didn't know and another who didn't like anyone from Desparre PD after a debacle six months ago with one of her officers. She frowned, looking for friendlier faces, but she mostly saw FBI jackets, plus a handful of people covered from head to toe in white protective gear. Evidence technicians, probably more FBI. All of them flown up the four hundred plus miles from the FBI's Anchorage field office.

Movement off to her side caught her attention and then an adorable black-and-tan dog plopped down at her feet, staring up at her expectantly. Behind the dog was a man with dark curly hair, perfectly smooth light brown skin and hypnotizing dark brown eyes. He had more than half a foot on her five-foot-six-inch frame, was probably a few years older than her thirty-five years and he wore an FBI coat.

"That's Patches," he told her, in a smooth, deep voice that would have put her instantly at ease if it hadn't made awareness clench her stomach. "And I'm Jax."

He tilted his head, and she had the distinct feeling he was cataloging everything about her.

She stood a little taller, feeling self-conscious in her civilian clothes—comfortable jeans with a warm sweatshirt under her jacket, and a pair of heavy-duty boots that could kick in a door.

"Did you know one of the victims?" he asked as Patches nudged her hand with a wet nose.

Keara smiled at the dog, petting her head as she told Jax, "No. Well, I don't know. Maybe." She cleared her throat, held out her hand. "Keara Hernandez. I'm the police chief in Desparre." She gestured vaguely in the direction of the mountain. "We're Luna's neighbors."

His eyes narrowed slightly, assessing her without any of the visible surprise she was used to from Alaskans when they heard about Desparre's female police chief. Then his big hand closed around hers, warm and vaguely unsettling. "Jax Diallo. Victim Specialist for the FBI. Patches here is a therapy dog."

"Therapy?" She looked down at Patches, who stared back at her calmly. "I assumed she was a bomb-sniffing dog."

"Nope. Patches and I are here to help the victims."

"Well, maybe you can give me some details, as a professional courtesy." She showed him her badge, just in case he thought she was lying, but he barely glanced at it. "I've got to answer to my citizens tomorrow. They want to know if they're safe."

"I can't really answer that, Keara." He drew out the *e* in her name slightly, *Kee-ra*. It was almost Southern, and it made her flash back to another case, another man, another time in her life entirely.

She'd been a brand-new patrol officer, assigned to partner up with a man who would eventually become her husband. Juan had frowned at her that first day, and although he hadn't said anything, she'd seen it all over his face. He didn't like being assigned to work with a woman.

Keara glanced away from Jax, not wanting him to see the emotions that were hard to keep off her face whenever she thought about Juan. But when she redirected her gaze to the right, all she saw was that blood.

It was a dark smear across the concrete, nothing like the thick, pooled mess that had surrounded Juan when she'd found him behind their house seven years ago. His eyes had been open, glassy, his cheek already cold to her touch.

"Keara?"

She jerked at the feel of Jax's hand on her elbow, the concerned tone of his voice. Shaking off the memory, she forced her gaze back to the Victim Specialist. "Is there someone I can talk to about the case?"

"Not right now. But I'm here if you want to talk about—"

"Sorry. I've got to go." Keara gave Patches one last pat, then spun back the way she'd come, suddenly uncaring that she'd driven all this way and hadn't gotten any answers. Because right now what she needed most was to get out of here.

Away from the bloodstains and the bomb remnants. Away from the unexpected memories.

Hopefully, the FBI would do their job fast. Hopefully, the people of Luna would get the answers they deserved about the person responsible for this bomb, the closure that would help them move on with their lives.

Without it, they could try to move on. She'd tried damn hard. She'd left behind everyone in her life and moved across the country, given up the job she'd dreamed of as a detective to become the police chief in a sleepy little town where she might spend six months of the year snowed in.

But she'd never actually found the peace she'd desperately searched for, the peace she'd almost convinced herself she'd achieved. Not if the sight of one smeared bloodstain could bring it all rushing back like this.

She'd never found her own closure. Not with her husband's killer still out there somewhere.

Chapter Two

Desparre's police chief walked away from him at a pace that looked purposeful, rather than desperate, the stomp of her boots echoing behind her.

Jax stared after her, intrigued. Even dressed down, she looked like someone who was used to being in charge. The dark hair she'd pulled back into a severe bun highlighted the sharp lines of her face, the thick eyebrows and exaggerated Cupid's bow of her lips. She looked like she had Mediterranean heritage, with perhaps a hint of Irish. It was hard to downplay beauty like hers, but she was obviously trying, with little to no makeup. Probably an attempt to get people to take her seriously. Women in law enforcement were the minority; women in high-level law-enforcement jobs even more so.

She was young for a police chief, although a place like Desparre probably didn't get a lot of crime. It was the sort of town where people came to disappear. Usually, those people weren't dangerous. They were running from a tragedy in their lives or from someone who meant them harm. Hiding out in the vast Alaskan wilderness, in somewhere like Desparre, which rarely rated mention on a map, would be a good option.

Keara probably didn't see much crime of this scale. When a tiny town like Desparre—or Luna—faced a threat, they often didn't have the resources to handle it. Their police forces were small, too; their training often less than ideal.

But Alaska could be tough. With the constant threat of natural dangers, like blizzards or avalanches, frostbite or even wild animals, the people here learned to get tough, too, or get out, Jax had discovered.

Until six months ago Jax had lived in DC, working on the FBI's Rapid Deployment Team. Victim Specialists on that team worked a three-year term responding to mass casualties all over the country. When his time was up, Jax had been more than burnt out. Working as a private therapist for trauma victims had been intense in its own way, but it couldn't compare to the sheer volume of victims he could see in a single day, at a single site, with the FBI.

Moving to the Anchorage field office had felt like his chance to slow down. A chance to relax in Alaska's wild open spaces instead of DC's city center. He'd just finished training the puppy he'd found abandoned and scared, teaching her to work with victims. Coming to Alaska had felt like the right time to get her started as an official FBI dog.

He was the first Victim Specialist in the Anchorage office. Although they'd been unsure what to do with him initially, that had changed fast, putting him and Patches in high demand. Still, he hadn't been to any mass casualty events in Alaska until today.

Shaking off his exhaustion, Jax turned away from Keara Hernandez's retreating form as two agents jogged his way.

Ben Nez was a couple of years older than Jax's thirty-eight, with years of experience working in Alaska, since he'd spent most of his FBI career here—and before that, a good chunk of his life. His partner, Anderson Lync, was four years younger than Jax, and the office's designated "FNG." As Ben had explained it the first time Jax heard the term, Anderson was the "effing new guy." Because even though Anderson had been at Anchorage six months longer than Jax, they only gave agents the FNG designation, not mere Victim Specialists.

"We've got seven dead," Ben announced without preamble.

Anderson knelt down and pet Patches, probably as much to comfort himself as to be friendly. The younger agent looked worn out, his normally perfectly styled blond hair sticking up, exhaustion leaving half-moons under his eyes.

"Six died at the scene, one more at the hospital," Ben continued, speaking rapid-fire like he'd been mainlining coffee all day.

Or maybe after more than a decade with the Bureau, an agent just gained the ability to set aside the horror and exhaustion and be fueled simply by the desire to find those responsible. Whether it was getting numb after seeing a huge volume of tragedy or knowing from experience that pushing through was the only way to find answers, Jax wasn't sure.

"Twelve others are being treated in the hospital, and some are critical. Given the location choice…" Ben paused to gesture around them meaningfully, and Jax realized how serene this park must have been before the bomb. "We're probably looking at an intended target—or maybe targets—rather than someone trying to create fear or make some kind of statement. We'll need to get a lot deeper in this investigation to be sure, though. What have you heard from the victims, Jax?"

"Not much about a possible motive." Besides Akna and her mom, he'd spoken to a pair of locals who'd come by to see for themselves if it was really true, the parents of a victim who'd already been transported to the hospital and a handful of people who'd been near the park when the bomb exploded. Then he'd fielded calls from various family members asking for updates on the case's progress and collected as many details as he could about the victims so he could follow up with them personally. "So far all I'm hearing is shock. No mention of anyone with enemies. But right now my focus is getting them help."

"What about the soccer game?" Ben asked, not sounding surprised.

Normally, when Jax got called to a scene, he'd go with the investigators to interview victims, not do it himself. But often information came out when victims or family members were talking to Jax about details they didn't think were important or had forgotten to mention to the agents. Sometimes, it was one of those small details that led them to the perpetrator.

"It was posted on some kind of online community board." Jax repeated what Akna had told him. "Sounds pretty last-minute, but we can pull it up and check the time stamp."

"I already did," Anderson said, standing up, while Patches scooted over to Ben, and the veteran agent took his turn petting her.

What most agents didn't realize was that while the therapy dogs were there for the victims, they helped the investigators cope, too.

Anderson pulled out his phone and scrolled through notes, his lips moving silently until he finally said, "Eight a.m. About half an hour before the game started and an hour before the bomb went off."

"Not much time for someone to plant it if they were targeting one of the players," Ben mused. "Not to mention that not everyone who responded used their real names. Some of them are just screen names. Unfortunately, the guy who posted the idea about the game, Aiden DeMarco, died at the scene."

"But not all of the players were killed," Anderson said. "Maybe the bomber was going after one of the other people at the park. Or even someone who was supposed to be here, but left once they saw a game in progress."

Ben nodded slowly. "Or they'd been targeting one of the soccer players and they planted it quickly when they learned that person would be here this morning. That game drastically increased the number of people who were hurt or killed today."

"Was the bomb on a timer?" Jax asked. "Or did someone set it off remotely?"

"Looks like it was set off remotely," Ben replied. "Probably with a cell phone, but we'll know more after the lab techs get their hands on it. We sent it to the lab six hours ago. Hopefully, we'll have the answer tomorrow. In the meantime..." He stared meaningfully at Jax.

"You want me to come with you to the hospital? See if any of the victims saw anything?"

"The fresher it is in their minds, usually the better," Anderson said.

"No problem," Jax agreed, even though he knew that was only partially true. Sure, memories faded over time. But with trauma, the mind could block out pieces. Sometimes, those details only returned later.

He gave Patches an encouraging smile. "Want to go help some more people?"

Woof!

Ben jerked slightly at Patches's enthusiastic reply, but Anderson just smiled. "She handles this part of it better than any of us."

"Kind of," Jax replied, but Ben and Anderson were already heading toward the SUV.

The truth was, dogs were susceptible to depression from this kind of work, too. They needed breaks, just like people did. But there was no denying that Patches loved cheering people up. Right now she was staring at him expectantly, then glancing toward the SUV, knowing she had more work to do.

He smiled at her, then lifted his arm, directing it toward the vehicle. "Okay, Patches, let's go."

The hospital was going to be his next stop anyway. He ignored the growl of his stomach reminding him he hadn't eaten anything since the quick sandwich he'd grabbed four hours ago. He had hours left before his day would be over.

Hopefully, one of the victims at the hospital would have answers that would get them closer to the bomber. Because if Anderson was right and the intended target of the bomb hadn't been on scene, would the bomber try again?

AFTER SEVEN LONG years alone, the memories shouldn't have been so close to the surface.

Keara stared into the whiskey she'd ordered hours ago, but had barely touched. The amber liquid reflected back a distorted version of the hand under her chin, a hand that had once worn a thin gold band, no diamond to get in the way on the job.

She hadn't had such a vivid flashback to Juan's murder in years. The bomb scene was nothing like her husband's murder. The thick jagged slice across her husband's neck, the blood pooled underneath him, the crickets chirping happily in the background. Her scream echoing through the tiny yard, making a neighbor call the police, because she was too traumatized to move. Too shocked to do her own job because she'd known with a single look that he was already gone. And she'd never even suspected there was a threat.

When the investigation began, she'd been told repeatedly to stay out of it. It was her husband, but it wasn't her case. She'd understood that, believed in her fellow detectives, believed Juan would get justice. But a year later the case had gone cold, the detectives insisting they'd done all they could, that they'd loved him, too. In that moment she'd known she couldn't stay. Not with the Houston PD, not in the life she and Juan had built together. Not if she wanted to be able to move forward.

It's over, Keara reminded herself, squeezing the whiskey glass but not lifting it to her lips. She'd made her choice when she moved to Alaska. Let go or drown in it. Those had been her options six years ago and she'd picked *let go*.

At least she thought she had.

Except here she was, failing to do her job because of the past. Pushing the whiskey away from her, Keara glanced around the old-fashioned bar on the outskirts of Luna. Between the claustrophobic closeness of the booths jammed together and the heater turned up to battle the chill that slid underneath the ill-fitting door, the air was stuffy and beer-scented. She'd chosen it because she'd wanted to be alone in a room full of people, rather than truly alone in her vehicle and then her house.

Although it was nearly twice the size of tiny Desparre—in terms of population, if not geography—there weren't many options late at night in Luna. She'd hoped a quiet booth and a short glass of whiskey would calm her nerves. Instead, she'd choked on the only sip of whiskey she'd taken. And there was nothing quiet about this bar.

Since moving to Alaska, she'd become a loner. It was a trait many of her citizens shared, for myriad reasons. For her, it was partly because of her job. A chief of police didn't fraternize with colleagues or civilians too much. Especially not a female chief of police who was new to Alaska and wanted to be taken seriously.

The rest of it, of course, was Juan. Although people in Desparre usually let you keep your secrets—because they often had their own they didn't want to open up about—real friendship dictated honesty. After living here for six years, Keara still wasn't sure if she was ready for honesty.

Now she glanced around the bar, wondering if all the small decisions she'd made to isolate herself had brought her right back to where she'd started. Sinking into grief.

She needed to go home. But there was something vaguely calming about having people around her, people she didn't know, who mostly left her alone. The bar was closer to Luna's lone hotel than it was to downtown. She didn't recognize anyone, and the snippets of conversation that reached her said most of these people were outsiders.

There was a group of guys in jeans and T-shirts who'd been drinking since before she'd walked through the door and already hit on her more than once. A loner at the bar drinking soda water and eyeing the hard stuff. And a couple at the other end of the bar who'd jammed their stools as close together as possible while they flirted. She'd bet a week's pay that none of them had been in Alaska longer than a few days.

Still, they weren't immune to what was happening here. In between lewd jokes from the group of drinkers, the alcohol-tainted conversation beside her would shift to the bombing.

"I heard a couple more died in the hospital."

"No one else died, man. But I think one of them had to have a leg amputated because it was blown mostly off in the explosion."

"Someone was trying to kill one of those soccer players."

"Nah, this is terrorism. You'll see. They'll start hitting bigger parks next, take out more people."

Only the two men hunkered down near the door sharing a couple of pints looked like locals. One of them periodically patted his friend's shoulder awkwardly and glared at the out-of-towners. The guy getting the sympathy had red-rimmed eyes, ruddy cheeks and a knocked-over pile of shot glasses beside him.

She'd recognized the look as soon as she walked into

the bar and chosen a seat on the opposite end of the place. Against the wall, where she could see everyone, but she tried to avoid glancing their way. One of them had lost someone they loved tonight. Keara couldn't bear to hear about it.

She dragged her gaze away from him and tried to focus on what she needed to do next. It was after eleven, well past the time when the Luna Police Department shut down for the night. But after the bombing—even with the FBI on the case—maybe someone would still be there. She could stop by on her way home, hopefully get some real answers she could share with her officers, with her town.

Setting aside her whiskey, Keara stood. She wasn't ready to face the drive up and down the mountain, or the emptiness of her house that she knew would feel more lonely than usual tonight. But she was still the chief of police. And she had people who needed answers.

"Hey, at least there's only six dead," one of the guys at the rowdy table slurred. "Could have been way worse."

Before Keara could maneuver free of her booth, the big guy who'd lost someone he loved was up and screaming.

Then he was diving across the small bar, leading with fists and grief. His punch landed, sending the guy who'd spoken to the floor. Then the guy's friends jumped on his attacker, and suddenly, everyone seemed to be in the fray. Even the loner at the counter grabbed an abandoned beer bottle off the bar and chucked it. The way he swayed violently when he did it told her that although he'd been drinking soda water since she'd arrived, he'd imbibed plenty of alcohol beforehand.

Only the couple near the door leaped up and ran out of the bar, away from the fight.

The bartender reached under the counter and Keara knew what was coming. She tried to get ahead of it, holding up her badge and screaming, "Police. Stop!"

But the bartender was quick, yanking his shotgun up and over the top of the bar, racking it loudly.

Keara heard it and flinched, but no one else paid any attention, not even when the bartender yelled, "Stop it or I'll shoot!"

"Sir, put the shotgun away!" Keara yelled at him, but the bar had gotten louder.

One of the men in the group closest to her spotted her badge and yelled, "Cop!"

Then the group was shifting, a furious mob coming for her fast.

She backed up, trying to protect her weapon as she pulled out her mace and sprayed it across the group. The noxious fumes spilled back toward her, clogging her throat and making her eyes water.

The group kept coming, too drunk or unthinking.

Keara backed up another step, but then her back slammed into something protruding from the wall and there was nowhere left to go. The four men who'd been hitting on her were rushing her from one direction. The two men who'd been grieving got in the mix, too, still going for the drunken group.

She was about to get overrun by them all.

Chapter Three

Twelve hospital rooms, filled with pain and fear and disbelief. Twelve victims, trying to recover from burns and deep cuts and in one case, an amputation. Twelve families, furious and scared and feeling helpless.

Jax and Patches had visited them all this evening. Some as briefly as five minutes, when the victims or the family didn't have the energy or inclination to talk to the FBI. Others as long as half an hour, the longest the agents would allow since they wanted to talk to everyone before the night ended.

Jax glanced at the base of his bed back at his hotel, where Patches had the right idea. Her tongue lolled slightly out of her mouth, her feet periodically twitching in her sleep. As soon as they'd returned to the hotel, she'd hopped up into bed and fallen fast asleep.

He needed to do the same. But despite being emotionally worn out, he was still hungry, since he hadn't ever found time for dinner. Part of him was still amped up, feeling the pressure from all directions. A need to help the victims and families move forward. A need to help the investigators get information to find the person responsible.

Slipping quietly out of the hotel room, he slid on his coat and trudged down the stairs. The hotel didn't have its own restaurant, and as far as he could tell, the only thing nearby that was open was a bar. He didn't want a drink, but maybe they'd have food. At this point he'd settle for peanuts.

He zipped his coat up to his chin and huddled low in it. Springtime in Alaska was beautiful, but it wasn't warm.

On his way out, he waved to Ben and Anderson, who were still slumped in the lobby chairs, trading case notes.

"Where to?" Ben asked, raising an eyebrow when Jax answered, "Bar down the road."

Jax looked them over, in the same spot he'd left them after they'd returned from the hospital. "Did you two ever eat dinner?"

"Power bars," Anderson said. Without looking up from his phone, he tossed one to Jax. "I always travel with them."

"Thanks." The protein-heavy power bar was probably better than anything he'd get in the bar, and Jax hesitated, debating returning to his room. But he was too antsy to sleep and although he liked Ben and Anderson, he needed a break from the case. "See you later."

When he stepped through the door out into the frigid Alaskan air, Jax knew it was what he needed. A walk probably would have been better than the bar, but he didn't know the area and he didn't want to get lost or run into a wild animal. So instead, he walked quickly toward the log-cabin-style establishment. The walk was long enough to make his nose and ears sting from the cold, but not long enough to clear his head.

He heard it when he was fifteen feet away. Yelling and crashing sounds. Probably a fight, definitely too many people involved.

Then a couple holding hands darted out of the bar and ran toward him.

"What's happening?" he asked.

"People are mad and drinking," the woman said, only

pausing briefly as they continued past him, toward the hotel. "It turned into a big fight. I wouldn't go in there."

Yanking out his cell phone, he texted Ben and Anderson a message.

Bar fight. Call the Luna police? Or earn your community badges today...

A bar fight was a local PD problem, not the purview of the FBI. But the agents were close and Luna police had a lot to manage right now. Jax didn't know which option Ben and Anderson would choose. But he figured doubling up couldn't hurt. He'd just started to dial the Luna police chief directly when a female voice cut through the yelling. A voice he recognized, slightly husky and naturally commanding. But right now underlaid with definite panic.

Dropping his phone into his pocket, Jax raced inside.

Five angry and obviously drunk men were crowded near the side wall, some of them holding beer bottles aloft like weapons. All of them were yelling, most of it incoherent, but what Jax could make out were a mix of violent threats and juvenile insults. Two were facing off against each other, shifting back and forth, glowering.

A sixth was passed out half on a table, half on the floor, and looked like he needed stitches. A seventh stood near the bar, holding his own beer bottle and watching the spectacle with a wide grin. The bartender stood behind him, brandishing a shotgun but looking uncertain.

Where was Keara?

Jax strained to see, then realized. She was behind the pack of men, ordering them to back up. From the way his eyes started watering and his throat was suddenly on fire as he took one step farther inside and the door slammed shut behind him, he realized she'd sprayed them with mace. It seemed to have only made them angrier.

Fear tightened his chest, knowing she was trapped behind the angry group. Could he wade into them, give Keara a chance to slide free?

He rejected the idea immediately. There were too many of them, fueled by alcohol and fury, likely to take any physical contact as an invitation to resume fighting.

Still, he had to do something. The two who'd been circling each other had turned toward Keara, and from the way they shared a sudden look of agreement, they were about to rush her.

Jax wasn't armed. Even if he was, it probably wouldn't help, based on the bartender's worried shake of his head.

"I already called the police," the bartender yelled at him. "If I fire this now, it might go through those guys and hit the lady back there. She's in trouble."

Jax swore and looked around for something he could use as a weapon, even though he knew it was useless. What he needed was Ben and Anderson, a way to even the numbers.

Leaping on top of the bar, Jax bellowed, "FBI!"

As one, the group turned toward him, but they only lowered their fists and bottles for a split second. Then they were up again, and the group was turning back toward each other.

Faster than he would have thought possible, while the men were distracted, Keara slid along the wall, breaking free of the group. She had her pistol out and leveled at the man who seemed to be the primary instigator.

"I'm chief of police in Desparre!" she yelled. "And the man on the bar is with the FBI. Put the bottles down and back away right now!"

For a moment it seemed like it might work.

Then the big guy in front swayed a little and yelled back, "You can't get us all, bi—"

"People died today!" Jax cut him off as Keara took a slow step backward, closer to him.

They froze, their attention redirecting his way. "We're searching for a *bomber* right now! You really want to end up in jail for threatening a police chief?"

Two of the men shook their heads, set down their bottles and stepped away from the group, holding up their hands.

Two of the others hesitated, their bottles lowering slightly.

But the big guy in front flushed an even deeper, patchy red and announced, "You're not FBI! You're not even armed!"

A flash of movement below Jax caught his attention. Too fast for Jax to move out of the way, the loner who'd been watching with glee grabbed hold of his leg and yanked hard.

Jax flung out his arms, trying to brace himself, hoping his head wouldn't smack the top of the bar as he crashed downward, sliding awkwardly, painfully, off it. Broken glass sliced through his arms, and his back scraped the edge of the bar as his legs slammed into the bar stools, knocking them over.

Then he was on the ground, trying to catch his breath and focus through the pain in his head, and a bottle was crashing toward his face.

Knowing it wouldn't be fast enough, he tried to roll away.

The guy over him suddenly stiffened, his eyes going unnaturally wide. Then he toppled over, the bottle crashing down inches from Jax's face and luckily not shattering.

Behind him, Keara had her gun trained on the group who'd frozen again, and her other arm directed his way, wires extending from the Taser in her hand to the guy on the ground beside him, still stiff and moaning.

Then the door burst open and Ben and Anderson were there, weapons out, yelling, "FBI!"

As they rushed into the room, giving Keara an approving nod, Ben glanced down at him with a mix of concern and amusement.

"You've got to stop playing agent, Jax."

SHE'D GOTTEN LUCKY.

Although no officer was immune to the danger of being caught alone and outnumbered, at least in Houston, backup tended to be relatively close. You might get caught in a dangerous situation—and it wasn't uncommon—but you'd probably be in the thick of it with other officers. In Alaska, the danger was far less persistent. But you were way more likely to be caught alone. The distance it could take the closest officer to come to your aid could be deadly even if you held off the threat for a long time.

Keara had been reaching the end of that time when Jax had walked into the bar.

She glanced at him now, sitting across from her on a couch in the lobby of the hotel down the street from the bar. He was grimacing in a T-shirt, his bloodied sweater in a bundle next to him along with his coat, as one of the agents—a tall, lean blond guy who'd introduced himself as Anderson—wrapped his arms with gauze.

"There's no glass left behind," Anderson said. "I was SWAT for a while in DC, so I had to get some basic medical training, but you still might want to go back to the hospital. Most of these cuts will close up, but this one—" he pointed at the last, deepest cut he'd bandaged "—might scar unless you get it stitched."

"I'm fine," Jax said tightly.

"Yeah, I get it. I wouldn't want to go back there, either," Anderson said. "That was a rough evening, talking to all those victims. Especially the one who lost her leg, whose fiancé died in the blast. I don't know how—"

"You should have stayed outside," Ben cut his partner

off. "You keep forgetting—you're not an agent." He glanced at Keara, eyes narrowing as he studied her. "Was this all drunken, overemotional idiocy or did you hear anything we might want to know for our investigation?"

She didn't have to glance at Jax to feel his embarrassment, but the truth was, she'd needed him tonight. Law enforcement or not, his presence—and presence of mind—had definitely saved her from getting hurt. Maybe even from getting killed.

"Idiocy," she confirmed, trying not to cringe as she subtly probed her lower back with her fingers. Between the time she'd maced the group and Jax had arrived, she'd been shoved into the wall, right where some kind of decoration hung. The bruise ached with every quick movement.

"And grief," she added, remembering the man who'd burst into tears when Luna police arrived and cuffed the whole lot to escort them to cells. His younger sister had died in the explosion.

Her hand shook as she stopped pushing on the bruise and it wasn't all from pain. The bruise was nasty, but she didn't need medical care, just time to heal. It was also adrenaline, still pumping as if she hadn't left that bar. As if she hadn't gotten away from the crowd of men towering over her with bottles and fists and anger they were willing to redirect at the nearest available target. Especially one who'd just sprayed them all with mace.

With six years on the police force in a big city like Houston—five of them on patrol—Keara had faced plenty of dicey situations. Most of them with a partner at her back, but a few alone. Back then she'd lived with a different level of awareness at all times.

In Alaska, she'd gotten used to needing to be wary of the elements more often than the people. She should have positioned herself near the door. Should have ignored her emotional desire to avoid the grief-stricken man there and picked a spot near the exit. She still might have been overrun, but she probably could have gotten to a safe distance to pull her weapon sooner. Maybe stopped the brawl faster, without anyone getting hurt.

"So Keara," Ben said as Anderson finished patching up Jax, "you were at the scene a few hours ago."

When he stared at her assessingly, as if waiting for her to confirm what he already knew, she nodded.

"Did you notice anything unusual? Anyone hanging around who seemed off?"

Ben didn't need to clarify as all three of them stared at her, waiting for an answer.

At the scene of a bombing, in a small town full of people who liked their business to be their business, it would be easy to slip into the edges of a group. Pretend to be sympathizing. Pretend to be there out of safety concerns or empathy for neighbors, while actually reveling in your handiwork.

Police officers—especially someone like her, who'd spent years on patrol in a busy city—learned to spot the outliers. People who were trying to blend in, but were just a little too focused. On the woman alone, walking in front of them. Or the fire blazing in a building, origins unknown. Or the devastation of an attack, like a bombing.

Keara mentally reviewed the people she'd noticed at the edges of the scene, near the hastily assembled memorial made of candles and flowers and stuffed animals, or down the street, pointing and shaking their heads. Everyone had looked the way she'd felt. Shocked. Horrified. Like a veneer of safety had just been ripped away, revealing a vulnerability they'd never expected.

She shook her head. "I don't think so. I don't know everyone here. Not even close. But many of the people on scene I recognized at least vaguely. If the bomber was there, he's a good actor."

"Or she," Anderson put in.

Keara shrugged, acknowledging that truth, although as far as she knew, bombers were more likely to be male. Running murder investigations in Houston had told her that men liked to kill violently: strangulation, bullet wounds, stabbing. Women were less likely to murder in the first place, but more likely to use arson or poison. And they were more likely to kill a single person; men were significantly more likely to kill multiples or commit mass murders. Of course, those were generalizations. Bombings weren't something she'd ever investigated.

"What about this?" Ben asked, sounding like he already expected the answer to be negative. "This is a bomb fragment. Does the symbol on it look familiar? Does it mean anything to you?" He held out his phone, zoomed in so she could see the detail, the series of interconnecting loops.

Distantly, she felt Jax leap up and grab her arm as she swayed. She heard Anderson's surprised "You know it?"

But she couldn't focus enough to answer. The lobby around her spun in dizzying circles as her whole body seemed to catch fire and her lungs couldn't get enough oxygen.

She'd seen that symbol once before, seven years ago. On the wall at a murder scene in one of Juan's last investigations before he was killed.

Chapter Four

Could their bomber be connected to a case Keara's husband had investigated seven years ago?

Jax's heart thudded too hard as he watched Keara, her olive-toned skin too pale, a sudden tightness around her eyes and mouth. The knowledge that she was a widow surprised him, filled him with sadness for what she'd experienced, along with a tinge of jealousy. Ridiculous and inappropriate, but he was self-aware enough to recognize why. He'd been instantly intrigued by her, attracted to her. Seeing her in trouble in the bar, then seeing her in action, had only increased those feelings.

None of that mattered. Not when she was staring back at them, trying to get it together after she'd announced that her dead husband had investigated a case with the same symbol. Not when she might have the key to the investigation.

Ben and Anderson were staring at her, too. Ben's fingers tapped a frantic beat against his chair and Anderson was leaning toward her, hanging half out of his seat. But both of them were experienced enough not to rush her.

Finally, her fingers loosened the death grip they'd had on the couch since he'd helped her sit. "I haven't seen that symbol in seven years."

"Are you sure it's the same symbol?" Ben asked.

She held out her hand for his phone, then zoomed in and

stared at it a long moment. "I'm pretty sure. It might not be exact, but it's close enough to look connected."

"Tell us about this case," Anderson requested.

"It was a murder," she said and some of the intense energy radiating from Ben and Anderson instantly deflated.

Jax had been part of enough investigations—even though he was on the periphery—to know why. A murder was pretty different from a bombing.

"The victim, Celia Harris, was fairly well-known in Houston. She owned a popular chain of bakeries and was always volunteering her time to local charity events. The press picked up news of her murder fast, maybe because she had two young kids and was killed in a back alley in a bad part of town. Probably also because the murder was violent. That symbol was spray-painted on the wall behind her. I didn't work the case, but I know Juan and his partner suspected it was going to be the start of a series of killings."

"They thought it was a serial killer?" Ben asked. "Why?"

"None of the obvious suspects panned out. There were signs Celia had been abducted and probably not by someone she knew. They thought the symbol was a serial killer's signature."

Anderson scooted back in his seat, looking less anxious the more Keara spoke. "But…"

"But there were no more killings that matched. They never saw the symbol again. Well, Juan's partner didn't. Juan died a few weeks into the investigation."

Jax didn't ask the question he most wanted to know the answer to right now: What had happened to her husband?

Instead, he glanced from Ben to Anderson. He knew them well enough to recognize their waning interest. They didn't think this was connected. But the symbol was unusual, an odd series of interconnecting loops that he'd heard the agents say earlier didn't mean anything they could identify.

"Any idea what the symbol means?" Jax asked Keara.

She shrugged. "Juan and his partner thought it was the killer's own design."

"How sure were they that the killer actually drew the symbol? Couldn't it have been spray-painted before the murder happened?"

Keara shrugged, suddenly looking exhausted. "I didn't ask for particulars. I just knew they'd determined it was put there by the killer. You can contact the Houston PD for more details. Juan's partner is still there, as far as I know. I don't keep in close touch with the department, but I don't think the murder was ever solved."

Ben nodded and Anderson wrote down the contact information for Juan's partner, but Jax didn't need to ask to know it was low on their list of priorities. They'd follow up—they were both good agents—but despite the strange symbol, they didn't think it was connected. And he understood why. The symbol was too generic, the crimes too different. Besides, there were too many variables. They couldn't even be sure the murderer in Keara's husband's case had been the one to draw the symbol. Alleyways were often filled with random graffiti, especially in a big city like Houston.

Keara stood, flinching in a way that told him that he wasn't the only one who'd left that bar with injuries. The closed-off expression on her face said she wouldn't welcome him asking about it, so instead he asked, "Are you okay to drive home? Desparre isn't exactly close."

"Out here, it's about as close as you get," she replied, her chin tilting up just slightly. "Thanks for the help," she added, her gaze sweeping the three of them, lingering briefly on him before she headed for the door.

"The symbol is unusual," Jax said once she'd left the hotel and it was just him and the agents in the brightly lit lobby.

"It's not connected," Ben said, rubbing a hand across his eyes.

"I'll call the partner and follow up anyway," Anderson added, "but Ben is right. It's strange, but coincidences happen."

"I don't know—"

"Jax, you want to talk to her about this more? Be my guest," Ben said, glancing at his watch and standing. "But you know as well as we do that it's unlikely there's a solid link here. Yeah, the symbol is odd, but it's not particularly unique. And we can't even be sure the killer in her husband's case is the one who drew it. She said it was spray-painted on an alley wall. Could have been some random tagger practicing. Our symbol was literally on the bomb fragment. That's pretty different."

"Maybe, but—"

"An alley in downtown Houston at a murder site. And a bomb fragment in the middle of nowhere, Alaska. A single murder and a bombing that's already killed seven and injured at least twelve more. You've got the psychology background, so you tell me: How likely is it that a violent murderer turned into a bomber?"

"Not very," Jax agreed, trying not to be distracted by the way his arms stung, the way his back and legs and head throbbed. The two aspirin he'd gotten from the hotel desk hadn't done much to ease the pain.

From the type of murder Keara had described, the killer had wanted to get up close. He thrived on the brutality, on causing someone else to suffer, on watching that suffering up close and personal. He'd probably loved the attention, the big press coverage in a big city. A bomber was a different personality type. Someone who *didn't* want to be hands-on for the actual kill. Someone who wanted to see more destruction, but choosing a place so far off the map meant maybe he wasn't looking for the intensity of news coverage.

"Still…"

"What?" Anderson prompted when Jax went silent.

Jax's specialty was working with trauma victims, helping them reclaim control over their emotions and their lives. He'd spent time analyzing the motives behind the perpetrators, but only if it was in service of the survivors.

But the more time he'd spent working for the FBI, the more he'd realized that the specialty translated. And not just as a Victim Specialist, but also in providing real insight into the way the perpetrators thought.

He didn't know enough about the case Keara's husband had investigated to be able to say if it was connected or not. But something about it kept nudging his brain.

"The symbol was on the bomb fragment," Jax said. "That means it's important. But maybe the bomber didn't expect it to survive the blast. Maybe he drew it for himself."

"Maybe," Ben agreed.

"So maybe he never expected it to be connected to a seven-year-old murder."

"Is there any news on the Luna bombing?" Tate Emory, an officer she'd brought on to the Desparre PD just over five years ago, leaned his head into her office.

Tate was one of her most easygoing officers, with a calm under pressure none of her veterans had expected. Of course, they only knew Tate's cover story, believed he'd been a true rookie when he joined the force. But Keara knew he'd been a police officer before hiding away in this remote Alaskan town. Because she'd kept his secret, he was one of the only people here who knew anything about her past.

Still, she wasn't about to share the possible connection to one of her husband's cases. Not when the FBI had grown less and less interested the longer she'd spoken. Not when the light of day was bringing her own doubts.

Last night she'd been so certain. This morning, back at work in Desparre and fielding calls from concerned citizens about their neighboring town, she wondered if she was wrong.

It had been seven years since she'd seen that symbol. Yes, years on the force had enhanced her skills of observation and memory. But maybe it wasn't the same. Even she had to admit it didn't look like much beyond doodling. Or maybe both a murderer and a bomber had seen the same symbol somewhere and used it themselves.

"The FBI is managing the investigation." She told Tate what he'd surely already seen on the news. "I couldn't get anything useful out of them."

An image of Jax, crashing down from the top of that bar after he'd tried to help her, filled her mind. There was something compelling about him. And it was more than the tall, dark and handsome thing he had going for him, or the adorable dog who followed him around.

It was the eyes, she realized. The way they'd fixed on her, given her one hundred percent of his attention. A psychologist's trick, surely, but it had felt personal.

"They have no suspects?"

Keara shook off thoughts of Jax and focused on Tate. The officer was only a few years younger than her own thirty-five, but the way he carried himself made him seem like he'd seen a lot over those years.

"If they do, they didn't share the details with me." She thought about the exhaustion on the two agents' faces in the lobby of the Luna hotel last night, going over evidence after a full day at a bomb site. "I think they're struggling to figure out a motive."

"That was a big blast. Seems like it was someone who had experience making bombs," Tate said. "Then again, these days any criminal-minded sociopath can find a recipe to make a bomb on the internet."

Keara nodded, her gaze moving to the open door of her office. Resisting the urge to ask him if he'd dealt with bombings in his previous job, she said, "I got cards from several FBI agents and their Victim Specialist. I'll stay in contact."

"Sounds good."

As Tate turned back for the bullpen, Keara said, "Close the door behind you, please."

Once she was alone, she dialed a number she hadn't called since she'd moved to Alaska. For all she knew, he'd changed it. A small part of her—the part that really did want to leave the past behind her—hoped he had changed it.

"Fitz," he answered on the first ring, his voice a deep grumble created by years of smoking and drinking.

The familiar voice instantly took her back to the swampy summers in Houston, to responding to a dangerous call one last time with Juan before he took the promotion to detective and partnered up with veteran Leroy Fitzgerald. Leaving her to work with a rookie for a year, before she made the jump to detective herself. But by then, they were engaged and rules prohibited them from working together anymore.

"You talk or I hang up," Fitz snapped.

"It's Keara Hernandez," she blurted, relieved when her voice sounded only slightly strained.

She and Fitz had never gotten along. She'd tolerated him because he was Juan's partner and a partner's trust on the force could be the difference between life and death. He'd tolerated her for the same reason.

"Keara."

His voice softened in a way she'd only come to know after Juan had died, when Fitz had been sidelined like her, and two other detectives were assigned to investigate. Unlike her, Fitz had been allowed to stay close to the investigation, even tag along at the end.

"How's Alaska?"

His voice was neutral, but she'd always suspected he was glad when she left Houston. When she stopped hassling him and everyone else for details on her husband's case. When she'd stopped making all of them feel guilty for failing, no matter how hard they'd tried. She'd been the final holdout, the last person to accept the case would never be solved.

If the sudden pain burning its way up her chest was any indication, she'd never truly accepted it. She'd only run from it.

"Peaceful, mostly." She got right to business, not wanting to hear about life on the force she'd left behind—assuming he was still on the force. "I'm calling because there's a case up here with a symbol that I think matches the one from that murder you and Juan caught at the end. The one you thought was a serial?" She was purposely vague about the Alaskan case, phrasing it in a way that wouldn't be lying if she had to admit it wasn't her case at all, but hopefully not inviting questions.

"Really?" He sounded surprised, but only vaguely interested. "Another murder?"

"Not exactly. Could you fax me the details? I want to see if my memory is as good as I think it is. See if the symbol really is the same."

There was a pause long enough to make Keara silently swear, before Fitz asked slowly, "I'm guessing since you called me on my personal line that this is an unofficial request?"

"Yes."

"Is this about Juan?"

The pain that had been creeping up her chest clamped down hard. "Why? What do you mean?"

"Nothing. I just... I figured if I ever heard from you again, it would be because you'd finally started investigating Juan's death on your own." He let out a forced laugh. "You always were dogged. Kind of a rule-breaker."

It was a much more polite version of what she'd overheard some of her colleagues in Texas saying about her when she'd been a patrol officer, even after she'd become a detective. They were traits she'd tried hard to tame when she'd come to Alaska.

Follow the rules, for the most part. Definitely not date anyone within her ranks. She'd barely befriended them, determined to keep her distance. Not just to maintain her authority, but also to protect herself. Being a police officer was a dangerous profession, even in a quiet little town like Desparre. The officers here had become her responsibility and she took that seriously. If someone died on her watch, she needed to be able to stay removed enough to do what had to be done, to keep the rest of the team going.

Of course it was important to be persistent, to chase down the truth no matter what. But there was also value in learning when to let go.

It was something she thought she'd succeeded in.

"Is there some reason to think Celia Harris's murder was connected to Juan's death?" she asked tightly. If there was, they'd all kept it from her back then.

"No," Fitz replied.

"Are you sure?" she demanded, suddenly certain he was keeping something from her.

"Yeah, I'm sure. As sure as I can be. I mean, we don't know who the hell took Juan out. Just because Juan's case went cold six years ago doesn't mean we all gave up on it."

It was only the hurt underneath the anger in Fitz's voice that kept Keara from snapping at him. When the case had officially gone cold, she'd done the only thing she could do to survive it. She'd tried to shut down that part of her life entirely, remove herself from any reminders that she'd ever been married, that she'd ever faced such a loss. And she'd done it in spectacular fashion, by running as far away as she could.

"Have you found anything?" she demanded, anger seeping into her own voice. Whatever Fitz thought of her decision to leave Houston, she was still Juan's wife. She still deserved answers.

"No."

In that single word, she heard all of the defeat she'd felt six years ago, when the chief had officially called off the active investigation, told the detectives on Juan's case they had to move on.

Closing her eyes, Keara let out a long breath, trying to regain her composure. "Tell me about Celia Harris's murder, then. Please. You never found any likely suspects, did you?"

"Well…"

Her eyes popped back open. "Who?"

"Your husband went to talk to someone whose car was near the scene of the murder. A hospital orderly with some minor criminal history named Rodney Brown."

A mix of dread and anger made her pulse speed up. "You remember the name all these years later? Why?"

"Juan talked to the guy on kind of a long-shot lead. I didn't go with him. He said it didn't look like anything, but that Rodney kept insisting the whole thing was a mistake. That he hadn't taken his car out at all. It struck Juan as a little weird, but he thought maybe Rodney was just nervous about being interviewed by a police officer. I wouldn't have thought anything of it, either, except Rodney disappeared a few weeks later."

Keara let the timeline sink in and her anger intensified. "A few weeks later. So you're telling me this guy disappeared right after Juan was killed?"

"We looked into it," Fitz insisted. "We couldn't find any evidence that he was involved in Juan's murder."

"You couldn't find any because it didn't look like he'd done it or because he disappeared and you couldn't find him?"

When Fitz didn't immediately respond, Keara jumped to

her feet. Through the glass walls of her office, she saw some of her officers staring at her with curiosity and concern.

She turned her back on them, knowing there was no way she could hide the horror she felt. "You think it was him."

"I did," Fitz said quietly. "But no one else agreed, Keara. And seven years later I wonder if I was just reaching for anything. For anyone I could blame. He was my partner. It eats me up every day that we couldn't solve his murder."

"Why the hell didn't you tell me?"

"What would you have done?"

Investigated on her own. She would have done whatever it took to find Rodney Brown and figure out if he'd killed her husband.

"That's why I didn't tell you," Fitz said, without her saying a word. "Because we chased that lead as far as we could. It was a dead end. And..." He let out a heavy sigh. "You deserved to move on. Juan would have wanted that."

Keara grit her teeth, trying to hold back the tears suddenly threatening. "Just send me the file, Fitz."

She hung up before he could say anything else, then planted her hands on her credenza for stability. Seven years. Someone who might have killed Juan had had seven long years to run. Seven long years for the trail to go cold.

Was it possible he'd shown up here, stepped up the volume of his kills by becoming a bomber?

Chapter Five

"Does this symbol look familiar to you?" Jax held up the digitally enhanced image that had been found on a bomb fragment.

Gabi Sinclair winced as she hauled herself up higher against the headboard of the hospital bed. Her sheet slid downward and she immediately hiked it up, avoiding looking at the leg that had been amputated below the knee yesterday. Her light brown skin was tinged with an ashy gray, her eyes bloodshot.

When Jax had met her last night, she hadn't been able to stop crying about the fiancé who'd died in the blast. Today she was all gritted teeth and desperate determination, wanting any information she could get about the investigation. A mix of numbness and anger that would only last so long before the grief bled through again.

Hopefully, when that happened, he'd be able to help her.

She stared at the symbol intently for a long minute, her free hand dropping down beside the bed to pet Patches, who'd been patiently waiting. Finally, she shook her head. "I don't know it. What is it?"

From slightly behind him, Jax sensed Ben and Anderson's disappointment, heard their suit coats slumping against the rough hospital wall. They'd taken the lead today, but asked him along to make the victims and their families feel more comfortable. The more rooms they visited, the more questions Jax asked. Technically, it was the agents' job to ask about the symbol, but for some of the victims, he suspected it would be easier to talk to him.

Gabi was their final hospital visit. None of the victims they'd spoken to had recognized the symbol.

"This was drawn on one of the bomb fragments," Anderson spoke up, stepping forward in the tight space. "We don't know what it means. It might be nothing. But we're checking everything."

Gabi frowned slightly, directing her gaze at Patches, who scooted closer to the bed and made the tiniest smile quiver at the corner of Gabi's lips.

"When we have some answers, we'll tell you what we can," Jax said, not wanting to overpromise what he might not be able to deliver, but also wanting to help start the healing process. If Gabi felt like she was cut off from real information, it would only increase the helplessness she felt.

She nodded at him, her hand stalling against Patches's head, her brow furrowed like she was trying to puzzle it out, too.

Despite research done by Ben and Anderson—and some curiosity searching Jax had done himself on publicly available sites—none of them understood it. They'd found symbols that were similar, but nothing close enough and so far, nothing else tied to a crime like this. If the bomber had been trying to send a message with the symbol, it appeared to be one only he understood.

Maybe the case Keara's husband had investigated would provide the break they needed. When Jax had pressed him on it that morning, Anderson said he was waiting for a call back from the Houston detective.

"Is there anything else you can remember from yesterday morning?" Ben asked, stepping up next to Jax, crowding him just slightly, like he wanted Jax to step back.

Gabi glanced from him to Ben, then shook her head. "Not really. Carter and I were just going for a walk." Her voice trembled on her fiancé's name, then she cleared her throat and kept going. "We'd stopped to sit on the bench for a few minutes when it happened."

"And you didn't notice anyone behaving strangely?" Ben asked. "No one leaving the park or staring at it from a distance?"

The FBI had gotten news back from the lab that morning that the bomb had been set off remotely. That made it more likely the bomber had been nearby, watching for the exact moment he wanted it to detonate.

Gabi shook her head quickly, but she'd answered these questions before.

"Thanks, Gabi," Jax said. "I know this isn't easy. But if you think of anything—even if you're not sure it matters—you can call any of us. And if you need to talk, I'm just a phone call away, day or night. You know Patches is always excited to come and see you."

Beside her bed, Patches let out an affirmative *woof!*

Gabi startled at the sudden noise, then gave his dog a tiny smile.

Anderson shot him a look, but Jax ignored it. Technically, telling a victim they could call in the middle of the night was dangerous territory. He'd known Victim Specialists who'd fallen into roles halfway between personal therapist and best friend by being too available. But he worried more about not helping enough than being overwhelmed by a victim's needs.

As Jax and Patches started to follow the agents out of the room, Gabi's voice, more tentative than before, reached him.

"You're going to catch the person who did this, right?"

"That's why we're here," he assured her. "The FBI brought us in all the way from Anchorage because Agents

Nez and Lync, and their colleagues, have a lot of experience. This case is the only thing they're investigating right now. It's our biggest priority."

"That's not an answer," she said, more grief than anger in her words.

He nodded soberly. "I'm not going to make you a promise I can't guarantee. But I'll tell you this—we're putting everything we have into this investigation. And when it comes to finding bombers, the FBI is *very* good. I'd bet on us."

He stepped a little closer, wanting her to read on his face how much he believed it. "I can also promise to I'll keep you informed. I believe we'll get this person. You let us worry about that. You focus on getting better. Deal?"

She swiped a hand across her face, wiping away a rush of tears he pretended not to see. "Okay."

He gave her an encouraging smile, then followed Ben and Anderson into the hall.

It wasn't until they were outside the hospital that Ben halted suddenly, turning to face him and making Patches stop short. "You want to act like these victims' personal therapist, that's your business. I know you're good at your job, so I'm not going to question your methods. But Anderson and I know what we're doing, too. So let us do our jobs."

Jax put his hands up, pasted an innocent look on his face.

"We asked you to come along because it makes the victims more comfortable. They connect with you and it reduces the stress of feeling like they need to give us information or we won't find the person who killed someone they love. Or the stress of having to relive what happened to them. We're happy to have you with us. But you're not an agent, Jax. You need to remember that."

Ben shook his head and spun around again, striding for the SUV.

Anderson gave Jax a sympathetic look, but he didn't disagree with his partner, just followed.

Patches stared up at him, reading the tension, and Jax stroked her soft fur. "You did a good job, Patches. I'm the one who's in trouble."

She shifted, pressing all sixty pounds against him. She wasn't that big, but she was strong.

He laughed, giving her an extra pat on the head. "Thanks, Patches. Let's get going."

She strode alongside him, her gait full of puppy energy. Sometimes, he forgot that at a year old, technically she still was a puppy. Despite the tough job he'd given her, despite the difficult start in life she'd had—being tossed onto the street to fend for herself at a few weeks old—she was always cheerful.

The perfect fit for a job like this. But sometimes the job still got to her.

Right now it was getting to him. And it wasn't talking to the victims, as hard as that was.

He'd come to the FBI from private therapy to help stop perpetrators before they could become repeat offenders. He knew he made a difference here. But despite his training, despite how much he loved what he did, sometimes being a Victim Specialist felt too far on the sidelines.

Sometimes, it just didn't feel like he was doing enough.

THE STATION WAS empty and dark.

Normally, Keara would be gone by now. Actually, if things were normal, she probably wouldn't be working at all on a Sunday. But with worried citizens needing reassurance, and a town that needed extra vigilance because of a nearby bombing without an obvious motive, she'd come in early and stayed late.

Heading home didn't mean she was off the clock. In a small town like Desparre, there was no such thing as truly off the clock. If something happened after the station was officially closed for the night, the officer—or chief—who was closest to the action would get the first call.

Tonight she didn't want to get on the road. Didn't feel like making the relatively short drive to her house.

She'd been distracted all day, moving on autopilot. In a job like hers, that was dangerous. But knowing that didn't make it any easier to focus.

After she'd returned home from Luna last night, images of her life with Juan had taunted her sleep. She'd woken on a scream, on the memory of returning home from work that horrible day.

She'd been exhausted, frustrated by a case she hardly remembered, one she'd subsequently solved. She'd wanted nothing more than to settle on the couch in front of the TV with a delivery pizza and a bottle of red wine. To simply snuggle with her husband and forget the argument they'd been having on replay every few weeks.

The house had been lit up, the front door locked, no sign that anything was wrong. She'd walked inside and headed straight for the shower, a holdover habit from her days on patrol. Forensics said the timing wouldn't have mattered, that Juan had been dead before she even arrived home, but the shower still bothered her. The fact that she hadn't suspected for a second that anything was wrong, that she'd had no idea the man she'd loved so deeply was already gone.

And then, afterward, the hint of annoyance when she'd walked through the house and couldn't find him. The sigh she'd heaved as she'd realized the back door was open, that he hadn't bothered to come in from the garden when she'd arrived. The way she'd desperately tried to suck in gulps of air once she'd fallen to the ground beside him, but her lungs still screamed, telling her she wasn't getting enough oxygen.

The investigation had determined that someone had hopped the fence into their backyard while Juan was relaxing on a lawn chair. They'd slipped up behind him and slit his throat.

If he'd realized anyone was there, the knowledge had come too late. There were no defense marks on his arms or hands. No awkward angle to the slice across his neck, which might have happened if he'd tried to turn at the last minute.

She hoped it meant that it had all happened too fast for him to suffer. But even an instant of pain, even a flash of insight that everything he'd fought for in his life was over, was too much.

It was too much for her, too. For six years being in Alaska had kept the memories at a survivable distance.

Now the bombing was bringing it all back. But if the person who'd killed Juan had come here and set off a bomb, why had he chosen such a different crime?

Fitz hadn't sent her the case file from Celia Harris's murder yet, but if that killer was responsible for the bomb, too, something drastic had changed. She'd seen the evidence photos from Celia's murder; the whole office had. They'd been gruesome enough, with such an unlikely victim, that Juan and Fitz had consulted briefly with the rest of the detectives.

Celia hadn't been killed in the alley where she'd been found, and her killer had taken his time murdering her. Although Keara's cases tended to be the standard sort—motivated by more obvious reasons like greed, jealousy or anger—Houston wasn't immune to serial killers. She'd understood immediately why Juan and Fitz had thought there'd be more murders.

But a bombing seven years later? Even if the bomber had stood nearby and watched the pain and death his handiwork caused, was it really the same as wielding a knife? She'd never heard of a violent killer becoming a bomber.

Maybe she was reaching, grasping at a similar symbol because she still needed answers, despite how far she'd run.

The crackle of the intercom from outside the entrance of the building, followed by a familiar voice asking "Keara? Er-Chief Hernandez?" startled her.

The distinctive voice made goose bumps prick her arms. Keara rubbed them away as she stood and strode to the front of the station, swinging the door wide.

"How did you know I was here?"

Woof! Patches answered, making a smile break through the mask of competence and calm that Keara used automatically on the job.

"Yours is the only civilian car in the lot."

He'd noticed what car she was driving? She studied him more closely, taking in the focused stare belied by a relaxed stance. Maybe psychologists were more like police officers than she'd thought, both needing to be observant and analytical.

"You have news on the bombing?" As she asked it, she realized the only reason he'd tell her in person was if it was connected to her past. Bracing her hand on the open door frame, she asked, "Is it connected to my husband's death?"

"What?" Jax's too-serious expression morphed into concern as he took a step closer.

Too late, she remembered that he knew her husband had investigated a murder where the symbol was found, but not much more. He didn't know anything about Rodney Brown, or the fact that her husband's murder had never been solved. Or even the fact that her husband's death had been a murder.

She took a step back, losing the stability of holding on to the door frame, but also escaping Jax's cinnamony scent. She didn't know if it was aftershave or cologne or if he just liked to mainline chai, but it was the sort of scent she wanted to keep breathing in.

It was distracting. *He* was distracting.

Something bumped her leg and Keara looked down,

finding Patches there. The dog had followed her inside.
Jax was coming, too, but moving more slowly.

Keara kept her gaze on Patches, petting the dog while
she tried to come up with a way to redirect Jax, a way to
avoid talking about what had happened to Juan.

"I don't have anything new to share about the bombing," Jax said, his voice slow and soft. "And Anderson is
still waiting on that file from Houston PD. Is there more
you need to tell me? Some other connection we should investigate?"

When she didn't immediately answer, he put his hand
under her elbow.

The contact startled her, warmth from his hand making
her realize how cold the rest of her body felt. She jerked her
gaze back up to his. "Maybe. I'll know more once I get a
look at that case file."

Jax stared at her, his dark brown eyes hypnotic. Finally,
he nodded, stepping just slightly closer.

She had to tilt her head back to hold eye contact and she
put a warning in her gaze. She liked Jax, but she'd been a
police officer too long not to see what was coming. He
was trying to make a connection, sympathize with her so
she'd trust him enough to tell him what he needed to know.

A slight smile tilted his lips and Keara wondered if she
needed to put a different kind of "back off" vibe out there.
Nerves fluttered in her chest and she put it down to how
long it had been since she'd had to let anyone down easy.
Since she was their police chief, thankfully, people here
mostly considered her off-limits as a woman.

"I'm not an agent."

His words were so far from what she'd expected to hear
that it took her a few extra seconds to digest them.

"And you have no jurisdiction in Luna," he continued.

She crossed her arms over her chest, refusing to take

a step backward and let him know his closeness affected her. "And?"

"The case you talked about feels psychologically different—the MO, the location, everything. But I can't get that symbol out of my head. It might have been an accident that we were able to recover it on the bomb, but it wasn't an accident that the bomber made it. It means something to him. That suggests the cases are connected somehow. I can't let this go. And since you're waiting on a case file you really shouldn't be requesting, I'm guessing you can't, either."

Keara frowned, trying to keep her expression neutral as Patches nudged her leg, looking for attention. Despite all the memories that had resurfaced tonight, she couldn't help but smile at the dog, with her tiny matching brown spots at the top of each eyebrow, and bigger spots on her muzzle and chest. Keara silently pet Patches again as she waited for Jax to continue.

"I think we should work together," Jax finished, staring at her expectantly. "Quietly, on the side. If we come up with anything, we share it with the agents."

It was a mistake for a lot of reasons.

Keeping information from the investigating agents—no matter how small or seemingly inconsequential—could be the difference that prevented the case from being solved. Besides, if she and Jax worked outside the official team, they wouldn't have all of the information.

After this was over, Jax would go back to Anchorage, but she still had to live in this community. She'd have to answer to her citizens if something went wrong, and she'd lose the support of their closest neighboring town, too.

Then there was Jax himself. Although she had no concerns when it came to her self-control around the handsome Victim Specialist, she couldn't deny that he ignited a tiny flicker of attraction whenever he was near.

Juan had been gone for seven years. She wasn't totally

closed off to the idea of moving on someday. But it didn't feel like the time, not even for a fling. Not if this case could be the key to solving his murder.

"Okay," she agreed, the word bursting free before she could hold it back. "Let's work together."

Chapter Six

Something was wrong.

Jax could see it through the window of the tiny diner on the outskirts of Desparre, somewhere Keara had told him they were less likely to attract attention. It had been an hour drive for him after spending the day all over Luna with Ben and Anderson, talking to victims and families. He'd left discouraged and exhausted, with the bruises on his back and legs aching, but judging from the unguarded torment on her face, Keara's day had been worse.

He pictured the look on her face yesterday when she'd asked if the bombing was connected to her husband's death. That meant her husband had been murdered—and presumably, that the murder had never been solved. He'd desperately wanted to ask about it, but he couldn't turn off years of working as a psychologist. It had been the wrong time. But maybe today would be different.

"Come on, Patches," he said, leading the way into the diner. Keara had told him that the owner was low-key and didn't mind letting working dogs inside.

True to her promise, the diner was mostly empty and the waitress who nodded a greeting just cooed "aww" when she spotted Patches.

By the time Jax joined Keara at her booth, she looked serious and in control. The ability to mask her emotions that fast was probably a necessary skill for a police chief. But it still surprised him. And if he was being honest with himself, he was a little disappointed that she felt the need to hide from him.

You barely know her, he reminded himself. Yes, people usually opened up to him faster, probably because knowing how to reach people was a job requirement he couldn't just turn off outside work. And yes, last night they'd agreed to work together, so he'd expected more honesty. But mostly, he was just intrigued by her. He had no idea how long he'd have to get to know her before the case was solved and he had to go back to Anchorage.

"Is anything wrong?" Jax asked, keeping his voice neutral.

Patches took the more direct route. She went to Keara's side of the booth and put her head on the seat.

From the surprise and amusement on Keara's face, Patches had looked up at Keara with her soft puppy eyes, a tactic that rarely failed.

The smile twitching at the corners of Keara's lips burst into a true grin as she pet Patches. "She really knows how to put on the charm, doesn't she? Is that something you taught her when you trained her to work for the FBI?"

"Nah, she came by that naturally. I was biking home from work one day and—"

"You *biked* to work in Anchorage? Must have been summer."

"This was almost a year ago. I was working in DC then. Getting to and from FBI headquarters took forever in traffic, so I bought a bike. Anyway, I was on my way home and I saw something moving in the bushes and then this tiny little puppy jumped out. She gave me this look like she wanted me to take her home."

He'd had to swerve his bike, had almost tipped it. But he'd always felt like she'd been waiting for him to come along.

Growing up, he'd had a dog, so he'd known instantly that Patches was too young to be away from her mother. But she'd been totally alone, so he'd scooped her up, walked his bike the rest of the way home and then taken her to a vet.

Keara's smile curled downward. "Someone left her out there?"

"Yeah."

She shook her head, still petting Patches. "Kids and animals," she muttered. "Those are the worst calls, because they're trusting, relying on someone to care for them. Not that I want to get called to any scene where someone is hurt, but at least as an adult, you've seen enough of the world to know. If you're paying attention, there are threats everywhere."

She was staring at his dog when she spoke, letting Jax study her more closely. He'd worked with law enforcement long enough to know how terrible their jobs could be. He wondered how being a chief in Desparre compared to being a detective in Houston. The latter was surely bloodier, but the former put a lot of responsibility on her shoulders.

Deciding to keep the conversation light, he continued, "It's lucky I found Patches when I did. The vet thought she was about six weeks old. But she was feisty and determined from the start. I'd been working for the FBI for two and a half years by then and there are a few Victim Specialists who have therapy dogs in DC. I immediately thought she'd be good at it. She officially started at six months. Youngest dog they've ever used."

He heard the pride in his voice as Keara's gaze finally swung back to him. There was something pensive in her gaze, something that made him want to lean across the table and get a little closer.

"Can I get you anything?"

The nasally voice startled Jax and he realized the waitress was standing next to their table.

"Just a coffee would be great."

"Make it two, please," Keara said.

"And for her?" The waitress nodded at his dog, then smiled. "Does she want a bowl of water? Or we can bring her a dog c-o-o-k-i-e."

Woof! Patches's head appeared over the top of the table, swiveled toward the waitress.

The waitress laughed. "I see she spells. Okay, two coffees and a dog cookie it is!"

When she left, Jax returned his attention to Keara. But whatever he'd seen in her eyes was gone now, replaced by a seriousness that told him they were about to get to work.

"So the woman who was murdered seven years ago? Celia Harris? Apparently, Juan, my husband, and his partner, Fitz, had a possible suspect. I mean, they looked at a lot of people and I guess this guy didn't stand out more than anyone else, at least not initially. But then, a week after my husband was murdered, Fitz went to talk to him again. I think it was kind of a distraction assignment, honestly, to reinterview any witnesses or suspects that Juan had talked to alone. You see, Fitz wanted to be part of the investigation into Juan's death and the chief wouldn't let him."

She didn't have to tell him that she'd also tried to insert herself into the investigation of her husband's murder. Just talking about it was making her eyes narrow and her lips tighten.

"What happened to your husband, Keara?"

"He was murdered." Her expression became even more pinched. "In our own backyard."

"I'm sorry."

"Me, too." She straightened, and he saw her game face come on. "It was never solved, which is why…" She took a visible breath, shook her head and started over, her voice calmer. "So about a week before he was killed, Juan went to talk to Rodney Brown. His car was pictured close to the scene near the time of Celia's murder. Fitz said Juan returned from that interview without feeling like he'd gained much, but the guy lied about the car being near the scene. And when Fitz went back—a week after my husband's throat was slit—the place was totally cleared out."

Jax felt himself cringe at Keara's description of how her husband had died. He could tell from the anger and pain wrapped up in those few words that she'd been the one to find him. An ache formed in his chest as he watched her, trying to be clinical. How much worse must it have been, as an officer of the law, knowing the person who'd killed him had gotten away with it?

"Fitz spent a lot of time trying to track down Rodney Brown. Apparently, he worked as an orderly at a hospital in Houston, but he just stopped showing up. His work history before that was a little spotty, so it wasn't totally out of character. And his family told Fitz that he was flighty and not great about staying in touch. Back then none of them were all that surprised that he'd just cleared out of his apartment. Fitz has been checking for signs of him over the years, even got a warrant to watch his credit report to see if he popped up somewhere else in the country. But there's been nothing."

"So you think he killed Celia Harris and your husband, too?"

"It's pretty suspicious timing to disappear."

"Yeah, it is."

"And now there's a bomb here with the same symbol. But…" She frowned, shook her head.

"You're thinking the same thing the FBI is," Jax concluded.

Her eyes narrowed at him, but she held off on saying anything as the waitress dropped off their coffees, and Patches started greedily chewing on her dog biscuit.

After the woman was gone, Keara demanded, "What do they think?"

"They don't know about your husband. No one from Houston mentioned that angle. And I'm guessing Rodney Brown's name is in the file, but he didn't stand out. The main thing is that—"

"A violent killer—someone who obviously enjoys the kill itself—is unlikely to become a bomber?"

"Pretty much," Jax confirmed. "You're right that the symbols are eerily similar. But if it's the same person, why a bomb? And why here? Why *now*, so many years after the murder in Texas?"

FITZ WAS RIGHT. Rodney Brown was a ghost.

Keara leaned back on her couch and took a sip of red wine. It had been another long day, full of questions from her citizens that she couldn't answer, full of worry about a case she wasn't even supposed to be investigating. She wasn't usually much of a drinker, especially while she was pondering a case, but tonight she was on her second glass.

Maybe that was why she reached for her wedding album, instead of returning to her laptop. In those first months after Juan's death, she'd sobbed over the pages. But since moving to Alaska, she'd tucked it into the corner of her bookshelf and hadn't opened it again.

Now she ran her finger over the shape of Juan's face, frozen in a slightly nervous smile as he waited at the altar for her. When she'd first met him in that Houston roll call, seen the way his shoulders slumped and his mouth tightened at hearing he'd be partnered with her, she'd been sure they'd never be friends. But after a year of tough calls, patrolling a dangerous area together, they'd developed a mutual respect that had slowly blossomed into more.

Now he was gone. The constant, overwhelming grief she'd felt in that first year after he died had slowly dulled into something she could push to the back of her mind. But with each day that passed since she'd seen that blasted symbol, the gnawing ache was returning, along with the certainty that she'd failed Juan.

Fitz was right. She'd played by the rules in Houston, let her fellow detectives handle the case because she'd been sure they'd find justice for one of their own. And because it had been hard enough to function at all during those early days and months, let alone constantly look at pictures and details of what had happened to Juan. When the case had gone cold, she should have taken it up herself and damn the rules, damn the consequences. Instead, she'd run away.

Since coming to Alaska, she'd followed the rules, too. She'd tried to be a by-the-book chief. But not anymore.

She took another long sip of wine and closed the album, pushed it away from her. Tipping back the rest of her glass, she yanked the laptop into her lap and stared at the notes she'd compiled on Rodney Brown.

The guy was a loser. He'd had a handful of arrests as a minor for getting into fights. More of the same as an adult, usually bar fights. Plus a single sexual assault charge that had later been dropped. From what Keara could tell, it was more because the victim didn't want to go through a trial than for lack of evidence.

Serial killers were often sexually motivated. But Celia Harris hadn't been sexually assaulted. Fitz's investigation had never turned up any similar kills. Although Rodney Brown clearly had a violent streak and a problem with women, there were no signs he'd ever crossed paths with Celia Harris. And he didn't seem sophisticated enough to have pulled off the risky abduction and then committed such a violent murder without leaving behind useful evidence.

Juan's murder had been almost professional. A quick hit and then the killer had disappeared. No one in her neighborhood had noticed anyone who didn't belong or seen anyone running away at the time of the murder. Yes, it made sense that a violent killer of women who thought the police were onto him might try and take out the detective who'd questioned him.

But Rodney Brown had only been questioned once. After a few weeks of silence, would he seek Juan out and murder him? The closer she looked at the details of the case, the more unlikely that idea seemed. Taking all of the pieces together, she understood why Fitz had decided the two weren't connected.

Except the timing was pretty hard to ignore. And the fact that Rodney Brown had so completely dropped off the map suggested a sophistication that perhaps he'd hidden in the rest of his life.

As for the bomb, sure, anyone could dig up the basics on the internet. But pulling it off was another thing. And no matter how she looked at it, the long gap in time and the change in MO made it pretty unlikely that all three crimes were connected.

Cursing, she tossed her laptop onto the couch beside her. Tears of frustration blurred her vision, but she blinked them back.

Yes, cold cases were harder than fresh investigations. The adage of the "first forty-eight hours" was true. Over time, memories faded, witnesses forgot, evidence that had been missed the first time often disappeared for good. But that didn't make them impossible.

Keara pictured the symbol from Anderson's phone, with the series of interconnecting loops, drawn onto the bomb with a thick black marker. Different enough from the symbol over Celia's body in that alley, spray-painted onto the stucco wall of the adjacent building in bloodred. But the design itself was the same, the loops that looked almost childish. If all of this was connected, if she had a shot at solving her husband's murder, that symbol was the key.

The melodic ring of her doorbell startled her, made her glance at the credenza in the corner where she'd stashed her weapon. Few people knew exactly where she lived. Even fewer would visit.

She considered ignoring it, but curiosity got the better of her and she strode to the door. When she peered through the peephole, there was Jax on her front porch, shivering in a dark coat and looking tired. Patches was at his side, her head swiveling from him to the door, as if she knew Keara had stepped up to the other side.

It had been a long time since she'd felt attracted to someone. Sure, she'd had brief flashes of awareness in Alaska when she crossed paths with someone, but nothing that lasted more than a few minutes. With Jax, the attraction seemed to grow each time she saw him, with each new detail she noticed. The surprising muscles in his arms when he'd stripped down to a T-shirt in the hotel lobby, the intuitiveness of his gaze when she was holding something back, the hint of a dimple that popped on his right cheek when he gave a full-blown grin, usually at Patches.

More than simple attraction, though, she felt a *connection* with Jax. Some invisible pull, a desire to simply sit beside him and soak in his presence. She'd tried to ignore the feeling, but right now she felt that pull even more than usual.

"It's the wine," she muttered, resting her forehead against the door, anxious at such a simple decision. Open the door and let him in? Or pretend not to be home?

Woof!

A smile burst free and Keara had to smother the giggle that wanted to follow. Any man who could inspire such loyalty from a dog like Patches had to be a good one. And maybe the fact that he lived so far away was a plus. Anchorage was definitely past the point of being practical for a relationship, so that alone should avoid any awkwardness when it was time for him to leave.

He might be FBI, but he wasn't a law-enforcement officer. He wasn't in the thick of danger, wasn't someone she'd have to constantly worry about.

Not that it really mattered. She didn't want anything serious. Not now. Probably never again.

But a fling with a handsome, intelligent, sensitive man? Maybe it was time.

Taking a deep breath, Keara opened the door.

Chapter Seven

The door swung open and Keara swayed forward, her gaze locked on his and lips parted. He'd never seen her hair down before, but right now it hung long, silky and loose, perfectly straight over her shoulders. She was dressed casually, in jeans and a well-worn long-sleeved T-shirt that looked soft to the touch and showed off curves her police uniform hid. Even her expression was less guarded, softer.

"Come in," she said, her voice huskier than usual.

Patches bounded inside at the invitation, but warning bells went off in Jax's head, despite the desire stirring in his belly.

He could see it in her low-lidded gaze. She thought he was here for a totally different reason than the agreed-upon plan to investigate together. Of course, she'd never given him her address, never invited him over. It had been foolish to show up without calling. Especially at nine o' clock at night.

But after yet another day of nonstop visits with victims and family members, feeling no closer to bringing any of them real closure, he'd just wanted to see Keara. To sit across from her and watch the way her lips pursed when she was deep in thought, see the determination in her gaze and posture when she thought she was onto something. To soak up her presence and soothe his own frustrated nerves.

So he'd managed to get her home address out of Luna's police chief, under the pretense that he was keeping her apprised of the investigation, and she was keeping them informed of anything suspicious in Desparre.

It had been stupid and selfish, he realized now as Keara raised her eyebrows at him, the corners of her lips twisting up in an expression that looked like a dare. Red wine stained her lips with a hint of purple.

He tried to come up with an excuse to leave, but then she licked those lips and he was moving forward without conscious intent.

She pushed the door closed behind him, leaning against him as she did it, and the brief contact made his mouth go dry.

This close, he could see the ring of slightly lighter brown at the center of her coffee-colored irises. He could smell a rich cabernet, subtle enough that he doubted she'd drank a lot. And it wasn't just her well-worn T-shirt that was soft; it was also her skin.

She blinked up at him, her chest rising and falling faster, and he could feel his own breathing pick up in response.

He'd been drawn to her from the first day they'd met. So when she swayed forward again—or had he leaned toward her?—he ignored the voice in his head telling him this was the wrong time. Threading his fingers through hers, he tugged gently and then she was pressing against him, up on her tiptoes.

The first contact of her lips sent a spark through his body like he'd given himself an electric shock. Then he closed his mouth around her bottom lip and tasted the cabernet she'd been drinking.

She let out a noise that was half-sigh, half-moan and pushed higher on her toes, her free hand tangling in his hair and pulling him closer. Then her tongue was in his mouth and her kisses turned fast and frantic.

Jax wrapped his free hand around her back, molding her body to his, and his heart rate skyrocketed. He had a solid seven inches on her and yet somehow, the fit was perfect.

Woof!

Patches's bark registered in the back of his mind as Keara kissed him harder.

Then Patches let out several more, higher pitched barks.

The insistent sound returned him to reality, helped his mind take the lead back over from his body. He pulled away slightly, trying to catch his breath as he stared over Keara's head and down the hall.

Patches stood in Keara's hallway, leaning slightly forward, as if ready to bark again or run toward them.

Unwinding his arm from around Keara's back, Jax tried to calm his pounding heart. The scent of her—a mix of that wine with something sweeter and more subtle—invaded his senses, making it hard to focus, especially when she leaned in again.

He stepped back, quickly enough that she stumbled toward him before righting herself.

"This probably isn't a good idea," he forced himself to say.

Keara blinked at him a few times, then that professional mask slipped back over her features. But not before he saw a flash of hurt in her eyes.

She was as attracted to him as he was to her. But he'd be a terrible psychologist if he didn't recognize that they were both acting on it for the wrong reasons.

Flings weren't his thing. They never had been, but at thirty-eight years old, he felt way past them. And even if Keara was emotionally available, she lived four hundred miles away. He might be here for a month or a break might come in the case tomorrow and that fast, he'd be on a flight home.

Besides, Keara hadn't kissed him because of that attraction. She'd kissed him because she was emotional and frustrated, probably over the thread-thin connection between her husband's death and the bombing.

He took another step away from her, as the idea of her kissing him because she missed her dead husband cooled the rest of his desire.

"You came to talk about the case?" Keara asked, her voice as detached and remote as the expression on her face.

When he nodded, she spun and headed into the interior of her house. "Come on, then."

As soon as she reached Patches, the dog turned to walk with her. Keara stroked Patches's head as they strode away, his dog's tail wagging.

Running a hand through his hair, straightening the spots where Keara had tugged and tangled it, he followed. With every step, he took a deep breath, trying not to watch the sway of her hips as she led him into her living room.

It was exactly what he would have expected her personal space to be. Cozy, with a fireplace centered in the room. Comfortable, with a couch that looked perfect for curling up on. There was even a wool blanket thrown over the back of it. And peaceful, with big curtained windows diagonal from the fireplace that had to open to a spectacular view of the forest behind her.

There was an open bottle of wine and a single empty wineglass on the live-edge wood coffee table. Beside it, a laptop and a wedding album.

A mix of regret and pain—some for her, some for himself—tensed his chest and then dropped to his stomach.

Her gaze went from him to the album, then back again. "If there's a connection between all of this, it's that symbol. We need to know what it means." Her expression gave nothing away, but her voice was slightly shaky as she sank onto the couch. "You've got a psychology background, right? Any ideas?"

Jax settled on the big leather chair beside the couch, not surprised when Patches pushed past him to sit beside Keara. His dog always knew who needed her most.

"That's profiler territory," Jax said. "I used to be a psychologist, so yeah, I definitely have insight into some of these criminals. But this symbol doesn't represent anything I can decode."

"It's the only thing connecting the crimes," Keara said, the frustration in her voice edged with grief. "Nothing else is similar. Fitz sent me the file from Celia Harris's murder. And I know everything about Juan's murder. The only possible link is the timing and the fact that Juan questioned a possible witness shortly before he was killed—and shortly before that witness disappeared. But the bombing? Nothing about it seems remotely connected. Except this damn symbol."

Jax leaned forward in his chair, resting his forearms on his thighs. "What if that's because the murder—or possibly murders, if your husband's case is also connected—were the anomaly? What if he was always a bomber?"

Keara twisted slightly to face him, her eyebrows twitching inward. At her interest, Patches pivoted, too. "What do you mean?"

"Maybe the kill was personal. Maybe the bomber knew Celia Harris. Maybe bombs are his thing and this was the exception." He could hear the excitement in his voice as he turned it over in his mind. "It could make him easier to track if he's really a bomber. Maybe there have been others."

Keara's shoulders dropped, her excitement obviously waning. "I don't think so. Juan thought Rodney was suspicious mainly because he so vehemently denied being near the crime scene when it happened. But he couldn't find any personal connection between Rodney and Celia. If this was a serial killer, that wouldn't matter so much. But a personal kill?" She shook her head. "After Juan died and Rodney disappeared, Fitz dug deep, looking for a connection. He never found one, either."

"You said Rodney was flighty, right? That he didn't tend to stay in one place for long, that even his family wasn't all that concerned when he cleared out?"

"Sure, but it's pretty coincidental timing," Keara insisted.

"Exactly," Jax agreed. "What if Rodney leaving *is* just a coincidence? Maybe Celia's murder and this bombing are connected. And it's possible your husband's death is, too. *Maybe*. But what if it's not Rodney? What if we're looking for someone else?"

"WHAT IF IT's not Rodney?"

Jax's words from last night had run through Keara's mind during a restless night of sleep and again duringher drive into work this morning—when she wasn't distracted by memories of kissing him. She'd been attracted to him from the start, so she'd expected to enjoy those kisses. What she hadn't expected was the intensity.

The man kissed with a singular focus, until she'd felt consumed by the feel of him, by the taste of him. He might not have been law enforcement, but after plastering herself against him, she suspected he worked out with his agent colleagues, because his chest was rock-solid.

It was better that he'd stopped it before things went too far.

He was a colleague. He was also her best chance at connecting the Luna bombing to her husband's murder—if in fact they were connected.

He was also dangerous. A fling was one thing. A fling was temporary, a distraction from the fact that she'd chosen a profession that sucked away a lot of her personal time. A distraction from the fact that even if she had more personal time, she had no one to spend it with. But a single kiss from Jax and she'd felt herself wanting. Physical wanting, of course. But emotional wanting, too. And that was territory she didn't want to revisit.

"Everything okay, Chief?"

Keara looked up from her desk.

Tate Emory was standing in her doorway, too-perceptive concern in his dark eyes. He was the closest thing she had to a friend on the force. Not that she didn't like just about everyone on her team, but Tate was different. She knew his secret, had given him a job in a tricky situation, so it was easier to share things with him in return. She'd kept his confidence, so he'd keep hers.

But not this. Not the guilt that filled her like nausea when she thought about kissing Jax when she should have been focused on getting justice for Juan.

She forced a smile. "It's been a tough week. We're four days out from that bomb and neither the FBI nor the Luna police have much more to go on than they did when it went off."

By Wednesday morning—a full ninety-six hours after the bomb had detonated—she'd expected a solid suspect, maybe even an arrest, but at the very least, a manhunt. Instead, the FBI's semiregular news conferences beside Luna's police chief focused more on reassuring a scared public that they were working on it, and asking them to come forward if they had information that could help.

What the public didn't know—what Keara had learned from talking to her colleagues in the Luna Police Department—was that the FBI still had a long way to go. They still had no idea who or what the intended target was, or what goal the bomber was trying to accomplish. Was there a message? If so, no one knew what it was. They still weren't even sure if the bomber had been going for a bigger death toll by waiting until the impromptu soccer game happened or if that was unintentional and he'd expected few—or maybe even no—dead.

"Hey, at least it's finally May," Tate said, his tone more enthusiastic than the forty-five-degree weather warranted.

It would be a while before they hit temperatures that didn't require a coat. But at least it was sunny.

She gave him a halfhearted smile, acknowledging his attempt to cheer her up.

"I'm going to take a trek up the mountain today," Tate said, apparently giving up on that.

"Take Lorenzo and Nate with you. I doubt we're going to magically run across someone who knows something, but let's be honest. If Desparre is a good place to hide out, the mountain takes it to the next level."

The mountain that separated Desparre from Luna was a great place to get lost, even more lost than the relative isolation offered by the rest of Desparre. Five years ago they'd discovered kidnappers had hidden five kids on that mountain for many years. They'd also found a murderer, running from a decades-old charge in Kansas. It wasn't a stretch to imagine a bomber hiding there, too.

All of her officers were using their extra time between calls to chat with citizens, both to reassure them that the bombing investigation would be solved and also to see if anyone had useful information. So far it hadn't borne any fruit, but there had to be a reason the bomber had targeted such a tiny park. Luna and Desparre weren't that far apart, at least not in Alaskan terms. So there was a good chance someone around here knew something, even if they didn't realize it.

Lorenzo Riera was one of her veterans, a steady officer who'd once faced down a grizzly bear who'd gotten a taste for people food and wandered downtown four years ago. He'd just as readily had her back at a more standard bar fight breakup last month. His partner, Nate Dreymond, had barely passed a year on the force. Since Tate's partner, Peter, had left a few months ago, Nate was the force's rookie.

Having Lorenzo at his side would be good backup for Tate if he ran into trouble, and having Nate tag along would give the rookie a chance to watch two great officers at work.

"Got it," Tate agreed. "But you know, maybe you should reconsider the K-9 unit. If I had a K-9 partner, you wouldn't have to keep putting out those failed job postings for another officer."

It was a request Tate had been making almost from his first day on the force. Usually, Keara cited their lack of funds. But after seeing Jax work with Patches, she wondered if the cost might be worth it. "I'll think about it."

Tate's mouth opened and closed, as if her response had totally thrown him.

"Let me know if anything pops," she said.

He nodded and took the cue to leave.

She should do the same. Being chief meant a certain amount of politics and paperwork, but in a town as small as Desparre, it still required her to be out on the streets, too. Or maybe that was just the kind of chief she'd chosen to be.

She'd been out in her town every day since the bomb had gone off, reassuring citizens and doing the same kind of low-key investigative work as her officers. But right now the question of Rodney Brown's involvement was still messing with her focus.

Jax's claim that Rodney's leaving was just coincidence could be right. Twelve years in law enforcement had taught her that stranger coincidences happened. The problem was, it had also taught her to always be suspicious of them, because too much of a coincidence usually meant it wasn't actually a coincidence.

Then again, maybe something bad had happened to Rodney, too. But what? And why?

Rodney Brown killing Celia Harris and then killing Juan

was a real possibility she couldn't drop. But the bombing connection felt more tenuous.

What if they were two different people? The idea made Keara jerk straighter in her chair, making it roll slightly backward and bump the credenza behind her.

Two different people didn't mean they weren't connected.

The theory made her heart rate pick up, sent a familiar rush through her body. The thrill of the chase, when her gut was screaming she'd hit on something. She'd felt it regularly as a detective. As a chief, she had less opportunity to be in the center of a case in the same way.

Grabbing her cell phone, she hit redial on a number that had started to appear constantly on her list of recent calls.

"Jax Diallo."

The deep, relaxing tone of his voice sent a little thrill through her that Keara tried to ignore. "Jax, it's Keara."

"Keara."

The way he said her name, the way she could practically see his slight smile, made her stomach clench. Pushing forward, she told him her new theory. "What if you're right about Celia Harris's murder being personal? What if the person who killed her is still out there, but it's not Rodney Brown?"

"I don't—"

She kept talking, adrenaline pumping, her words spilling out faster as the idea continued to take shape. "What if the killer knew Rodney, knew the symbol he liked to use, and spray-painted it above Celia's body to lead police in the wrong direction? Or maybe they'd had a falling out and it was a 'screw you' kind of move?"

"So you're suggesting Rodney is the bomber?" Jax asked, not sounding anywhere near as excited by the theory as she felt.

"Yes! When Juan came to talk to him about the murder,

he was pissed because his symbol was used. He killed Juan to keep him from connecting it to his own crimes. Then he left town."

"So you think Juan is the one who let it slip about the symbol? But what about Rodney's car being near the murder scene?" Jax asked, still sounding confused.

"We know Rodney was near there at the time of the killing. Maybe it really was coincidence. Or maybe he knew what was going to happen and drove by, but he wasn't the killer."

"Then, the real killer told Rodney he was going to murder this woman? Why would he do that?"

"Maybe they had a sick friendship. You can't tell me you haven't seen criminals connect before, give each other ideas, trade stories about what they've done, even cooperate with each other. Maybe give each other alibis. Maybe play a one-upmanship game."

"Well, sure," Jax said, his tone still skeptical.

"Maybe that's what happened here," Keara said, holding in her frustration. "And whether or not Juan mentioned the symbol, Rodney knew about it. So maybe that was his real worry. He wouldn't know that Houston PD isn't like the FBI. We don't have bomb databases. We wouldn't know if he'd used that symbol before, not if it was outside our jurisdiction."

She blew out a heavy breath, tried to slow her adrenaline along with the speed of her words. "What I'm saying, Jax, is that maybe the killer and the bomber *aren't* the same person. But maybe they know each other, even schemed together at one point. And Rodney killed my husband because he was onto something bigger than a single murder."

Jax sighed. "It's a good theory, Keara, but there's a problem."

"What?"

"The FBI ran the bombing details through our database,

specifically that symbol. They finished reviewing everything today and confirmed it. We've never seen a bomb
with this symbol before. Not in Houston, not anywhere."

Chapter Eight

With every large-scale crime scene, Jax found at least one person whose resilience awed him. From the Luna bombing, that person was Gabi Sinclair.

The young woman was a fighter. She'd lost a leg, lost a fiancé. She was definitely angry, grieving and in pain, but she was also strong. She had a lot still to get through, but he knew she'd come out the other side of it.

He went to see Gabi at her mom's house in Desparre, where she was staying while she healed. He was hoping she might remember something more, since she'd been at the edge of the park, maybe at a good vantage point to see the bomber leave the scene. But she had nothing new to offer him, just like he had nothing new to share about the investigation. The most he was able to do was return her fiancé's watch, which had been processed by the FBI.

"They told me in a month, I'll get a preparatory prosthetic," Gabi said, fighting through the pain as she settled herself on her mom's couch, with Patches beside her good leg. "After a few months I'll be able to get fitted for something permanent. Then I'm going to learn to run again."

She said it all with her chin tipped high, with her mom clutching her hand and fighting tears. Gabi only broke down once, when he handed her the watch and she told him about her fiancé's funeral, which had been put on hold long enough for Gabi to be released from the hospital.

As Jax and Patches climbed into his rental SUV, Gabi's broken words echoed in his head. "I thought Carter and I had so much time. We had so many plans. Now all our dreams for our future together are just gone."

Instead of seeing Gabi's tearful gaze, he pictured Keara, stoic and frustrated as she tried to get closure, seven long years after her husband had been murdered.

It wasn't his job. Not to investigate the bombing outside his role with the victims. Definitely not to try and connect it to an old murder case. But he'd seen what a good investigation could do for those left behind. Knowing who was to blame, being able to see justice done for those they loved. It made a difference. It was why he'd left private practice to join the FBI. Maybe he could help Keara find her own closure.

"Call Keara Hernandez," he told his phone as he started up his SUV, heading toward downtown Desparre instead of back to Luna. Even before she picked up, his pulse increased at the thought of seeing her.

"Hello?"

Her tone was cautious, as if she wasn't sure what to expect, and he wondered if it was because of their kiss last night or his less-than-enthusiastic response to her theory this morning.

"I'm in Desparre and I was hoping we could grab a coffee before I make the drive back to Luna," he told her, surprised at the nerves in his belly, like he was asking for a date instead of a chance to talk about the case.

He could have just swung by the police station, but he didn't want word getting around that he was spending too much time talking to the Desparre police chief. Ben and Anderson were already suspicious. As much as he respected them, he wasn't in the mood for their only-partially joking jabs at him "playing agent." Especially since he didn't plan to stop. Not for this case, and not when it might help Keara.

When the pause on the other end of the phone went on too long, Patches chimed in. *Woof! Woof!*

Keara laughed. "Okay, Patches. I can do that." Then her voice got more businesslike. "This isn't Anchorage. We don't have a dedicated coffee shop in Desparre. But there's a spot we can go outside downtown with good coffee. You have a new idea about the case?"

"I wish I did. I just thought we could talk it over again, see if we can come up with something new." He didn't say the rest of it: he wanted to see her.

There was another pause, like Keara was reconsidering, but then she said, "Okay," and gave him an address.

It was actually closer to Gabi's mom's place than driving all the way into downtown, and Jax pulled into a gas station and did a quick U-turn to get onto a different street. According to his GPS, it was a quicker route to The Lodge, the spot where Keara had recommended they meet.

"You ready to see Keara?" he asked Patches, glancing at her in his rearview mirror.

As she barked an affirmative, Jax frowned, squinting at the huge dark blue truck behind him. It looked like the same vehicle that had been behind him on the road from Gabi's. But why would it now be going this way? Had it also turned around at the gas station?

Was someone following him? And why did that vehicle seem slightly familiar, like he'd seen it before today?

He eased up on the gas, slowing to ten miles below the limit, hoping the truck would pass him on the otherwise deserted road. But it slowed, too, staying just far enough behind him that Jax couldn't get a good look at the driver.

His heart rate picked up, even as he told himself he was being paranoid. Why would anyone follow him?

It was probably just a coincidence. Still, when a street appeared to his right, Jax yanked the wheel that way.

Patches barked and he could hear her sliding across the seat at his sudden turn.

"Sorry, Patches," Jax said, his gaze darting back and forth between the road ahead and the rearview mirror.

After a minute passed and the truck didn't appear again, Jax let out a heavy breath and eased his foot slightly off the gas.

Despite telling himself he'd been overreacting, he didn't fully relax until he reached the restaurant Keara had chosen. Apparently, it had once been a lodge and even the outside looked more like a log cabin than a small-town restaurant.

As he let Patches out of the SUV and scratched her ears, an apology for his erratic driving, he couldn't help glancing around for the big blue truck. Then he shook his head and muttered, "I think I needed a longer break, Patches."

She stared up at him, her soft brown eyes telegraphing sympathy.

He'd considered taking a vacation between finishing his term on the Rapid Deployment Team in DC and moving out to Anchorage. But the job opening had seemed perfect and the idea of Alaska had felt so different and enticing that he'd jumped on it. He'd been sure the cases he'd see here would be tiny compared to the mass casualty events that had burned him out over the previous three years. But this bombing was bringing it all back.

Apparently, that stress was making him imagine threats where there were none.

Movement in the distance made him jump and his gaze darted to the woods bracketing the restaurant. Then he froze in awe.

A moose, much bigger than he'd imagined the animals to be, paused and stared back at him.

When Patches took a slow, curious step forward, Jax grabbed her collar and his rapid movement sent the moose running.

Letting go of a breath along with Patches's collar, he said, "Let's go see Keara."

Woof! Woof!

Grinning at his dog's suddenly wagging tail, echoing his own feelings, Jax led her into The Lodge. There were small tables scattered throughout the main space, centered around a fireplace. Near the front was a section that carried food, like a small specialty grocery store.

It wasn't very big, so he could tell immediately that despite his detour, he'd still beaten Keara here. Probably due to his erratic driving. Good thing there hadn't been a cop around to pull him over for speeding. That would have been embarrassing—and not just because Keara would have heard about it.

Jax ordered himself a chai latte, while the teenage girl behind the counter cooed at Patches, and then he sat at one of the cozy tables. It looked like a spot to take a date, not the sort of place you'd sit and talk about an old murder and a new bombing.

His nerves picked up again, for an entirely different reason, as Keara entered the restaurant. She spotted him across the room, a hesitant smile tipping her lips before she turned and ordered herself a drink.

Then she was walking toward him and Jax couldn't stop himself from cataloging all the differences from last night. Her hair was tied up in its typical tight bun and as she unzipped her coat, he discovered she was wearing her police uniform. Everything about her—including the serious look on her face—broadcasted that today was all business.

He tried to respond in kind, but he couldn't stop his gaze from dropping to her lips. Couldn't keep his mind from revisiting the feel of those lips against his, the taste of her mouth as she'd kissed him. The sudden desire for a big glass of cabernet filled him.

When he dragged his gaze back to her eyes, they were slightly narrowed. The hands around her mug whitened at the knuckles. Her gaze drifted to his mug and then a smile quirked her lips. "Are you drinking chai?"

"Yeah."

That smile quivered again, making him wonder if he'd missed something, and then Keara cleared her throat, her expression turning serious.

"So there are no other bombs with this symbol?" she demanded. "Not anywhere in the country over the past seven years?"

Woof! Patches went to Keara and nudged her, making her reposition her mug to prevent her drink from spilling.

From the smell that wafted toward him, she'd opted for hot chocolate. He tried not to wonder what that would taste like on her lips.

"Sorry, Patches," Keara said, taking a seat and petting his dog.

Finally, she turned back to him with raised eyebrows.

"No. And when it comes to bombs, since the FBI has the biggest lab in the country dedicated to bomb evidence, we probably would have seen it. Unless—"

"Unless the other bombs exploding destroyed the symbols," Keara finished for him. "Maybe we were never intended to see that symbol at all. Maybe that's why Rodney had to kill Juan, because even if Rodney didn't kill Celia, the crime was now connected to the symbol."

"Killing Juan doesn't change the case file," Jax reminded her.

"No. But Juan was the only one showing any interest in Rodney," Keara shot back, her expression as desperate as it was determined.

Jax stared at her, dread sinking to his stomach. This

tenuous connection between the murder in Texas and the bomb had reignited Keara's hope that her husband's case could be solved. Based on the way she'd responded to the symbol the first time she'd seen it, that was something she'd given up on until now.

This new chance could be making her see connections where there weren't any. Was his hope that she could move on making him do the same?

If so, were they both fooling themselves that they could possibly solve Juan's cold case?

SHE NEEDED TO keep her distance from Jax.

Maybe not physically, since he was helping her investigate the bombing—and hopefully her husband's murder. That was giving her access to information she'd never be able to get from the FBI otherwise. So simply staying away from him wasn't an option. But separating herself emotionally was.

Sighing, Keara signed another document in the huge stack of paperwork on her desk and set it in her outbox. Being chief, even in a small town, meant a lot of paperwork. It had taken her several years to get used to the amount of time she spent at her desk, rather than out in the field. A small town in a place like Alaska—with more than twenty percent as much land as the whole of the lower forty-eight, but the lowest population density anywhere in the country—meant she still had to take calls personally. That fact had made the transition easier.

Slowly, she'd gotten used to being the boss. Of maintaining a certain distance between herself and her colleagues. Of being tougher on her officers than she would have wanted in their place, because she knew how important it was not just to maintain her authority, but also to keep them safe.

It wasn't easy. Not just the loss of the camaraderie she'd

had when she was just one of the force, but also being hard on her officers. She'd even fired one, a rookie who'd had tons of promise and she'd liked personally, too. But he'd ignored direct orders, actually broken the law. Yes, he'd done it to save someone, and in his place, she might have done the same. But that didn't matter. Not now.

She had to do whatever it took to make sure none of her officers' spouses ever faced what she'd experienced. It was a responsibility that weighed heavily on her every day.

Still, most days she loved being a chief in Desparre. She loved the way a town known for its self-sufficient, independent citizens would pull together and look after each other when needed. And she was proud of the officers who worked for her, proud to call herself their chief.

There were definitely days when she missed being a detective. Missed working closely with a partner, unraveling a puzzle to give someone justice. She'd made the conscious choice to put that role behind her after Juan's death had gone unsolved. But now…

She shook her head and pushed her chair back from her desk, then stood and stretched. She'd been dealing with paperwork for hours, ever since she'd left The Lodge.

Coffee with Jax and Patches had felt more like a date than a professional meeting, despite the fact that they'd only talked about the case. Her fingers pressed against her lips, remembering the feel of his kiss, wishing she could get it out of her head.

She hadn't dated since Juan had died. Not really. Sure, she'd gone on a few "you'd get along so well; what's the big deal; give it a try" kind of setup dates. The kind where she'd met a guy for a drink, tried not to feel uncomfortable as he asked her what it was like being new to Alaska, what it was like being a police chief, then finally gone home. A couple of times, the guy had called for a second date and she'd let him down easy.

She'd told herself it was just too awkward to date in a town where she was the top law-enforcement official. She'd told herself that one day this would feel more like home and the timing would be better. But maybe that was an easy excuse. Because somehow, here it was, six years later, and Desparre *did* feel like her home. Yet, she hadn't gone out on a single date since those early setups.

Maybe it was pure bad luck, because she'd also never felt a connection to anyone like she'd been feeling with Jax over these past few days. At least, not since her husband.

The thought made her fingers drop away from her mouth and her stomach cramp up. Why did the first man who'd made her think about moving forward have to be one who was also forcing her to face her past?

Spinning away from the glass wall that gave her a view into the bullpen where some of her officers were working, Keara stared through the small window at the back of her office. The view was relaxing, the edge of a dense forest that butted up against this part of town. On the rare occasions that she opened the window, it filled her office with the chirping of birds and occasionally the call of a wolf. Once, she'd spotted a bear off in the distance.

When she'd first walked into this office, knowing it was going to be hers, she'd felt like she could breathe deeply for the first time in a year. Alaska had given her solace, a place to start over and hopefully, to heal.

Now, for the first time, she wondered if her family was right. Maybe she wasn't here to move on. Maybe she was here to escape the constant reminders that had been everywhere in Houston. The home she'd shared with Juan, their favorite restaurant, the streets they'd once patrolled together. Even the shared friends, the family who meant well but cringed and didn't quite meet her gaze when someone mentioned Juan's name.

Being in Houston, knowing Juan's killer was out there

somewhere, walking free while Juan was gone, had filled her with a constant rage on top of the grief. And then there'd been the weight of failure, the knowledge that she—a police officer, a *detective*—hadn't been able to get Juan justice.

Coming here had made it all fade into the background. But it was returning now, that familiar weight that seemed to suffocate her from the inside.

She couldn't run forever. Maybe the bombing wasn't connected to Juan's murder. But whether it was the key or not, regardless of the fact that she had no jurisdiction, she was going to investigate.

The thought made the grief and anger and frustration burning inside her coalesce into something more powerful. Determination.

Keara glanced at the picture she kept framed in a corner of her office, almost hidden behind stacks of paper. Juan stared back at her, serious and proud in his police uniform from when they'd first started dating.

"I promise you," she whispered to that picture, her voice cracking, "this time I'm not giving up. I'm not running away. I'm going to figure out who killed you."

Chapter Nine

"Has there been *any* progress in the FBI's investigation? Are we any closer to knowing who did this?"

Justin Peterson's questions were full of frustration, but far less anger than when Jax and Patches had last visited the man. Maybe that was because today the visit was in his home, instead of the hospital.

"Absolutely," Jax said, leaning forward even as Patches continued to do her work.

She'd sat beside Justin as soon as the man led them into his living room. He'd been absently petting her ever since. His three-year-old daughter, Lily, was sprawled on the floor, chatting nonsense to Patches.

Every few minutes Patches would suddenly drop to her belly, full of puppy energy, and Lily would burst into giggles and pet her.

"What is it?" Justin asked, but this time he cracked a smile as Patches did more of her antics and Lily laughed again.

"I know it seems like a slow process, but doing it the right way now means we won't damage evidence that might help us later. It means that we're checking everything carefully so we get the person responsible. And we will. The FBI has a lot of experience with this kind of crime. And the lead agent managing this case, Agent Nez, has investigated a lot of bombings in his career."

Justin nodded slowly, finally seeming to believe the words Jax had been repeating for five days now. "Someone should pay for this."

His gaze dropped to his leg. He'd pulled up the fabric of his pants on his right side to show Jax before Lily had come into the room. A nasty scar traveled all the way from his ankle to his knee, where doctors had dealt with the large piece of metal that had been lodged there. "It ain't pretty. But at least they saved my leg. At least I'm still here."

Tears filled his eyes that he quickly swiped away as he glanced at his daughter, oblivious as she rolled over and Patches did the same.

A laugh burst free and Justin muttered, "Maybe we need to think about getting a dog."

"Yes, Daddy!" Lily screeched, leaping up and throwing her arms around Patches's neck. "A dog like Patches!"

Woof! Patches jumped to her feet, too.

"Better ask your mom," Justin said and Lily went racing out of the room. "Careful!" Justin called after her.

"We'll continue to be in touch," Jax said, shaking the man's hand as he stood. "I'm glad you're home. I'll keep you updated about the progress. And you can call me if you have questions."

"I appreciate it." A genuine smile lit Justin's face as his daughter screeched from the other room, "Mommy said yes!"

"Good luck," Jax said, then turned to his dog, who was staring in the direction Lily had disappeared. "Come on, Patches."

She followed him out the door and Jax felt his own smile break free. He was helping these victims. Slowly, but surely, they were all starting to move forward. Some were taking smaller steps than others and some had much harder journeys, but they'd all get there.

It was why he'd made the jump to the FBI. He was good at this. Maybe Ben and Anderson were right. Maybe he needed to stick to what he knew best, his own job.

As much as he wanted to help Keara, as much as he wanted to be more directly involved in stopping the person responsible, everything that was emerging from the FBI investigation suggested his and Keara's theories were off base.

There were no other bombs with the symbol. It was possible, though unlikely, that this was the only time the bomber had used the symbol. A bit more likely was that it had only been recovered in this particular bomb. But when Jax had floated that idea with Ben, the agent had seemed unconvinced. More likely, this guy was solely a bomber and the murder in Texas was unrelated. It was what Ben and Anderson believed. They even questioned if the symbols really matched. The loops were so random, they wondered if it was just coincidence, and that Keara, desperate to find connections to the old murders, was seeing what she wanted to see.

And yet… Jax couldn't shake the feeling he'd had when he'd first seen that symbol, the certainty that it meant something. He couldn't shake the memory of Keara's eyes widening, the way she'd swayed and gone pale, when she'd seen it.

Once he and Patches climbed into his SUV, Jax didn't bother to start the engine. Instead, he pulled out his cell phone and dialed Ben.

"Ben Nez," the agent answered. Even over the phone, he sounded commanding, the tone of someone who'd been an agent for a long time and was comfortable being in control.

"It's Jax. I'm just leaving one of the victim's houses and I have a question."

"A question or information on the case?" Ben asked, a warning tone in his voice, like he knew what was coming.

Ignoring it, Jax pushed forward. He could take the snide comments about being a wannabe agent. What he couldn't take was worrying that he'd kept quiet when speaking up might have made a difference. "I'm just wondering if we have any more details on the bomb. You've got a lot of experience with weapons like this. Does it seem like it's the work of someone who's been doing it a long time? Do you think whoever did this has made bombs before?"

A heavy sigh, meant to be heard, greeted him, followed by a long silence.

Finally, Jax broke it. "This isn't idle curiosity. What do you think?"

"It's hard to say," Ben said, his tone cautious. "The bomb itself wasn't very sophisticated. You can learn how to make something like this on the internet if you know where to look. But the fact that no one noticed anything unusual, that we don't have any cameras that caught anything suspicious, suggests this guy isn't an amateur. Plus, we've been looking hard for a motive, since the most likely reason to target this location is to take out a specific person. So far we haven't come up with anything promising."

"So—"

"You're a great Victim Specialist, Jax," Ben said, cutting him off. "And if there's information you're getting from the victims that could help us figure this out, I want to hear it. If you're asking about this because it's going to somehow help you in your role, then fine. But being an investigator isn't something you do off the side of your desk, no matter what you might have seen on TV."

Jax stiffened. He'd worked side by side with Special Agents and other members of the FBI for four years. He understood all too well how many people—agents, evidence technicians, victim specialists, analysts and more—came together to solve a crime.

"I know I'm not an agent," Jax said, wishing the words didn't feel just a little bit bitter. "And I'm not trying to be one." That much was true. Despite the burnout he was feeling, despite the desire to be more embedded in the investigative side of things, he did love his job. "But this case is different. This case—"

"This isn't the first time you've stepped outside your lines," Ben contradicted. "I don't know if this is how things ran when you were on the Rapid Deployment Team…"

"Not really," Jax admitted. Yes, he'd shared his insights when he could, but he'd often worked with big task forces. And his time at a particular crime scene had been very focused.

Alaska was different. The field office was big, but so was the area they covered. When he'd had psychological insight into a case, the agents had listened. To be fair, that had always included Ben.

Maybe he was stepping over the line with this case. Thinking of his clandestine meeting with Keara just that afternoon, Jax mentally crossed off the *maybe*.

"I'm sorry," Jax said. "You're right. It's just that the symbol is really bothering me in this case."

"We're looking into it," Ben said, but his tone told Jax the truth.

They'd already decided it wasn't important.

"I'm not an agent," Jax said again, sitting up straighter and making Patches stick her nose between the seats.

Absently petting her, Jax insisted, "And I'm not a profiler, either. But my background is in psychology. That means I understand a lot about human motivation and people's desires, especially the ones they can't seem to help. All of my training, all of my experience, is telling me there's something to this symbol."

There was another pause, but this one was shorter. "Fair enough," Ben said. "Do you know what?"

"No. But the fact that you haven't been able to connect it to anything else? The fact that this strange symbol was also near a murder? There's something here."

He'd been trying to deny it, but he couldn't shake the gut feeling he'd had from the beginning. "I need a favor."

"Okay," Ben said, reluctance in his tone, but less hostility.

"Run the symbol through the FBI's database again. This time do it without the bomb specification. See if that symbol has appeared at the scene of any other type of crime."

"I'll do it," Ben said, "but look, I've been down this kind of rabbit hole before, trying to make connections that aren't there. Be prepared for disappointment."

IT HAD BEEN six long years since she'd been embedded in a case like a detective, sorting through the evidence and clues. But sitting in her relaxing Alaskan home—her escape—with her laptop open to two case files and a mug of coffee that had long since gone cold, a familiar buzz filled Keara.

She loved being a police chief. She liked and respected all of the officers on her force and admired the spirit of the people of Desparre. Moving here had done so much for her mental health. It had made her feel like she was allowed to have a life again, that it wasn't a betrayal to keep living it, without Juan.

For the most part she hadn't really missed being a detective. That role came with too many memories. The surprise party Juan had thrown her when she passed her detective's exam and got promoted. The initial thrill of working a desk in the bullpen close to him. Working as partners had been against policy, since they'd just gotten married when she was promoted. But seeing him across the detectives' area each day had reminded her of their early times together, patrolling.

She'd expected being a detective would bring them closer, feel more like it had at the beginning, when they'd worked together every day. But too quickly, discussions about their cases had started interfering with their relationship. Most of it had been subtle, like the slow deterioration of their romantic dinners into sharing case files over takeout.

Then there'd been the expectations Keara had never seen coming. Being a patrol officer was dangerous, in Juan's opinion. But with Keara in a detective's seat, he'd wanted to try and have kids immediately. While she'd been working late to fit in—being a detective was still a bit of a boys' club—he'd been imagining babies. Toward the end of his life, when Keara thought they had plenty of time to figure it out, they'd started fighting over what they wanted, and when. Now it was all too late.

She minimized the case file for her husband's murder that Fitz had sent her unofficially. It hadn't been easy to go through, though thankfully, Fitz had left out the crime scene photos.

Seven years had dulled some of her grief, taken it from a sharp-edged pain that made it hard to breathe to something duller and more manageable. But she couldn't help wondering if things might have turned out differently if she and Juan hadn't made a pact to stop talking business and focus more on their relationship in those last six months. Would she have seen the threat coming? Would she have been able to prevent it?

"You can't change the past." Keara repeated the words her police-employed psychiatrist had told her seven years ago, when she wasn't ready to hear them. "You can only impact what happens in your future."

Ironic that more and more, the key to moving on seemed like it would involve revisiting her past.

And yet, was it too late? Seven years was a long time in the investigative world. There was a reason those cases were considered cold. A reason they were set aside and detectives' time reallocated to newer cases. A reason they were rarely reopened, unless some new evidence suddenly came to light.

Rubbing the back of her head, where a headache had started to form, Keara skimmed through Juan's interview with Rodney Brown one more time. The notes were slim, the interview itself a long-shot possibility. No matter how many times Keara reread them, she didn't see anything now that her husband hadn't seen back then. Except…

Keara jerked forward, yanking her laptop closer as an offhand mention describing Rodney's house caught her eye. "Lives with a roommate, not home," Juan had written.

Juan had originally gone to interview Rodney thinking he might have seen something relevant since his car had been photographed near the crime scene the night Celia Harris was killed. Although it was good police work not to rule anyone out as a suspect too quickly, Rodney hadn't been considered one initially. The only reason Juan had left that interview with even mild suspicion was that Rodney had denied driving his car anywhere near the crime scene.

Happening to be near a crime scene wasn't a crime. Still, Juan had thought it was more likely Rodney was just afraid of police after his various assault arrests rather than a legitimate suspect, especially since he had no apparent connection to Celia. While the assault charges and the probable sexual assault told them he wasn't a nice guy, the specifics didn't suggest possible serial killer.

Like hundreds of other people who'd been interviewed in the Celia Harris murder, Rodney Brown had been pushed to the bottom of the list of people who might know something. But what if Juan had been approaching it from the wrong angle?

What if the reason Rodney had so vehemently insisted he hadn't been driving anywhere near the crime scene that night was because he hadn't? What if the roommate had used his car?

A thrill ran through Keara, a jolt of adrenaline she hadn't felt in a long time—the gut feeling that she was onto something with a case.

When Rodney had disappeared, the follow-up interview by Fitz said the house had been cleared out. So that meant the roommate had disappeared, too. Had they left together? Had they been in on Celia's murder together?

Or maybe her earlier theory had been right all along. Maybe the person who'd set the bomb had intentionally used the symbol from Celia's murder to throw suspicion on someone else—his roommate.

If she was right, that triggered a lot of new questions: Who had killed Celia and who had set the bomb? Which of those two had killed her husband, Rodney or his roommate?

And where were they both now?

Chapter Ten

Every officer in the Desparre police station turned to stare at Jax as he strode through the station, following Officer Tate Emory to Keara's office.

Jax tried not to feel self-conscious as he juggled two cups of takeout coffee, wondering why he was getting so much attention. He'd been here before; it wasn't like the officers didn't know who he was. Maybe it was the overstuffed bag he had slung over one shoulder, full of FBI case printouts Ben had handed him that morning. Or maybe they could read his newly cautious hope about what those printouts might contain.

As Jax gave subdued nods of greeting to the officers who met his gaze, Patches bounded around him, occasionally darting to a desk for a pat from one of the officers before running back to his side.

"What's going on?" Jax asked Tate softly.

Tate's gaze briefly scanned the room before coming back to him. "Something's up with the chief," he said, then knocked on the door to Keara's office before pushing it open.

From across the station's bullpen, through the glass walls into her office, Keara had merely appeared hard at work. From a distance, he'd assumed her normal professional face was on. It was calm and serious and confident, probably something that had helped her win Desparre's trust when she'd first shown up here, an outsider and young for a police chief job.

Jax had known from her frantic call at seven that morning—when he and Patches had barely been awake—that she was reenergized about the bombing investigation and its possible connection to Juan's death. He should have realized this new information about a roommate she'd discovered would only fuel Keara's desperation.

Up close, he could see the dark circles underneath her eyes that suggested she'd been awake long before she'd called him, maybe that she hadn't gone to bed at all. Jittery energy radiated from her.

As he stepped more fully into the room, she stood and reached for one of the coffees he held. "Is this for me?"

"Yes," he answered.

Woof! Patches circled Keara, tail wagging.

"Easy, Patches," Jax warned her, not wanting his dog to trip Keara.

"She's fine," Keara said, bending down to pet Patches and getting rewarded by a dog kiss across her cheek. Keara laughed, then took a long sip of coffee, closing her eyes like she'd badly needed the caffeine jolt.

Tate gave Jax a raised-eyebrow look that seemed to say "See what I mean?" before he left the office, closing the door behind him.

Jax took a minute to watch Keara while she had her eyes closed, exhaustion and hope battling on her face. All the while, she pet Patches.

His dog's tail wagged, but she glanced back at him, as if she also wondered what was going on with Keara.

What must it be like to have spent seven years knowing someone she loved had been murdered and not being able to do anything about it? What must it be like now, to have this sudden, long-shot hope again?

Dread tightened his chest, knowing he was partly responsible. If they were both wrong, how much worse would it be for Keara?

Her eyes opened, her gaze instantly locking on his like she'd read his thoughts. Instead of making him feel more guilty, the intensity there made his own hope ignite.

What if they were right? What if they could solve her husband's murder? What if she was finally able to get closure and move on with her life? He lived too far away to be a part of it in any meaningful way, but knowing that didn't stop a sudden longing.

She broke eye contact, standing, and her tone was all business when she said, "Let's get to work."

He'd spent the morning like he had almost every other morning since he'd arrived in Luna, talking to victims and their families. Today he'd mostly been returning personal effects. For some of the victims, it was a welcome visit, a sign of moving forward. For others, it was a stark reminder of what, or who, they'd lost.

At lunchtime, when his mind had been ping-ponging between the idea of Rodney Brown having a roommate and the needs of the bombing victims, Ben had asked to meet. He'd handed over a stack of printouts and told Jax, "This is your theory, so I'm going to let you run with it. It's not protocol and I'm definitely going to be reviewing all of this myself as soon as I get a chance, but I'm expecting you to return the favor. You find something—anything at all—and I want to be your first call. Deal?"

Jax had looked down at the massive stack of printouts, then back at Ben, who'd grinned and said, "Our databases aren't magic. I input the details of the symbol, but with parameters this wide—connected to any crime over the past seven years—it spit out a *lot* of cases across the country. There's a good chance none of them are connected to the bombing or the murder, because the system matches descriptions. And it's all different law enforcement entering them, not just FBI. It's you who has to pull up the actual pictures and do a visual comparison. Still…"

"There's a chance," Jax had said. "It's a deal. I'll call you if I find anything," he'd agreed, although the first thing he'd done when Ben left the room was call Keara and let her know he was coming to the station and needed her help. He knew Ben had thrown the material at him because he still felt doubtful about a connection to the symbol and was more than willing to let Jax do the heavy lifting on that aspect of the case.

"Let's see the cases," she said.

"There are a lot," he warned, pulling out the massive pile of paperwork. "The database spits out all possibilities. It's up to us to wade through them all and narrow it down."

She gave him a one-sided grin and held her coffee cup up like she was making a toast. "Welcome to the life of a detective, Jax. Let's take a look."

As she cleared off some space on her desk and gestured for him to take the seat across from her chair, she asked, "Does the FBI know I'm helping you with this?"

"No." He settled into the seat and set half the stack in front of him, passing her the other half.

Instead of sitting beside him, Patches followed Keara around to her side of the desk.

As Keara dug into her stack of files, Jax couldn't help but stare at her carefully tied-back hair and light, professional makeup. Even the first day he'd met her, dressed down in jeans and a raincoat, she'd looked like someone who was in charge. But the day he'd stopped by her house unannounced…

He smiled at the memory of her hair spilling over her shoulders, the cabernet staining her lips like a funky lipstick. It was a look he doubted many people in Desparre got to see, even on her days off.

"Stop staring and start reading," Keara said, without glancing up.

The smile grew and he held in a laugh. Why couldn't he have met her under different circumstances? Without her husband's unsolved murder hanging over her head like a dark cloud? Without four hundred miles between their homes?

As his smile faded, he asked, "Any luck finding the roommate?"

Her gaze met his, serious and determined. A look that said she would search as long as it took. "No. Assuming Juan was right, this guy wasn't listed on the lease with Rodney. I haven't been able to dig up so much as a name." Her lips tightened as she blew out a heavy breath. "Whoever he is, he's as much of a ghost as Rodney, maybe even more so."

As Jax stared at her, she broke eye contact, lines creasing her forehead. There was a hint of fear underneath her words as she said, "Seven years is a long time. I'm scared I won't be able to track him."

"We can do it," Jax said, resisting the urge to reach his hand out and take hers.

From the other side of the desk, Patches made a slight whining sound, her way of getting attention when she knew someone needed her but wasn't paying attention. From Keara's suddenly surprised look, Patches had also pushed her head into Keara's lap, insisting on being pet.

Some of the lines raking Keara's forehead disappeared as she pet Patches.

He said a silent *thank you* to his dog, then continued, "There is one piece of good news here."

She looked up at him again.

"If he's trying so hard to stay beneath the radar that you're struggling to even find mention of his name, there's probably a reason. We might really be onto our bomber."

"THERE HAS TO be *something* here," Keara muttered as she set aside yet another case description in her *No* pile.

She and Jax had been sorting through the huge stack of cases he'd brought for almost an hour. In that time, Jax's stack of unrelated cases had grown almost as high as hers. They had a few *Maybe*s, but years spent as an officer, then a detective, then a police chief told Keara none of them were likely to be connected to the bombing, Celia's murder, or Juan's murder.

She'd been so hopeful when Jax had walked into her office, carrying such a big stack of possibilities. After her sleepless night, having Jax to help—along with his calming presence and Patches's cute distraction—had made her feel like answers had to be in sight.

She wasn't so far removed from her time as a detective that she'd forgotten the slog of it all. The hours that felt unending and pointless until one small detail broke open a case. Both Juan's and Celia's cases had remained open for a year, with Houston detectives logging thousands of hours on them, and they still hadn't found that one detail.

Lately, Keara had spent too much time fighting a roller coaster of emotions, rocketing from a certainty she'd finally get closure to the fear that she'd get nowhere and just end up back where she'd been six years ago. Grief-ridden, brokenhearted and stuck.

Back then she'd reacted by finding a tiny job posting across the country, far from anyone she knew. Getting the job had been a surprise; when she'd taken it, her family and friends had all been shocked. Until five days ago, it had felt like a brand-new start.

"We've got a couple of possibilities," Jax reminded her, his dark brown eyes full of determination, like he was trying to lend her strength.

She gave him a shaky smile, both appreciating the effort and not wanting him to see too deeply into her soul. Working with detectives was hard enough—they were trained to see what you weren't telling them. But someone with years of experience as a psychologist and a therapist? The more time she spent with him, the more she wondered if he could tell everything she was thinking.

She redirected her gaze to her stack of cases before Jax could make out the other thing she couldn't help feeling when he was around—attraction.

He was so different from Juan. Half a foot taller, Jax was slower to smile but more likely to have it burst into a full-blown grin when he did. His skin was darker and smoother, his body more lean muscle than Juan's heavier bulk.

But it was more than just the physical differences. Her husband had been hard to win over, suspicious and wary until you proved you could be trusted. Jax seemed to approach everyone like his friend, until proven otherwise. Probably a result of their respective professions.

In other ways, she could see definite similarities. Juan could fill a conversation with lots of small talk so you didn't even realize you'd shared a lot more with him than he had with you. It was a skill that had come in handy as a detective, but frustrated her in the early stages of their relationship. Only once they'd been dating for a few years had he really started opening up to her.

From the little bit she'd asked about Jax's personal life, he hadn't seemed closed off at all. Still, he was good at pulling personal information out of others. It was certainly something that was helping him reach victims. Maybe that was why she'd connected so easily to him.

Was that all this was? Her projecting a connection because she needed someone to help her process the fact that Juan's death had gone unsolved? That she'd *let* it go unsolved, by running across the country instead of staying and trying to figure it out herself?

"No," Jax said and for a minute, Keara wondered if she'd spoken her thoughts out loud.

"What?"

He sighed, ran a hand through his hair that mussed it up just enough to make Keara long to fix it for him. "I thought maybe I'd found something, but I didn't."

He tossed the case summary printout on his *No* pile, then gave her an encouraging smile. "We're onto something. I can feel it." His eyes were already on the next case file as he muttered, "We just have to keep searching."

A smile pulled at her lips despite how discouraged she'd started to feel. For a minute she just watched him, then Patches nudging her leg made her refocus.

Petting the dog with one hand, Keara flipped open a new case file and her heart gave a hard *thump*. "No way," she breathed. She yanked the page closer to her face to scrutinize the scanned picture of a symbol. It looked eerily similar to the one found at the murder, down to the spray paint.

"What is it?"

Jax sounded distracted and Keara shook her paper at him, her excitement growing. "I think I found something. It's…" She shook her head, surprised at the crime. But there was no question that the symbol was the same. "It's an *arson* case. Unsolved, no promising suspects. It's from six years ago, in Oklahoma." She set the paper down. "Maybe that's why the detectives never found Rodney after Juan died. He'd already moved on to Oklahoma."

"Keara." Jax looked up at her, surprise and intensity in his gaze. "I've got something, too."

Her pulse jumped again as she leaned toward him across the desk, trying to see his case details. "Another fire?"

"No, another murder. Five years ago, in Nebraska."

Excitement filled her, churning in her stomach along with too much coffee. "He was heading north. He was slowly moving toward Alaska."

Jax's gaze met hers again and she saw her excitement reflected there. "Maybe."

"*Maybe?* No, definitely." The buzz she'd felt last night when she'd discovered Rodney had a roommate returned, headier now.

She tossed the case information into her *Yes* pile and kept searching. Over the next half hour, her excitement dimmed slightly, as no new cases looked connected. But then she and Jax found three more in rapid succession, until they had a stack of five with the exact same symbol. The symbol was drawn in different ways, found in different places at the crime scenes, but they had to be connected.

"We're onto him," Jax said, grinning at her over the newly divided stacks of cases.

The dimple just visible on his right cheek as he smiled at her almost made her smile back. Except…

"There's just one problem," Keara told him, dread already balling up in her stomach again.

"What? That we probably haven't found everything?" Jax referred to the fact that there was one time gap big enough that they'd agreed there was probably at least one more connected crime. "I'm sure another one will surface eventually."

"Not that," Keara said. "Every single one of these cases is in a different jurisdiction. Hell, every case is in a different *state*."

"Okay, but—"

"Jax, he set off this bomb in Luna, left behind this symbol." Frustration welled up, made her want to take it out at the gym on a punching bag. "This pattern suggests he commits one crime and then leaves. He's probably already gone."

He stared back at her, his grin slowly fading.

Beside her, Patches whined and nudged her leg.

Keara looked down at the dog and gave her a grateful

smile, tried to will forward some positive energy. They'd found the criminal's trail, but had it already gone cold here?

Boom!

A sound like thunder directly overhead exploded in her ears, making her flinch and instinctively leap to her feet, her hand already near her weapon.

Through the glass walls of her office, her officers were doing the same, glancing questioningly at one another.

Then the silence following the loud noise was replaced by screaming.

Before Keara made it to her office door, the door into the bullpen opened.

Charlie Quinn, one of her longest-term veterans, appeared, looking pale. Even from a distance, she could read the words on his lips.

"Bomb."

Chapter Eleven

There was chaos in her police station.

Her officers were all racing for the door, some grabbing weapons from desks and shoving them in holsters, others looking around with panic. The door into the bullpen was open—and probably the door to the station beyond that—so Keara could hear the panicked cacophony outside, too. Screams, crying and a persistent wailing that sent a chill through her entire body.

After yanking open the door to her office, Keara raced into the chaos and yelled, "Wait!"

Her officers stopped moving toward the exit, but their gazes still darted all around. Her veterans seemed filled with anxious determination, ready to find out what was happening and help. Some of the newer officers looked stiff with uncertainty. None of them had ever faced anything like this.

Neither had she.

Dread settled in her gut, her pulse picking up at the worry she wouldn't know how to manage this properly. Houston was a big city, but even there, she'd never been on the scene of a bomb. The closest she'd come was seeing the aftermath of the Luna explosion.

"Right now we don't know anything."

"We know it was a bomb outside, maybe on the street,"

Charlie interrupted, his voice deeper than usual with tension. "Lorenzo and the Rook are out there."

At his words, everyone started moving again.

"Stop!" Keara demanded. "Listen. We need to be careful. What we don't know is if there are more bombs set. Sam, I need you to stay here and manage the station. Field calls, deal with anyone who comes in off the street and get paramedics on scene. Then call the hospital in Luna and tell them to expect injured. We might need their medevac helicopter. Line it up."

Sam Jennings nodded. He was a five-year veteran who was typically cool under pressure and great at multitasking, especially when it involved tech. But his movements were shaky as he headed toward the front of the station.

"Everyone else, keep your eyes open and stay in contact with each other. Let's go."

As her officers started running for the door, Keara turned back toward her office to ask Jax to inform the FBI.

He met her gaze immediately, and there was worry in his eyes, even as his attention seemed to be half on the phone at his ear. Moving the mouthpiece backward, he called to her, "I'm on with Anderson. The FBI is on the way. They're coming with agents and evidence techs. They'll handle the bigger investigation—they assume it's connected to Luna. They want you to focus on helping the injured and securing the scene."

Keara didn't bother being offended at the FBI instantly calling jurisdiction. They had more experience, more resources. She was happy to focus on the safety of her citizens and let the FBI take the lead. Nodding, Keara delayed a few seconds to take in the calm steadiness of Jax's presence. Then she took a deep breath and raced after her officers.

As soon as she stepped outside, a wisp of smoke wafted toward her, the acrid taste of it filling her mouth and then her lungs. Her eyes watered, partly from the smoke, but mostly from the scene in front of her.

The grassy park down the street from the police station—a popular place for citizens to dog walk or picnic—was now a bomb site. Flames leaped out from a small gazebo at the back of the park, close to the woods. The charred ground around it, a blackened patch where bright blue wild irises had just been starting to bloom, reminded her of the scene at Luna. The set of swings at the center of the park were warped and partially collapsed, one swing completely missing. People were scattered around, some lying on the ground, some hunched over, and others stumbling away.

She'd known some of the victims at the Luna bombing. She knew almost everyone who lived in Desparre.

Keara ran faster. She heard the heavy police station door slam closed and looked back to see Jax hurrying after her. She immediately glanced toward the ground at his side, but he'd left Patches in the station. Probably because of the debris that might be dangerous for her to walk on.

Whipping her gaze back to the park, Keara scanned the area, trying to take in everything at once. There were people staggering backward, their movements and expressions full of shock. Others seemed frozen. Still others were helping, moving toward the park instead of away from it, risking their own safety for their neighbors. That included her officers.

Whoever had done this was either fearless or making a statement. The park was less than a hundred feet from the police station.

Slowing to a stop as she neared the park, Keara searched for anyone whose reaction seemed out of place. Either too calm or worse, pleased. But everyone appeared shocked and scared. No one was hurrying away from the scene, either.

She glanced at Jax, who'd paused next to her. His expression was serious and troubled, but he still managed to radiate a certain calm. No wonder people gravitated toward him in a crisis.

He shook his head at her and she realized he'd been looking for the same thing, studying people with a psychologist's perspective.

Whoever the bomber was, he was either long gone or one hell of an actor.

"Chief!"

At the tearful tone of Lorenzo, one of her steadiest veterans, Keara's gaze whipped back to the park.

At the edge of the grassy area, near the road, Lorenzo was bent over someone.

The dread in her gut intensified, bubbling up a familiar grief. She didn't need to see the face of the person on the ground to know who it was. The newest and youngest member of her force. Lorenzo's partner, twenty-year-old Nate Dreymond.

Rushing over, Keara dropped to the grass next to Lorenzo.

Nate was prone on the ground, eyes closed and face ashen. There was blood on his head, and his arm was stretched out at an unnatural angle.

"We were heading out for patrol. Someone in the park called us over. I'm not sure who it was or what they wanted." Lorenzo's words were rapid-fire, his voice shaky. "Rook was ahead of me. When the bomb went off, something flew this way and slammed into him. I don't know what it's from, but—" he gestured to a piece of metal, twisted and unidentifiable, and covered in blood "—the force of the blast knocked me down, too." His hand, shaking violently, went to his own head.

When he met her gaze, his focus seemed off, too. "When I could get up, I came over here, but—"

"No," Keara whispered, the image of another man's

blood filling her mind. She leaned down, pressing her ear to Nate's chest. She expected to hear nothing, but a weak *thump thump* came through.

"He's in bad shape," Lorenzo finished.

Letting out a long breath, Keara sat up again and barked into her radio, "Sam, get that medevac from the Luna hospital. Nate needs it."

She scanned his prone form, looking for injuries that needed immediate attention. She'd gotten basic training in first aid over the years in Houston. It had been a long time, though, and she frantically ran through the mental checklist she used to know by heart.

She didn't see any way to help him. He was unconscious with a clearly broken arm, but the blood on his head wasn't still flowing.

"Medevac is coming," Sam's strained voice informed her. "They're twenty minutes out."

"Help!"

Keara's head popped up at the cry. She put her hand on Lorenzo's arm and asked, "You okay?"

"Fine," Lorenzo said.

There was no doubt he needed to get checked out by a doctor, but she nodded. "Stay with Nate. Call me if anything changes."

Then she pushed to her feet and hurried across the park to the person calling. The grass felt strange beneath her boots, crunchy where it should have been soft. As she ran, she passed by other Desparre citizens, some simply looking dazed and others clearly injured.

There was a family, fairly new to Desparre, with a six-year-old and a new baby on the way, hugging each other and crying. The owner of Desparre's downtown bar, wrapping his bleeding arm with his own shirt. A loner who lived up the mountain and came into the park every few weeks but still stuck with his own company, sat on the ground, looking dazed. He had a hand to his head and both legs were bleeding, but nothing was gushing.

Keara scanned each of them, but kept moving. None needed immediate attention.

The fire at the gazebo was growing, flames devouring most of it now. The structure was relatively far from other buildings, but it was close enough to the woods to be a concern. She lifted her radio and said, "We need to manage this fire."

"On it," Tate Emory answered and from her peripheral vision, she could see he was also on his cell phone, probably with the tiny fire department. They were located on the edge of Desparre and they served the whole county, including Luna and other neighboring towns. They were also all volunteer and had similar hours as her officers.

"I've got some citizens lined up to bring buckets from the bar while we wait for the fire department," Tate told her. "We should be able to keep this from jumping."

"Good. Radio if you need more help," she instructed, then jammed her radio back into her belt.

At the edge of the gazebo, she discovered who had called for help. Talise Poitra owned the grocery store in downtown Desparre. She was friendly and quick to advise outsiders, which Keara had discovered her first week in town. Talise had celebrated her seventieth birthday last month and hung balloons all over the grocery store. She'd stopped by the police station with cake and told them she insisted the entire town celebrate with her.

Right now the woman with the long gray hair, easy smile and deeply weathered skin from a lifetime in Alaska was holding her leg with one hand and her ear with the other. A deep gash ran the length of her right thigh and blood spurted out at regular intervals.

Swearing, Keara yanked at the sleeve of her police uniform until the arm ripped off. She dropped to her knees and tied the fabric around the top of Talise's leg. But no matter how hard she yanked the knot, blood was still pumping.

"I got it," Jax said, suddenly beside her, his belt in hand. "Brace yourself," he told Talise, then tightened the belt over the fabric.

Talise went pale, her eyes rolling backward as she swayed. But she stiffened before Keara could grab her. Her hands dropped to the ground, bracing herself, and Keara saw more blood on the woman's right ear.

Fury overlaid the dread she'd been feeling. This was *her* town. These people were *her* responsibility.

She put her hand on Talise's arm, trying to comfort her, even as her gaze met Jax's.

"Two bombs," he said, his tone filled with meaning she didn't understand.

She shook her head and he added, "Two bombs in less than a week. Just one town apart."

The implications sank in fast. The crimes they'd been poring over this afternoon had been filled with differences. The only commonality they'd shared besides the symbol was that the perpetrator hadn't struck again in the same jurisdiction, or even the same state.

"It's not the same person," she breathed.

Chapter Twelve

The day had gone by in a blur of blood and fire and pained cries. But rushing from one person to the next hadn't been able to fully distract him from the panic.

Over his years on the Rapid Deployment Team, he'd gotten used to mass casualty events. They didn't get any easier, but the fear and panic of his first few scenes hadn't returned in years. Not until today.

Only after most of the victims had been checked by paramedics and Keara was helping put out the last of the fire had he realized why. A flame had sparked, creating a loud *boom* that sounded like a bullet, and his gaze had leaped immediately to Keara.

In that moment it hit him. He was worried about her safety. He was worried about *her*.

Recognizing where the panic was coming from created a different kind of worry, but he'd pushed it aside and spent the rest of the day focusing on the victims.

Jax was exhausted. So was Patches, who'd joined him at the scene as soon as it was clear enough to be safe. The two of them had talked to as many victims as possible. They'd also spent time comforting the Desparre officers, who had never seen anything like this.

For all of his exhaustion, the people around him were even more tired. Ben and Anderson coming in with their

FBI team had taken the weight of the investigation off the Desparre PD, but it hadn't taken away the responsibility.

He could see it as he eyed Keara from his peripheral vision, trudging beside him, leaving the bomb site. There was soot smeared across her forehead, someone else's blood on her arms and a furious determination on her face.

As she glanced back at the scene, barely visible in the moonlight, he told her, "There's nothing else you can do there tonight."

Walking between them, Patches nudged Keara with her nose, always sensitive to people's needs.

Keara smiled fondly down at his dog, petting her head as she refocused on their destination: the police station.

Anderson jogged up beside them, shivering even with his FBI jacket zipped all the way up. The agent had come from Los Angeles and even after being in Alaska longer than Jax, he still hadn't acclimated. His normally perfect hair was sticking up in all directions and there were dark craters under his eyes. "We'll be taking another look at that symbol now that we've seen it at a second bomb site."

Jax felt his heart thump harder. "It was on this bomb, too?"

"Not on the bomb. We found it on a tree behind the gazebo. It was carved there, pretty recently, judging by the state of it."

Keara frowned, looking more perplexed than encouraged by the news.

Anderson glanced from Jax to Keara and back again. "Ben said you were combing through other crimes that might have the same symbol. Any luck?"

Jax gave a frustrated shrug. "We thought so, but now I'm not so sure they match. I'll flag them for you guys to look, but…"

"Seems like more than one person is using the same symbol," Anderson finished, not sounding surprised.

Jax glanced at Keara, wanting her take on it, and she gave a discouraged nod.

"This symbol means something we don't understand yet," Anderson said. "You were right about that, Jax. Whatever the meaning, it sounds like it's important to more than one criminal. Maybe it's connected to an organization, possibly some kind of underground group."

"But *what*?" Keara muttered. "The Houston PD researched it seven years ago. *I* researched it this week. None of us came up with anything."

Anderson shrugged, covering a yawn with his hand. "Or it could be more personal. Maybe we have a couple of criminals who were a team once and now they're both taking the symbol to their own crimes."

Keara's troubled gaze met his and he could practically read her thoughts: *If the symbol was from some personal event, how would they ever figure it out?*

Patches nudged her again as they reached the police station and Keara pet her once more before holding open the door.

Jax filed inside with Patches, but Keara stayed there, holding the door open and thanking each of her exhausted officers—and all of the FBI agents, too—as they walked past her.

She was a good chief. It couldn't have been easy for her, being the only woman on the force, being so young for her role and being an outsider, too. But it was obvious her officers respected her. Despite how personally each of them had been touched by today's tragedy, they mustered up weak nods for her in return.

Even the FBI agents, who could sometimes get frustrated with small-town officers who had little experience dealing with major crimes, seemed impressed by Keara and her team.

As Keara finally followed them inside, Sam stood up behind the front desk. "Any news on Nate?"

Keara swept her gaze over her officers, who had all stopped in the entryway of the station to listen. "The hospital is going to update us when there's any change. I'll keep you all informed."

Keara's youngest rookie had been in bad shape when the helicopter had lifted off. So had its other occupant, the grocery store owner who was far stronger than she looked to have held on until the medevac team arrived. Five other people had been taken to the hospital, too, but they'd gone by ambulance, taking the hour ride up and down the mountain to get to Luna. But at least—as of right now—no one had been killed in this bombing.

"We're going to relocate over to Desparre," Ben said, moving to the front of the crowd.

The seasoned agent, who'd lived in Alaska most of his life and managed other scenes where explosives had been set off, was holding up better than most of them. But even he had cracks in his stoicism, with a tight set to his jaw that suggested this case had him worried.

"There's a hotel just a few miles outside of town," Keara said. "It's called Royal Desparre. It's a nice place, but we don't get many tourists here. They'll have vacancies."

"Thanks," Ben said. "Let's go," he called to the other FBI agents and employees, and then he told Keara, "We'll be back in the morning."

As they trudged out of the station, Jax lagged behind. He didn't want to leave without a chance to talk to Keara alone. He wanted to see how she really felt about the new bombing and what they'd found this afternoon. But it was more than that. He also wanted to be able to talk to her outside her official capacity, away from people who relied on her to set the tone and be a leader. To make sure she was really okay.

"You coming?" Anderson called to him as Keara's officers all started heading out the door, too.

Jax looked at Keara and found her gaze already on him. "I have a pull-out couch," she said, loud enough for Anderson to hear. "In case they won't let Patches stay in the hotel."

Anderson didn't look like he bought her reasoning, but Jax jumped on it. "That would be great. Thanks."

Patches gave her own *woof* of approval.

Keara nodded stiffly at him, then turned away, checking on each of her officers individually. She made sure each one was able to drive home, then waited until they'd all left the station before she finally returned her attention to him.

"How are you holding up?" he asked.

Patches hurried over to her side again, sitting next to Keara and staring up at her. But it wasn't the look Patches gave when she was trying to help someone; this was his dog becoming attached.

Jax stared at Patches as Keara began to pet his dog, and new anxiety filled him. He was becoming attached to Keara, too. Whenever the end of this case came, he wasn't sure he was going to be ready to stop seeing her every day.

Keara pet Patches for a long moment without answering. Then her troubled gaze met his. "How do you do this, case after case?"

"What do you mean?"

"This." She gestured toward the front door. "How do you come to these scenes, tragedy after tragedy?" Her voice cracked as she continued, "How do you wade into them, again and again, hearing about the worst thing someone has experienced?"

He shrugged, gave her a small smile. "I'm good at it. Patches is good at it."

Woof!

Another smile broke free as he told her, "That's right,

Patches." Then he said to Keara, "It's not easy. But knowing that I've helped someone makes it worthwhile. What about *you*?"

She laughed, but it was short and bitter. "The type of crime scene I've probably been called to most often in Desparre is a bar fight. This is way outside of my comfort zone. I didn't experience anything like this, even in Houston."

Jax flashed back to the dangerous situation in the Luna bar the day he'd met her. His arms were still healing from being sliced through with broken bottles when the drunk had yanked him off the bar. He could still feel the panic when he'd jumped into the fray, worried the mob of men was going to overrun Keara at any moment.

"I mean, how do you handle constantly running into danger?"

"It's part of the job. I accepted the danger a long time ago, when I took the oath to become a police officer. But I've been at this career since I was twenty-three. I still get scared on calls sometimes, but I trust my training and I trust my officers to have my back. And I believe in what I do. That's worth the fear."

She frowned, staring at the ground, her hand pausing on Patches's head. Her voice was almost a whisper when she admitted, "It's not the physical danger that really scares me. It's the cases I can't solve. That's what keeps me up at night."

When her gaze met his again, he saw years of pain reflected back at him. "What scares me is the idea that I'll never be able to solve Juan's murder. And that as long as it remains unsolved, I'll never be able to fully move forward myself."

KEARA WOKE UP disoriented, a headache pounding at her temples and the smell of smoke lodged in her nostrils. Against her back was a strong, warm body.

In a flash, the night before returned to her. Making the short drive from the police station to her house, every second stretching out as she'd fought to keep her eyes open. Jax in the seat beside her and Patches lightly snoring in the back.

When they'd finally pulled up to her house, she'd barely had the energy to trade the uniform she'd worn to the crime scene for joggers and a long-sleeved T-shirt. She'd leaned over the sink and scrubbed her hands, face and arms, but sleep had sounded more appealing than a shower.

She'd returned to her living room to find Jax already changed into sweatpants and a T-shirt emblazoned with Fidelity. Bravery. Integrity. Apparently, he carried extra clothes everywhere he went.

In that moment, with the weight of the town's expectations and Juan's unsolved case, Jax—half a foot taller than she was with the body of a federal agent and the eyes of a therapist—had seemed like the perfect person to help her shoulder some of it. So when he'd walked over and put his arms around her, she'd sunk into his embrace.

She vaguely recalled him walking her over to the couch and coaxing her to lie down against him. As soon as she'd laid her head on his outstretched arm, the exhaustion had overcome her.

Despite the horror of the day before, despite the gnawing worry about her ability to solve Juan's case so many years later, it was the best she'd slept in years. She glanced at the floor below her, where Patches was just starting to stir, her feet twitching and her eyes opening.

When she met Keara's gaze, her tail started to thump against the wood floor and Keara whispered, "Shhh."

Nerves made her feel clumsy as she slowly slid forward on the couch, carefully lifting the arm draped over her waist. She barely breathed as she tried to slip away from Jax without waking him.

It had been seven long years since she'd woken up with a man's arm draped over her.

She finally took a deep breath as she sat up and Jax didn't move behind her. Carefully setting her feet down so she wouldn't step on Patches, she slid forward, hoping to stand without disturbing him.

"It's morning already?" Jax asked.

His voice was slightly deeper with sleep, and it sent a jolt of awareness through her, even as she cringed at having woken him.

"Yep," she said, her voice too cheery. She stood, heading toward the connected kitchen and resisting the urge to run a hand over her hair, which felt like a tangled mess, the bobby pins half out of her bun. "Coffee?"

Patches leaped up, racing after her, sliding as the planked wood floors of her living room gave way to slicker tile in the kitchen.

Keara couldn't stop the laugh that escaped as Patches ran around her in a circle, tail wagging. She looked more like a puppy than a therapy dog and Keara knew Patches was catching her nervous energy.

"Sounds good," Jax said from the living room.

She could hear him standing, probably stretching, but she didn't glance back. Her neck and face felt warm with the knowledge that he knew exactly why she was trying to busy herself. It didn't take a psychology degree—which he had in multiples—to recognize that she was uncomfortable with what had happened between them last night. The fact that it had been a lot more innocent than the kisses they'd shared a few days ago didn't matter. Spending the night in his embrace had felt more intimate.

As she scooped coffee grinds into the machine, Jax joined her in the kitchen. From her peripheral vision, she saw him lean against her island and watch her.

Before she could get her scrambled brain to come up with small talk—or better yet, a coherent discussion about the investigation—he asked, "What did your family think about you moving across the country to be a police chief?"

"They weren't thrilled." She spun to face him and even knowing where he'd been standing, even though he was still a couple of feet away, it felt too close. His hair was slightly mussed from sleep, making her realize how curly it was, making her want to run her hands through it.

Fisting them at her sides, she continued, "But then, they kept hoping Juan's death would be a wake-up call that I needed to find another profession."

"They worry about you."

"Yeah. I'm an only child, but as my dad likes to joke, with Irish on one side and Italian on the other, we're not a small family. My aunt was a police officer and I was really close to her growing up. She worked a night shift during most of my childhood, and since my parents worked days, she'd pick me up from school every day. She was killed on the job the same year I got my badge."

"I'm sorry."

Keara nodded. The year her aunt had died had been the same time she'd been paired up with Juan. It had been a hugely bittersweet time in her life. She'd wanted to follow in her aunt's footsteps since she was a kid. She'd always imagined them working together someday.

"I've lived here for six years now and they still ask when I'm moving back on a pretty regular basis." She shrugged, even though it frustrated her. "At least it's coming from a place of love."

"What if we solve Juan's case?" Jax stared at her, his gaze so focused that even Patches quieted down.

Her heart jumped at the idea that he still thought it was possible. Jax wasn't an investigator, but over the past week, she'd discovered he made a great partner. "What do you mean?"

"If we solve it, would you consider moving back to Houston?"

She'd never thought about it. Moving to Alaska had been a concession; her way of admitting that Juan's murder would always remain unsolved.

The Houston PD would probably take her back, if they had an opening. She'd had a good relationship with the officers and chief there. But what had started as a self-imposed exile and escape had become her home.

She shook her head. "I don't think so. I should visit more. I miss my family. But that was a different chapter of my life. Alaska is my future."

Saying the words out loud, she realized how true they were. It freed something inside her, made real happiness seem possible again. And staring at the Victim Specialist in her kitchen made even more seem possible.

Diverting her gaze before he read her thoughts, she spun back to the coffee machine, filled it with water and hit Brew.

When he didn't move, she turned back toward him, bracing her hands on the counter behind her. "This is my town, Jax." She sighed, the responsibilities crashing back around her. "I'm glad the FBI is taking lead in the new investigation. They have a lot more experience than I do. But when they leave, this will still be my home. These people will still be my responsibility. I'm officially involved now, so we don't need to be investigating on the side."

He pushed away from the island, his mouth opening.

She cut off the argument she could see coming. "That doesn't mean I want to stop working with you. I don't care what your title is. I want your psychological insight on this. But what we saw in the cases we dug up yesterday? They don't match what's happening here."

He frowned, lines creasing his forehead. "I know."

"If this were one person so savvy and determined to stay off police radar by jumping jurisdictions—hell, jumping *states*—between his crimes, why set off two bombs in less than a week? Most likely, this is still connected to the crimes we dug up *somehow*, if we can figure out that symbol. But right now we have a bigger problem."

Jax nodded. "We're looking at a serial bomber."

"Yeah. And with two bombs in six days, he's probably not finished."

Chapter Thirteen

Jax had a tendency to overanalyze things, but right now he knew exactly what he wanted.

He stared across the Desparre park at Keara, frowning as she talked to Ben and Anderson. As if she sensed his gaze on her, her focus shifted to him briefly. Then her head swung back to the agents.

Patches nudged his leg with her nose a few times and he pet her head.

"Sorry, Patches. You're right. We need to be working."

Although yesterday had been horrific, with people bleeding and crying and the gazebo blazing, the aftermath of the destruction was terrible, too. The once-cheerful white gazebo was now a pile of charred wood, splintered edges reaching into the air. The ground beside it was burned and bloodied. Scattered across the park were discarded personal items that hadn't yet been tagged and collected as evidence. The FBI's Evidence Response Team members walked among them, gathering anything relevant.

Somehow, it all felt more jarring after the awkward bliss of his morning. While Keara had showered, he'd made scrambled eggs. They'd eaten at her kitchen table and he'd pretended not to notice when she fell for Patches's sad eyes and fed her some under the table.

He'd never dated anyone in law enforcement, despite

working so closely with them, despite some mutual interest a few years ago when he'd been in DC. He'd never wanted the constant fear that came along with it. But Keara? His gaze darted to her once more, took in the serious determination in every line of her body. Being with Keara would be worth it.

The four hundred miles between Desparre and Anchorage wasn't ideal, but it suddenly didn't seem impossible.

The bigger hurdle was Keara herself. Her reaction to waking up next to him this morning had been equal parts adorable and frustrating. But even if she was willing to try and pursue something long-distance, would her heart really be in it? Or would she never be able to truly give him a chance while her past was unresolved? Her words at the police station ran through his mind:

What scares me is the idea that I'll never be able to solve Juan's murder. And that as long as it remains unsolved, I'll never be able to fully move forward myself.

As he stared at her, hoping this case would be able to shed light on her husband's murder, would be able to give her that closure, he also hoped he could find a way to breach her walls even if it didn't.

She'd been closed off for years, running away to Alaska but never able to escape her husband's unsolved murder. It probably made her feel like a failure in some ways, and it wouldn't matter how often someone told her that wasn't true. She'd always wonder if she should have done more, if she should have insisted on staying on the case. He didn't need training in psych to guess that. At the very least, he wanted her to find some peace, and maybe it could be with him.

Patches nudged him again, harder this time, and Jax smiled down at her. "I know. Let's do some work."

He angled his arm toward the big tree behind the gazebo, with fresh tape around it marking it as part of the crime scene.

She tilted her head at him, as if questioning why there were no people in the direction he was telling her to go. But she walked that way anyway, periodically glancing back to make sure he was following.

This wasn't part of his job, but he needed to see the symbol himself, needed to evaluate how similar it was to all the others he'd seen in case files yesterday.

The white spruce was charred like the gazebo, strips of wood dangling from the tree. The lower leaves were charred, too, and a few branches had snapped off. But on the side facing away from the gazebo was a familiar set of loops. It wasn't an exact match to the other symbols, but only because they all had some small variation—mostly due to the materials used. This one was neatly carved, suggesting that the person who'd done it was skilled with a knife, and Jax couldn't help but think of the way Keara's husband had been murdered. With one quick slice across the neck.

A chill darted up his arms and Jax shivered, his gaze going to the surrounding forest, dense with trees and places to hide. He didn't have a lot of experience with serial bombers, but it wouldn't surprise him to learn that they liked to stay close, admire their work.

Woof!

Patches's reminder that he needed to get to his own job—and hers—was overlaid by Anderson calling, "Jax!"

The agent was standing across the street from the park, beside a couple Jax remembered from yesterday. When he'd first seen them, they'd had a young girl between them. Now the woman had a hand curved protectively over her stomach, which had just enough of a swell to tell him the reason she'd climbed into an ambulance yesterday, despite looking okay. She'd been checking on her baby.

Jax jogged over, Patches at his heels.

He hadn't had a chance to meet the family yesterday before they'd all taken off, the dad and daughter jumping into their car and following the ambulance out of Desparre. He was surprised to see them back here today.

"Jax is our Victim Specialist and Patches here is a therapy dog," Anderson introduced them. He gestured to the petite Black woman with worried eyes. "This is Imani." Then he motioned to the man beside her, a mountain of a guy whose thick beard and pale skin patchy with anger made him look like someone who could handle Alaska's wild terrain. "And her husband, Wesley."

"Nice to meet you," Jax said. When he noticed Imani eyeing Patches, he added, "She's technically still a puppy. If you want to pet her, she'll love it."

A smile peeked free and Imani reached her hand out toward Patches, who rushed over and sat on her feet.

Wesley pet her, too, keeping his other arm wrapped protectively around his wife. "We saw you at the park yesterday," Wesley finally said.

Jax nodded, letting the couple lead the conversation, knowing that Anderson had called him over for a reason.

"You were taking to the chief after she helped the officer who was hurt." Wesley and his wife shared a glance full of worry. "Is he okay?"

"He's critical." Jax told them the news Keara had gotten this morning. "But he's a fighter."

"It's our fault," Imani said, her voice tearful. "We called him over and that's when the blast went off."

"That's not your fault," Jax said. Deep down, she knew it. But it often helped victims to hear someone else say it. "But why did you call for him?"

Anderson nodded at him as Imani and Wesley both pet Patches faster, their anxiety suddenly palpable.

"We saw this guy skulking in the woods by the gazebo," Imani said.

Jax's pulse leaped as Anderson leaned in. Had the guy they'd seen been lurking there because he was carving a symbol into the tree behind the gazebo?

"We were here with our daughter," Wesley continued. "We were heading to the swings when we spotted him. It's a park. Why does anyone need to be hiding in the woods? Unless he's there to watch kids. So we called the officers over. We hoped they could talk to the guy or scare him off."

"Who was it?" Anderson asked. "Did you recognize this guy?"

Imani shook her head. "No. We're new to Desparre. We don't know that many people yet. After the blast, he was gone."

"What did he look like?" Anderson asked.

"He was white," Imani said. "In his thirties, probably. Brown hair, I think."

Excitement thrummed along Jax's skin and he suddenly understood how the FBI agents probably felt when they got a promising lead. He'd seen it on their faces before, the sudden thrill of the chase, but he'd never felt it so intensely himself until now.

Rodney Brown had reddish-blond hair, but from a distance it might seem brown. And he was white, would be in his thirties now.

"Anything else you remember?" Anderson pressed. "Height, maybe? Or facial hair?"

Imani shook her head. "No facial hair. But he was pretty tall. Close to my husband's height, I think."

Jax frowned, studying Wesley, who was probably only an inch shorter than Jax's six foot one. Rodney was five foot eight. Then again, the distance between the swing set and the woods was probably twenty feet. If the guy had been skulking close to the trees, maybe that had thrown off her perception, made it hard to get a good look. Plus, a bomb had gone off shortly after she'd seen him.

Then again, maybe it hadn't been Rodney she'd seen. Maybe it was Rodney's elusive roommate.

KEARA SLIPPED INSIDE the police station. She checked in quickly with Sam, who was sitting at the front desk again today, then let out a relieved breath when she reached the empty bullpen.

She'd been at the bomb site and talking to members of the community since 7 a.m. Checking the time on her phone confirmed it was now past 3 p.m. She hadn't stopped for lunch and there was only so long the scrambled eggs Jax had cooked that morning could hold her. She didn't have an appetite.

Not after seeing the blood staining her park. Not after talking to the hospital, hearing the words *extremely critical* and *coma* when she'd asked about both Nate and Talise. But her stomach growled and her head pounded, and the coffeepot in the bullpen was calling her name. So was a quick break and a little solitude, before heading back out to talk to more people, find out if anyone had seen something that might help them find the bomber.

After dumping the sludge at the bottom of the pot that someone had brewed early that morning, Keara started a fresh one. Then she leaned against the wall, started to close her eyes.

Just before they drifted shut, she saw the stack of files on her desk through the glass walls of her office. The cases with the symbols.

Technically, they all belonged to the FBI. She probably wasn't even supposed to look at them. She definitely wasn't supposed to have them.

Pushing herself away from the wall, Keara grabbed the coffee carafe and poured everything that had brewed so far into a mug. Then she strode into her office, pushed the door shut and sat at her desk, staring at the stack of *Yes* files she and Jax had been so excited about yesterday.

There were four murders and an arson in those files. Add in the murder of Celia Harris in Houston and the bombs in Luna and Desparre and what did it all mean?

Keara slapped her hand against the desk in frustration, making it sting. Then she took a long sip of her coffee, willing the headache away, and got to work.

First, the murders. Celia Harris had been abducted, left in an alley, her killing brutal, from multiple stab wounds. She'd been a tough victim to grab, a pillar of the community with young kids and a husband at home. The symbol had been spray-painted onto the wall behind where her body was found. That had been seven years ago in Texas.

Skipping over the arson for now, Keara opened up the next murder. Five years ago, in Nebraska. The victim was a nineteen-year-old boy, on his way home from college. He'd disappeared from one side of town, only to show up on the opposite side a day later, with the symbol drawn in permanent marker across his back. He'd been killed in the time in between, from blunt force trauma to the head. He was a popular kid, a basketball star at his college. But he'd also been brought up on two sets of sexual assault charges and was estranged from his parents.

Four years ago, in Iowa. The victim was a middle-aged man, an ex-marathon runner scheduled to speak at the small town's high school track meet. The event was a big deal in the town and when he hadn't shown up, it had caused a huge uproar. His body being found later that night in a cornfield was the biggest crime they'd seen in more than a decade. He'd been shot three times, the symbol drawn thickly in pen on his arm.

Three years ago, in South Dakota. The victim was a popular middle school teacher who'd survived a heart attack the year before. She'd been grabbed and killed within a few hours, but a witness to the kidnapping had only been able to say her killer was a white male. She was strangled, found on a playground with the symbol spray-painted on the slide behind her.

Two years ago, in Montana. The victim was the newly elected mayor of a small town, with deeply polarizing views. He'd been last seen staggering drunk out of a bar. He was found a day later, in his own backyard, dead from a blow to the head. The medical examiner hadn't been able to determine if he'd fallen and cracked his own skull open or if someone had done it for him, but there had been a strange symbol spray-painted on the back of his house.

Keara stared at the glass wall into the bullpen of the station she'd come to call her own. The symbol undeniably connected these cases in some way, but the manner of death was different across all of them, the symbol never exact. It was possible there was a single killer making his way north to Alaska, committing one murder a year. Perhaps there'd been another crime in the gap after Montana and before the two bombs in Alaska, maybe in Canada while he made his way farther north.

Maybe one person had committed the murders and someone else—someone with the same knowledge of the symbol—had set the fire and the bombs.

She flipped open the arson case from Oklahoma six years ago. A brand-new rec center, the pride of the community, had opened the week before. The fire had destroyed half of it and damaged the other half so badly that it would have needed to be razed anyway. The city had never rebuilt it. Behind the rec center, on the brand-new basketball court, the symbol had been spray-painted from one end to the other.

Frowning at the case, Keara downed the last of her coffee and debated getting more. But even though it was calming her headache, her too-empty stomach was protesting. Setting the mug aside, Keara leaned back in her chair.

How similar was setting a fire and setting off bombs? They seemed pretty different to her, both from the practical standpoint of knowing how to do it and from the potential motivations. But maybe the killer was also the arsonist and the bomber had just gotten started.

It didn't feel right. No matter how she arranged the crimes in her mind, it didn't make sense. She couldn't imagine one person killing in so many different ways, with so many different victim types. And she couldn't imagine a pair of killers grabbing victims together, then randomly switching to arson, then later to bombings.

But she wasn't a psychologist. What she needed was Jax's insight.

A brief laugh escaped. Yeah, she wanted Jax's help right now, but that wasn't the only thing she wanted from him. She wished he were sitting across from her to lend his quiet support, too. So she could stare into his dark brown eyes and calm the frustration boiling inside her over all the pieces of this case that didn't quite fit together.

It had been a long time since she'd wanted to work with a man on a case in quite this way. Seven years, to be exact.

Guilt flooded, followed by an image of Juan staring contemplatively at her. The ache of missing him had faded with time, but moving on now would be a betrayal of everything they'd had together.

She was a cop and her husband had been murdered. There couldn't be room for anything else until she'd found the person responsible and made him pay.

Chapter Fourteen

If Jax was home in Anchorage on a Friday night, he'd be having dinner with friends, or maybe talking a couple of the agents into taking him to the shooting range. He'd thought he was mostly finished with the travel when he'd left the Rapid Deployment Team. But Friday night while he was in the middle of a big investigation with a lot of victims who needed him was just another night.

Tonight, though, instead of wanting to grab a quiet dinner and crash, Jax wanted to see Keara. "What do you think, Patches?"

She seemed to know exactly what he was thinking, because her tail started to wag as she stared up at him.

The two of them were on the outskirts of Desparre, back at the diner where he'd met Keara on Monday. Knowing they'd let Patches in had made it an obvious choice for a break. He'd ordered a sandwich. Enough to calm his grumbling stomach, but not so much that he couldn't eat again if Keara was up for dinner. Beside him, Patches was happily chewing the treat the restaurant owner had handed her, ignoring the dog food Jax had brought.

"Spoiled," he told her and she wagged her tail again.

Giving her a quick pat on the head, he dialed Keara, anxious to hear her voice. Although they'd gone to the crime scene together that morning, she'd left way before he had, to canvass the community. He'd spent the day in Desparre, too, but he'd been focused on the victims and families with the biggest emotional need. He and Keara had talked to the same people several times today, but never at the same time.

He missed her.

Her phone rang and rang. Just when he was expecting voice mail to pick up, Keara answered, sounding distracted. "Hello?"

"It's Jax," he told her, although he assumed she knew it from the display on her phone since she'd long since entered his contact information.

He could hear papers shuffling in the pause that followed and then finally she sighed and asked, "Did you speak to Imani and Wesley again today? Did you see the artist's rendering of the person they saw near the woods?"

After Jax had left to talk to more victims—starting with the families of Officer Nate Dreymond and Talise Poitra— Anderson had called in a sketch artist to work with the couple. He'd asked Anderson to send him the picture once it was finished.

"Yeah," he said. "I mean, people change. The picture we have of Rodney Brown is from seven years ago. But—"

"It doesn't look like him," Keara cut him off. "The nose is wrong. The cheekbones are higher. I know Rodney could have started going bald in the past seven years, but the hair seems off, too."

"Sketches aren't perfect," Jax reminded her. "Imani and Wesley weren't that close to the guy and it sounds like he tried to get out of view when he saw them looking at him."

"I know. But the thing is, I spent the afternoon reviewing the cases your system spit out. I know we already agreed the bombings don't seem connected to the earlier crimes, but Jax, I'm not sure any of them are connected."

Jax frowned and set down his sandwich. Since the second bomb had gone off, he'd been thinking they were off base, too. But there was some reason the same symbol was showing up across so many cases. He couldn't imagine a group of killers across the country, all equally skilled at evading police and all committing one crime before going dormant. "It could be a pair," Jax reminded her. "Rodney and his roommate."

"Maybe," Keara agreed, but she didn't sound convinced. "Jax, the thing is, we flagged all of the cases based on the symbols. I even considered sending the symbol to an anthropologist in case it has some kind of ancient significance, but it doesn't seem worth it. It's too rough and random, with nothing to indicate it means anything at all. I mean, you're a trained psychologist, and you haven't seen anything in it to give us a clue to its meaning. I went back and reviewed the details of the cases, too. They're just as…inconsistent. Victimology is all over the place, and the MO is different each time, too. I've never chased down a bomber before and I've never had a serial murder case, either, but nothing I know about them fits what I saw in those case files. If you take the symbol out of it, they don't seem connected at all."

"But we can't take the symbol out of it," Jax reminded her.

She let out a frustrated laugh. "No kidding. But the victims don't fit. Jax, we've got a rec center that was empty and set on fire. The murder victims were a female baker in her thirties who was a pillar of the community, a nineteen-year-old college boy with a couple of sexual assault charges on his record, a fiftyish man who used to run marathons, a popular middle school teacher in her forties and a sixtyish man with a really polarizing platform who was just elected as mayor. Then we've got the bombings, where we haven't identified the target. What ties all of these people together?"

Leaning back against the vinyl seat, Jax contemplated the list Keara had just given him. She was right. They didn't make sense as targets of the same person. They didn't even make sense as targets of two people.

The explosions in Luna and Desparre weren't the first bombings he'd assisted on. And he'd worked with two victims of a serial killer that the FBI had managed to rescue, helping them through the legal process for almost a year. He wasn't a profiler, but he'd learned way more about how serial killers worked during that case than he'd ever wanted to know.

Most serial killers had a specific type. Even when there wasn't specifically a sexual component to the crime itself, many of them were sexually motivated. Such a wide range of victims wasn't unheard of, but it was unusual. And when it happened, there was almost always a specific method of killing that was most important to the killer.

Still, the symbol… It felt almost like a signature to him, a specific thing the killer felt compelled to do, something that marked the crime as theirs. They might be able to change their MO, but a signature would remain.

But was drawing a series of loops on or near the bodies really a compulsive behavior? Or was it being used by a group of criminals, maybe individuals who'd found each other somehow and made a pact to leave behind the symbols to confuse authorities?

Except if that was the case, then why hadn't they seen additional matching crimes in each jurisdiction?

Rubbing his head, Jax admitted, "It doesn't make sense to me. I talked to Ben a bit about it today. He had a quick look at the cases we pulled. He admitted that if we'd found a series of bombs with the symbol, they'd be chasing that lead full-throttle. But across singular killings like this, he thinks it's far less likely to be connected."

"The FBI is still looking into it?" Keara pressed.

"Yeah. But obviously, the bombs are the first priority. Two so close together are a pattern that can't be ignored. And then there's the psychology of a bomber versus a killer."

"Bombers like chaos," Keara said. "They like to create fear and destruction."

"Yeah," Jax agreed. "And a serial killer who murders his victims up close probably isn't going to want to watch from a distance, like with arson or a bomb. It seems like two different personality types to me."

"And unless our murderer is also just determined to try out every method of killing possible, the single murders in each state don't really seem connected, either," Keara said.

Jax sighed. He'd initiated the call feeling hopeful, almost nervous. He'd been planning to suggest they get dinner and distract themselves from the stress and horror of the case. He'd been hoping dinner might lead to an offer for him and Patches to stay on her couch again, even though he'd confirmed that the Royal Desparre allowed dogs. He didn't expect her to join him on the couch this time, but right now being close to her was enough.

Now he felt exhausted and discouraged. Even Patches, catching his mood, let out a whine and lay on the ground.

"Where do we go from here?" Keara prompted when he didn't speak for a minute.

Jax rubbed his head, pushing aside his sandwich, no longer hungry. "I have no idea." And that was true of more than just the case. Equally frustrating was his inability to help her personally, help her move forward. Without that, there was no chance of this attraction between them going anywhere.

KEARA HADN'T BEEN back to Texas in over a year. Even then, so many years after her husband's murder, being in Houston had given her anxiety, brought back all of her anger and frustration over Juan's case having gone cold. But maybe it was time to return. The thoughts ran through her mind the next morning as she lay in bed.

Once the bombing was solved, she could take some personal time. If she could convince the Houston PD to reopen the case, if she could work it unofficially, maybe she could finally get some closure.

Seven years was long enough. She needed to be able to move forward. And for the first time, she wanted to truly move forward, to start living her life fully again.

It wasn't hard to identify the reason. She'd never known a man like Jax Diallo, never connected so quickly to anyone.

He lived on the other side of the state, but that might actually be a good thing. It would keep any relationship from moving too quickly, from getting too serious before she was ready. Because wanting to move forward wasn't the same as wanting to dive headfirst into a serious relationship. Still, she didn't want to say goodbye when the bombings were solved.

She was pretty sure he was interested. Best of all, although he worked for the FBI, he wasn't a law-enforcement officer. He wasn't constantly running into danger. He was helping victims, but he wasn't interacting with the suspects.

Sure, there were no guarantees. Everyone faced some level of risk just walking around in the world. Being a cop for so many years had definitely taught her that. But Jax was a much safer man to love than Juan had ever been.

The unexpected thought made anxiety and guilt bubble up and Keara shoved off her covers, stepped onto the cold wood floor in her bedroom. *Love.* That was an emotion way off in the future, if ever. Right now she had much bigger things to worry about.

Glancing at the clock on her bedside table, Keara groaned. Almost 8 a.m. It might have been Saturday, but she still had a long day ahead of her and she had planned to get an early start.

So much for that plan. Debating whether to jump into a fast shower or just start making phone calls, Keara opted for the phone. She started with the hospital, heart pounding faster as she waited for news on Nate and Talise.

"Both of their conditions are the same," the nurse who finally came on the line told her.

She tried to quell the disappointment. At least they weren't deteriorating. Both had faced serious injuries. Talise had gone through emergency surgery for her leg and Nate had gotten his head stitched up, only for doctors to open it up again a few hours later to release intracranial pressure.

Hanging up with the hospital, Keara sighed and headed to the kitchen. She couldn't stop herself from glancing at the couch where she'd slept—much less fitfully—the night before last. Couldn't stop herself from wishing Jax and Patches were sitting there to greet her again this morning.

When she'd spoken to Jax late last night, he'd been at a diner on the outskirts of Desparre. They'd talked about the case and then he'd had to let her go, to take a call from one of the agents. Even though she'd gone through everything she'd needed to tell him about the cases, she'd half expected him to call back. When she hadn't heard from him, she'd heated up a frozen dinner, done a little kickboxing to combat her frustration, then headed to bed.

As she turned on her coffeepot, Keara pulled up Jax's number. Before she could hit Call, her phone rang. It was a number she didn't recognize.

"Chief Hernandez," she answered.

"This is Ben Nez."

The last of Keara's sleepiness cleared away. Was there a break in the case? "Agent Nez. What's happening?"

"We've been running down all of the victims in the two bombings, trying to nail down a potential target."

From the beginning, she'd heard the FBI theorizing that a specific target was likely, since the bombs could have easily been placed in more populated areas or spots that would have gotten more publicity. Although the bombs had definitely made the news in and around Desparre and Luna, they hadn't been large or spectacular enough to make much of a blip on the national news.

"Any luck?" she asked when he paused.

"Well, I wanted your take on something. We just discovered that one of the people who was killed at the Luna bombing is actually related to a victim in Desparre."

"Who is it?" Keara asked, frowning. The connection was news to her.

"Aiden DeMarco was the victim in Luna. He posted the idea about the soccer game on the chat room, so the bomber would have definitely known he'd be there. He was eighteen, planned to leave Alaska to go to college in California. We looked into him early on, didn't see any reason for him to be targeted, but we could have missed something. His aunt on his mom's side, Gina Metner, was injured in Desparre."

"I know Gina," Keara said. The woman was a transplant from the lower forty-eight. She'd moved up to Alaska to be near her sister and escape from a violent ex. But the ex had since died and Gina had decided she wanted even more solitude than Luna offered, so she'd found herself a home in Desparre. She worked part-time at the library in Luna and part-time at the grocery store with Talise.

"Gina talked about her sister and her nephew, but I didn't know his name," Keara told Ben. "I didn't realize he'd been killed in the bombing."

"Can you think of anyone with a grudge against Gina?"

"No one living." Keara explained about the violent ex,

then added, "Gina and I got to talking a year ago, when she first decided to move to Desparre. She gave me a bit of a rundown on her life. But otherwise, she's pretty quiet. She's got a couple of friends here we can talk to, but I can't imagine her having made a ton of enemies since she moved to Alaska two years ago."

"We spoke to Gina already," Ben said. "She said the same thing. It could be a coincidence." He sighed. "But I was hoping we might have stumbled across the connection we've been trying to find."

"Gina wasn't badly hurt in the bombing," Keara said. "She was leaving the park when the bomb went off. She got checked out since the blast initially impacted her hearing, but she got the all clear to go home the same day. The only thing she needed was a couple of stitches and not even directly from the blast. It was when the explosion knocked her down and she hit the pavement."

"Right. So if the bomber was targeting her and he was nearby, maybe the couple who spotted him and called the police over threw him off. Maybe he was distracted and ducked into the woods to hide, didn't get farther away quickly enough. He wouldn't have wanted to be that close when the bomb went off. Assuming the bomber is the same person Imani and Wesley saw near the tree with the carving on it," Ben added.

"Luna and Desparre are pretty small towns. It's not really surprising that two of the victims would be related."

"Yeah, well, you know what they say about all the bases," Ben said.

Keara mumbled an agreement, trying not to let him hear how disheartened she felt. This kind of investigation was more like a marathon than a sprint. A bomber savvy enough to have set off the bomb in Luna—which hadn't yielded any significant leads more than a week later—probably wasn't going to be easy to find.

"What about the sketch of the suspect?" Keara asked.

She hadn't recognized him. Neither had anyone on her force. That was a little bit surprising if he lived around here, since they were a small town. Then again, Desparre was known for being the sort of place where you could come to disappear. They had a lot of land to get lost in and if you wanted to stay off everyone's radar, there was a whole mountain to hide on. If the bomber was hiding here, it wouldn't be the first time the town had a criminal in their midst.

"We're still showing the sketch around," Ben told her. "So far no one knows this guy."

If the bomber *was* the same person who'd been responsible for the murders and arson in the lower forty-eight, it made sense that no one knew him. He'd be staying far below the radar. But there had been five days between the Luna bombing and the one in her park. It had now been two days since the blast that had been close enough to shake the walls of the Desparre police station.

If he'd gone from a once-a-year, once-a-location killer to a serial bomber, how much time did they have before he struck again?

Chapter Fifteen

When Keara walked into the police station half an hour later, the rest of her department, and most of the FBI agents, were already there. Thankfully, it looked like they were just getting started.

She nodded at her officers, who were all working serious overtime. Since they were a small town, they were constantly on call. But the station was typically closed from 9 p.m. until 9 a.m. In the past two days most of them had been there until midnight.

Then her gaze was drawn to Jax. As soon as she made eye contact, he smiled at her. Patches did him one better, letting out a happy *woof!* and racing across the room, sliding to a slightly uncoordinated stop at her feet.

Keara laughed, grateful for the moment of levity. She wondered if the intelligent therapy dog had done it on purpose. "Hi, Patches."

Patches wagged her tail, staring up expectantly until Keara pet her.

Then Jax was standing beside her, his presence somehow managing to make her more calm and nervous at the same time.

"Today we're hoping to get more information on motive and our potential suspect," Ben announced, his voice carrying over the few conversations and making everyone go quiet.

"Since you know the residents here better than we do, we're hoping to pair agents and officers," Ben said. "The goal is twofold. First, to figure out if anyone knows of a reason one of the victims might have been targeted or anyone who'd want to do them harm. Second, to show them the sketch we got from two of the people on the scene. See if anyone recognizes him."

"What about me and Patches?" Jax piped up.

"We're hoping you can drive back to Luna, talk to Aiden DeMarco's family and see if they have any idea why both their son and his aunt might have been targeted."

Jax nodded, looking unsurprised, and Keara hid her disappointment.

He wasn't an agent. He wouldn't have been paired with her anyway. And if he had been, she would have needed to protest. Although talking to residents wasn't dangerous in theory, it could lead them to a bomber. Hell, they could actually end up knocking on the door of the bomber. Keara didn't know everyone who lived here, especially those who chose to hide on the mountain, who didn't want to be known.

Desparre was a small town only in terms of population. When it came to size—and the distance backup had to travel if you needed them—it was definitely large.

"I've got a list of pairings," Ben continued, "and a stack of printed sketches you can show people. That way, anyone with low vision won't have to squint at your phones. And there's no chance of anyone trying to snatch that phone away from you."

He said the last part like he'd experienced it and Keara raised her eyebrows at Jax, who just shrugged in response.

"Does that work for you, Chief Hernandez?" Ben called across the room.

Everyone's attention swiveled her way and she nodded, appreciating that he wasn't just trying to railroad over her small department. The FBI had more experience, but her officers knew the area and the people better. "The plan makes sense. Everyone stay safe out there. If you get a lead, call it in on the radio before you pursue it. And make sure you stay in contact. I want everyone checking in with regular status updates."

Her officers nodded somberly. Normally, she might have gotten a couple of rolled eyes at that request, but not today.

Policing a small town could get tedious, make you let down your guard. You thought you knew the people, thought you knew the dangers. But out here, where it was common to take calls alone, communication was their best defense. It was something she preached on a regular basis.

"I've got pairings up here," Ben announced, and everyone headed his way.

Keara turned to Jax and lowered her voice. "Did you talk to Ben and Anderson any more about the other cases and the inconsistencies?"

"Yeah. They're as confused as we are. They think our best chance of figuring out what the symbol means is to follow the other leads right now." Jax's lips pursed. "I still think there has to be a way to use the symbol to find the killer, but I don't know how."

It wasn't his job to know how. His psychological insight was useful, but he'd already stepped into profiler territory by confirming that the symbol was important, that it linked these crimes somehow. Jax wasn't an agent or a detective. It was her job—and Ben's and Anderson's and all of the other agents and officers—to follow the leads and uncover the bomber.

"You should focus on the victims," she told him. "I've seen the difference you and Patches make."

Woof!

Keara smiled and pet Patches more, as Jax stared at her pensively, his expression unreadable.

Had he felt insulted that she didn't think he should run leads? Would he feel the same way if he knew it made her more comfortable pursuing something romantic with him when he was sticking safely on the outskirts of the case?

His lips twitched, like he could read her thoughts.

"Let's get going," Ben said and Keara gave Patches one more pet, nodded goodbye to Jax and hurried over to see who she'd be running leads with today.

"It's you and me," Anderson announced before she reached the more senior agent.

"Great," Keara said. Anderson seemed pretty easygoing and professional. "Where are we headed?"

"Up the mountain. The place most likely for a bomber to be holed up, don't you think?"

"Let's do it," she agreed. She glanced back once more at Jax as she headed out the door and she could have sworn she saw him mouth the words, *Be careful*.

As she led Anderson over to her police SUV—specially equipped to handle Desparre's rough roads and danger-ous weather—she wondered if Jax worried about her. She wanted him far away from danger, didn't want to have to fear finding another man she cared for the way she'd found Juan. But she'd understood the dangers with Juan because she faced them herself. What must it be like for Jax, somewhat on the outside, to hear that she was head-ing into a remote area that would be a good place for a bomber to hide?

Pulling out her phone before she hopped into the car, she sent Jax a quick text:

Let me know how it goes with the victims today. I'll keep you updated, too.

It felt like the sort of thing she'd text if she was actually dating him. Hoping she wasn't making assumptions about plans that weren't reciprocated, she tucked her phone back into her pocket.

Climbing into the driver's seat, she asked Anderson, "Which part of the mountain? You know it's pretty massive, right?"

"We have one of your veterans paired up with one of our longtime agents. They're hitting the far side of the mountain. I thought we'd handle the closer side. We'll do as much as we can today and see what pops."

"Sounds good," Keara agreed as she started up her vehicle.

Some people headed this far north in Alaska just to find a good adventure. But most of the people who landed in Desparre were looking to be left alone. Usually, there was nothing sinister about it. Maybe they were running from a tragedy, like she was. Or maybe they were running from a threat, like Tate Emory was. Sometimes, though, they were hiding because the law was after them or because the vast spaces of Alaska seemed like a great place to stay off law-enforcement radar or hide a victim.

For the first ten minutes of their ride, Anderson was quiet, just texting or watching out the window. Then he slid his phone into his pocket and shifted toward her. "So this symbol…"

She glanced briefly at him, then back at the road. In the spring driving up the mountain wasn't dangerous like it could be in the winter, with the heavy snow and avalanches. But the roads were still narrow, the vehicles here usually large. On a couple of occasions, she'd had to hit the brakes for an animal. Once, it had been a bear.

"What about it?" she asked. "You have a theory?"

"Maybe. I've been thinking through what Jax told me this morning about how different the victimology and MOs in each of the cases has been, even the way the symbol was written. In marker or spray paint or even pen."

"And?" Keara prompted, her hands tensing around the wheel, hoping he had a new idea that would make sense of it all.

"We know savvy criminals learn from each other. What if we've got a group of them on a dark web site, not just trading insight into how to avoid getting caught, but also sharing this symbol?"

"Why?" Keara asked. "You think it's a way to mark their own kills? Keep track and try to outdo each other? But wouldn't using the same symbol defeat the purpose?"

"No," Anderson replied. "I was thinking more like a game, coordinating a single symbol across all these different places and crimes to confuse police."

The tension across the back of Keara's shoulders and neck notched tighter. "That makes sense," she admitted. Not only would it confuse the authorities if they connected the crimes through the symbols, but it also added a cooperative-competitive element that she could imagine appealing to a killer or a bomber. Attention from an eager audience without the risk, since they were all criminals, too.

If Anderson was right, the bomber wasn't committing the other crimes. If the communication was happening in a chat room on a dark web site, then the bomber probably didn't even know who the other people were.

A familiar frustration welled up. Even if they caught the bomber, would it get them any closer to Juan's killer?

Or was her dream of finally solving his cold case just that?

Chapter Sixteen

Talking to Aiden DeMarco's parents had been brutal. All of their dreams for their eldest son had been shattered in a single moment. Jax and Patches had been able to offer them support over the whole day that Jax knew they needed. And he'd managed to gather as much information as he could about what Aiden's parents—who'd been nearby when the bomb went off—had seen. But they had no idea why anyone would target their son or his aunt. Neither did Jax.

Frankly, he didn't think anyone *had* targeted either one.

Halfway through the day Ben had called him after checking in with Anderson. He'd shared the other agent's theory about a group of criminals coordinating on a dark web site. It had Ben excited and the cybercrime unit back in Anchorage pivoting to the theory as a priority.

If they were right, a serial bomber with the knowledge and connections to access a site like that probably wasn't using bombs as a messy way to kill a few specific people. He was way more likely to be an indiscriminate killer more interested in watching the chaos he created.

The fact that they hadn't found other bomb sites with the symbol could have meant his earlier bombs weren't as perfected and the symbol he'd intended to leave behind had been destroyed in the blast. Or evidence had been poorly collected or missed. Either way, this seemed like a practiced criminal.

Someone like that was prepared. He was well hidden, might have even booby-trapped his home in case law enforcement ever figured out his location.

Keara was driving around on top of a secluded mountain, searching for him.

The idea had lodged a ball of fear in his chest that had just gotten worse as the day turned into evening and the sun set, descending the town into darkness.

He'd heard from her again early in the afternoon, letting him know they were at the top of the mountain and hadn't had luck so far, but nothing since then. Jax had resisted calling or texting her, not wanting to distract her at a crucial moment. She was a seasoned law-enforcement officer with more than a decade of experience under her belt, about half of it in a busy city with a much higher crime rate.

Right now, though, making the lengthy drive back from Luna with Patches asleep in the backseat, he'd been alone with his worry for too long. He'd be at the Desparre police station in five minutes, but he wasn't sure if anyone would be there since it was after nine. He knew Ben had gone back to the hotel, but he didn't know whether Anderson and Keara had made it down the mountain yet.

Was this what it would be like if he could talk her into giving a relationship with him a chance? This constant fear about whether she'd make it home? Was that something he'd be able to handle long-term? Because despite the distance between Anchorage and Desparre, if he and Keara started something, he couldn't imagine ever wanting to stop.

"Call Keara," he told his phone.

From the backseat, Patches let out a quiet *woof*, then he heard her sitting up.

It rang twice before Keara picked up. "Hi, Jax."

She sounded happy to hear from him, but he could tell

from the exhaustion underneath that the trip hadn't yielded anything promising.

Woof! Patches chimed in loudly.

Keara laughed. "Hi, Patches."

"I take it no one recognized the picture?" Jax asked.

"We had a couple of vague 'he looks sort of familiar, but I don't know where from' kind of answers. But no one had a name and address handy."

"So he might live up on that mountain," Jax said, feeling more encouraged than Keara sounded.

"He might," Keara agreed. "We'll definitely have officers canvassing again tomorrow. The thing is, the mountain is huge. People stake out land and build without permits or actual ownership. It's not like we can stop them if we don't know they're up there. Some of it is pretty far off the beaten path. And if you've got someone willing to venture off the road a ways—which we definitely do—it can be nearly impossible to find them."

"It sounds like the stereotype of Alaska," Jax commented. "That you can just venture off and get yourself completely off the grid, if you're not afraid of the harsh elements."

He'd seen some truth to that when he'd gotten here, but Anchorage was a pretty developed, populated area. Still, he could drive about an hour outside town and find solitude at a glacier if he wanted. He and Patches had done it a half dozen times since moving here and only once had he run into another person.

Compared to Anchorage, Desparre was the wild north.

"Well, sometimes the best thing about a place can also be the worst," Keara said.

He heard her turn signal in the background and the knot in his chest loosened up, knowing she had to be off the mountain to need a turn signal. "Are you going back to the station now?"

"I've already been there. I dropped Anderson off and now I'm almost home. I was just about to call you, actually."

"Oh, yeah?" His long day suddenly seemed less exhausting.

"How did the trip to Luna go?"

"Nothing new, really." He sighed, remembering the devastation on the parents' faces, the confusion and grief in every movement of his three younger siblings.

"I guess I'm not surprised." He heard her car door slam, then her voice got more distant, maybe as she juggled the phone and opened the door to her house.

"Me, either, but I was hopeful. The fact that one of the Luna casualties, Aiden DeMarco, was the one who set up the soccer game and then his aunt was also hurt in a bomb? It seemed like maybe there was something to that."

"I don't think this bomber was after a specific—" She broke off on a mumbled curse.

"Keara?"

"Someone's been in my house."

"What?"

"My office doesn't look right."

"What do you mean? Are you sure?"

From the backseat, Patches whined, picking up on his anxiety.

"Yeah, I'm sure."

Her voice was hard and determined and he imagined her pulling her gun from its holster.

Jax punched down on the gas, wishing he was closer to her house. "I'm coming to you. Get out of the house, Keara."

"I'm a police chief, Jax. And I'm already inside. I can handle a walk-through."

"You need backup!"

"I'll call them," she promised, "But I need to go."

"No! Just wait for backup. That has to be proced—"

"*Jax*. It doesn't look like anyone is in here." Her voice had dropped to a whisper and he had to strain to hear her final, "I'll call you when it's all clear."

"No—"

He swore as he realized she'd hung up, then hit the gas harder, taking curves too fast. If a Desparre police officer pulled him over, all the better. Then he'd have backup.

He wasn't an agent. He'd gone to the shooting range with the Anchorage agents enough to be a pretty good shot, but he didn't carry a weapon. That wasn't how Victim Specialists worked. On some level probably the agents' teasing about him being an "agent wannabe" bothered him because it was true. Some part of him would have loved to get into the nitty gritty of an investigation, follow a trail of clues until an arrest and been the one to slap handcuffs on perpetrators. But he'd never pursued it, knowing the role he had now would ultimately fulfill him more.

At this moment, though, he wished he'd made a different decision. Wished he could be real help to Keara.

"Call Desparre PD," he told his phone as Patches whimpered.

"Desparre Police Department," a tired voice answered. It was familiar, but he wasn't sure which officer had phone duty that night.

"It's Jax Diallo," he blurted. "Someone broke into the chief's house. She needs backup right now."

"*What?*" The officer's surprise was overridden only by his sudden state of alert. "Okay, we're on it. Do you know details? Is the person still there? Are they armed?"

"I don't know. But *Keara* is there." He couldn't remember ever feeling this helpless.

"I'm sending help now," the officer told him, then hung up.

Jax punched down a bit more on the gas, even though he knew he was approaching dangerous speeds. Then he called Ben.

From the sound of the agent's voice when he answered, Jax had woken him up.

"I need agents at Keara's house. Someone broke in," Jax cut off his greeting.

He didn't bother ending the call as he whipped his vehicle into Keara's drive and slammed it into Park.

From the backseat, Patches slid across the seat and yelped.

"Sorry, Patches," he said, then added, "Stay!" as he jumped out of the SUV and closed the door behind him.

He could hear police sirens in the distance, getting closer, but the house in front of him was mostly dark, only a porch light giving him any real visibility.

It wasn't enough. For a house far from neighbors, set in the woods, it wasn't nearly enough to see if a threat lurked nearby.

Jax glanced back, watching for the police cars. But they weren't close enough yet.

He couldn't wait. He ran around to the back of his vehicle and dug underneath the spare tire, hoping the rental company wanted their renters to be prepared. Relief filled him as he found a big metal hexagon wrench. It wasn't a gun, but it was better than nothing.

He was racing toward the house, holding the wrench too tightly, when Keara stepped out the front door.

"It's empty," she told him, holstering her gun. "Whoever was in here was gone before I got home." The hard fury on her face was only undermined by the vulnerability in her eyes.

His grip on the wrench loosened and he realized his hand hurt from how tightly he'd been gripping it.

Her gaze drifted to the wrench then back up to his face. "You were going to rush in here with nothing but that?" Her lips pursed with what looked like anger, but her forehead crinkled with confusion or concern and she went silent.

He didn't bother to answer, just tried to breathe deeply, encourage his frenzied heartbeat to slow.

From the car, Patches called *Woof! Woof! Woof!*

Keara walked over to Jax, put her hand on his arm and he looped his free arm around her, yanking her against his chest.

Even with the sirens getting louder and louder, there was no way she'd miss his rapid heartbeat; no way she'd misunderstand his fear. But he didn't say anything. Right now as much as he wanted to pursue something more, they were only colleagues. He'd known her for eight days. He had no right to tell her how to manage a crime scene at her own home.

But she whispered against his chest, "I'm sorry I worried you. I should have gone outside and waited for backup."

As if her words had summoned them, a pair of trucks came screeching into her drive, portable sirens blaring.

Jax glanced behind him, letting go of Keara as officers jumped out of their vehicles, weapons ready.

Keara held up a hand. "It's all clear. But someone was in my house."

The officers holstered their weapons as Keara continued, "I don't think anything was taken. It barely looks disturbed. I think whoever was here hoped I wouldn't even realize it. But they definitely went through my office, especially all of my documents."

"Any sign of forced entry?" Charlie Quinn asked. There was exhaustion in the dark circles under his eyes and an invisible weight that seemed to pull his whole face downward, but his voice was focused and clear.

"No." Keara looked troubled as she admitted, "I'm not sure how they got in."

More vehicles raced into the drive and then FBI agents poured out.

Keara looked embarrassed as she said, "I've already cleared the house. It was a break-in, but nothing was taken."

Ben strode toward them, looking purposeful and focused. "You get a lot of break-ins around here?"

She shrugged. "Some."

"Do people know this is the police chief's home?"

She nodded slowly. "I don't advertise it, but this is a small town. So yeah, I'm sure some people have figured it out."

"Ever had any problems here before?"

She shook her head.

Ben nodded briefly at Jax, then asked Keara, "Any chance this is connected to the bombings?"

Jax's calming heartbeat took off again as he stared at Keara, watched her consider it.

"I don't know. But someone was interested in what I had in my office. I don't bring police cases home, except on a laptop, which is in my SUV. My paper files are mostly personal."

Ben nodded. "Just in case this is connected, how do you feel about letting the FBI's evidence techs go through your office?"

Keara nodded slowly. "All of our officers are trained in evidence collection. But in the interest of collaboration, that would be appreciated."

Ben nodded at her, then started calling out orders to the other agents as Keara directed her officers to head home.

Then she turned to Jax, all the vulnerability he'd seen in her eyes earlier gone now and replaced by anger. "What do you think? Why would the bomber come here? He assumed I'd have case files in my home and it would be an easier target than a downtown police station? You think he hoped to find out what we knew about him?"

Jax stared back at her, all his worry over her home being targeted fading into the background as he remembered the first time he'd seen her at the bomb site. Then the expression on her face when she'd identified that symbol for them. A symbol that, as far as they could find, hadn't appeared on a crime scene in Alaska until the Luna bombing.

"I think we were right from the beginning," he realized. "I think the bomber *is* connected to your husband's murder."

"What? *Why?*"

"I think all of the cases are connected," Jax said, the theory gaining strength in his mind as he said it out loud. "I think we just found the missing motivation."

"What do you mean?" Keara asked.

"I think the missing motivation is *you*."

Chapter Seventeen

Dread mingled with fury and residual adrenaline as Keara stared at Jax. The excitement in his gaze told her that he thought his new theory was right.

"How could I be the motivation for these bombings?" Keara asked. "I didn't have a close relationship with any of the victims—unless you count the fact that Nate works for me. I wasn't even there when the Luna bomb went off. And if he wanted to target me in Desparre, he could have come out here earlier, planted the bomb at my house."

The thought that the bomber knew where she lived, that he could have been in her house, looking through her personal items, made her home somehow feel less *hers*. The idea that he might have seen her photo album from her wedding sitting on her coffee table, might have flipped idly through the pages, smiled at the memory of killing her husband, made her fists clench.

The bomber coming here to find out if they were onto him made sense. But him setting bombs *because* of her didn't.

When Jax stayed silent, his lips twisted and his pupils rolled slightly upward, like he was still working it out in his mind, she prompted, "You need to explain this theory to me."

Behind her, the other agents had gone quiet, but stepped

closer. They were all listening, too, waiting with enough patience that Keara knew they valued Jax's psychological insight as much as she did.

"What if we've stumbled on to a serial killer who isn't interested in a certain victim type or a particular weapon?" Jax asked slowly.

Keara held in her immediate rebuttal: they'd already decided this wasn't a serial killer/bomber *because* there wasn't a common victimology or MO. "Then what's his motivation?"

"He gets off on outwitting police," Jax said, a mix of surprise and certainty in his voice.

"Police in general?" Keara pressed. "So not me specifically?" She didn't like the idea either way, but the thought that a serial killer was somehow focused on her, motivated to kill because of her, was really unsettling.

"Yes," Jax said, his hand reaching out like he was going to take hers, then dropping back to his side. "Sorry. I didn't mean that it was you personally motivating him. I think he's motivated by whoever is working to solve the crime he committed. It's like a game to him—can he keep committing crimes without the police finding him?"

Keara frowned. Behind her, she could hear the agents shifting, like they were impatient and unconvinced, too.

"Every serial killer wants to outwit police," Ben spoke up. "I don't think that's enough of a motivation alone."

"Why not?" Jax countered, crossing his arms over his chest. "You thought a group of criminals were playing games by using the same symbol and laughing at police on a dark web chat room."

"Sure," Anderson said. "But—"

"Hear me out," Jax interrupted. "It could explain why there have been so many different locations. Because he's looking for a new challenge each time, a new police office to test, to see if he can find a worthy opponent."

"Or he's just trying to outrun the investigations by changing jurisdictions," Ben countered. "A lot of serial killers try that."

"Sure," Jax agreed, not looking deterred. "But you didn't think it was a serial criminal responsible for everything, because of all the differences. What about the similarities? How likely is it really that we have six different criminals—murderers, an arsonist and a bomber—all using the same symbol *and* all equally skilled at leaving behind such clean crime scenes? Not to mention, all of them only committing one—or maybe two—crimes before stopping?"

The agents behind her were silent as Jax stared at them with raised eyebrows. Keara thought about each of the case files she'd read, about the total lack of progress in each of those cases. They'd all eventually gone cold, just like her husband's murder.

"Okay," Ben said, sounding like he was reluctantly getting on board with Jax's theory. "Then why bombs now after a series of murders and one arson?"

"Because the weapon isn't the point," Jax said, the excitement in his voice growing.

It set off an excitement in her, too, a hope that they were getting closer to finding the person responsible for all of the crimes. Including Juan's murder.

"When serial killers get away with it, they get bolder, right?" Jax asked, his gaze on Ben.

Keara shifted, so she could see them both.

On Ben's face was interest, the thrill of being on a solid lead that she recognized. The excitement was catching. All the other agents were slowly nodding.

"Usually," Ben agreed.

"Sometimes, they go for bigger challenges, too, right?" Jax leaned in and his familiar cinnamon scent wafted toward her. "They'll try to grab victims who are more high risk for them. They'll spend more time with the victims, leave the body in a more public place, maybe."

"So you think this is just a progression?" Keara asked. "He started with murders, tried an arson—and presumably got more attention with the murders, so returned to them? Then he came here and decided bombs would have a bigger impact, get more of a law-enforcement response?"

Jax nodded. "Yes. And maybe some of this was also him learning what he liked. Maybe initially he figured he'd get more of a thrill from the killing than he did. When he discovered it was actually watching the law-enforcement response—seeing the police scramble to try and find *him*—that became more of his focus."

It made sense in a weird way. Celia Harris's murder almost certainly wasn't the guy's first kill. It was too perfect, too precise, the victim too high risk, the body dumped in a place too close to public areas. He'd probably started with easier victims, people who were less likely to be missed, dumping the bodies in places he hoped they wouldn't be found. The symbol could have evolved over time, too.

"So if this is all a progression, if it's really about this guy trying to outwit the police, then what about Juan?" Keara asked as fury and grief and determination entwined inside her. "He got too close to the truth, didn't he? This guy thought he was outwitting police and then Juan showed up at his door and the bomber decided he needed to kill him, didn't he?"

Jax nodded slowly, her own pain reflected in his eyes. "That's my guess. I think you were onto something all along with Rodney—or, more likely, given that the sketch we have doesn't match Rodney, his roommate. I think Juan was killed because he got too close to the truth."

"And the crimes were much bigger than he'd ever realized," Keara finished.

KEARA'S GAZE WAS troubled as she demanded, "Do you think the bomber came here because he knew I worked here? Because he knows I'm Juan's widow?"

The agents behind her all cringed. It was barely perceptible, because they were all trained and practiced at hiding emotion. But no doubt they'd all dealt with loved ones who were afraid of one day getting the dreaded call.

Jax's heart gave a pained kick, but he tried to consider all the angles before he answered. This wasn't his job. This wasn't his specialty. Yes, he had a lot of training in psychology, a lot of experience working with the victims this type of criminal left behind. But there were other professionals out there, profilers who focused on the other side of it: knowing the mind of the criminal.

"I doubt it," he said finally. "But it can't hurt to get a profiler's thoughts on that." He glanced at Ben, who nodded slowly, but didn't seem anxious to get a second opinion.

"If I'm right, then it took him a long time to get to Alaska. If he came here for you, then why stop in so many states along the way? Why take so many years to get here? It seems like it was probably a coincidence."

"He was jumping from one jurisdiction to the next," Anderson said, "changing locations once each case went cold. Unless we just missed some of his crimes, this guy is patient."

Ben nodded. "A year is a long time in between crimes for a serial criminal, if that's really what we've got here."

"Right," Anderson said, sounding excited by Jax's new take on the perpetrator. "But for big investigations like the ones we're talking about, it seems reasonable that police would be actively investigating for a year. Those investigations would slowly ramp down until they were deemed cold and set on the back burner."

"This guy probably wouldn't know exactly when that happened," Ben said. "But once he couldn't see police activity, once the news coverage died down, he moved to a new state, studied a new victim, planned a new crime." He gave Jax an impressed look. "It makes sense. And it explains a lot of things that just wouldn't fit together otherwise. I think you're onto something here, Jax."

It would take a methodical, patient killer. But each of the cases Jax had reviewed with Keara suggested that kind of criminal. Someone who had studied how to avoid leaving forensics behind, who had watched his intended victim beforehand to avoid witnesses, who had scoped out the location he planned to leave the body. Someone who followed the police investigation, followed the officers investigating, without being noticed.

Jax flashed back to the moment he'd been driving to meet Keara and had thought someone was following him. A dark blue truck that had turned another way when Jax started driving erratically. Had it been the bomber, looking for insight on the case? Had he followed Jax in the past, maybe even to Keara's home? Had that been how he knew where she lived?

Guilt flooded, along with a rush of relief that Keara was okay. What if the bomber had been waiting in her house instead of just going through her files? What if he'd been standing in the dark with a knife, ready to do to Keara what he'd done to her husband?

The idea made nausea flood through him and he tried to push it back, tried to keep thinking through his new theory as impartially as he could.

Keara stared back at him, her eyes narrowing as if she could read his emotions.

She probably could. She was a trained investigator, after all. Would it scare her off, the intensity of his feelings for her? How had they gotten so strong, so fast?

"If this guy is following the investigation as closely as you're suggesting, and it is someone who's been here less than two years, then he's been at the scenes," Keara said with certainty. "He's been talking to people. That means someone has seen him. We need to keep circulating that sketch. Has it been shown to all of the victims and anyone else who was near the scenes at the time of the bombings?"

"We've shown it to all of the victims who are able to look at it right now," Anderson said, reminding Jax that there were still two Desparre victims in comas, still three from the Luna bomb who were critical and unresponsive, as well.

"And? No one recognized him?" Keara pressed.

"Some of them said the sketch looked kind of familiar," Ben replied. "But no one could give us a name. Same result as the general canvassing today."

"He's good at blending in," Jax said. "He's got a lot of practice fading into the background."

"This is a small town," Keara said, frustration in her voice. "We notice outsiders. Yeah, we let them have their privacy, but unless they're hiding out on the mountain all day, we see them." She frowned, a ripple of anger rushing over her features. "Of course, I thought that five years ago, too, and we had a kidnapper living among us. People knew him vaguely, but no one seemed to know who he was."

"We'll find this guy," Jax said, hoping he sounded confident. But would they? Why was he still here if it was the same person? "He figured out who you were," Jax breathed, the final pieces that didn't quite fit falling into place in his mind.

"He figured out that I was the chief of police or that I was Juan's widow?" Keara demanded, sounding like she already knew the answer.

"He was probably planning to move on after the Luna bombing like he had with all the other crimes. But you showed up that night," Jax realized. "Or maybe he followed me when I came to Desparre to talk to you about the case." He told Ben about the blue truck and the agent nodded, jotting notes.

"I'm sorry," he told Keara.

She waved a dismissive hand. "We don't know that was him. And if it was, you shook him. Anyway, if he's sticking around because he realized who I was, that gives us more of a chance to bring him down."

"He's breaking pattern now," Ben said, a warning in his voice that Jax felt deeply himself.

"I know," Keara said, glancing at the other agent. "My husband almost caught him. Maybe he's worried I'm just as good."

"With a personality type like this, if he's breaking pattern, he could be fixating on you," Jax said, the worry he felt coming through in his words.

Keara nodded, fury in her own voice. "He can fixate all he wants. I'm fixated now, too."

"Keara." He stepped closer, trying to block out everyone else, everything else, as she tipped her head up slightly, meeting his gaze.

"I think you could be in danger."

Chapter Eighteen

The air felt stuffy and uncomfortable inside Jax's SUV. Or maybe that was just all of Keara's pent-up anger.

She took a deep breath. The anger and grief over her husband's murder had settled over the years, buried deeper where it was less likely to bubble up at any moment and overwhelm her. But right now, knowing the person who had done it was probably here, trying to destroy the new town she'd chosen to call home, had pushed it all to the surface again, as strong as it had ever been.

It wasn't fair to take it out on Jax.

She glanced at him, saw the worry in his tense profile, in the focused gaze that kept jumping between the dark road ahead and his rearview mirror, like he was watching for a tail. It was obvious he felt guilty, thinking he might have led the bomber to her.

"It's not your fault," she told him.

He glanced at her briefly, pensively, then back out the windshield.

"For all we know, this guy found out where I lived by talking up the locals."

"And no one recognized him?" Jax countered.

"Judging by that sketch, he's not exactly a memorable-looking guy." The couple who'd seen him—assuming the person they'd seen *was* the bomber—said he was just shy of six feet, with thinning brown hair. He'd been wearing a shapeless coat, maybe to disguise his build, and sunglasses on a not-so-sunny day. When asked if there was anything memorable about him, Imani had just shrugged and called him "average."

Keara glanced at Patches in the backseat, sound asleep with her head resting on Keara's overnight bag. "This really isn't necessary." She repeated what she'd said back at her house, when everyone else had either headed home or gone inside to gather evidence. When Jax had insisted she come stay at the hotel where it was safer, she'd rolled her eyes and blurted harshly, "Don't be ridiculous."

Ever the therapist, he hadn't taken offense. Probably he'd recognized her misplaced frustration and fury.

Even now he just said calmly, "We agreed you'd be safer at the hotel. Plus, Patches will love the company."

Woof! she chimed in from the backseat.

Keara twisted to look at the Labrador retriever and couldn't stop her smile. The puppy had been wound up an hour ago, jumping over the seat in Jax's SUV where she'd been shut inside, barking and trying to get someone to let her out. As soon as Keara had given in—and given herself a welcome distraction while federal agents combed through her office, looking for evidence—she'd nudged repeatedly at Keara, like she was mad it had taken so long. Then she'd lain down at Keara's feet and promptly fallen asleep.

She'd been asleep for most of the ride from Keara's house toward the Royal Desparre Hotel, too. But apparently saying Patches's name woke her instantly.

"Can't argue with that, can you?" Jax asked, giving her a tense smile as he pulled into the hotel parking lot.

As he put the SUV in Park and shifted to face her, focusing those compelling deep brown eyes entirely on her, Keara resisted the urge to fidget. She was a police chief. She didn't fidget.

"Jax, look, I don't mean to be rude, but let's be honest here. You're not law enforcement. You can't protect me."

He shrugged, only a brief flicker of offense in his eyes. "Well, then it's a good thing this hotel is full of FBI agents, isn't it?"

"Then what's the point of me staying with you instead of just getting my own room?"

Woof! Woof! Woof! Patches seemed to argue from the backseat.

"If I'm right, then this guy has gotten away with it for at least seven years, Keara," Jax said, sounding tired as he retread the argument they'd already had at her house.

It was an argument he'd won, since she was here, with her bag packed with her uniform for tomorrow and her work laptop. She'd left her personal vehicle in front of her house, hoping it would seem occupied if the killer decided to return.

Still, the idea that she was leaving the house empty, making it easy for him to go back through it if he wanted, made her antsy. She'd finally agreed to come with Jax when he suggested that if she didn't want to stay with him, she should bunk with one of her officers. The idea of staying with Jax was making her nervous, the attraction between them palpable in the air. But asking one of her officers to lend her their couch felt too close to admitting she wasn't up for being their leader. And that was something she'd never do.

"You know I'm armed," she said once more as he opened the door and started to climb out. "Maybe you don't know this—I'm a damn good shot."

He leaned down, met her gaze with his own less patient one. "Your husband carried a gun, too, right? And this could be the same asshole who killed him, only now he's got seven more years of practice."

Jax held her gaze for a long moment, surely seeing the

horror and grief rush across her face at the low blow. Then he stood and shut the door behind him, before opening up the back for Patches.

His dog stared at Keara for a long moment, offered up a *woof!* then climbed out, too.

Keara sat motionless in the SUV, imagining the beautiful sunny day she'd found Juan dead in their backyard. He'd been caught completely by surprise, even when the killer had slipped up right behind him to slit his throat.

Swallowing back the surge of tears that threatened, Keara reached into the back to grab her overnight bag. Then she followed Jax silently into the hotel.

JAX OPENED HIS eyes to find Keara staring at him.

She immediately redirected her gaze, sipping a cup of coffee he'd somehow slept through her brewing. She'd gotten dressed while he was sleeping, too, changing out of the joggers and long T-shirt she'd put on before climbing into the second bed. Now she was wearing her uniform, with the four-star emblem on her collar designating her role as chief of police.

He tore his gaze away from her still-loose hair and makeup-free face to check on Patches. When his dog had realized Keara was staying last night, she'd run in circles for a minute, then leaped onto the bed with Keara and slept at her feet.

His dog was still at the end of the bed, her front paws dangling off the edge. When she saw him looking at her, her tail thumped the bed.

He grinned. He couldn't believe someone had tossed her out. It was hard not to smile when you saw her. "Hi, Patches."

Throwing off his covers, Jax climbed out of bed and asked, "How did you sleep, Keara?"

He'd zonked out. He wasn't sure how, with the woman

he was falling for only a few feet away from him, but it had been a long, stressful day. Apparently, it had caught up to him.

But right now he felt refreshed, reenergized and determined. And the woman he was falling was still only a few feet away.

Her eyes widened as he stepped closer and she set her coffee down, her mouth moving like she was getting ready to speak.

When he stepped closer still, into her personal space, she surprised him by looping her arms around his neck. "I slept fine. Not quite as well as I did on my couch, though." He could feel her heart rate pick up as she stared at him, giving him a small, sassy grin.

He flashed back to the feel of her spooned against him on her couch and couldn't help but smile back. He wanted to stay in this moment, savor the feeling of being with Keara as if they were a long-established couple and not a pair of colleagues who'd barely known each other more than a week. But her lips were too close to him, her gaze broadcasting a mix of uncertainty and desire.

As he slowly bent his head closer, one of her hands slid into his hair and the other stroked along the back of his neck, making all of the nerve endings there fire to life. He pressed his lips softly to hers as she sank into him. The gentle meeting of their lips sent sparks through him, but he kept his kiss slow, wanting to linger in the moment.

She tasted like coffee with cream and sugar. She smelled faintly of the lavender soap in the hotel bathroom. She felt exactly right in his arms, like she belonged there.

Too soon, she was pulling back, her gaze serious, despite the passion that still lingered. "Sorry I was hard to deal with yesterday."

He laughed, surprised at the admission. "Thanks for letting me win the argument."

A grin burst on her face, her own laugh soft and short, and somehow, in that moment, he knew. However many dangers she faced because of her job, he still wanted to be with her.

Pulling free of his embrace, she told him, "I may not have known you long, Jax, but I'm figuring you out. And I didn't want you and Patches trying to stand guard at my house." She picked up her brush, started to pull her hair up into its customary work bun. "Much as I appreciate it," she added.

He watched her a minute longer, gave her an easy smile when she glanced questioningly at him. It wasn't time to talk about anything serious. He knew she wasn't ready. But maybe if they could resolve this case, that would change.

Mentally shifting into work mode, he said, "If we assume the killer was planning to stick to pattern and leave after he set the bomb in Luna, that means most likely he spotted you at the scene at some point. Do you think he could have recognized you from Houston?"

Keara froze, one hand holding up all of her long hair, the other holding her brush. Then she continued working it into a bun, her voice steady but underlaid with anger as she replied, "It seems unlikely, but I guess it's possible. More likely he heard my name and recognized that. Then he might have started digging up details on me. There was a picture of me in the paper back in Houston from Juan's funeral. I'm sure that would come up if you dug enough."

"So either he heard someone at the scene say your name or he talked to people, asked who you were," Jax continued, thinking out loud.

"Probably," Keara agreed, jamming bobby pins into her hair and then slapping her hands on her hips. "What are you thinking, Jax?"

At her insistent tone, Patches jumped off the bed, ran

to her side and plopped down at her feet, staring up at him, too.

Jax couldn't help another laugh. "Okay, Patches. I'll get to the point." He redirected his attention to Keara. "I'm the one you've had the most contact with from the team in Luna. Maybe the killer followed me, maybe not. But we know he's been paying attention to you. We can assume he knows who I am."

Keara's eyes narrowed. "And…"

"We also know he didn't get any information about the status of the investigation when he broke into your house."

"Assuming this whole theory is right and it was the killer who broke in, then that's true," Keara agreed. "I don't have any information about the bombings—or the killings or arson—at my home."

"So he's still looking for information."

"And you have an idea," Keara said.

"He might have already seen the sketch of himself, so I'm sure he's being careful. Maybe he's tried to change his appearance. But if he's still here, he'll want to find out the status of the case. Who better to get it from than the guy who's been giving *you* information?"

"Okay," Keara said slowly, her narrowed eyes telling him she didn't like where this was headed.

"What if I go back to the scene in Desparre? The FBI has finished processing it, but I've seen residents there every day, leaving signs and stuffed animals for Nate and Talise, looking for information. They all know Patches and I are here to help the victims and the community. We can stick around, let people know we're there for anyone who's struggling to process this, to share what we can about how the investigation is going."

"You hope he'll hear about it and come talk to you," Keara said, her expression telling him she liked this less and less with every word.

"Yes." He stared back at her, trying to project confidence, even though it felt like a long shot. But a long shot was better than nothing.

She started to shake her head and he cut her off. "It's daytime, so there are going to be plenty of people around. He's not going to set off a bomb in the same spot twice."

When she scowled even more at that, he insisted, "Hitting twice in the same state is already a departure for him. Yes, he's been getting away with his crimes for a long time. But that's because he's smart and he's patient. This is a pretty low-risk thing for me to do. It's not really even that far from what I'd normally be doing right now. But maybe it will work. You and some of the agents can set up at a distance and watch. What do you think?"

She sighed and gave him a reluctant-looking nod. "Let's call Ben and get his opinion."

As Jax headed to the bathroom to get changed, he heard her on the phone with the FBI agent. She talked through his idea impartially and fully, even though he knew she would have preferred not to have him involved. But when he stepped out of the bathroom, ready for the day in his standard dark dress pants and a button-up shirt with an FBI jacket over it to let citizens know who he was, she nodded.

"We're on."

Twenty minutes later he was standing next to the temporary short fence that had been erected around the crime scene to keep anyone from hurting themselves before the damage could be repaired. As he looked around the empty scene, Jax wondered if his plan was a mistake.

Three days after the bomb had gone off in Desparre's downtown, people were starting to get back to normal. Instead of congregating near the stash of signs, candles and teddy bears that had been piled high with messages for the dead and wounded in both Desparre and Luna, residents were giving it a wide berth today. Their gazes darted his way briefly, pausing with grief and fear, before they resumed their business. Apparently, they'd hit the point where they hoped to move on, try to forget while they waited for good news on the victims and the suspect's capture.

Jax sighed and knelt next to Patches, who looked as dejected as he felt. She whined a little and he scratched behind her ears.

"I know, Patches. You want to work."

Her tail thumped lightly at the word as she stared up at him, then glanced toward the part of Desparre with all of the shops, with all of the people. It was Sunday morning and in the distance, he could see people in dress clothes starting to stream toward the church down the street from the police station.

His gaze shifted from the far end of town with the church, to a little bit closer, at the police station. From an attic Jax wouldn't have guessed existed in the police building, Keara, Ben and Anderson were watching him through binoculars. So far there was nothing for them to see.

"We'll give it another half hour here, then go find people to talk to," he promised Patches.

Her tail wagged and he grinned at her.

Then dirt sprayed up from the road in front of him, pebbles stinging his legs as a distant *boom* sounded.

For a second he was confused, even as Patches started frantically barking, already standing.

Then the sound registered. Someone had just taken a shot at him. But from where?

Panic followed, tensing his whole body as he glanced around frantically, looking for the shooter, looking for a safe place to go.

Then there was another *boom* like a firecracker going off and a metallic screech as the bullet hit the small fence behind him.

"Run, Patches!" Jax yelled, angling his arm toward downtown. Toward the police station.

She barked, staring up at him, waiting for him, and he took off, too.

He ran as hard as he could, Patches keeping pace at his side, even as he wished for her to outrun him, to get to safety faster.

He was pretty sure the person shooting at him was using a rifle. Which meant either they weren't a great shot or they were playing with him, forcing him to run for his life even though they could end it at any time.

Chapter Nineteen

"Wait!"

Ben's voice echoed behind her as Keara leaped down from the attic in the police station, skipping the entire ladder and landing hard on the floor below.

Pain jolted up from her legs, making her teeth slam together, but she ignored it the same way she ignored Ben. She'd agreed to Jax's plan to try and fool the man who'd killed her husband and now he and Patches were in danger.

She couldn't survive losing another man she loved.

The unexpected thought made grief and dread clamp down hard, almost doubling her over. It was too soon. Way too soon.

"Keara!" Ben yelled. "Get someone up here with a long rifle!"

"Okay," she gasped at him, but she didn't even need to yell the order, because Tate Emory and Charlie Quinn were already rushing toward her, both holding rifles.

They didn't know where the shooter was, but they knew his target.

Maybe she'd make a better one.

There was no time to grab a bulletproof vest, so Keara just straightened and kicked into gear again, running for the front of the station. She blew past her officers, warning them, "Active shooter! Gear up before you come out!" Then she raced outside.

Yanking her pistol from its holster, she ran into the center of the street. Near the church, residents were looking around in confusion and she yelled at them, "Get inside!" Then she spun the other way, toward the park.

Jax and Patches were still running toward her, but there hadn't been any more shots fired. If the killer was smart, he was already trying to disappear. Even with a rifle, there was only so long he could hold off police. They were too close.

They could get him. She could get him.

The thought fueled her, added fury to her fear and determination to her strides, lengthening them even as she kept her gun ready. She'd been one of the best shots in the Houston PD back in the day and she still kept up her practice. If she saw the shooter, he was finished.

As Jax met her gaze, he waved his arm, made a motion at her that clearly meant "turn back."

"Move!" she barked at him as she got close and he started to slow, like he was planning to grab her arm and try to turn her.

His gaze lingered on her, his head pivoting to watch even as he followed her orders and kept going, Patches keeping pace with him.

Then he was behind her and her focus sharpened, her gaze sweeping the empty street in front of her. The killer couldn't be far.

She kept pushing, legs and arms burning as she ran hard toward the park. Her lungs ached, too, out of practice at this kind of running, especially with the chilly Alaskan air sending an icy blast down her throat with every breath. Where would a shooter have the best angle?

As she drew alongside the park, she realized. Down the side street that bisected Main Street, ending just past the park. He'd be able to see Jax, but Jax would be unlikely to

see him because the woods continued that way, offering
plenty of places to hide.

Boom!

Keara instinctively cringed, even as she dodged left and
then right. It wasn't a rifle this time, but the sound of a pistol firing. As she rounded the corner onto the side street,
nearly skidding off her feet, she saw him.

About Jax's height, wearing dark green—a good choice
to blend into a forest—he was running hard, too. And there
was a dark blue truck parked on the street ahead.

She could yell out a warning, shoot him when he inevi-
tably spun and fired at her. Or she could tackle him, bring
him in. Force him to admit all the things he'd done, force
him to serve time the way he deserved.

Keara hunched inward, pushed her strides as long as
she could, as he slid to a stop alongside his truck, stopping
himself by grabbing the side mirror.

Then he was spinning toward her, aiming his gun again.

Keara dove for the ground, twisting as she flew through
the air, trying to get her own gun up as another gunshot
blasted. She slammed into the hard-packed earth with a
grunt that stole all of her air and made her vision momen-
tarily fuzzy.

Then he was in the truck, the tires spitting dirt as she
lined up her pistol and fired. She heard the *ping* of her bullet hitting the truck, but it wasn't enough.

The truck careened around the corner and out of sight.

JAX'S HEARTBEAT REFUSED to slow.

He'd been back at the hotel for half an hour, but his body
was still amped up, the adrenaline overload not subsiding.
He wasn't sure it would until Keara walked through that
door and he could see for himself that she was okay.

Kneeling on the floor, he wrapped his arms around
Patches's neck, hugging her.

She whined a little, pushed her head up into the crook of his neck. She'd seen a lot of terrible things during her six months as a therapy dog—and she'd definitely had a rough start in life. But she'd never been in danger while she'd worked for the FBI.

Fury and guilt mixed as he stroked the soft fur on her back, whispered, "We're okay, Patches. Keara is okay, too."

She whined again at Keara's name and he knew she had to be wishing for the same thing he was.

As he'd reached the safety of the Desparre police station, a small group of officers had poured outside, wearing bulletproof vests over their uniforms and helmets on their heads. They'd looked serious and nervous, but moved confidently in pairs toward the threat.

Not long afterward, Ben and Anderson had climbed down from the Desparre Police Department's rarely used attic, frowning and shaking their heads. "He got away," Ben had told him. Then he must have seen Jax's panic, because he'd added, "Keara is okay. We're putting out an APB on the truck. Dark blue, like you said."

Now, back in the hotel room where he'd been escorted by a pair of police officers and told to "stay put," Jax wondered: If he'd done something differently when he'd seen that truck, would they have already caught the bomber?

Pushing aside the frustration, he continued to pet Patches until her presence calmed his raging heart. She seemed to relax, too, and she pulled her head off his shoulder to glance at the door.

"I know, Patches. You want Keara."

Her tail wagged and new nerves filled him. Keara hadn't been hurt chasing down the killer, and hopefully they'd get lucky and catch him quickly with the APB. But then he and Patches would be leaving.

He'd been putting off telling her how he felt, putting off telling her that he wanted to pursue a relationship, despite the challenges. He'd been waiting for the right time, hoping this case would end with her getting closure on her husband's murder and make it easier for her to move on. But there was never going to be a perfect time to talk, not even if that happened.

He needed to act.

As if on cue, there was a knock at the door and Patches leaped to her feet, giving an excited bark as her tail whipped back and forth. A reaction like that could only mean one thing: Keara was here.

His heart rate picked up again as he looked through the peephole to confirm it before letting her in.

Keara looked formidable, despite torn sleeves and the dirt covering her once-crisp uniform, despite the strands of hair pulled loose from her bun, and the smear of dirt across one cheek. Determination blazed in her eyes and there was a hard set to her expression that said it didn't matter how far the bomber ran, she was going to find him.

He stood staring at her, watching her gaze run over him like she was reassuring herself he wasn't injured, as Patches ran in circles around her.

Finally a shaky smile broke and she bent down to pet Patches, before standing and moving closer to him. Close enough to touch, but the intimidating, focused expression was still in her eyes, mixed suddenly with a fear he knew he'd caused.

"Are you okay?" she asked, her voice barely above a whisper.

"We're fine," he reassured her. "I'm not sure he actually wanted to hit us."

She blew out a heavy breath that he felt across his face. "We lost him." She shook her head, and her hard mask broke, showing all the frustration underneath. "The FBI is working with my officers to find him, and we've coordinated with all the surrounding towns to be on the lookout for him or his truck. I got a partial plate, which will help, but…"

She sighed again, ran a hand through her hair that just pulled out more pieces of her bun. "We found the rifle, too, and we're running it for prints. The bastard was wearing gloves, but there's a good chance he loaded it without them, so hopefully we'll get a hit there."

"We'll get him," Jax said, discovering it was easy to inject his voice with confidence. This killer was savvy and he'd gotten away with it for a long time. But the Anchorage agents were very good and very dedicated. And Keara? Jax knew this was the most important case of her life. She wasn't going to rest until she found him. And he'd bet on her over anyone else.

It was something he needed her to know. "Keara—"

"Shh." She put a finger to his lips, then stepped closer. She blinked and the last of the frustration and angry determination faded, leaving behind residual fear and need.

"Are *you* okay?" he asked as he settled his hands on her hips, desperate to pull her to him, desperate to hold her until the threat was gone. But he needed to hear her say it.

"I'm okay now." She pushed his hands aside, unstrapped her holster and set it up on top of his TV. Then she looped her arms around his neck, pushed up on her tiptoes and fused her lips to his.

It was nothing like the kiss they'd shared this morning. Instead of going slow, her grip tightened as soon as his lips started to move against hers. Her tongue breached the seam of his mouth and she moaned, sending his pulse skyrocketing.

Gripping her hips again, harder this time, he pulled her closer until there was no space between them. She was a perfect mix of lean muscle and feminine curves, and her tongue was dancing around the inside of his mouth in a way that made his eyes roll back in his head.

Her kisses were fast and frantic, and Jax met her pace, learning the curves along her body with his hands as she looped a leg around his hip.

Then she pulled back slightly, breathing heavily, her eyelids at half-mast as she panted, "I can't stay long, Jax. I have to get back out there."

As she was leaning back in, he whispered, "We have all the time we want, Keara. Anchorage and Desparre are only a jumper flight apart." His lips sought hers again, desperate for another feel of her before she went off chasing a killer.

But she pulled away, her hands dropping from around his neck and her leg returning to the floor.

When he opened his eyes, she was still breathing hard, but the desire in her gaze was fading. She nodded, stepping out of his embrace so quickly he almost stumbled, and he tried to figure out what was happening.

"You're right," she said. "And those jumper flights happen every day. The killer has obviously targeted you, Jax, and I don't want it to happen again. You need to get on one as soon as possible. You and Patches should go home."

He stared back at her, his own passion cooling as understanding dawned. Keara wasn't here right now because the overwhelming relief that he was okay had made her realize she wanted something more serious.

She was here to say goodbye.

Chapter Twenty

Patches whined and glanced from Jax to the closed hotel door.

"I know," he said softly, petting her. The look Keara had given them as she'd grabbed her overnight bag and paused at the door, before shutting it softly behind her, was lodged in his brain. It had been full of regret and sorrow. But it had also been full of finality.

She believed he'd follow her advice. She believed she was never going to see them again.

It had been hours since she'd left and he hadn't heard from her since. He knew she was out there somewhere, searching for the bomber. She'd thrown herself into danger while she asked him to run away from it. For the FBI's part, they didn't like that he'd been targeted, either. Ben had called to check in on him. The agent hadn't suggested that he go home, but he'd sounded discouraged as he advised Jax to stay inside.

Jax had agreed, but asked for a favor in return. When Ben had originally run the symbol through the FBI database, they'd focused on the past seven years, since Celia's murder. But today Jax had asked Ben to run the symbol for a ten-year stretch about thirty years ago.

After Keara had left, he'd needed something else to focus on. Sitting in the quiet of his hotel room with no victims to help and nothing else to do made it too easy to think about the expression on Keara's face as she'd walked out the door. He wasn't about to give up hope of changing her mind.

Still, it was one thing to wish for this case to be solved, for her husband's murder to be solved. For Keara to get closure. He believed in her. She was dogged and a damn good investigator. Maybe it wouldn't happen quickly, but he believed she'd find the person responsible.

But after what happened this morning, he wasn't sure closure would be enough to make her move on. At least not with him.

His job wasn't usually dangerous. Still, he enjoyed using his knowledge of psychology to help investigations. If the opportunity arose again, he didn't want to turn it down. Even if he was willing to promise that, maybe Keara just couldn't bring herself to ever date someone connected to law enforcement again.

He understood it. He'd seen the details from her husband's case file. The murder had been gruesome. He couldn't imagine finding someone he loved that way. He definitely empathized with her need never to lose anyone violently again.

It was why she'd backed away from him. And it wasn't a fear he was sure he could breach, no matter how hard he tried.

Patches whined, nudging his leg, and Jax nodded at her. "You're right. I need to focus."

She slid to the floor, looking dejected, and he wondered if she understood exactly what was happening with Keara, if she was just as upset over it.

Giving her one last pet, he clicked to the next result in the files Ben had sent over. Thirty years ago the FBI's system to compare unsolved crimes was newer. There were fewer entries, so fewer possibilities to go through. But maybe he'd get lucky.

Because the thing he'd realized as he'd tried to find a way to distract himself from Keara's departure was that he'd been right from the very beginning. The symbol meant something. And if it was being used by a single criminal, it was probably connected to that person's childhood.

Working with the victims of a serial killer last year had been brutal. It had taught him that human beings were capable of far worse atrocities than he'd ever seen before up close. It had also taught him that many of the perpetrators came from violence themselves. Instead of learning empathy from it, they'd sought it out, tried to inflict pain on others.

Maybe the bomber was the same. Maybe the symbol came from a traumatic incident in his childhood and he was now marking his own crimes with it. Maybe...

Jax sighed and set aside one more case, wondering if he was wasting time. Even if he was right, the symbol could have been overlooked or never entered in the FBI's voluntary database.

Then his pulse spiked as he flipped to the next case. Here was the symbol he'd seen at two bomb sites, staring back at him from a twenty-nine-year-old case. A murder that had happened in Texas, not far from Houston.

He read fast as Patches sat up, scooting closer and resting her head on his leg. Although the FBI database was meant for unsolved cases, the police in this case had known exactly who the killer was. They just couldn't find him.

Arthur Margrove had been known around the community as a violent man. Prone to picking fights with anyone—including his wife—he'd been arrested repeatedly for assault. He'd served multiple short sentences in jail, but never learned his lesson. After being fired from yet another job, he'd returned to his job site, broken in and smashed everything he could find. Then he'd gone home and murdered his wife.

Today Arthur would be in his sixties. He wasn't the bomber.

But Jax tapped the computer screen, his fingers marking the information he'd been searching for all afternoon and into the early evening. Arthur Margrove had a son.

Todd Margrove had been five years old at the time of the murder. He'd been standing beside his mother's body when police came looking for Arthur, covered in her blood, probably from trying to help her. Both of them were underneath a bloody symbol drawn on the wall. A symbol that had now been replicated across the country.

Jax grabbed his phone and dialed Keara's number. Frustration gnawed when the call went to voice mail, and he left a tense message:

"Call me back, Keara. I know who the bomber is."

KEARA GLANCED AT the readout on her phone as she drove down the mountain. Jax was calling.

She gripped the wheel tighter as she debated whether to answer. She'd spent the day running leads with her officers, the fury and frustration in her chest building and building until it felt ready to burst.

Nothing was panning out. Thinking about what had happened with Jax in the morning just added fear to the mix.

Whatever Jax wanted now, it wasn't to tell her he'd gone home; she knew that much. She hadn't spoken to him since she'd left his hotel room that morning, but she had talked to the FBI agents, suggesting they get him a flight. Ben had raised his eyebrows at her and told her Jax understood the threat and was staying off the streets. The FBI didn't believe he was in real danger. They thought if the bomber wanted him dead, he wouldn't have missed.

They thought today's shooting was a message. The

bomber knew what they were doing and he wasn't falling for it.

He was having fun with them, because after all, if Jax was right, this was what he wanted anyway. A strong opponent to chase him, the thrill of getting away despite their best efforts.

It wasn't going to happen. Not this time.

They might not have prints to give them a name, since the rifle had come up empty. But they had a partial license plate. They had a sketch.

Her phone stopped ringing as Keara rounded another bend, riding the brakes because this stretch of road was steep. She'd gone up to the top of the mountain to talk to the loner who'd been at the scene of the Desparre bombing. He'd called the station and implied he might have seen the person in the sketch. He'd asked for her personally, and because he was a recluse who'd opened up to her in the past, she'd agreed.

Charlie Quinn and his FBI partner had spoken to him yesterday and reported back that he was crotchety and uncooperative, but didn't have any useful information. It seemed unlikely he'd have something new today, but she had to check. Plus, it gave her some time to herself.

But when she'd arrived, no matter how many ways she asked, the information he'd claimed to have didn't surface. Instead, he'd spent the entire discussion digging for details on the case. Maybe it was because he'd suffered some minor injuries, cuts to his legs that had required stitches. Or maybe he was just one of those guys who got off on crime scene details.

He wasn't the bomber. In his late fifties, in poor health and bad shape, not only did he not fit the description, but he'd lived in Desparre too long.

Still, Keara's radar was up. As soon as she'd returned to

her SUV, she'd called the station to update them, let them know she was heading back in.

The whole thing had been a waste of time. Peering up at the sky through her windshield, she scowled at the fading light filtering through the towering trees. Pretty soon it would be dark. Her officers had been working a lot of overtime in the past four days. The shooting downtown today meant they'd needed to spend as much time reassuring the public and keeping a visible presence there as running leads.

The more time that passed from when the bomber had shown up in the park, the farther he could run. Yes, he'd found a police department—and a group of federal agents—to try and outwit. But he hadn't made it so many years without being caught by being stupid. Maybe the shots at Jax had been his parting ones. His way of telling them they'd gotten as close as they ever would. His own form of goodbye, before he showed up in some other state, committed some other crime.

Rounding another corner, Keara's SUV jolted as it ran over something in the road. The back of her vehicle did the same and then the tires started making a rhythmic *thump thump thump*.

Flat tires.

What the hell had she hit?

Glancing around her at the darkening woods, Keara put her SUV in Park and pulled her gun as she stepped out of the vehicle.

Scanning the area and seeing nothing unusual, she walked to the back of her vehicle. There was a plank of wood driven through with upward facing nails directly behind her back wheels.

Adrenaline rushed through her, all her senses on alert as she lifted her weapon. She spun around just as something flew toward her head.

Keara ducked, trying to center her weapon at the figure that had rushed out of the woods, but the slab of wood still made contact with the top of her head.

Pain exploded in her skull, bringing tears to her eyes. Her feet came out from underneath her and her arm slammed down on the edge of the board of nails, making her lose her grip on the gun. It skidded away from her, out of reach.

Then the man she'd seen only from a distance that morning was filling her vision, a smile on his face. The bomber, murderer, arsonist. The man who'd shot at Jax. The man who'd killed Juan.

He wavered in her sight, her vision blurry from the hit to the head, her lungs screaming from the hard landing. Fighting the urge to throw up, ignoring the burning pain in her arm, Keara shoved herself upward, launching at him.

But he moved fast, swinging that slab of wood again.

Even though she threw up her arm to block it, the wood still made contact with the side of her head.

She hit the ground again, head throbbing, nausea welling up hard.

Then she was moving, her head bumping over every uneven piece of ground, into the woods.

Her vision went in and out, as dizziness threatened to overtake her, threatened to suck her into unconsciousness. Panic erupted, flooding her system with terror, but keeping her awake. She was weak from the blows to her head, too dizzy to stand. Too dizzy to fight.

He left her for a moment and she swallowed the nausea, tried to move, but her body wouldn't cooperate. Then the bushes in front of her were moving and she blinked, trying to right her swaying vision, until she realized it wasn't bushes she was seeing.

They were camouflage, broken branches strategically covering the truck he'd hidden just off the road. He planned to put her in that truck, to take her somewhere else.

It wasn't a quick death he planned for her, but probably a painful one.

Keara rolled onto her belly, biting down on her cry of pain as her vision swung one way and then back again and her head throbbed violently. *Where was her gun?*

Too soon it didn't matter because she was being lifted, thrown over his shoulder with frightening ease. He carried her around to the back of the truck where a metal gun box was propped open.

Keara kicked, raking her fingernails over the backs of his arms, still coherent enough to think like the cop she was. To get his DNA on her.

He yelped and swore and then he was swinging her fast enough to make her nausea overwhelming, make her vomit on the ground beneath him. Soon the ground disappeared altogether and she was being stuffed into the empty gun box.

She shoved upward, trying to escape, but he'd dropped her into the box awkwardly, making it hard to move. The multiple blows to the head and the new wave of dizziness slowed her down, too. The lid closed, leaving her in darkness.

As she heard him move away from her, she took deep breaths to reduce her panic, then slammed against the metal lid, trying to open it. The lid buckled slightly, but held. Then the truck started to move, taking her away with Juan's killer.

Chapter Twenty-One

"Have you heard from Keara?" Jax asked Ben over the phone, trying not to give in to worry. He'd called the agent after Keara hadn't picked up, and told him the same news he'd given Keara's voice mail.

"No. She's on her way back from talking to someone up the mountain. She got a weird vibe from it, though. Said she'd stay in touch on her way down." There was a pause and Jax imagined Ben frowning at his watch. "If I don't hear from her in the next ten minutes, I'll give her a call."

Could she have followed a trail right to the bomber's home? Or maybe he'd followed her up there, ambushed her on her way back?

Jax only halfway paid attention as Ben went on about what a great find Jax had made and said he'd start running the name Todd Margrove immediately. Then he asked if Jax thought it was Rodney's elusive roommate from back in Texas. From the way he asked, Jax had a feeling he'd repeated the question a few times.

"Yeah, maybe. Look, let me call you back, okay?" He hung up without waiting for an answer, dread forming in his gut.

Maybe he was overreacting because he'd been shot at that morning, but he suddenly couldn't stop picturing Keara in trouble. "Come on, Patches. Let's go for a drive."

Woof! She leaped to her feet, danced around him even as she didn't get the usual laugh out of him.

He moved faster the closer he got to his SUV, scanning the semidarkened parking lot. He opened the back door and Patches jumped in, then Jax got behind the wheel.

"Hold on, Patches," he told her, driving faster than was legal as he whipped out of the parking lot and headed for the mountain. It was closer from here than the police station and he couldn't wait the ten minutes for Ben to follow up with Keara, then call back and tell Jax he was overreacting.

He could hear Patches sliding around a bit in the backseat as he rushed toward the base of the mountain, where the main road led up to the best place in Desparre to hide out. But were there other roads off it? He had no idea.

"Sorry, Patches," he told her, wondering if he should have left her in the hotel room. But most likely he *was* overreacting. And if he caught up to Keara coming down the mountain, maybe she'd be more open to talking with an adorable dog begging for her attention, too.

"Almost there," he muttered a few minutes later as the road that led off the mountain came into sight.

Before he reached it, a dark blue truck sped away, making a turn in the opposite direction Jax was coming from.

It was *the* truck.

Jax's pulse picked up as he instinctively punched down harder on the gas. Had Keara run into the bomber on the mountain? Had he hurt her? Was she still up there?

Yanking his phone out of his pocket, he told it, "Call Ben Nez!"

As he reached the base of the mountain, Jax's gaze pivoted from the road that went up the mountain to the street heading out of Desparre that the blue truck had taken. Should he go search for Keara up the mountain? Or follow the bomber?

He clenched his teeth, panicked at the thought of making the wrong choice. *Go after the bomber.* It was Keara's voice in his head. He could imagine her insisting she could take care of herself, to keep the bomber in sight and get the police and FBI on him now.

"Ben here. What is it, Jax?"

The way Ben said his name, the stress in his voice, told Jax he'd repeated himself again.

"I found the bomber. Coming down off the mountain in that same truck. He's heading out of town. I'm following him." Jax's voice sped up as he made his decision. He passed the road up the mountain, hoping he'd made the right choice.

"*What?* Jax, where are you exactly?" Ben asked.

Jax gave him the road, then demanded, "Did you hear back from Keara?"

There was a pause that made dread drop to Jax's stomach, then Ben admitted, "She's not answering her phone. Anderson and I were just about to head up the mountain."

"Should I turn around?" Jax demanded, trying not to panic. Maybe Keara couldn't answer because the roads were dark. He'd heard agents the other day complaining about how narrow they were, how the sudden drop-offs alongside the road in places were startling. Maybe she didn't want to dig her phone out of her pocket and be distracted from driving.

"No," Ben insisted. "Stay on the bomber. Just make sure you stay at a distance. You don't want this guy spotting you, okay? Just stick behind him and keep giving us updates. We're on our way."

"No," Jax insisted. "Send someone else. You need to go find Keara."

"Jax, if Keara's in trouble, it's probably connected to that truck," Ben said, his tone darkly serious, noises in the background suggesting he was already heading for his vehicle. "But we'll send officers up the mountain just in case.

We're coming to you. Just be safe. The road you're on leads out of Desparre. It eventually goes into a neighboring town so small they don't even have their own police department. What they do have is a lot of secluded, wooded areas where a bomber might hide. One of Keara's officers was just talking about it earlier today as a place where the bomber could be if he wasn't in Desparre or Luna."

"Okay," Jax agreed, only half listening as he focused on the road ahead. It was empty except for him and the blue truck. He didn't want to get too close and tip the bomber off that he was being followed. He also didn't want to lag too far behind, have the guy take a sudden turn and disappear before Jax could catch up.

"This guy is a killer, Jax," Ben stressed, as if Jax needed the reminder.

He knew all too well what the bomber had done to Keara's husband, what he'd done to Keara's life.

"If you think he's spotted you, turn around. Give us his last coordinates and we'll be right behind him," Ben insisted. "Don't risk your life. You're not an agent. You're not trained for this. Do you hear me? You do *not* want to end up alone with this guy."

"Okay," Jax agreed, not sure if he meant it. Where was Keara? Why hadn't she called him back? Why hadn't she answered Ben's calls?

"Shit," he swore as the truck suddenly sped up, whipping off the road and onto a bisecting trail into the woods.

Jax hit the gas, and as he headed farther away from town, Ben's voice came through a burst of static. "Jax! Did you hear me? Don't engage!"

From the backseat, Patches yelped as she slid across the seat.

"Hang on, Patches," he said, slowing as he reached the turn the blue truck had taken. He eased off the gas entirely, until his SUV was just creeping forward, until he could crane his head and stare down the road.

Boom!

Jax punched the gas again as the gunshot blasted, and his SUV raced forward. Hopefully, they'd pass the road before the bomber could hit them. Hopefully, the bomber wouldn't follow, but would use that opportunity to keep going.

Patches yelped again as Jax gripped the wheel hard, ducking his head low, hoping neither of them would be a visible target.

But as they passed the trail, the truck was still stopped, the brake lights lit up. A hand disappeared back inside the driver's side window, and the truck started up again as if the driver was going to take this chance to get away.

He had a brief instant of relief. Then the gun box in the back of the truck popped open and Keara partially emerged from it.

KEARA GASPED IN the cool night air as she finally got the lid free. She pushed herself upward, desperate to get out of the box that had felt like a too-small coffin.

Ironically, it had been the truck slamming to a stop after taking that nausea-inducing turn that had given her the right angle, just enough leverage, to shove open the box. Now she ducked low again as the unmistakable sound of a bullet pierced the air.

Was he shooting at her?

As quickly as the thought entered her head, she realized it was wrong. The bomber was shooting at Jax, who was amazingly behind them. His SUV had been racing past the trail where they were stopped, but then his eyes widened in the window, his expression caught in the glow from the bomber's brake lights.

Jamming the box lid fully upward, Keara pushed un-steadily to her feet, ready to leap out and race for Jax's SUV.

Then the bomber hit the gas.

Her upper body went flying forward, wrenching her mostly out of the box and into the truck bed. The metal lid of the box slammed against her calves, but she barely felt the pain over the jolt to the rest of her body as she landed hard, then slid toward the edge where the back of the truck bed had popped open.

Catching herself before she slid right out, Keara grabbed the edge, holding on. Her fingers sliced open on the metal as she held on hard, as she tried to angle her legs to brace herself against the side. She eyed the ground below, moving rapidly enough to intensify her dizziness. They were going too fast. She'd missed her chance to jump.

Then Jax's SUV backed up and spun wildly onto the road, chasing them.

The truck jerked to the side and Keara lost her grip on the edge as she flew sideways across the truck bed. She slammed into the side of it, grabbing the edge there as her body spun and her legs dangled off the vehicle, hanging in midair. Head pounding, she scrambled to get fully back on the truck as it swerved again and the *boom* of a bullet fired.

Maneuvering onto her knees, she peered into the front of the truck, where the bomber leaned out the window, slowing slightly as he fired backward at Jax.

Gritting her teeth, Keara pulled herself slowly, painfully, up the truck bed, smearing blood in her wake. Could she get to the left side, near the front of the truck bed? Could she reach the bomber's hand, yank the gun free? Shooting him while she was in the bed of his moving truck wasn't her best plan, but it didn't seem like her worst option, either.

The truck sped up again and Keara's knees slid out from underneath her. She swore as she slammed against the truck bed again, and her arms were yanked hard as she kept her grip on the side. Ignoring the sharp ache in her arms and shoulders, Keara kept dragging herself forward.

She glanced back and saw Jax gaining. She wanted to tell him to get off this trail, get himself out of danger, but she was also grateful for the backup, grateful that she wasn't completely alone with a practiced killer.

Taking deep breaths to try to ease the pounding in her head and the throbbing across her entire body, Keara grabbed the front of the gun box. Painfully, far slower than she would have liked, she moved on her knees across the front of the truck bed, pulling herself with her bloodied hands.

When she was halfway there, the bomber twisted to look at her. His eyes inches from hers through the glass startled her, almost made her lose her grip.

There was a darkness in his gaze Keara had never seen before in over a decade of policing, a fury to his scowl that said he was going to make her pay for daring to go up against him.

Keara glared right back, refusing to show him any fear. Today this ended. And it wouldn't be with her painful death. It would be with his arrest.

Lurching sideways, Keara made it to the left side of the truck. Adrenaline or determination was helping her vision even out, pushing the pounding in her head to the background. Now that he knew she'd gotten free of the gun box, would he hold his pistol out the window again? Would he be expecting her to make a grab for it and not take the risk? Or would he focus it on her?

Glancing behind her, she saw Jax. He was gaining on them, close enough now that she could make out the grim determination on his face.

Then the bomber hit the gas again, hard.

Keara swore as her knees came out from under her once more and she banged into the edge of the gun box headfirst, slicing a cut across her forehead. Holding on tighter to the side, she scrambled, trying to wedge her legs against the front and side of the truck. No way could she let go at such a high speed, with the way he kept wrenching the wheel back and forth slightly. No way could she make a grab for his gun if he tried to fire at Jax again.

But from the corner of her eye, she saw Jax getting closer. He was almost on top of them now, gesturing for her to do…what? Try to jump onto the front of his SUV? She shook her head at him, knowing that was a move made for movies, and would probably be deadly at this speed.

Then the bomber slammed on the brakes and Keara's grip came loose from the truck edge. She was thrown against the front of the truck and the gun box, but barely felt the pain as she twisted toward Jax, and the SUV still racing for her.

He was going to hit the truck. At that speed, with that much force, it would probably kill her.

She took a deep breath and tried not to show any fear as she stared back at the man she'd somehow fallen for in such a short time.

It felt like everything was moving in slow motion as his eyes went huge, then his jaw clamped down.

The SUV wrenched sideways as Jax must have yanked the wheel hard. The right wheels came off the ground and for a terrifying moment, she thought he was going to flip it. Then the SUV came back down again and he must have hit the brakes. But not hard enough, because the front of the SUV slammed into one of the trees lining the trail and the whole front of the vehicle crumpled inward.

"No!" Keara screamed as the bomber hit the gas again, and she went flying to the back of the truck.

She grabbed hold before she was tossed over the edge, her hands shaking with the desire to let go, let momentum carry her. But if the fall didn't kill her, the bomber would surely get out and finish the job while she was incapacitated or out cold.

Praying that Jax had survived the crash, Keara stared at the SUV, hoping to see him climb out. But all she could see was smoke billowing from the front of the vehicle, and then too soon, the bomber turned off onto another trail.

Trying to push Jax to the back of her mind, Keara scanned the truck bed, searching for something she could use as a weapon. But there was nothing here. The gun box had been empty, too. But it was old, dented from her twisting inside it and slamming her boots into the lid. Could she rip it off? It wasn't much, but it was better than nothing.

Before she could even start to pull herself back to the front of the truck, the bomber slowed and then came to a stop.

Shoving herself to her feet, Keara glanced over the top of the truck at a tiny cabin, tucked deep into the woods. Swearing, she leaped off the truck, ready to make a run for it.

Too fast, she heard the truck door open behind her and the bomber snapped, "Do it and I shoot you in the back."

A small part of her, knowing it was probably the least painful way to go, wanted to do it anyway. But that wasn't her. She was a fighter, right to the end.

Gritting her teeth, she turned toward him.

He laughed, surprise evident in the sound. "That was a rougher ride than I thought, wasn't it?"

Ignoring the jibe, she tried to throw him off guard, give him a reason to think she was still a worthy opponent, not worth killing yet. "So where's Rodney Brown? Is this all your doing or are you two working together?"

He let out another sound, somewhere between a laugh and a grunt, and his gun lowered to his side. "Rodney has been dead for seven years."

Surprise jolted through her as he continued, "I borrowed his car when I killed Celia Harris. You know I did that, right?" He nodded, a slight smile forming. "I didn't expect anyone to come looking for the car. Rodney was belligerent with the cop, of course, and I couldn't take any chances."

Pain and anger filled her, overriding her physical pain as he spoke of her husband.

His smile grew, as if he could see it. "Rodney has been dead since the day that cop—your husband, right?—came to the house. I dumped his body in the ocean. Then I tracked down the cop and slit his throat."

Keara felt herself sway at the words, felt a familiar, incapacitating grief rip through her as the bomber shrugged and added, "And then I moved on."

He lifted his gun again as she tried to breathe through the pain. "And I'll tell you, you've been a lot of fun, but it's getting a bit dicey for me here. I think it's time for me to move on again."

Chapter Twenty-Two

Something was burning.

Jax groaned and lifted his head off the steering wheel, not sure if he'd blacked out or if he'd just hit his head when he'd slammed his SUV into the tree, trying to avoid smashing into Keara.

Keara!

Opening his eyes, he saw nothing but white. The airbag had deployed. He groaned again as he twisted his head, peering around it out the side window. The truck was gone.

Woof!

Jax whipped around in his seat, and his chest and shoulder screamed in protest. "Patches! Are you okay?"

She whimpered and he cursed himself for having brought her along.

"I'm sorry, Patches. I'm coming." He tried to smash the airbag out of his way and the movement sent a tearing pain through his left arm. Cursing, he unhooked his belt and twisted, ignoring the way his shoulder screamed as he slid out from behind the airbag.

Peering into the backseat, he saw his dog on the floor. She stood when he met her gaze, her tail wagging slowly, pointing downward.

"Are you okay, Patches?" He reached back with his right

hand, letting his left arm hang limply. Had it been wrenched out of the socket in the crash? He wasn't sure.

When he pet Patches, she leaned closer, stretching her head between the seats and licking his face.

His gaze ran over her, searching for injuries, but she looked okay. Then she leaped up, putting her front paws between the seats, and relief filled him. If she could move like that, she probably hadn't broken anything.

Resting his head on hers for a second, Jax tried to take deep breaths. It hurt his chest a little, but he was pretty sure it was the way he was twisted, pain radiating from his shoulder.

Then the hint of smoke hit him again and he spun forward, peering out the front. There was a lot of smoke coming out of his vehicle, but he didn't see fire.

The whole front of the vehicle was smashed in. Would it still drive?

He turned the key, giving it a try even though it seemed pointless. It didn't even make a noise.

Swearing, he slid over to the passenger side and opened the door. He half fell, half climbed out of the SUV and then Patches was outside next to him, having leaped over the seats.

How far had the bomber taken Keara? And where was his backup? Had they driven right past this trail, sticking to the road Jax had given Ben on the phone?

Jax stuck his head back into the SUV, fumbling around for his phone, which had been in the center console. When he finally found it underneath the passenger seat, he discovered the screen was smashed. He tried turning it on anyway, but nothing happened.

"Damn it!" Heaving out a sigh, Jax glanced back toward the road he'd followed the bomber down, the road that presumably his backup would be rushing to. Then he looked the other way, in the direction the bomber had probably taken off.

How far had he gone? Jax could see another trail bisecting this one up ahead, but the trail he was on continued as far as he could see, too. The sun was very low in the sky now, casting pinks, oranges and yellows over the tops of the trees. He wasn't sure where he was or where exactly this trail led. But it was going to be completely dark soon and one thing he did know: they were far from help.

Woof! Patches ran down the trail slightly, then glanced back at him, barking again.

"You want to find Keara?"

Woof!

Jax nodded. Hurrying to the back of his SUV, he grabbed the tire iron that had been useless the last time he'd pulled it out. But it was the closest thing he had to a weapon. Not much use against a gun, but better than nothing.

Then he jogged after Patches, breathing through the pain that rattled in his head each time he put his foot down, and the sharp ache that kept searing through his left arm.

She stayed ahead of him, glancing back periodically to make sure he was following. When she reached the connected trail, she turned onto it without hesitation.

Jax followed, his heart thumping harder from adrenaline and pain, but also fear of what was up ahead. Was Keara here? Was he already too late to help her?

He jogged forward a few more steps, caught up to where Patches had stopped to stare back at him. And then he saw it. A driveway with a dark blue truck in it. Behind that, a small wood cabin.

Putting his finger to his lips, he knelt beside Patches and whispered, "Shhh." He glanced at the drive again, searching for any sign of Keara or the bomber, but he didn't see either one.

Hugging his good arm around Patches, he kissed the

top of her head, then stood. Angling his arm back the way they'd come, he told her, "Go back to the car, Patches. Wait there."

She glanced behind her, then stared up at him, confusion in her soft brown eyes.

"I need you to go back to the car," he repeated, knowing she understood the word. Eventually, Ben and Anderson would find his vehicle, even if they needed to contact the rental company and run a trace on it. If Jax was dead by then, he knew the agents would find Patches a good home.

"I love you, Patches. You're such a good girl," he told her, trying not to let his voice crack.

She sat down and he shook his head, angling his hand again.

"Go, Patches," he said, then turned away from her, creeping toward the cabin. He knew she didn't want to do it, but she *was* a good girl. She'd go and at least she'd be safe.

Taking deep breaths, Jax tried to block everything out: fear for Patches, fear for himself, fear for Keara. He tried to just focus on his surroundings as he crept up to the cabin.

They were inside. They had to be.

Praying that Keara was still alive, Jax slunk up to the edge of the cabin. The windows at the front were totally covered, so he slid along the side of the house, searching for a view inside, some idea of what he was getting himself into.

Feeling hyperattuned to every sound, Jax cringed as dead leaves from last fall crunched lightly under his feet. The edges of fir trees brushed against him as he crept alongside the cabin. His adrenaline was pumping hard, but he felt focused. He gripped the wrench harder, hoping he'd be able to use it.

Then he came up to another window, with a small space where the curtain hadn't been fully shut. Inside the cabin the bomber was standing with his back partially to Jax, a gun held loosely at his side. Across from him, Keara was swaying on her feet, blood on her forehead and her uniform, a dark bruise across her cheek. But she was alive. And she looked fighting mad.

Relief and fury mingled, and Jax picked up his pace, slipping around to the back of the house. There was a door here.

Jax tested the handle and it turned under his hand. Heart pounding, he eased the door open and slid inside.

The bomber didn't turn. If Keara saw him, she gave no indication of it.

Taking light, careful steps, Jax moved forward. His breath was shallow as he tried not to make a sound, as he lifted the wrench, got it in position to smash it down across the back of the bomber's head.

One more step...

The bomber spun toward him, gun lifting fast, a smile rushing over his face. "Welcome to the party."

Jax was here.

Keara tried not to look past the bomber as he stared at her, snarling the way he'd been doing for the past few minutes. She'd thought he was going to shoot her on the driveway, but then a distant noise had made him frown and usher her inside.

Since then he'd bragged about paying off the loner on top of the mountain, laughed at the police response to his Desparre bomb. He'd done it all with a slight smile hovering on the corner of his lips, like he was hoping she'd rush him. Hoping to infuriate her before he shot her.

She'd gritted her teeth and stared back at him with as unaffected a look as she could manage. But she'd known he was just working himself up to something she couldn't withstand. He was working himself up to Juan's murder. Maybe to Jax's, too, if he hadn't made it out of that SUV.

But now Jax was here. Alive and somehow in this cabin. Just as he raised a big metal wrench over his head and

Keara thought it was all about to end, the bomber spun and told Jax, "Welcome to the party."

Keara wouldn't have dared trying to rush the bomber when he was that close to Jax, the gun pointed. But he spun back to keep them both in his eye line quickly.

The bomber shook his head, said to Jax in a mock-sad tone, "And here I let you live at the park." But he couldn't seem to stop a smile from breaking.

Jax slowly lowered the wrench, dropped it to the floor with a *clang* that made Keara flinch.

"If you killed me, then how would I be able to rue how much smarter you are than me?" Jax asked, his tone and expression even.

The bomber's eyes narrowed, like he wasn't sure if Jax was mocking him. Then he shrugged and said, "Like I told Keara, you've given me some fun here. I like a challenge. But the heat is getting a little too close. It's about time for me to move on. And I'm afraid you can't come with me."

"Where to next, Todd?" Jax asked.

Keara's attention jolted from Jax to the bomber, who visibly jerked.

Then he gave a forced smile. "You're better than I thought you were. How'd you get my name?"

"An old case," Jax said and the bomber's eyes narrowed as he shifted more to face Jax, his gun lowering slightly as he took his attention mostly off Keara.

Her breath stalled. She had no idea how Jax had come up with Todd's name, with details of his past. But if Jax could keep Todd talking, keep his attention, maybe she could rush him. She wasn't at full strength—not even close—but she had rage and desperation on her side. She would *not* watch another man she loved die.

"How old?" Todd asked, his voice squeaking slightly.

"Twenty-nine years old," Jax replied evenly, his gaze never shifting to her. "Committed by your father."

Todd scoffed. "He was no *father*."

"Then why use his symbol?" Jax asked. "Why repurpose it as your own?"

Todd grinned slowly, and the evil there made a shiver race over Keara's skin.

"That might have been his kill, but it's always been my symbol."

"You smeared your mother's blood on the wall?" Jax asked, surprise in his voice that told Keara he hadn't found all of the answers. "Why?"

Todd scowled, shook his head. Something in his expression told Keara even he wasn't sure of the answer. "Does it matter? That's my symbol."

"And what about the man who killed your mother? It didn't bother you that people thought it was his symbol?" Jax asked.

Keara slid forward, one tiny millimeter at a time, holding her breath, trying not to listen too closely to the horrible tale of Todd's childhood. She needed to get close enough to launch herself at him and she needed him to be distracted enough that she'd land before he could lift his gun and fire. But she had to be completely focused.

"I dealt with him. Right before I killed Celia Harris," Todd said, his head tipping up, pride and hate in his words.

Jax nodded slowly, not looking afraid. "It gave you the courage to try a riskier kill."

Todd scowled again. "I didn't need courage, but yeah, I went for someone people would actually miss." He shrugged, then gave a broad grin that told Keara she needed to move soon. "And then I discovered how much *fun* it was to fool the police."

He started to turn back toward her and she knew: this might be her only chance.

But he was twisting too fast, his gun lifting again.

She wouldn't make it. But she had to try.

Keara launched herself off the ground even as Jax's "Keara, no!" rang out and Todd's smile shifted into a sinister smirk.

A familiar *woof! woof! woof!* came from behind Jax and a blur of brown and black fur raced through the doorway.

Todd's smirk slipped as he twisted back in the other direction.

Then Keara landed hard, roping her arms around Todd, trapping him beneath her as they hit the ground. The force of it reverberated through her body as she focused on his gun hand. Ignoring the searing pain in her own hands, the slippery blood making it hard to hold on, she gripped his middle fingers and twisted them backward.

He yelped and lost his grip on the gun.

Keara shoved it away from him as she leveraged herself into a crouched position over him, yanking his arms up behind his back like she was going to cuff him.

Before she could, he rolled, shoving her off him.

Then he was pushing himself off the ground.

"I wouldn't do that," Jax said, his voice low and deadly.

Keara glanced up.

Jax stood with his feet braced apart like he was on a firing range, the pistol in one hand as the other arm dangled strangely at his side. Patches stood beside him, her teeth bared in a way Keara had never seen.

Todd lowered himself back down and then the room erupted in noise as the front door crashed inward and Ben and Anderson rushed inside.

"You're under arrest," Ben yelled, weapon directed at Todd as Anderson yanked Todd's hands up behind his back and cuffed him.

Jax lowered the pistol he held and gave Keara a shaky smile.

It was over.

Epilogue

A week later Keara stood in front of her officers in the Desparre Police Department, trying not to choke up. "It's been an honor working with all of you for the past six years," she told them.

They stared back at her, giving each other uncertain looks, not having expected this speech on her first day back in the office.

She'd spent the past week at home recuperating. Although the most concerning of her injuries had been the repeated hits she'd taken to her head, everything had looked normal on all the tests. It was the small puncture wounds across her arm from the nail board, her sliced-open hands from hanging on to the edge of the truck and the split on her forehead requiring stitches that had actually kept her away longest.

"Desparre has truly become a home to me," she continued, wanting to get it all out before she became overemotional. "It's going to be hard to leave."

"You're leaving?" Nate Dreymond asked, surprise and disappointment in his tone.

He wasn't officially back on duty yet and wouldn't be for a few weeks, at least. But ever since he'd been released from the hospital, he'd come in each day to see his colleagues.

Talise, too, had woken from her coma. She was still in the hospital, but doctors expected her to make a full recovery.

The town was moving forward. With Todd Margrove behind bars and expected never to be free again, it was going to help everyone heal. Including her.

"It's time," she told them, even though she'd never expected to be leaving the place that had given her so much after Juan died. It had given her a reason to live again, a purpose to help her move on. And it had led her to Jax.

She glanced behind her, where Jax and Patches stood in the doorway. Patches was fidgeting, more full of puppy energy than Keara was used to, her tail thumping whenever Keara glanced her way. Jax was more subdued, his arm still in a sling, the sympathy in his gaze lending her strength.

He knew this wasn't easy for her. But she'd come back to Desparre someday, to see the people and the place that had changed her life.

"Where are you going?" The way Tate's gaze shifted briefly to Jax when he asked it, he probably already knew.

"I'm moving to Anchorage. I'm going to be a detective again."

She'd officially had her interview over the phone two days ago, gotten the call that they wanted her yesterday. It probably hadn't hurt that a longtime agent of the FBI had contacted them and said they'd be crazy not to hire her.

The officers glanced at each other again, and she could feel the mix of emotions in the room: still some confusion and sadness, but they were happy for her, too.

Technically, being a detective was a step down. And moving across the state, to a place where she barely knew anyone, was definitely a sacrifice.

It was also fast. Fast enough that it scared her a little. If she was being honest with herself, it scared her a lot.

She'd known Juan for more than a year before they started dating, had been with him for nearly three years before they got married. But she'd only spent a year as his wife before losing him.

She didn't want to waste any time with Jax, didn't want to look back and have regrets. Not everyone got a second chance like this and she wasn't going to let it go because she was afraid.

She hadn't wanted to fall for him. Hell, she hadn't wanted to fall for anyone, especially not someone who was remotely in harm's way. And despite Jax's official title, he was too good at psychoanalysis to stay completely removed from the investigative side of things. He would never be one hundred percent safe.

Then again, no one was.

"Congratulations," Charlie said, his voice booming over the silence that had fallen.

Then all of her officers were chiming in, offering her congratulatory handshakes and hugs.

Twenty minutes later she walked to the door, giving the room one last, long look. She wasn't officially leaving for a few weeks. She was going to help find her replacement, so she wouldn't leave the town she loved in a lurch. But today felt like goodbye.

As she reached him, Jax took her hand and she smiled at him. Today also felt like a new beginning.

Woof! Patches said and Keara laughed, bending down to pet her. Then she stood and took Jax's hand again.

"Are you sure this is what you want?" Jax asked as they stepped outside into the brilliant sunshine. "You know I'm willing to do any amount of jumper flights. Patches and I can try to be here every weekend if you want to stay."

He gestured at the police station where she'd spent so

many of her waking hours in the past six years. "I know these people have become like family to you."

Keara squeezed his hand tighter. "I've loved being a chief. And you're right, I'm going to really miss everyone in Desparre. But being a detective is in my blood."

She let out a cleansing breath. "After Juan's murder went cold, I didn't want to do it anymore. Every part of being a detective was just a reminder that he didn't have any justice. But I'm ready now."

She stared up at him, knowing he could probably read her nervousness in her smile. "I want to do it near you. If you don't think it's too soon."

"Too soon?" He laughed. "I was ready to profess my love a week ago."

She felt herself jerk slightly, at the surprise of his words, at the fear they evoked inside her. But she pushed the fear down. There were no guarantees in life, but Jax had faced down a murderer for her. They'd both come out of it alive. And for as long as they both had left, she wanted to be with him.

A grin burst free, the fear suddenly overrun by an absolute certainty that she was doing the right thing. "I love you, too, Jax."

Woof!

Keara laughed, the sound louder and more gleeful than expected, as she bent to scratch Patches's ears. "I love you, too, Patches."

As she stood again, still holding tight to Jax's hand, he tugged her toward the park. Work was already well underway to return it to its previous state.

Keara took a deep breath of the crisp, clean Alaskan air and glanced around at Desparre's downtown. People were walking around, smiling and laughing, unafraid.

Then she turned back to Jax, the last of her fear fading into the background. She was ready to live that way, too.

She was ready to forge a new future, with him and Patches.

* * * * *

COLTON BULLSEYE

GERI KROTOW

To my dad, Ed—your love has made all the difference.

Chapter One

"I am being careful, trust me. It's my job. If I'm not on my toes, I'll never get to the bottom of Charlie's murder. I'm starting with the man who falsely accused him and whose testimony put Charlie behind bars." Dominique de la Vega focused on driving in steadily increasing traffic as she entered downtown Grave Gulch, Michigan. Her morning call to her fraternal twin, Soledad, was over her car's hands-free option.

"I get what you think your job is, sis, but I'm worried. You're pushing your luck too far. If Charlie really was murdered, as you suspect, there are bigger forces at work here than one or two criminals." Soledad's concern made Dominique wish they were speaking face-to-face, so that she could better reassure her sister.

"I'm telling you, Soledad, Charlie was innocent. And I'm chasing down the best lead since his death, since he was convicted." Ever since she'd started teaching creative writing at the county prison two years ago, Dominique's investigative-reporter instincts had gone into full alert mode. One of her students there, Charlie Hamm, had convinced her that he'd been wrongfully convicted and imprisoned; he'd insisted that the drugs he'd been accused of dealing were never his. He'd claimed the witness who'd testified against him had lied, and that false evidence had been planted, too. When he was found dead from an "apparent prison brawl," she'd wished she'd acted sooner on Charlie's claims of innocence. The least she could do now was dig until she uncovered the truth.

"I get it, Dom. You want justice for Charlie. He was one of your best students and his poetry touched you. He convinced you he's innocent, and I have to agree that it sounds like he was. That's fair. But what kind of justice would it be if you get hurt, or worse? You said this possible lead is about who put Charlie behind bars in the first place?" Interest reflected in Soledad's voice, but Dominique also heard distraction. Her sister was baking up a storm, as usual. As the owner of Dream Bakes bakery, it was her life.

Dominique stopped at a traffic light on Grave Gulch Boulevard in the center of the city and gave herself a heartbeat to answer her perceptive sister. If she told Soledad who she was really interviewing, or where exactly she was going to in Grave Gulch, her sister would relay the information to their father in two seconds flat. He'd flip out when he discovered she was willfully going into a part of town she wasn't familiar with, in the midst of a drug cartel's attempted takeover of their beloved town. If her father had read last night's police blotter in today's *Grave Gulch Gazette*, he'd have figured out that she was going to where drug-related crimes had occurred last night. To complicate matters, there was a serial killer on the loose in Grave Gulch, too, which added to Rigo de la Vega's worries over his family. Dominique appreciated his concern, and while she felt not a little guilty that her actions caused him any angst at all, she wasn't going to stop doing her job. She was in her third decade of life and had ventured into dicey situations all over town and the state for countless stories over the years.

She didn't disagree that any part of Grave Gulch was downright dangerous when it came to ferreting out information from a probable drug dealer and, at the very least, false witness. The particular street she was headed to had seen several serious crimes this past week, all opioid related. As much as GGPD wasn't cooperating with her on this story as she'd like, she felt for them. Every time it looked like the heroin scourge had been tamped down, it popped up again without warning. ODs often happened in clusters, depending on where the dealers were peddling their lethal wares. Dominique had learned long ago that getting the whole story often meant taking risks but getting her dad on board was another matter. Especially difficult to convince was her father, Rigo, who was beyond protective of his twin daughters, and always had been.

"Yes, the lede in my story is about Charlie's key accuser. I'm going to get to the bottom of why he lied. Then I hope to tie it into Randall Bowe." She believed Charlie's case was yet another instance of GGPD's forensic scientist deliberately tampering with evidence. "You know he's suspected of planting the false evidence that almost put Everleigh Emerson in jail for murder for good, and several others, right? Thank goodness Everleigh was cleared." She gripped the steering wheel in frustration. "GGPD is in over its head, if you ask me. Now that it's solid truth that Bowe planted false evidence against Everleigh, GGPD has clammed up about the other cases, including Charlie's. It'll be more difficult for me to figure out why Bowe went after Charlie but trust me, I will." Randall Bowe was in her sights, and she wasn't letting up. Charlie's death placed his case at the bottom of the GGPD priority list, as other investigations Bowe deliberately damaged involved the living. It wasn't going to keep Dominique from getting justice for Charlie, though. "Look, sis, I can't give you more information right now. You'll tell Dad." She never could hide her thoughts from her sister.

"Maybe I will, Dominique. You sound like you're already in trouble. Where are you, anyway?" The clang of utensils and aluminum sheets sounded over the connection.

"I'm in Grave Gulch, downtown. I just drove past you. Trust me, I wouldn't walk into a place unprepared, or in a dark alley or anything like that. Plus, it's broad daylight."

"Don't patronize me, sis. We both know that evil knows no time of day or place."

Dominique sighed, wondering why she'd told Soledad about any of this in the first place. Why hadn't she kept their morning connection time simple and allowed her sister to do most of the talking?

You're nervous.

Yeah, she was a little on edge. Going in to find and ask for an interview from the man, according to Charlie, who'd lied to put Charlie behind bars wasn't what she'd consider usual, even for her job. Usually she'd leave the investigation of criminal activity to GGPD. But first Randall Bowe had evaded questioning, and now GGPD was locked down about Bowe's involvement in rigged prosecutions. She had to do something, and that meant going after the false witness. Ever since she'd taught the creative writing and poetry night class for inmates in the county correctional facility, she'd established a bond with the men and women who had found them-selves behind bars, rightfully or wrongfully.

She'd listened to those who claimed wrongful imprisonment, agreeing to use her skills as a reporter to investigate what she could, but made no promises. Again, this wasn't her job, it was GGPD's. As she had expected, she found many allegations to be unfounded. When confronted with the facts, most inmates had stopped insisting on their innocence. But not Charlie Hamm. Charlie had always proclaimed his innocence, and had never given up on the hope that he'd be released early, once someone proved his case. He was arrested a year before he'd been arrested again and sent to prison, both times for dealing. Dominique believed his heartfelt admission that he'd deserved the first arrest, and that it had scared him straight. Charlie swore he'd been in the wrong place at the wrong time, trying to help users and dealers break free of the sordid life. He'd been brought up on drug dealing charges with what appeared to be minimal but solid evidence in the form of an eyewitness and a single fingerprint. When the reports of Randall Bowe's alleged evidence tampering began to leak out of GGPD, her reporter senses had tingled. Besides the possibility of a fake witness, evidence against Charlie, in the form of the fingerprint on a suitcase full of opioids, had been handled by none other than Randall Bowe. She knew GGPD was up to its neck in work with the confluence of a serial killer on the loose, the increasingly powerful opioid cartel and the recent kidnapping of a young child who'd been thankfully found safe and sound. All separate incidents. It would be unrealistic to expect GGPD would get answers on Charlie's case with any sensible timeliness.

Charlie had provided her with all of what he knew, and she'd taken copious notes. He'd believed that a cartel kingpin was at the heart of his wrongful imprisonment. When she'd pressed Charlie for names, he'd balked, claimed that "the drug ring in this town is nothing for a lady like you to worry about." Charlie had always maintained that he was in recovery for his own heroin addiction and was a reformed part-time dealer, as well. His goal was to help others and he'd claimed that's all he'd been doing when the event went down that got him in jail this time. Dominique wasn't a novice and knew that addicts were often gifted liars—it was a dark side of the disease. But Charlie was unlike any other addict or dealer-turned-legit she'd ever interviewed. He'd had such a positive outlook, even while imprisoned. If only she'd pushed harder, Charlie might still be here. She still struggled to accept he was gone.

Charlie Hamm had been found dead in his cell from internal bleeding suffered during a prison fight. Some of her students told her that they suspected the fight was staged—Charlie was targeted by the drug cartel's boss because Charlie had specific information pertaining to the drug ring, including the names he never provided her—but they wouldn't tell her more, wouldn't give her one iota of information. They were afraid for their lives, too. Which led her to wonder if Charlie knew the actual kingpin, a name that so far had eluded law enforcement, as far as she knew.

To make matters worse, she'd uncovered facts that made it appear that Grave Gulch PD hadn't done all their homework when Charlie was arrested. Point in case was the faulty evidence, processed at GGPD's small but highly capable forensics lab. Dominique wasn't certain, or convinced, that Randall Bowe's reason for planting the fingerprint against Charlie had anything to do with the cartel. But GGPD wasn't letting her in on their findings, so she had no choice but to follow the drug cartel lead.

Charlie never should have been brought to trial. Her heart ached for him, as much as her fury gnawed at the possibility of his fatal injuries being a premeditated murder. His suspicious death and all he'd told her previously triggered her reporter instincts into rapid-fire, and fueled her quest to solve Charlie's case.

"Please don't go to Dad, Soledad. Not yet. You know that this story is vital not only to my career, but for the *Grave Gulch Gazette*, as well."

"No offense, sister of mine, but I don't give a beaver's butt about the Pulitzer Prize. I want you safe. Alive." More clatters sounded over the connection as Soledad worked. Dominique didn't bother to correct her sister. Sure, she wanted to one day win the coveted journalism award for her paper as much as anyone, but her first allegiance was to the story. The truth. She'd add justice in there but knew that the local courts would handle that part. If she could make sure the bad eggs at GGPD were called out and meted punishment. First she had to get some evidence that Charlie's jail time was for a crime he might never have committed.

"Are you making any of your snickerdoodles today?" Her stomach grumbled at the thought of the buttery cookies, cinnamon baked into their crisp outer edges.

"Remember what I said about patronizing, sis?" Soledad wouldn't be sidelined by Dominique's distraction technique.

"Sorry. Trust me, sis, I'm good. I've got to go, but I'll stop by later if I can." She enjoyed all of the confections her sister created but had to limit herself as her sweet tooth was a serious downfall. As she passed a too-familiar apartment building, the memory of eating hot cinnamon rolls in Stanton Colton's bed flashed in her mind. The deep pang of regret it triggered was immediately followed by frustrated annoyance. She'd split from the dangerously attractive bodyguard two years ago. Ever since she'd taken on Charlie's story, though, Stanton had been occupying more space in her head. Probably because she'd always relished sharing her research with him, getting his perspective as a security expert. Memories of him and their short-lived—but passionate—relationship belonged in the past.

"You sound distracted." Darn Soledad's ability to read her, even over the phone. Dominique got it; she was equally able to sense where Soledad was emotionally, sometimes physically. They definitely had the twin connection.

"I was for a minute. This traffic is nuts. I'm good, though, no worries. I should probably let you go. We both have work to do."

"We sure do. I'm proud of you, sis. But for the record? It's my prerogative to worry about you. Know I love you and nothing is worth any fancy journalism prize." Soledad's sincerity infused Dominique's center with a sense of peace. It wasn't the first time she'd realized how blessed she was to have her sister in her life.

"Love you, too." She disconnected and continued to drive down Main Street, passing all of her favorite haunts, including a used bookstore and nearby coffee shop. Her description of where she was headed hadn't been completely honest. She was well into the east side now, where in a matter of a block the cheery storefronts gave way to run-down buildings and littered sidewalks. Making sure she was as close to the desired cross street as possible, she parallel parked in front of a dilapidated building that had splintered plywood boarded over every window and the door. Still, it was better than driving into the depths of the narrow road she'd have to walk to get to the interview.

Dominique quickly reviewed the address and map on her phone, committing her next steps to memory. Her subject, Johnny Blanchard, was her ticket to the truth. The witness had been difficult to chase down, and he refused to speak to her on her cell phone, opting to leave her messages on the *Gazette*'s landline only. Before Charlie's death she would have thought Blanchard might be slightly paranoid, but her perspective about what was happening in Grave Gulch had changed. The more information she gleaned, the more deadly Charlie's case seemed to have been, from the moment he'd been arrested. The fact that Charlie wouldn't give her names, in his attempt to protect her, was telling.

Grabbing her trusty, purse-size notebook, she locked her wallet in the glove compartment, shoved her favorite bag under a blanket she kept on the back seat and held on to her keys and phone as she exited the car. Once on the street, she pocketed both in her wool cream trench coat. She was grateful for the warmth it gave her on the almost-spring day. April here meant snow and cold temperatures as Lake Michigan slowly woke up from its long winter of freezing conditions.

Her choice of outfit was deliberate. It was important that she looked like her profile photo on the paper's website and her social media, so that Johnny knew it was really her. Otherwise, she'd never get close to Johnny; he'd take off the minute he spied her from the window or peephole of his apartment in this part of Grave Gulch. Which was why she'd opted to not dress down but maintain her preferred style.

Everything she relished about living in Grave Gulch—the large, diverse community with a small-town feel, being able to recognize many faces at her most visited restaurants and coffee shops, the ability to enjoy all four seasons with gusto—faded as she turned off the main street and walked deeper into what could be low-income housing in Anytown, USA.

Except this was her home, and it made her heart ache to see the suffering too many endured on a regular basis. She'd reported ad infinitum on the opioid epidemic's effect in Michigan, but nothing ever prepared her for the harsh separation between the addicted and those who'd either never touched the stuff or were in solid recovery from addiction. Dominique regularly read the published police blotter, and when GGPD hadn't been so shut-down against giving the press case information she'd ask officers for more specifics. Last night two drug deals had been reported on this same street. GGPD had captured one dealer but the other was still at large. The street wasn't abandoned, but the sense that she was being watched hung like a thick wet blanket about her shoulders. It was to be expected; drug dealers were always looking for a new source of income.

How many people had taken this same route to their

eventual death as they sought the fix for their addiction to prescription painkillers?

You can't fix everything. Work on fitting your piece of the puzzle.

Only three more blocks and she'd be where the answers to Charlie Hamm's wrongful conviction, and maybe even his murder, began. A shiver struck her nape and shocked down her spine. Soledad was right; this might be her worst idea yet, coming here alone. Her toes itched for her comfortable and serviceable running shoes. She'd remembered the address, the location on the street grid. But she'd forgotten how quickly a situation could go sour.

You're being ridiculous.

She was. It was the middle of the day and she was here to ask a person a few questions. No need to make a dramatic case out of it. Let the drama stay where it already existed: in Charlie's probable murder.

Dominique breathed in rhythm with her steps as sweat trickled down her back, soaking her blouse under the wool coat. It wasn't one of her usual forest hikes, with hawks, eagles and trees overhead, but only a few blocks.

Only a few more steps. She forced herself to appear confident, without fear. It was only human to be wary when the ravages of several crises saturated Grave Gulch's normally upbeat atmosphere.

You know you fanned the flames unnecessarily.

Admittedly she'd been fired up when she'd used her personal social media to basically threaten the local cartel with retribution for their crimes against Charlie, along with pushing GGPD until all information pertaining to cases Randall Bowe had worked was released. She'd vow to not stop until she had the truth. Her last post had been a bit softer, as she'd promised to seek justice for Charlie and wouldn't stop until she had the entire truth. But the meaning was indisputable.

The address was in her sights. She stepped across a tiny break in the sidewalk, kept going. The interview wouldn't take long if Johnny cooperated.

A big *if*. Interview subjects were notoriously fickle when the stakes were high. Soledad's words haunted her. Was she risking her safety for nothing?

No. Justice was *always* worth fighting for. But she picked up her pace, anxious to get her story and get home.

STANTON COLTON USED his best security and protection skills to follow Dominique without being detected by the intrepid reporter. Typical of her defiance against what any normal person would consider "too dangerous to go it alone," she was making her way up a street that had appeared on the GGPD's reports from last night.

He had double-checked that he had a weapon both at his waist and ankle before he left his vehicle. He'd parked several spaces behind where Dominique had left her modest SUV on the east side of Grave Gulch. It wasn't the flashiest of cars, and its black paint looked to be covered with an extra layer of dust. He briefly wondered if she was still partial to hiking through the

Michigan forests for hours on end. It would explain what looked like long pine needles piled in the corners of her windshield, plus the fresh pollen on the auto's hood. They'd enjoyed hiking the one spring they'd been together. As well as what they'd done before and after the outdoor excursions. Sometimes, during.

Nope. Not going there. Since they'd split two years ago, he'd kept a tight leash on his mind's wanderings regarding Dominique. She'd knocked him to his knees, something no woman before or since had ever done. And he'd promised himself he'd never again be so foolish, leaving his heart that vulnerable to a woman. Fortunately, his workload as CEO of Colton Protection left him little time to worry about being alone.

Dominique picked up her pace and he matched it, careful to stop into doorways or behind battered building corners as needed. He knew it was only a matter of time before she discovered he'd been hired to protect her, but Stanton wasn't ready to come completely clean about the assignment he'd accepted from Rigo de la Vega, Dominique's fortress of a father. Not until he had to. Dominique was in all likelihood going to give him a hard time about protecting her, and while he understood her viewpoint, he also had great respect and compassion for her dad. The man was frustrated by his daughter's refusal to see how her job as an investigative reporter put her life at risk, and he was desperate to keep her safe. Whether Dominique wanted to be protected or not wasn't on Rigo's radar. Rigo's words had been persuasive enough for Stanton to agree to accept the job. He'd reminded himself repeatedly over the past hours that was all this was. An assignment. A contract. It had nothing to do with his and Dominique's past.

Sure, it doesn't.

If he were to be honest with himself, Stanton was curious about where she was headed. He'd scoured the *Grave Gulch Gazette*'s digital archives for her reports from the last six months, which in fact was only a review of what he already knew. He never missed one of her articles. Dominique was a gifted journalist and while his business required mostly the nuts and bolts of crime reports to keep his clients safe, he always appreciated the more human, personal take that Dominique's reporting highlighted. Whether she was covering a crime victim or a high school student who'd been awarded a university scholarship, Dominique put her all into every report.

Stanton hadn't learned anything new from her reports, but when he'd checked out her social media page, his breath had lodged in his chest. Dominique had waved the equivalent of a red cape at the local cartel's kingpin. She hadn't mentioned the cartel or even drug dealing, but had made it clear she was going to uncover "every last criminal" who'd caused Charlie Hamm harm. And taken shots at GGPD, which made his head hurt for his sister, Chief of Police Melissa Colton. Then, as he'd scrolled further, he saw the "anonymous" posts threatening Dominique. He'd bet his professional reputation that the unknown posters were directly connected to the cartel. It made his gut twist to think about the sheer hatred aimed at her.

They'd parted ways two years ago and yet he'd never been able to let go of his instinct to protect her, to keep her safe. At least, that's what he told himself. If he dug deeper into his emotions, the truth was probably more related to the fact he might still have some remnant of feeling for her.

They were over, though, had been for two years, and he wasn't letting his thoughts wander back into that soul-sucking black hole. At least not during work hours. He had to stay in his lane, which for the foreseeable future was protecting Dominique.

And it was in her best interest to not alert her of his presence just yet. Letting her know he was here, and not leaving her side from here out, would cause a scene and draw the most unwelcome attention. Because no way in Hades was Dominique de la Vega going to accept his services without a fight. She insisted on doing things her way; this much, he'd wager, hadn't changed about his ex.

Her figure swayed with what he'd affectionately told her once was her ability to hypnotize him with a single step. She was clad in dressy wide black pants and a belted, short white trench coat that emphasized her hourglass figure, and he had to consciously work to keep his head in the game. He was here to guard Dominique, keep her safe from the deadbeats who were blasting her social media with vile and vitriol. He might be called to protect her from the kingpin of a major drug cartel operating in Grave Gulch. Not to stare at her ass nor think about how her skin had felt under his fingers.

Reviewing what Rigo had told him, which lined up with what Stanton had read on her social media posts, infuriated him. She'd put herself at unreasonable risk, and if he had his way, he'd talk her out of pursuing this story. Or at least wait until the dust settled from the blowout that was certain to ensue once she realized he wasn't going anywhere. His gut churned as he followed her, knowing dang well that Dominique was incapable of letting anything go if it involved unearthing the truth.

And then this morning's post. What on earth had possessed Dominique to announce publicly that she was looking for sources and intended to uncover "corruption in the Grave Gulch Police Department"? It was pure madness on her part. Sure, she was a reporter and he was all for her exposés and her investigative journalism. Free press was important. But it was best to leave the riskiest aspects, including anything to do with hardened criminal figures, to law enforcement agencies, or LEA. Let the local, and national as needed, LEAs handle it. Except Dominique seemed convinced that she couldn't trust her local LEA, GGPD. It stuck like a jagged piece of glass in his awareness because he had so many Colton family members who worked at GGPD, including his older sister, Chief of Police Melissa Colton.

Dominique's passion for justice was one of several characteristics that had attracted him to her in the first place. In his current position as her bodyguard, though, it made her a prime target for a bad guy at the top of a

local drug ring, as well as a bad cop, or police support-
ers who misread her motives. The threats facing her
were myriad and made his heart pound, his stomach
twist. If anyone hurt her—

You've made a mistake.

Yes, accepting this job was pure madness. It would
have been smarter to pass this assignment off to one of
the half dozen fully trained and capable agents on his
payroll. Colton Protection had earned its sterling reputation by protecting high-visibility clients from poli-
ticians to judges to A-list Hollywood celebrities. If he
didn't get his head completely in the mission, which
meant blocking off any thoughts of his previous asso-
ciation with Dominique, he risked blowing their until-
now untarnished image.

*Rigo made it clear—he's hired you to keep his
daughter safe, period.*

She turned right and made her way up a side street
that wasn't nearly as traversed as the one where they'd
parked. He mentally envisioned the side alleys, all memorized. Passing the first side street without a problem,
she didn't look over her shoulders once. Dominique
seemed to be pretty certain of where she was headed.
He scanned the street, approaching the next alley. A
hooded figure emerged from behind a large tree and
Stanton paused, keeping Dominique in view. The hairs
on his nape rose as he saw the man quickly close in
on her.

Stanton broke into a jog, then a full run as the figure's hand reached into his pocket.

"Dom, look out!" he yelled at the top of his lungs, but not before he saw the thug grab for Dominique.

Chapter Two

A shout behind her sounded exactly like her name and she halted, frozen in place. No, it couldn't be. It had sounded like a male voice was calling "Dom." Only one man ever called her that and he wasn't here. Not since their breakup.

She pushed forward, quickened her step. Her progress was harshly interrupted by hands that felt like a pair of vise grips on a shoulder and her hair, yanking her backward without warning.

"Ow!" She grunted in surprise, pulled off her feet as though she weighed no more than a bag of flour. Fear drove her to fight like the devil as she was dragged into the alley and then over a threshold, through a door kicked open by the attacker, and shoved into a dark corridor. Her assailant slammed the door closed with his heel as she kicked, twisted and screamed. Anything to gain purchase. Putrid smells of urine and body odor assaulted her and she knew this was a place where people came to use. To die.

"Shut up! Knock it off or you're dead." The thug's

hand clamped painfully over her mouth. His voice was low and ugly, and left her with zero thoughts of reasoning him into letting her go. He had her from behind, one beefy arm around her neck, holding her body against his. He smelled like cheap cologne and bubble gum, not much of an improvement over the stench of the building.

She knew she was going to die whether she resisted or not, so she sunk her teeth into the vile-smelling hand. He swore and let go of her mouth, and she sucked in a breath to yell as she tugged away from him. Her scream was cut off by a hard slap to the side of her head. Stars floated in her vision but didn't stop her training and that internal voice that urged her to keep going, to give it all she had. She reverted to the basic hand-to-hand combat techniques she'd learned years ago.

She jutted her elbow back into his gut, which felt like hitting a brick wall, but her stomp on his instep elicited a hiss. Cheered by his discomfort, she did the same with her other leg, taking time to drag her heel down his shin first, then press into his foot with all her might.

He responded by whipping her around and shoving her up against the wall, which forced her head back against the plaster. More stars floated, but not enough to preclude her vision. A mean mug of a man stared at her, his breath foul no matter the huge wad of pink gum he chewed on. Pure menace glowered in his gaze as his hands encircled her throat and he cut off her airway.

Dominique fought for her life, unable to gain enough space to breathe. Using the technique to take her shoulders under his arms and force her arms up to release his proved impossible, as each of his limbs was built like an oak tree. She clawed at his leathery face, kneed his groin repeatedly. He flinched but kept the pressure on her throat. Panic rose and, unable to get his hands off her neck, she gave his head a hard slap.

"You bi—"

An explosive sound, and a burst of light as the door was kicked open. Her attacker let go and Dominique collapsed to the ground, gasping in short breaths as her airway let in precious air. Heavy footsteps sounded, fading through the building.

"Dominique. Look at me."

The voice she'd recognize in her deepest depths of despair broke through her panic and gave her what in the past several minutes had grown dim. Hope.

Stanton had saved her; he was here. With great effort, she turned her head and looked into the deep blue irises that had haunted her every night since their breakup two years ago.

"What the heck are you doing here?" Instead of sounding authoritative and irritated, her words creaked out like a baby frog's first ribbit. Scratchy and weak. "Please tell me you're not stalking me."

He helped her to her feet and put his hands on her head, tilted it to one side and then the other, ran his fingertips over her throat. She batted his inspection away and made to walk out the door of the crusty building. But her wobbling legs betrayed her and if not for his guiding arm, she'd have fallen.

He swore under his breath and pulled her close, encasing her in his arms. It wasn't a bear hug or a greeting, but something to help ground her and convey that she was safe, not alone.

"Stanton, I'm okay. Really." She spoke with the same raspy voice into his shoulder, involuntarily inhaling the spicy masculine scent that was proprietary to Stanton. It was as though his very essence held the elixir for all that ailed her. The bruises that would soon begin to throb, the constant quest to get the best story, to find justice for Charlie. The long lonely nights since they'd broken up.

No.

She pushed against his chest and refused to meet his gaze again. Not yet.

"I'm ready to leave now. By myself. Feel free to finish whatever you came here for. Why are you here, by the way?"

"I believe 'thank you' is a customary response in these situations." His crisp enunciation, the inflection of gentle mocking in his maddening baritone, triggered a waterfall of emotions and memories that she wasn't in any place to handle. Not after being so brutally accosted.

"Sorry, yes, thanks so much. I'm… I'm fine." She lifted her chin but still couldn't meet his knowing gaze. They were on the concrete sidewalk, and the daylight seemed dimmer than it had only minutes earlier. As if they were in a black-and-white movie and the bad guys were all around. She ignored the part about the sexy man who'd saved her life. "I have to talk to—"

"You're not talking to anyone but me until we get out

of this godforsaken part of town." He placed her arm through his bent one and urged her forward. "If you can't manage it, be honest." She remembered this tone of his deep voice all too well. Stanton was on a mission. He'd hoist her over his shoulder and carry her out of this derelict neighborhood without a second thought.

"Wait. I can do it myself." She stopped and leaned on him as she took off one, then the other, shoe. "Let's go." Free of the treacherous heels, she still accepted his support but was able to set a much faster pace as they strode toward Main Street. Away from the danger, and her attacker.

Away from finding out who had murdered Charlie Hamm.

"HERE'S MY CAR." Dominique pulled away from Stanton, but he held tight, keeping her walking past the black SUV. He was concerned not only about her throat and body bruises, but her feet. She'd walked five city blocks in stockings. Or whatever kind of thin socks she wore.

"We're leaving it for now. I'll have one of my agents pick it up later." All he wanted was to get her into his vehicle and get them both out of here. If it was up to Stanton, Dominique wouldn't leave his sight until he'd eliminated the threats against her.

"I only need to get inside it, to take my tote bag. I keep an extra outfit, plus workout gear. I have a pair of running shoes and socks. Let me get them. Then I'll go with you." Her softly mumbled response made the hackles on the back of his neck stand up. She'd been injured worse than he'd been able to assess. Nothing less would explain her agreeing to his direction.

"Where's your bag?"

"Back seat. My wallet's in the glove compartment."

He set her against the trunk of a tree lining the main street while he opened the back door and retrieved her bag, then her wallet. When he straightened, she reached for the strap and he shook his head.

"I've got it. I'm parked here, too." He nodded at his vehicle, a few spots behind hers. "I'll get your car back to you within the afternoon, Dominique. It's the least of your worries right now." He helped her into the passenger seat of his Jeep, specially outfitted for Colton Protection. It was their bulletproof, armored, VIP vehicle. They had another SUV and two similar sedans, but he'd chosen the Jeep for this job. It had the fewest memories of his time with Dominique. Unlike one of the sedans where they'd made love, during that insanely passionate stretch of time they'd dated.

He didn't want any distractions while he was protecting Rigo's daughter.

"What put you here the same time as me, if you're not following me?" Her voice was returning, though if he wasn't bent over her, his ear so close he felt her breath, he didn't think he'd be able to hear her as well.

"My new assignment." He clicked the seat belt in place for her. "Hang on." He shut her door, walked around the front of the vehicle, doing a 360-degree inspection of the street. Satisfied no one was lurking, ready to follow them, he got into the driver's seat and started the engine.

"Let me guess—your assignment is paid for by one Rigo de la Vega?"

"I haven't even started driving, Dominique." Her brows rose and he hated the sight of smudged lipstick on her cheek, grotesquely elongating her downturned mouth. That bastard had done that to her.

Cursing under his breath, he turned away from the distraction of her face and shifted into gear. He executed a U-turn and headed back toward downtown Grave Gulch. Taking Dominique to safer ground. Anywhere but here.

"Yes, I accepted the job from your father. He's concerned about the threats you've received over your social media posts. He had every reason to be, I'd say."

"He, you—*both* of you—have no right to interfere in my work." Her voice, softened by the attack, didn't hide her outrage. He wished he'd reached her sooner, prevented that rat from laying a single finger on her. Anything to have her be her usual high-energy self. This shell of the woman he knew as strong and invincible frightened him.

She's safe. Focus on keeping her that way.

"Perhaps your work is none of your father's concern, and that's an argument you can take up with him, but you can't tell me you're not grateful that I showed up when I did." Maybe verbal sparring would bring her back from the scare.

She remained silent and he inwardly cursed. Dominique had survived a brutal attack only minutes before, and while he'd argue with her later about his "right" to protect her, he definitely had no business goading her while she was in such a vulnerable state.

Problem was, Dominique didn't do "vulnerable." She was as far from that as any woman he'd ever met, including trained agents.

"You taught me well." Her admission startled him.

"What's that?"

"When you insisted I learn hand-to-hand techniques and defensive maneuvers. All the stuff you taught me? They paid off." He saw her reach for her throat, rub it, in his peripheral vision. "It's true, what you said over and over again. I'd automatically do what I had to, if the time ever came, and it did. I was almost free of him but he was awfully big. I couldn't get his arms to budge once he had a grip."

"I'm glad to hear the training helped. You handled yourself incredibly well, Dominique." His heart had constricted, then pumped with fear, rage and purpose when he saw the thug grab her. He'd been so afraid he wouldn't reach her in time... "Did you hear me shout?"

"I did, but I didn't know it was you. Not at first." Or had she, but she just didn't want to tell him?

"It wouldn't have mattered, as by the time I saw him it was already too late. He came out of nowhere." Stanton hated that he hadn't seen him sooner.

"I feel stupid that I didn't hear or notice him in that alley. I was paying attention to the street."

"I'm sure you were. Don't beat yourself up over

this." His choice of words hit him and he grimaced. "I mean—"

"It's okay." She let out a hollow laugh. "I understand what you're saying. I think it'll take me some time to process, is all."

He nodded. "It always does." He turned off the main drag onto a wide boulevard.

"You sure would know. You've been beat up enough times." Dominique's voice held memories that he'd fought so hard to keep behind the mental wall that he never broached. Where their time as a couple resided. How she'd nursed him after an overzealous fan had tried to grab his client, or the time she'd made love to him after work when he thought the agency was taking an economic hit. He needed to stop reviewing the many times they'd made love, but it was difficult to keep the memories at bay when she was right next to him.

"Where are we going? I'm not going to the hospital, Stanton." She looked out the windshield, consternation on her face. He silently thanked heaven that she hadn't noticed their destination until now.

"You're getting checked over." He pulled up to the emergency room entrance of the main city hospital.

"I don't need the ER. I'm fine, really. I didn't lose consciousness, and I can walk. If I'm hurting tomorrow, I'll call my doctor."

"Save it. A thug with hands bigger than my head just tried to squeeze the life out of you. And there's already bruising on your neck." He swallowed. That jerk had come too close to doing permanent, life-taking damage.

She slumped against the seat. "Fine. But you're getting me an oat milk latte after this."

The reminder of her favorite comfort drink should have put his defenses up, reminded him to stay emotionally detached as he protected her. Instead, a tiny sphere of warmth lit, deep inside.

Too close to his heart.

"HERE YOU GO." Stanton set the covered paper cup in front of her and she immediately wrapped her hands around it, craving the warmth. After a relatively quick ER visit, he'd made good on her demand and they'd slipped into her favorite café. It was pretty hopping for a midweek morning. She'd noticed a man at the counter, who'd looked at her with unguarded interest when they'd entered, and her first reaction had been to turn and run until she realized why he was staring. She knew she was a sight, had seen her ghastly reflection in the hospital restroom. But she'd settled for simply splashing water on her face and running a hand through her long hair. It required too much effort to fully put herself back together. Thankfully none of the other customers paid her a second glance.

"Thanks for this." She kept her gaze downcast, giving herself imaginary space between her defenses and Stanton's overwhelming presence. It hadn't changed, two years later. At least, not for her. The constant sexual tension still arced between them as if she'd never walked away from him.

"I learned long ago to take your threats seriously.

Heaven forbid you don't get a latte when you want it." He took a sip of his green tea, which appeared to be scalding hot as steam rose from the open cup. She knew he preferred to sip his beverages without the plastic cover. Funny, the things she remembered.

"Are you satisfied with what the doctor said?"

"Why wouldn't I be?" The trauma surgeon had been called in to look at her throat X-rays and do a physical exam. She'd told Dominique that she'd heal in time and there was no lasting damage. "The ER doc seemed to know her stuff."

"Some bruises don't show up on X-rays. They can take days, weeks to surface." His mouth was a grim line that underscored his concern.

"Why do I get the feeling you're talking about something other than today's injuries?" She glared at him, or rather, tried to muster the energy to give him the evil eye. Instead she watched his familiar poker face. The only hint of his passion lay in his laser-blue eyes. She swore she saw white-hot sparks in their depths as he considered her.

"I know I'm the last person you want to have to spend any time with, but your father was convincing in his arguments that your life was in danger. I owed it to him, to your family, to take the job."

"Whatever you needed to do, I understand, but I don't have to like it. My sister is the one really responsible for Dad's involvement. I talked to her this morning and I had a feeling she was going to call him."

"Unless you spoke to her about your interview's location before ten o'clock last night, Rigo was ahead of it." Stanton's declaration cut through her wanting to blame Soledad, or Stanton, for her father's overprotective ways. "He told me to start this morning."

"Of course he was on to me sooner. He always is." She sipped her latte, relishing the creaminess of the oat milk, but it did little to soothe her fraught nerves. In all her years as an investigative reporter she'd never faced a life-threatening situation. Criminals, sure. Menacing notes sent to the *Gazette*, meant for her. But not a direct physical assault. That had to be why her hands were still slightly shaking. "And it turns out he was correct. More fool me." Appreciation flowed through her veins as she realized her father had in all likelihood saved her life. As had Stanton.

"You were focused on your job, is all. Getting the story. It's normal for you to dig deep."

She looked at him, ready to see the sarcastic expression on his face. Instead a soft smile played on—

Stop.

"You understand that much, don't you? That my job is my entire focus. It has to be. You never allowed our, um, your personal life to interfere with your job. It's no different for me, Stanton. It has to be all about the story." As her safety would be his single focus as long as she was his assignment. A prescient shiver traveled down her spine and she didn't want to examine the cause. Because the part of her that had never let go of Stanton, of what they'd shared, was jumping up and down in giddy anticipation.

"I do understand." He didn't elaborate, for which she was grateful. The last thing she needed was any more reminders of how well he'd once known her.

They sat in companionable, or rather, bodyguard-and-person-in-danger silence for several minutes. Stanton had chosen the small bistro table in the corner, away from most of the customers who frequented the busy café. Her eyes took in the familiar surroundings and she tried to allow herself to relax. When her gaze passed over the barista station and she saw the same man staring at her, her back stiffened.

"What is it?" Stanton missed nothing. She wanted to believe it was all about her, but it was why he was such a great security professional. Stanton was an observer and had superb intuition.

"There's a man sitting at the counter, at the far right, who I noticed when we came in. He hasn't moved and has kept his eyes on me the entire time. It could be nothing—"

"There are no coincidences when you're being targeted by a drug kingpin, Dominique." At least he didn't add in the part about how she'd attracted the unwanted scrutiny with her provocative social media posts. And she had the sense that Stanton knew a lot more about why she was a target than he let on.

"Is it the cartel I should be concerned about, or Len Davison the serial killer? What do you know about Charlie Hamm, Stanton? About Randall Bowe's habit of mishandling evidence? Or the drug cartel that's run rampant in Grave Gulch?"

He straightened in his seat, leaned in toward her. It'd be so easy to think he was about to tell her how much he wanted to make love to her again instead of preparing to fill her in on who wanted her dead.

Chapter Three

Stanton avoided giving Dominique an answer right away by checking out the man she was concerned about. He sat at the counter, his eyes on his phone, not looking like he cared an iota about them, or her. But Dominique wasn't about drama or paranoia. If she thought something was odd about the person, he trusted her instincts, even though he knew Dominique was testing him. Or maybe baiting.

She thought he was so busy doing personal protection that he was out of touch with what mattered to her, to the Grave Gulch community. He held back his defensive retorts, reminded himself he had to remain detached. Keeping his peripheral vision on the man of interest, he met her gaze.

"Charlie Hamm was imprisoned two years ago for dealing opioids, as part of a ten-year sentence. He was killed during a prison fight in the county jail last month. There's been speculation that his death wasn't a result of a random fight but instead a murder. Many in the local community think it's all a big conspiracy theory, though. Several people have been accused of crimes that didn't make sense, and the evidence against them all points back to GGPD's forensic scientist, Randall Bowe. There's a serial killer on the loose, Len Davison. If that's not enough, to swing back to Hamm, Grave Gulch has been slammed by the opioid epidemic, and with so many young victims, scores of families are still grieving. The last thing they want to hear is that a convicted dealer was wrongly incarcerated."

"You've been reading my work." Her eyes sparked and he reminded himself it was from professional pride and not from pleasure that he'd sought out her story. That she wasn't happy about being so close to him.

"I regularly read the local paper, among others. You know that much about me. Like most folks around here, I read the *Grave Gulch Gazette* every day. It's my job to stay on top of events, especially any crime that affects Colton Protection."

She nodded. "That makes sense. Still, it's always reassuring to know someone's reading my words." A grin let him know that no matter how brilliant a journalist she was, no matter how much success the *Grave Gulch Gazette* achieved, Dominique was a humble soul at heart. Her compassion for her fellow citizens had been part of what attracted him to her when they'd met. She'd been researching how well recent parolees integrated back into their community and had fought to find decent employment for a woman she'd first reported on when the woman was still an inmate. He wasn't surprised at all by her interest in another convict's story.

"This story, Dominique. Charlie Hamm, the cartel. Fill me in on what you haven't put in print yet. Do you have the kingpin's name?"

"Okay." She took a deep breath, sat her sore body up straight. "First, I don't have any names. That's one thing Charlie wouldn't give me. Do you remember that I was interested in teaching creative writing and poetry to inmates at the county prison? I followed through with it after, um, we split, and have been volunteering there at night and on weekends ever since. I had Charlie Hamm as one of my students. As you said, he was convicted. But he always proclaimed his innocence. Charlie was different, Stanton. He explained to me that he was put in jail on drummed-up charges by a user he was trying to help. The drug kingpin's honchos got to the witness and threatened him. They wanted Charlie out of the picture—he was making too much of a dent into their profits by referring users, and dealers who used, to the new public rehab that opened four years ago."

"The one halfway between here and Detroit, with costs billed according to economic need?" His agency had protected a handful of clients right after they left rehab, to keep them safe from the cartel, whose spiderweb reach often drew the newly sober back into their addictions.

"Yes. It's provided beds that Grave Gulch's three centers often don't have. At last count the rehab had processed over three thousand addicts. I don't have the statistics about how many have remained sober, but that's three thousand users who otherwise would never have received help. We simply don't have the space to treat them all in our town." The Grave Gulch community had risen to the occasion with public education and health resources. But it was never enough to stop the constant stream of vicious, drug-related crime.

"I thought the follow-up care was a problem, too." One of his agents on staff had a sister who'd been free of heroin for two years. It had required a geographical relocation and thousands of dollars that their parents took out of their retirement funds.

"It is. Most addicts don't want to do—or can't afford to do—the necessary geographical move to get them away from their usual haunts. The dealers certainly don't want to see their prime customers move away. Of course, they'll find more willing users any way they can." She took a sip of her latte. "This is very nice, thank you."

He nodded, ignoring the warmth under his breastbone her gratitude stoked. He always had ridiculous overreactions to Dominique.

"Charlie wrote the most touching poetry while he was in my class. It turns out he left his first wife for his second, in between arrests. The prosecutor used his sudden divorce against him, saying he wasn't to be trusted. He'd been picked up several times for various petty crimes but didn't serve hard time until the dealing charge. Did you realize the only physical evidence against him was a fingerprint on an old suitcase? And the unreliable witness's statement, of course. It was a false charge, in my opinion."

"Which brings us to your obsession with bringing down both the entire drug ring and rooting out corruption in the Grave Gulch PD."

"I don't appreciate the way you said that, Stanton. Is it my passion? Probably. My purpose? Absolutely. When you say 'obsession,' it discounts my motives. I'm not trying to 'bring down' the entire GGPD. And no matter how it looks, I'm not gunning for your sister. Melissa's always done her absolute best as chief. I understand the instinct to shut down discussion with the *Gazette* on a sensitive issue like Randall Bowe. But I'm not giving up on rooting out any bad cops or employees that are working there and have a history of corruption." Her chin jutted and her eyes blazed, resentment enunciating her intent. Had her emotions stayed bottled up deep inside her, the way his bitter disappointment at her rejection was shoved into the moldy basement of his heart?

Crap.

They were back to it, then. "This is where we left off, isn't it." He didn't pose it as a question, as they both knew the answer. Talk after talk, and eventually argument after argument, had led to this. The unscalable wall of discord between them. She never felt he accepted her for who she was. And Dominique had been right—he'd wanted her in a safer occupation, for certain. Since he worked a job that at times brought him face-to-face with his mortality, he had little room to judge Dominique's vocation. But he had a right to care about his girlfriend at the time, the woman he'd thought he wanted to marry, didn't he?

Not according to Dominique, who'd insisted the story always came first.

No matter, as he'd lost her anyway. And to heck with how much of his heart remained sore to this day.

"Stop it, Stanton. No more talk about what's passed between us. That remains in the past. *We're*—" she motioned between them "—over. If you expect me to allow you to follow me and give me your exceptional level of protection—" he didn't miss that she acknowledged his need to provide only the best that he could offer "—then you're going to have to back off trying to keep me away from doing my job. Otherwise I'm going to tell you and my father to shove your intentions—"

"Whoa, no need for cussing, ba—uh, Dominique." *Double dog doo.* He'd almost called her "babe." Letting out a long, extended breath, he flexed and fisted his hands. Wiggled his toes in his shoes. Cleared his mind of the emotions being with Dominique elicited. "Let me rephrase. Your sense of duty to get the story, to clear Charlie Hamm's name, moved you to post your concerns on social media."

"Yes. But lest you think I did that without any forethought, think again." She grinned and his lips twitched in response. "I put my intentions out there on my public profile in hopes of stirring up more witnesses and more sources about what's going on in the police department."

"You had to realize it'd catch the attention of the cartel, Dominique."

"I did. And how do you know it won't inspire a drug ring member to cash it in, give me the story and accept a plea deal, witness protection from law enforcement? I know GGPD's budget has to be stretched to the max right now but I've seen other reporters in similar circumstances get witness security. Melissa strikes me as someone who's all about keeping people safe, even if she won't let me in on the internal investigation." She shook her head. "I'd be further along, frankly, if it wasn't for GGPD. They have messed this case up but good, right from the start, with the either misidentified or clandestinely placed fingerprint."

"Now, wait a minute there. I've read the reports. The police on duty when Charlie's crime, okay, *purported* crime, went down all did their jobs well." His protection service worked in unison with Grave Gulch Police Department. It wasn't just about Melissa being chief, but about the GGPD's professional standing in the community. He kept GGPD informed, and they let him know salient points about cases and persons of interest. The two-way flow of information had allowed him to provide exceptional protection to several high-level political and local celebrity figures who'd found themselves stalked by criminals. Colton Protection had helped GGPD out by taking some of the load around personal security away and keeping intended victims safe while the police did their job to apprehend suspects.

"Maybe they did. But what about Randall Bowe?" She threw the forensic scientist's name out like a tie-breaking card in a poker came. "He's been under scrutiny for messing up evidence on several drug-related crimes. GGPD's apprehension rate was excellent, and they appeared to be making headway against the drug cartel. Until a number of the charges had to be dropped due to lack of evidence or witnesses. Tell me what's going on there, Stanton?"

"I can't tell you anything, Dominique, except that the police are on your, *our*, side. You know this better than I do, since you regularly report on them." He sighed. "I'll concede that there could be one bad cop, maybe two, including Bowe. That doesn't incriminate the entire department, though."

"It most certainly does if no one's trying to find the leaks and get rid of them. I know you're invested in GGPD more than most because of your family ties there."

"It's never as easy as it appears, Dominique."

"Kind of like us, right? We were matched perfectly on most issues, except one." She didn't say it and didn't have to; they both knew she referred to a permanent commitment. "It looked good on paper, made sense that we'd make a good pair, but then when it came down to it we had incompatible goals in life." Her dark eyes blazed with conviction, and color had returned to her cheeks under the bruises. He heard her, saw that she was trying to make a point about why they'd gone their own ways. Mostly agreed. But his mind kept seeing her in his apartment, before the breakup. When she was still his.

What on earth had he been thinking, agreeing to this gig for Rigo?

You still care. Too much.

"Stanton? Are you listening to me?"

STANTON BLINKED ONCE, twice, and she saw his focus come back on her. He'd drifted, and a pang of regret hit her sideways. It was one of his mannerisms that she'd found both annoying and endearing. A brilliant man, Stanton let his mind run miles ahead of everyone else's, putting together seemingly disparate pieces of information to form a full picture. It made him an excellent personal protection and intelligence professional. And it had made him second to none in bed. She didn't get the impression he was thinking of either, though. More likely he'd been recalling their disagreements, maybe even those last awful few minutes together. Shame hit her as hard as regret had. She'd been so immature, so overwhelmed at the weight of their connection.

"I'm fine, trust me. I heard you. You're juggling a lot of bowling pins, Dominique, that could end up hurting you, be it the cartel or your alleged bad player at GGPD. It's possible that more than one person would want you silenced."

Ouch. He hadn't said anything she didn't already suspect, but the bluntness of his conclusion stung.

"I know." She gave him his point. He was correct. The harsh set of his jaw, covered by its usual shadow of beard growth, was a perfect foil to the light in his eyes and conveyed his confidence. At least he couldn't read her mind as hers drifted. Back to their long hours in bed, how his skin felt against hers. How that light beard had scratched her inner thighs...

Refocus.

She tore her gaze away as a matter of survival. Her

eyes scanned over the familiar surroundings of the café and she tried to allow herself to relax, to forget that she was sitting across from the only man she'd ever given her entire heart to. Well, almost. When her gaze passed over the barista station a second time, she saw that the same man she'd seen earlier was still staring at her. Her back stiffened.

"What is it?" Stanton missed nothing. She wanted to believe his heightened perception was all about being with her, but Stanton had superb intuition.

"That man's still there."

"Right. We're leaving. Now." He stood and offered her his hand, which she waved away. Her legs were stronger, the shock having worn off.

She followed him back onto the street, pointedly not looking at the creepy guy at the counter. The fresh albeit chilly wind was refreshing and made her feel more human, less like a stalked opossum.

"I've got to go to the *Gazette* offices. You're going to be bored there." Maybe Stanton would agree to leave her there for the rest of the day, come back for her at close of day. It'd be nerve-racking, working with him next to her. "There's a security guard at the entrance. I'll be safe inside for the afternoon. You know the paper doesn't scrimp on employee safety."

"I do, and it doesn't change my job description, Dominique. No way are you going anywhere without me. And we can't be certain there aren't bad guys staking out the *Gazette*. I've got somewhere else we can go. Come on." Instead of going to his car, parked in front of the café, he put his hand in the small of her back and pointed her to the granite building next to the café. The first several floors were offices, but there were twelve floors of luxury apartments above the commercial spaces.

"I'm not going to your apartment." She halted, refusing to move forward.

"You don't have a choice right now. We need to keep talking about the case, and it's imperative we're not overheard." As he spoke, the man who'd been watching her exited the café and ambled in the opposite direction down the main drag of Grave Gulch, as if he was out for a Sunday stroll. Dominique had her doubts. She looked at Stanton and he was watching the man, too. He pulled out his phone and sent a quick text. When he finished, his gaze was back on her, and there wasn't an iota of compromise in his sapphire irises.

"Let's go."

"Fine." She fell into step with him. "We'll go to the paper after this, then?" She wanted to talk to her boss and fill him in on the most recent events. He deserved more than a text with news that she'd been attacked, needed backstory, no matter how much she'd reassured the senior editor that she was okay.

"Not today." He was resolute. Anger tried to spark in her center but all she felt was resigned. And bone-tired.

Neither spoke as they rode the elevators—first the public one to the tenth floor, then a private, residents-only lift to the penthouse. Memories whirled in her mind the closer they got to Stanton's apartment. When she walked through the familiar sleek doors into the contemporary space, it was impossible to not see every place she and Stanton had made love. On the foyer's tile floor the night after a particularly scary scenario he'd provided protection for, on the sofa that faced a wall of windows that overlooked all of Grave Gulch and to the countryside beyond.

"Let me take your coat." He was behind her, gently easing off her sleeves when she'd wanted to do it herself. "It's okay to accept help, Dom. I know you're hurting. I'd be sore, too, after a brute like that came at me."

She relented and allowed him to slowly ease the garment from her body. He laid it over the end of the sofa and walked to the kitchen, giving her a welcome modicum of privacy. As if he remembered she preferred to work alone, with minimal distraction. The thought of sitting still at her laptop, still in her gym bag, only made her aches hurt more.

"This view only gets better with time, doesn't it?" It was a shallow comment but she wasn't up for deep conversation. Not yet. She needed mental space after coming face-to-face with the memories of her and Stanton. The afternoon sunlight shone on the wooded areas surrounding the medium-sized city, varying shades of green offering hope for warmer spring weather soon. Winter struggled to let go of its hold on Michigan, keeping the mornings and evenings chilly well into May. Trees were a source of strength and peace for Dominique, and being able to appreciate this unique view on a regular basis had been one of many gifts she'd let go of when she'd left Stanton.

She'd missed this.

"My time to enjoy it gets less and less." He spoke from the kitchen counter. She heard a coffee machine and looked over her shoulder as she timidly sat on the edge of the leather sofa. "We just had coffee and tea."

"You didn't get to finish yours, and I need a shot of espresso. Keeping your insides warm will help you relax, too." He walked back into the room and handed her a pink mug. It had the logo of a local 5K run on it, an annual Grave Gulch fundraiser for breast cancer. It had been hers, something she must have left behind after their breakup. She looked at him, held up the mug.

"I'm surprised you kept this."

"Why? You thought I'd throw everything away? It's a good cup. Keeps my coffee hot the longest."

"There couldn't have been much to toss. I never really moved in here." She sipped and Stanton was right; she needed the warmth.

"No, you didn't." His tone was noncommittal. Why couldn't their relationship feel like that to her? Instead of making all of her emotions churn, with regret's bitter taste heavy on her tongue. "What were we discussing, again? Charlie Hamm?"

He'd thrown her a lifeline and she could have hugged him. No, no, not hug. Nothing that had to do with touching him. In a complete betrayal, her fingertips began to itch as if they'd die from never feeling his hard, smooth skin under them.

"Dominique?"

"Yes, Charlie Hamm. I know that if I can get to the bottom of his conviction, and who the force was behind it, I'll not only get justice for him, but upend the drug cartel that's done its best to decimate Grave Gulch."

"Again, it's imperative to leave the law enforcement to the experts. I'm not discrediting your investigative abilities or saying that your reporting doesn't have serious purpose. On the contrary, everyone needs to be able to understand what we've all been up against since fentanyl hit our streets. A good portion of my business has been protecting people waiting to go into the witness protection program or who don't want to have to lose their identity but the threat level doesn't warrant government-paid protection." He leaned his hands on the counter, his shirtsleeves rolled up and leaving his muscular forearms exposed. "I'm on your side, Dominique. At least as far as getting to the truth is concerned."

"But you're not going to support me going for the jugular. Putting myself back out there, making myself a target."

"There has to be a way to do your job virtually. Can't you call your interview subjects on the phone?"

"Absolutely not. I have to verify all of my sources, and I certainly have to speak face-to-face with the man whose testimony put Charlie behind bars in the first place. Only he can tell me who ordered him to lie on the stand. I have a feeling it'll lead me to the same person who ordered Charlie's murder."

"If indeed the prison fight wasn't incidental."

She shook her head, needing Stanton to believe her, to trust her judgment. "It wasn't like Charlie to get himself in any kind of altercation. He'd had a clean record the entire two years he was in jail. His dream was an early release, on good behavior."

Stanton's cell phone buzzed and he picked it up from the cocktail table, his thumb flicking across the screen. The play of light across his chiseled face mesmerized her. Her stomach flipped and she quickly reminded herself that he was off-limits. Failed previous relationship with him being reason number one, followed by the line of work he was in, and hers. Both were all-consuming, and his was particularly dangerous. Losing him once, no matter that it had been her decision, had been enough. It would be catastrophic to let herself get lost in him again, only for him to be taken out by a madman. Plus, Stanton made it clear that he had zero interest in picking back up with her. Even if he hadn't, she wasn't in the right place or frame of mind for any kind of romantic entanglement with anyone.

A soft groan escaped her bruised lips and she sucked in a breath, hoping he hadn't sensed her subconscious plea for attention from him. His immediate glance in her direction proved he had. Humiliation rushed heat into her face and she pointedly looked out the window, unable to meet his gaze.

"It's a text from Troy. He's on his way over to take your statement." Either Stanton didn't notice her discomfort or chose to ignore it. Instead of relief, disbelief at his words doused her embarrassment.

"Wha—wait a minute! I didn't agree to talk to the police." Anger fired through her veins, giving her a sense of purpose she hadn't felt since being so brutally assaulted.

Stanton stood up, paced to the panoramic window. It was what he always did when they'd argued. Gave himself space to think.

"You were attacked. I called my cousin the detective when you were getting your X-rays. He agreed to meet you privately, so that you don't have to go into the station. I thought you'd appreciate not facing down every cop in Grave Gulch right now. It's not like you're their favorite reporter at the moment."

"You think I can't take it? I don't care if all of GGPD hates the press. That's not my problem in the least."

"All of GGPD doesn't dislike the *Gazette*, and it's unfair to say that. You have to admit that it's hard to do your job when you're constantly being scrutinized. The *Gazette* hasn't let off GGPD—ever. And it's only gotten worse recently."

"If GGPD would keep the public informed about their internal investigation of Randall Bowe, it might ease a lot of the perceived tensions."

"It's called 'internal' for a reason." He stopped pacing, hands on slim hips, and glared at her. "The world isn't yours to exploit, Dominique."

"Exploit? Excuse me?" She stood up and said a silent thanks that she was able to do so in one steady movement. Her lower back hurt like heck and her shoulders were beginning to throb. She raised her hands in surrender. "I can't do this. Either pay my father back or assign one of your other agents to my case. I'm out." She moved toward the foyer, needing to be free of the constant nearness of him. His scent, his mannerisms, his voice.

"Dom, wait." At the use of his endearment for her she froze. This was the name he'd shouted earlier, right before the thug had grabbed her. In a moment of danger, he'd called out to her the way he knew she'd recognize it was him. So she'd know she wasn't alone. At some level, he must have known that she still trusted him. She turned back toward him and slowly closed the distance between them, but left several paces as a boundary when she reached the window.

"This isn't working, Stanton. It's not going to. We've been with each other for less than half a day and we're at fisticuffs again." Unwanted tears pooled and she blinked. "I'm not sad. I'm mad."

He ran his fingers through his hair, loosened his silk tie. She'd always appreciated how he insisted on a professional appearance, no matter how dirty his job got. The pale cream fabric highlighted the deep blue of his eyes. The cotton stretched over his broad shoulders, triggering more memories that were best forgotten.

His killer gaze pierced through all of her defenses, reminded her of all she'd lost. Constant stress at how they'd work out their demanding careers, yes. But also, long nights of intimate conversation, soul baring, and of course, lovemaking she'd never forgotten.

He ran his fingers through his hair again. "I'm sorry.

There's no need for us to be in each other's face like this. It's my fault. I'm protective of GGPD. It's in my blood. Literally." The reminder of how close he was to his sister triggered a pang of regret in her chest. It was one of the many things she'd found so attractive about Stanton, the way he respected and treasured his family.

"I'm upset and angry that an innocent man went to jail and served time, and while doing so was murdered. And yes, I think there's a dirty cop or GGPD employee behind it, along with the drug kingpin. But I have the highest regard for any man or woman who'd willingly put themselves in harm's way for our protection."

He nodded. "I know. But it's not easy, seeing the headlines day after day in the *Grave Gulch Gazette*. It's exhausting for all involved. And then the rumors that the paper will get acknowledged nationally—no one is against journalism or a local paper being rewarded. But—"

"But not if it makes local authorities, like your sister, look bad." She let the words slip out before she thought, and immediately wished she could take them back. Stanton was offering her an olive branch. His eyes widened slightly but she knew him well enough to know she'd angered him. "Wait, I'm sorry, Stanton. I shouldn't have said that."

"No, you're free to say whatever you want. You always have been." *Zing* right to her emotional solar plexus. He apparently hadn't forgotten their last conversation two years ago, when she'd blithely refused his marriage proposal. It'd been right here, in front of these windows, in the middle of the night after a particularly long round of lovemaking. She only figured it out afterward that he'd been planning it, when she realized he must have bought the ring ahead of time. But in the moment, they'd both been naked. Sated. Vulnerable. And she hadn't been ready for such a permanent commitment, not yet, but had begged him to stay together until she was. The pain of how he'd shifted gears, told her they weren't on the same page, their relationship wasn't ever going to work, still burned. But so did her attraction to him.

Their gazes met, and in his eyes she saw all she'd lost, all that could have been, and the man he was today.

"I—"

"No." He placed a finger on her lips. As stern and annoyed as his expression was, his touch was gentle. A whisper. "Stop talking, Dominique. Give me a minute here."

Give him a minute? Why did he need time? It wasn't as if he was as unsettled by her closeness as she was by his. He'd given no indication he was. Only then, on closer inspection, did she see how his pulse jumped in an erratic dance at the side of his strong jaw. His pupils were dilated, even with afternoon sunlight streaming into the penthouse. And his breath—he sounded as though he'd run up a flight of stairs as he closed his eyes, presumably to shut out her image.

Clarity hit and her breath hitched. While their minds knew they didn't belong together any longer, their bodies hadn't gotten the text. As if in a trance, her right hand reached up and stroked his cheek.

"Don't." His plea came out in a gravelly whisper, and he kept his eyes closed. But he didn't stop her. Her ire melted into compassion. She knew too well what it was like to fight it as he did now. She'd struggled to keep her physical desire in check from the moment he'd looked into her eyes right after he'd rescued her this morning.

"It's okay, Stanton. Isn't it normal to feel like this with an ex? We're not robots." She shouldn't be standing so close to him, shouldn't tempt fate by touching him at all. Her fingers explored his jaw, stubbled by beard growth, unable to get enough of him. No amount of touch with Stanton would ever be enough. She swayed toward him, unable to stop the desire-fueled momentum that pushed her closer.

"Dom." With no further preamble, Stanton's arms came around her waist and he tugged her flush against him. Air whooshed from her lungs as she felt his full length, including his erection, through their layers of clothing. She let her arms go to his shoulders and met him halfway as his mouth came down on hers.

Chapter Four

Stanton used every ounce of control to not take Dominique here and now, the way he remembered she liked it best, on the sofa. On the same cushion she'd been perched on like an injured bird, still stunned from flying into a window. If not for her earlier scare, he didn't think he'd be able to hold back. She'd recovered enough from her attack to be fully present in this moment, though, as her tongue met his with insistence, her lips pliant and delicious under his. It was as if they'd never stopped kissing since the last time he'd held her like this.

Stanton had never wanted Dominique more than he did in this moment. How had he waited two years to hold her again, to taste her? He shook with need as he held her but refused to manhandle her no matter what he knew—that she loved it when they both gave their sex life all they had to give.

The reminder of that relationship, and why it hadn't lasted, made him lift his head. He stopped the kiss but couldn't keep from devouring her with his gaze.

Her lips were wet, slightly parted, her eyes closed. No matter the bruises, the shadows under her eyes that told him she was working at full tilt on the Charlie Hamm story. Dominique was the most beautiful woman he'd ever known.

"Please, Stanton. Kiss me." Her whisper shot lust through him, and his arousal had to be apparent to her. He moved his hands to either side of her face. Slow. He had to take this slow. Savor it.

"Patience, babe."

He delighted at the moan that escaped her lips. He hovered, making her wait, until he couldn't stand it any longer. She leaned in as he moved in—

A loud buzzer sounded. His doorbell.

"Dang it." He rested his forehead against hers. They were both out of breath.

"Ignore it." Her lips moved to his jawline, down his throat. "We've waited too long for this."

The buzzer rang again and he grasped her hands, removed them from behind his neck. Tried to ignore the disappointment in her gaze. It echoed through his being, too.

"It's Troy. He's here to take your preliminary statement." Frustration rang in his every cell, poised to make love to the woman he'd not been able to forget.

You let her go, man.

He forcefully expelled a breath, moved toward the entrance. It was ironic. He was taking the same steps she had, after he'd proposed, and she'd countered with an offer his pride had been too bruised to consider at the time. He fought to bring his arousal under control. The buzzer rang another two times before he felt confident about opening the door to a trusted colleague and relative.

"Troy. Come on in."

"Hey, man. How have you been?" Troy's boyish face broke into a grin at the sight of his cousin. They shook hands and gave each other a bro hug as he stepped into the apartment. "You've been scarce at the station."

"I know, we've been swamped." It was true. Colton Protection had such an uptick in clients this past month that all of his staff was overworked. "I had to hire two new agents and their vetting took all of my time." And now, Dominique was exclusively his twenty-four seven for the foreseeable future. "Let's go sit down." When he turned and went back into the living room, Dominique was gone. He knew it was probably to the restroom, but seeing the sofa empty made his heartbeat stutter.

You need to take a pause here, dude.

"Is Dominique still here?" Troy sat in an easy chair opposite of the sofa.

"Yes. It's been a rough morning for her, but she's doing okay."

Troy nodded. "Good to hear."

"I'm here." She walked to the kitchen and stood next to the island, helped herself to a tall glass of ice water. "Nice to see you again, Troy. Can I get you something to drink?"

Stanton should have been the one to offer; it was his apartment, no matter how well Dominique knew her way around it. He hadn't changed it much since the breakup, pouring all of his energy into work. Anything to keep his mind off the memories. He remained in the living room, not wanting to examine how easy it would be to fall back into old routines with her.

"I'm good, thanks." Troy didn't seem surprised by any of this, another surprise. Was he like his entire family, who thought he and Dominique weren't through? He'd never been able to convince his parents, Frank and Italia Colton, that he and Dominique weren't going to reconcile. Now he wondered if they'd seen the parts of him that this morning had revealed. The factions of his heart that hadn't let go, not by a long shot.

"Stanton, do you want anything?" Dang it but she sounded as if she'd never left.

"No, thank you." His teeth ground together.

"Are you sure you're happy to see me, Dominique? Word on the street is that you've got it out for GGPD." Troy kept his smile but Stanton saw the barb for what it was. He'd thrown the same words at Dominique earlier, yet he had the urge to say something to shut Troy down ASAP. Didn't his cousin see that she was bruised, had been through hell today?

"You know you can't trust rumors, Troy." Dominique walked over to the sofa and sat on the end opposite of Stanton. He noticed she'd taken her athletic shoes off. Her one toe looked swollen and he made a mental note to ask her about it later. "Contrary to what seems to be the scuttlebutt, the *Grave Gulch Gazette* doesn't have any issues with GGPD as a whole. Unless you're covering up the truth. We look for the facts in every story, Troy. You know that."

Troy shook his head. "I do, Dominique, but when we have reporters snooping about all the time, it's hard to run a closed investigation. It breeds public distrust, too. Things leak out, factual or not."

"Then open it up. Tell us what we're asking for. Is there a corrupt cop on the force? In addition to Randall Bowe's deliberate mishandling of evidence?"

"You know we can't do that. And you shouldn't accuse someone of a crime unless you're certain."

Dominique and Troy squared off, staring at one another with open challenge. Stanton opened his mouth to cut through the tension, but Dominique spoke before he had to.

"Why don't we focus on you taking my statement for now?" She gave him a smile that didn't meet her dark, troubled eyes. Stanton felt the indecision coming off her. And it got right under his skin. This was why he'd fallen for her years ago.

"Excellent idea. Sorry about goading you, Dominique. But I'm not sorry about sticking up for the good public servants in my department."

"Nor should you be. Unless they're corrupt." Her words and posture remained unshaken but her tone was softer.

"Point taken." Troy's cheeks had reddened. He pulled out his phone, a notebook and pen. "Can you go over your entire morning with me, from when you left your house?"

Dominique complied, leaving no detail out. Stanton looked out the window as she spoke, unable to focus on anything but her voice. He needed to refocus on why he was protecting her in the first place, if he hoped to keep his emotions in check. His arms ached to hold her as she recounted the stunningly brutal attack that could have killed her.

You would have never held her again.

As messed up as he was over coming so close to kissing her again, he knew his inner turmoil was preferable to losing her. He'd already done that once, but knew she was safe and alive, living her life. He'd convinced himself she was free from harm, living in the apartment complex on the edge of town that abutted one of Grave Gulch's nicer suburbs. Her family and especially her twin, Soledad, who lived in the same apartment building, kept close tabs on her. He'd had to believe this, or he wouldn't have been able to let her go so easily two years ago. Recrimination welled again, reminding him that maybe he should have accepted her offer to wait on a marriage commitment. He'd been so stung by her refusal he'd acted before he thought it out, telling her it was either all-in or forget it.

"How exactly did you get the information that led you to your interview subject's address?"

Dominique paused and Stanton's glance strayed from the panoramic view. Her eyebrows drew together and she played with the hem of her blouse, normally tucked in but hanging out since the ER visit. Another sign of how hard all of this was on her, because Dominique was always turned out for work. For life. She rarely fit the description of "disheveled."

"The paper had a voice mail left on the main line, claiming to be Johnny Blanchard, the witness whose testimony helped convict Charlie Hamm. He said he had information I'd be interested in."

"He asked for you by name?" Troy was taking copious notes.

"Yes. Said it was about the Charlie Hamm prison fight." She leaned over and pulled one leg up on the sofa, sitting in the half yoga pose typical of her when she was working on her laptop or involved in a deep conversation. "My boss, the senior editor, gave me the information. I called the number and left a message with my cell number when no one picked up. My work cell, not personal. I have two phones." She shot a glance at both Stanton and Troy, and he thought she wanted to make certain they understood she didn't take her personal safety for granted. "Then he, assuming it was really Blanchard, texted me his address, which I didn't have before."

"Did you follow up with a search of the address?"

"Of course I did, but nothing came up. I wasn't surprised by that, as a lot of witnesses for major crimes go off the grid as far as the internet is concerned after they testify. And this witness had every reason to hide, since he lied on the stand and sent an innocent man to jail."

"You can't be sure of that, can you? Until you interview him and he admits to perjury?" Troy's query wasn't chiding; he appeared genuinely interested. Stanton wanted to warn his cousin that those were fighting words as far as Dominique was concerned.

"What I'm certain of, Troy, is that the Charlie Hamm I met in my creative writing course that I teach at the prison was a thoughtful, gentle man. He had a reputation for helping druggies on the street, and several sources verify this. From the local food bank to the homeless shelter, to the run-down rehab place at the corner of Main and Fifty-Seventh Street, Charlie was a good player. A positive change agent. You know the rehab I'm talking about, right?"

"Sure do. Had two heroin ODs in front of it last night."

Dominique swore under her breath and Stanton agreed with the sentiment. It never seemed to end, the countless victims of the epidemic. And yet the cartel continued to methodically expand their distribution ring, mixing higher and higher levels of fentanyl into the heroin.

"Both ODs made it, though. Thanks to the Narcan on site, and of course all of our officers carry it."

"Thank goodness." Dominique's evident relief smoothed the lines between her brows. "Did you know Charlie Hamm was the person responsible for getting Narcan into that facility to begin with? The social workers were swamped and he attended the training offered to the community by the rehab on the other side of town. Charlie believed all addicts deserve the same chance to live, to recover, no matter what side of town they came from. Does that sound like the work of a drug dealer to you, Troy?"

"No, it doesn't. But a lot of things don't make sense in Grave Gulch these days. Who knows what a dealer or user is thinking?"

"Charlie Hamm was innocent. Just like Everleigh Emerson was proven innocent, and Len Davison is on the loose because the evidence against him was destroyed. Multiple victims of false evidence and innocent people murdered by Davison. Now that we know that Randall Bowe is officially under suspicion of maligning evidence, all I need is the information pertaining to the fingerprint on the suitcase that sent Charlie to jail, along with proof that the testimony against him was bogus."

"I hope you get it, Dominique, I truly do. I'm all for catching any bad guy, in uniform or out. But I'm here because you were attacked while trying to do your job. It sounded like a classic setup and I wish you had called us before you went to interview your subject."

"If I'd let GGPD know, you would have checked it out and spooked the man." Stanton gave her points for not bringing up her concern over corruption at the department again.

"Which is exactly what's happened. He was scared away, but not by GGPD."

"What?" Stanton and Dominique spoke in unison.

"I took the preliminary information you gave me after the attack, Stanton, and paid my own visit to the area. The witness does indeed live at the address you had, Dominique. He's been there for the last month or so, working hourly at a local café in the kitchen. But he's fled the scene. Two neighbors said he was out in the apartment hallway, told one that he was waiting 'on an appointment.' But when word got out that there was a mugging going down, he took off. No one's heard from him and my bet is he won't risk coming back home for a good while. He might think that whoever went after you would come for him next."

"That sounds like a good assumption." Goose bumps rose on Stanton's forearms. He was glad that she had been correct, but more relieved that Dominique hadn't been hurt worse. The cartel wasn't in the business of scare tactics as much as flat-out murder.

"So it wasn't a setup by the witness, as you've both told me it could have been. My instincts and background work were spot-on. I couldn't have known in advance that I'd be targeted." Dominique's anger reflected in the furrow between her finely shaped brows. His fingertip itched to smooth her concern away. *Careful.* He tried not to frown at his conscience's internal prodding. It was a natural reaction to want to eliminate her stress and she'd had a particularly awful day. He checked his phone. It was only three o'clock. Five hours in her presence and his heart was screaming to take over from his brain.

"Except for your provocative social media posts." Troy held up his hands as if in surrender. "I'm not questioning how you or any other reporter does your business. But if you're going to dig into a case like Charlie Hamm's, it's bigger than any of us sitting here. No question, your interview subject is legit. Johnny Blanchard was the man whose testimony clinched the case against Charlie." Troy spoke with measured neutrality.

"Along with evidence falsified by a GGPD employee." She wasn't holding back any longer.

"If there was any malfeasance by an employee of GGPD, you can be assured we're working to get to the bottom of it, Dominique." Troy glanced up at Stanton. They'd been more like brothers as kids and he recognized the silent plea for a helping hand.

"It's not fair to keep labeling the entire GGPD because of the actions of one, or maybe two, bad players." Stanton repeated what he'd already said to Dominique earlier, hoping that this time she heard him.

"The *Gazette* isn't letting up until we have all the answers, Troy. You can tell the chief that." Dominique's arms crossed in front and he knew it had to hurt to sit like that. He'd bruised his ribs in the past and remembered any movement felt like torture.

"That's fair. It's your job. And I'll pass it to Chief Colton, when I run into her. We're all going pedal to the metal, Dominique."

"Well, then maybe the *Gazette* and GGPD do have something in common, after all."

Stanton silently groaned at Dominique's words. Did she have to throw down all the time?

And did he have to be so turned on every time she did?

"WHAT DO YOU mean she got away?" Pablo Jimenez's eyes were darker than their usual hellish black, and his face was screwed into a menacing scowl. "Your job was to get rid of both of them. Tell me Blanchard is taken care of."

Leo shuffled on his feet, wanting to look anywhere but at his jefe's face. But to look away was certain death.

"It was out of my hands. Blanchard took off before I ever arrived, and as I was about to finish her off, I was interrupted by an undercover cop." He was lying, a bit. Enough. He'd faced the witness and threatened him but he'd slipped away, faster than Leo was on his feet. And Leo had been focused on getting the reporter girl most of all. She'd openly threatened his jefe on the internet.

"What am I paying you for?" A large object, a crystal glass full of hundred-year-old Scotch, flew at him, and he had the sense to remain still, allow the pain to come. Jimenez liked pain, and to avoid the hand-thrown missile only revealed weakness, in the kingpin's view.

"I'm sorry. It won't happen again."

"You're correct, it won't happen again." Jimenez withdrew a long blade from his boot and Leo held his breath, certain he was about to meet *Dios*. "Next time, take more men with you. I want the reporter taken care of, and I should never have trusted that lousy dealer to be Hamm's witness. What good is it if he testified in court but now wants to spill his guts?" Jimenez spat into another crystal goblet, the amber liquid from his tobacco chew both revolting and mesmerizing to Leo. "Take her out, and the man who came to save her. I don't care if he's a cop. This local department refuses to accept who's in charge here. Me. If that doesn't work, we'll go after the reporter's family next."

"Yes, jefe."

No one argued with the jefe, ever. Leo knew his job.

"Go!" Jefe wasn't a patient man.

IF DOMINIQUE HADN'T felt the air leave the room previously, she'd have known by both Stanton's and Troy's expressions that she'd overstepped.

"I'm not saying we both do the same kind of work. Certainly you're on the streets every day, doing your best to keep Grave Gulch safe." She swallowed, her explanation hanging like the frivolous bunch of words it was. Stanton had returned to staring out the window and Troy looked at her with unabashed annoyance.

Troy stood, pocketed his phone. "I get it. Times are tense in Grave Gulch. It's worse than I've ever seen it. There's a killer roaming loose—I can't confirm if you have the correct name—we have internal issues at GGPD and we were slammed by the heroin epidemic. Not to mention some other cases that are popping up faster than the hungry alligators at the State Fair. Again, all of this is off the record. I don't want to see my words twisted and used as clickbait."

"Off the record. Got it." She wanted to explain how clickbait really worked, that she or any other reporter had no pull when it came to the titles of her articles. Once she sent her work to her editor, it was out of her hands. How much and how it would be published, as well as the headlines. Many times she'd complained to her superiors that she wasn't happy about exactly what Troy had mentioned—a hard-hitting story that had cost her hours, days, months, was all distilled into a misleading banner that ensured the online readers would click through. And that print readers didn't hesitate to buy the paper with their morning coffee. This wasn't a time for explanations, or worse, justification.

"I'll let myself out. Dominique, please come into the station as soon as you can, to file a full police report. I'll file a preliminary one to ensure we keep a lookout for a man matching the description of your attacker. Both of you, stay safe." Troy turned and walked to the door and she sat back down on the sofa, curling her feet under her. It was too hard to keep her guard up any longer. Exhaustion rolled over her but she knew it'd be hours, most likely days, before she enjoyed restful sleep.

"We'll be there within the hour." Stanton nodded at his cousin and watched him exit. Once the door clicked closed, he turned toward her. His eyes—still so startlingly blue—were full of ice shards. "Nice way to win friends and influence people there. I'm sure Troy won't hesitate to give you his next scoop." Stanton's lush mouth pulled up on the left side, his sardonic admonishment unnecessary.

"I messed up. I said as much." She leaned her head back and closed her eyes. If she could get five minutes to herself. "Don't you have work to do, you know, remotely? Where's that laptop you like to spend all your time on?"

"I'm not the same man you knew two years ago." She felt the sofa move as he sat at the opposite end. "I tend to leave work at work when I can. It means I'm at the office for longer hours, but at least by the time I get here, I'm done for the day."

"Except when you work hands-on, like with me." She blushed at the connotation. "I mean with protecting me. Now you're on the clock twenty-four seven. Seriously, I think you should think about delegating this assignment to one of your agents. Your leadership is needed at the helm of Colton Protection, isn't it?"

"You still think you know what's best for everyone around you. What about you? You're still chasing the Pulitzer like the Holy Grail. How has it worked out for you? You look exhausted to me, and it's not just from today."

She opened her eyes and stood, walked around the room on her sore feet. It was impossible to stay relaxed and quiet when Stanton was so close, and especially when he was grilling her.

"I'm the reporter, Stanton. I'll ask the questions. You know enough about what I'm working on. Let's turn the camera on you. How many more employees has Colton Security gained since—since two years ago?" She was still loath to mention their relationship, and disastrous breakup. Guilt nibbled on her conscience. It'd been brutal, the way she'd looked at Stanton in his naked glory, as he'd told her it was all-in with marriage, or nothing. She'd asked him to reconsider—still remembered the tears pouring down her cheeks—but he'd been adamant. "Marry me or we're through, Dominique." So hurt and confused by his hard line, she'd turned on her heel and gone to the bedroom, gotten dressed, then left. Except for the occasional run-in at a local event she was reporting on, where she did all she could to avoid him, they hadn't spoken since. Until he'd tried to warn her about the attacker this morning.

"Fifteen. Twenty-three employees total, if you count administrative staff. I've opened a second office in Los Angeles that's larger than here and appointed an office manager there. I've no desire to move to California. The occasional commute there is hard enough. But that hasn't changed the smaller staff here, where we have six bodyguards." He spoke in succinct syllables, without any hint of pride. His humility, no matter his incredible success, had drawn her in back then, made her want him all the more.

That was then, this is now.

"Was that the result of saving those big-name actors last year?" She'd read the AP report about a fan sneaking on a movie set, stalking an A-list actor who was guarded by Colton Protection. No one had been hurt, adding to Stanton's firm's stellar reputation.

"Mostly, yes." He sounded impatient and she turned from the window to see him striding across the room toward the kitchen. "I'm hungry. Lunch?"

"No, I don't think I can eat yet. I'd rather go to the station first, get this over with." She shuddered. It wasn't like her to go all vulnerable, but it wasn't every day she got blindsided by a vicious attack. Having to narrate her experience again in the sterile environment of GGPD did not appeal at the moment.

"Try a little something. We could end up waiting a

while for someone to take your statement." He pulled salad items out of the refrigerator and set them on the granite counter. "Steak, salmon or chicken with your salad?"

She froze. This was too familiar. They'd fallen into a routine when they were together. They'd meet here for lunch, or rather, lunch after sex, and then go to her apartment for dinner and often, a sleepover. Stanton had insisted he preferred her bed even though his bed, his apartment, was far more luxurious and accommodating.

"I, uh, whatever you need to get rid of." She'd lied, she was famished. But eating a meal in front of him, in his apartment, seemed so intimate. As if no time had passed, as if they were still together.

Too close.

He raised a brow but continued prepping two salad bowls, topping one with steak and the other salmon. He set hers in front of her at the island and ate his standing up. They shared half a whole grain baguette and he poured a small dish of olive oil for her, smearing his bread with the butter he always left out on his counter, just as his Italian-born mother did in the Colton house. Dominique didn't know where to put the surge of nostalgia that overwhelmed her. Tears pricked and she blinked, faux-coughing to cover it up. He'd remembered that she preferred salmon, olive oil with her bread. It touched something deep inside in the place she didn't allow her thoughts to wander if she could help it.

The place that remained exclusively Stanton's.

Chapter Five

Stanton remained standing on the other side of the counter, eating from his bowl as Dominique at first picked at, then appeared to relish, the meal. He hoped that by shoveling his salad into his mouth he'd avoid further dialogue with her. Any kind of communication with Dominique was lethal to his guard, his heart. As they ate he silently cursed himself for allowing her father to persuade—no, manipulate—him to take the case. But he couldn't lie to himself. Every day of the past two years since they'd been together, he'd scoured not only the news, but the police blotters, the reports, whatever his sister allowed him access to. All in an attempt to ensure no one was coming after Dominique. That she was safe. He'd never stopped worrying about her.

If he dug deeper, he knew it had to do with his regret over forcing the breakup. At seeing the pain etched on her face as she'd comprehended he was ending it. What had he been thinking, throwing a woman like Dominique away?

That worrying about her day and night wasn't your idea of a good time.

"Thank you for this, Stanton. I didn't realize how hungry I was." She picked up the paper towel he'd set down and wiped her mouth, her delicious, dark pink lips glistening with olive oil. Napkins were extra accessories he'd let go after she'd left him.

"I'm glad you finally ate something. You needed to eat before we go to the station." He was about to tell her that he didn't pick salmon just for her, or that the olive oil on the side was something he did for all his guests. But it would be lying. He'd never forgotten what she'd enjoyed, be it a favorite meal or position during their lovemaking.

He missed being with her, sure, but this overwhelming attraction, persistent thrum of his sexual awareness of her had to be from months with zero dates. He'd tried to find someone else…well, kind of.

"Left-swiping on an app is not dating."

His older brother Clarke's sardonic admonishment at a family dinner last weekend echoed in his memory. Clarke was a top PI who often liaised with GGPD and helped Stanton stay in the loop with cases, as appropriate to his protection services agency. His fiancée, Everleigh, had been framed by Bowe for the murder of her cheating husband, so he wanted to see the thug brought down as much as Dominique. But not at the cost of her safety.

Dominique stared at him and he wondered how long he'd drifted for this time. She did this to him. Made him think of things that had nothing to do with the matter at hand. His phone buzzed with a text from Troy. He set down his bowl to read it.

Two thugs hanging out around your building address. Suggest you come up with a different egress than the usual.

Showtime. His mind immediately shifted into body-guard mode, going over the mental checklist he'd used thousands of times before.

"What is it?"

"Troy's spotted some suspicious-looking jerks hanging around on Main Street in front of the building. We'll go out via the parking garage instead of the lobby."

"They're here? Now?" He watched her chew slowly, swallow. All the time watching him with the eyes that he was still able to read. She'd been turned on earlier, before Troy showed up. He'd do anything to bring that smolder back into her obsidian gaze. After he got her out of here safely. He hated seeing the fear that flickered in her eyes, quickly shut down by her stubbornness.

"Yes. I'm thinking that he couldn't get a photo without letting them know he's on to them, so we don't know if either one is the jerk who attacked you." He didn't bother telling her that cartel thugs were like cock-roaches in an apartment. Where there was one...

She speared a cherry tomato. He had to force his glance away from her. No way would he keep his mind on the case, on her dang safety, if he watched her eat.

Dominique ate her salad as if she hadn't a concern in the world. Didn't she remember the time they'd turned each other into their own personal salad bar, complete with sexual satisfaction?

"I'm not afraid of him, or any of the bullies Pablo Jimenez wants to throw my way."

"How do you know it's Jimenez?" He'd heard the name mentioned, read it in police reports, but so far no official pronouncement of the identity of the local cartel's kingpin had been made. Not by GGPD or any state law enforcement, and the DEA hadn't come forward with an exact ID yet.

"You're not the only one with connections at GGPD. Not everyone there thinks the media is the devil. I'm convinced it's Jimenez who's calling the shots. I'm going to get to the bottom of all of this. With a little luck, the truth won't give us justice for only Charlie and his family. It'll blow the drug ring wide open."

Her conviction sent a pulse of cold sober fear through him. "Dominique, you're not dealing with a local gang here. From what I know, you're correct. Jimenez is a statewide leader. He works for a network of very powerful men, with international connections." Men who were ruthless when it came to keeping their coffers full of billions brought in by drugs.

"That big network doesn't give a flip about a town of fewer than forty thousand people in Michigan, for heaven's sake. We're small potatoes for them." She ripped a paper towel from the roll he kept on the counter and wiped her mouth. "It's Jimenez whose pride's been stepped on. He thought he'd get away with silencing Charlie, and now Blanchard. And yes, me. He's not going to stop me."

"You really believe Charlie was murdered by them, right? If that's true, then you have a good idea of how resourceful Jimenez and his gang are. No leads, no witnesses are left behind. You're trying to disrupt that. You're a bug they're going to step on."

"A bug?" Her brow rose, and for the first time in over two years he glimpsed her sense of humor. How he'd missed her low, throaty laugh. How it rumbled across a room, echoed in his chest, wrapped around his heart.

Get a grip, man.

He nodded, scraped his bowl in the sink, rinsed both of their dishes, stacked them in the dishwasher. "A mere pest. Pablo Jimenez doesn't tolerate anyone looking into his business." He knew firsthand, as CP had provided a bodyguard last month for a witness to a fentanyl drug sale by one of Jimenez's guys. Said witness and his former client ended up going into federal protective custody.

"You know something you're not telling me."

"I know a lot of things, Dominique, but they're irrelevant to what we've got to do to get through the next days."

"I won't have this story in a matter of days, Stanton. Don't kid yourself. It's already taken me weeks to get this far, and I've been doing all the background work on the cartel for the last two years."

Interesting. It was the second time she refused to

refer to their breakup. Yet, like him, it seemed she used it as a reference point. He focused on the mission. To dwell on Dominique's motives for anything was a direct road to unnecessary pain. He'd sworn optional misery off after she'd left and he'd taken a long while to glue himself back together.

Are you whole again?

"You ready?" He prepared to leave, but when she straightened, leaned forward, all he saw was the countless times he'd kissed her over this counter. That one time, they'd ended up atop the granite, naked. Did the same mental videos play in her mind?

"Ready for what, Stanton?" She shot him a wary glance that didn't match the way she licked her bottom lip. Yeah, the attraction was still very much mutual. A small consolation when there was nothing they could do about it. Not yet, anyhow.

"We need to leave now if you're going to give your statement before close of business." He glanced at his smartwatch. Hard to believe that in two hours the working day was over for a good portion of Grave Gulch. Not that he worked banker's hours—providing security was a round-the-clock gig. "Get your bag and we'll go now."

"On it." She slid off the island chair but it wasn't with her usual grace. His bones ached for her as she took her time, held the edge of the island for a moment to make sure she had her balance. More telling were her hands, as they still visibly trembled, albeit slightly. He had to give her credit. She'd had a lousy day but was holding up like a champ.

"Let's take the elevator to the parking garage." He'd prefer the stairs but it'd be too hard on her. The door to the utility lift opened and he ushered her inside. It was spacious and bare, normally used by delivery services and the building doorman when a larger piece of mail had to be brought up.

"It would be easier to get into your car on the street. But I get the extra precaution." She moved a stray strand of her inky black hair from her eyes, tucked it behind her ear. A deep blue sapphire earring winked in the bright elevator light. His breath caught. He'd given her the earrings for her December birthday. Right after they'd started dating. He was inexplicably thrilled that she still wore a gift from him. Warmth rushed from his scalp, to his chest, pushed into his groin.

The thug who'd hurt Dom.

He conjured the memory of the man to keep from becoming visibly aroused. It had the desired effect but also reignited his anger, and not a little bit of despair. Would he ever get over her?

Do you really want to know?

The elevator dinged at the building's lowest level and opened to the garage's concrete floor.

He motioned for her to wait as he exited and cleared the area. There were security cameras on his vehicles and he'd checked them from the apartment before they left, on a phone app. The garage was well lit, clean, and there were no signs of bad guys. No matter, he'd feel better once he had Dominique safely in a car and they were en route to the police station.

"Okay, good to go." He held out his hand to her. It was an automatic gesture, but not one he'd do with a typical client. When she slipped hers into his, he vowed to stop overanalyzing himself, his thoughts. A lot of things were different when it came to guarding her. It didn't matter as long as the end result was the same: Dominique remained unharmed.

As they walked toward one of several CP vehicles stored in the parking garage, he allowed the naturalness of being with her sync with his protection skills. The mark of a good bodyguard wasn't how big or badass they were, although that helped. No, it was being able to accept one's surroundings and utilize them to your advantage. As long as Dominique trusted him enough to stay by his side and follow his lead, he'd keep her safe.

"Here." He held open the passenger door of a low-slung sports car and waited as she got in. Dang it, he should have considered her aches and bruises and picked the SUV parked next to it. But he wanted to ensure a quick escape if need be.

"You've improved your transportation means in two years." She spoke as he started the engine and backed out of the space.

"Business expansion." He was half listening as he prepared to egress the garage, his gaze constantly scanning the concrete floor, the walls, the spaces between other vehicles.

"The blacked-out windows are cool."

He drove up two ramps, entered the street-level floor. The exit was in view, onto a one-way, side-access street.

Traffic moved along, toward Main Street. The gate arm at the sentry station was down, but was automatic. It would rise as he approached.

"Stanton!" Dominique's scream pierced the air a split second before the gunfire exploded.

"Get down!" His arm reached toward her but then he pulled back when he saw she was already under the dash. He used both hands to maneuver, flooring it through the exit, past the garage tender's booth. Wood splintered as the barrier gate arm broke over the front hood and split in half on the windshield, which thankfully remained intact. Colton Protection had paid dearly for the precautionary extras, including bulletproof windows and double-framed reinforced doors. Still, depending upon the type of bullets flying, "bulletproof" could be a misnomer. He'd had an armored car shot at by tank piercers last month, in the desert between LA and Las Vegas. Their client, a multibillionaire oilman, had remained unharmed, as had the agent assigned, but the car was destroyed.

He drove through the exit, the pings of bullets ricocheting off the car's body filling his ears, and when he heard a definitive crack, he looked at the passenger side to see a long line across the passenger window, with Dominique's head popping up to take a photo with her camera.

"Stay down! What the heck are you thinking?"

"I wanted to get photos of the shooters." Triumph rang in her voice and he wanted to stop the car and make her see how risky this all was. The impulse rattled him, right in the midst of his automatic motions to keep her safe and his decision to trust her to stay under the dash.

"We don't need photos! We need to get out of here." He turned toward Main Street, clipping two parked cars and a bicycle chained to a lamppost as they sped down the narrow road. The car's extra layers of protection made it take turns a bit wider at times. He ignored the wreckage he left behind as well as he ignored the constant crunch of numbers his accountant fired at him for incidental damages. Colton Protection was insured for any vehicles damaged during the course of duty.

"They're blurry anyway," she grumbled but at least she was slouched down, as safe as she could be at this moment.

A black Porsche cleared the exit behind him and was on his tail almost immediately. The armored car's heft made it an easy target in the short run. Stanton knew Grave Gulch as well as the backyard he'd played in as a boy. He'd lose these jerks with a lot of concentration and a little luck.

Instead of turning left toward the station, he went right, then left down a side alley, turning onto the street that paralleled the main drag. Up and down the side streets, farther and farther away from the center of the city, he kept up the avoidance maneuvers until they were safely on the highway that led out of town, toward Lake Michigan.

"You're circling back, right?" Dominique's query broke his state of flow—the place his mind went during an op. Where nothing existed except doing whatever it took to keep a client safe. He finally let out a breath and risked a glance at her. Instead of her earlier pallor and the stressed posture, Dominique was the energized version of herself, her enthusiasm contagious. A bark of laughter escaped his parched throat.

"You get off on this, don't you?" The words escaped his mouth and he knew he wasn't over the adrenaline rush either, not by a long shot. It was always a kick in the pants to outwit the bad guys, no matter how many times he did it. But it wouldn't last for long, and he had to stay miles ahead of the cartel clowns.

"If by 'get off' you mean I had something to focus on other than my mind's replay of that loser's paws crushing my throat, yes. Where are we going, Stanton?"

"I'm thinking."

He gripped and released his hands on the wheel a few times, double-, triple-and quadruple-checked the side and rearview mirrors. He'd lost them. For now. He'd never expected Jimenez's outfit knew what his vehicles looked like, where he stored the extras. They wouldn't outwit him again.

"What can I do? I'll call 911."

"Hang on a sec." He used the hands-free phone to call in to GGPD, directly to his sister.

"Chief Melissa Colton." Melissa's warm voice answered with its customary professional clip.

"Melissa. Stanton. We're on speaker and Dominique de la Vega is with me. I called the station number because I'm reporting an attack." He outlined what had happened in the parking garage, and the ensuing pursuit. "Troy expected us to show up at GGPD to file a report. I assume you've heard that Dominique was assaulted this morning on her way to an interview with the trial witness for Charlie Hamm. Witness's name is Johnny Blanchard. Both Dominique and I agree that this is most likely the work of Pablo Jimenez. He's the only one has everything to lose if her story uncovers evidence of witness tampering. We're not heading into the station this afternoon after all. We'll swing in tomorrow, or the next day, whenever it's safe. I'm not messing around with threats from Jimenez."

"That's wise. Troy's filled me in about the attack. I'm sorry, Dominique. Glad Stanton was there to help out. Where are you and Dominique going? To Colton Protection headquarters?"

"No. I can't risk that they knew who I was, what I do. We're going to the lake house."

"Gotcha. Be safe, bro. And Dominique?"

"Hi, Melissa." Dominique's tone was wary.

"My brother's the best in the business. Best listen to him."

The call ended and he continued westward, as though drawn by a beacon.

"That was your sister's friendly way of telling me to stop bothering her police department. And it's pretty clear she still blames me for our breakup and hurting you."

He chose to ignore the reference to them, focused on the case. "Yeah, she's not happy about the *Gazette*'s endless inquiries. But she's as concerned as anyone about the possibility of corruption in GGPD." As chief of police, Melissa had done a fantastic job. Her efforts were currently buffeted by a constant barrage of crime, and the last thing she needed was the local paper questioning the integrity of her force. Stanton felt for his sister, but also hoped she'd get to the bottom of GGPD's bad apple barrel quickly.

"She must be stressed to the max. But still, then why won't she talk to me about it? She's refused every single request for an interview."

"You'll have to take that up with her."

"Please tell me that by the 'lake house,' you don't mean your parents' home." Dread soaked every one of her words.

He couldn't help it; he laughed. A record for him, to find humor during an op. And he'd done it several times with Dominique. "You used to love our weekends out there."

"Sure I did, when your family accepted me as one of their own, and not the traitor I became the minute we split. Answer the question, Stanton." Her icy tone told him she wasn't reminiscing about the times they'd skinny-dipped in the hot tub while the rest of the family slept.

He hesitated. He didn't have to take her to his parents' place. They could go out to his family's cabin, in the remote woods of Michigan's "mitten," but that was at least a five-hour drive on a good day. It was impractical for him, personally, to take her to his parents' place, but it was the best idea he had in terms of her safety.

Frank and Italia kept a very low profile for security reasons, as his father traveled frequently for his job since they'd become empty nesters, leaving his mother alone in the big, rambling home. There certainly was plenty of room at the house, so combined with the optimal security provisions, it was an ideal safe house.

"Stanton?" Annoyance weighed her words.

"Yes. We're going to my parents'."

She huffed sharply in displeasure and he knew if he took his gaze from the road he'd face her ferocious expression, the one that always made him think of a lioness.

"I'm not going. No way. A hotel would be a better idea. You lost the crooks—what does it matter where we hole up until the threat passes? Please tell me you're joking. Just circle back, and let's go to GGPD. You lost the shooters miles ago. I doubt they were able to follow us out of downtown even if you hadn't, with the traffic and construction."

"I'm not messing around here, Dominique. Someone tried to kill you this morning. Do you have any doubts that they meant to kill you? You don't seem to know when to stop. Last month you reported on Tatiana Davison, how her father's a serial killer. Besides digging into Tatiana's private life, how do you think Len Davison took you exposing his daughter like that? But getting yourself in the crosshairs of a serial killer isn't enough. Now you had to stir up the hornet's nest that is this cartel."

"I was doing my job. I am doing my job." She hadn't

been thrilled to report on Tatiana, but it was part of her assignment. "But yes, you're right. Those men who shot at us want me dead."

"Right. Jimenez will send in more men the closer you get to the truth. I can't risk keeping you at my place or anywhere in the city."

"What's wrong with my apartment? You know how to drive anywhere without a tail."

"Come on, Dominique. Stop being obtuse. I know how intelligent you are, remember? They already know where you live. We're talking about some very powerful people here. Think about it. If you want this story done right, you need to write it. That requires following leads that will be inconsequential if you're dead. You of all people know the resources a successful drug cartel has at its disposal."

He saw her blanch in his peripheral vision and he wished he could soften the blow for her, but if this was what was needed to make sure she didn't do anything to add to her risk, then so be it.

"I do know their power. They killed Charlie while he was in prison, a place they illegally sent him to."

"There are probably many other victims yet to be discovered. It appears they've infiltrated the legal system."

She nodded, her eyes downcast. "Okay. You've made your point." She sighed, and empathy for her situation yanked at the calm detachment that had taken over from the minute they left his apartment. "I can do this."

He gave a quick glance her way and bit back a laugh—Dominique looked like a victim about to walk the plank and not a grown woman en route to a luxury estate on Lake Michigan.

The more he thought about his decision, the better he felt. His family home was the best place for now. Removed from Grave Gulch, on a rural route, yet fully modern so that Dominique could access Wi-Fi and work. His parents were meticulous with their security, he'd made certain of it, and he'd double-check all of the systems once they arrived. Unless they were directly followed, they wouldn't find Dominique out here.

"You'll be able to hike all you want." He didn't want to examine why it was so important to him for her to have something to look forward to.

"It'd have to be with you, though." Her flat tone stung.

"Don't sound so enthusiastic. But yeah, you're not getting rid of me, not even in the woods." No place was safe until she had her story and GGPD had Pablo Jimenez behind bars, along with his troop of thugs.

"I have no problem with you doing your job. My father's paid you to do it. I'm not happy about being forced to spend time with a man who belittles me and thinks I'm 'obtuse.'"

Crap. He'd let the words fly when all he'd wanted to do was communicate that he knew how intelligent she was.

"I didn't mean it personally."

"Save it, Stanton. I've got to get back to figuring out my next steps. The sooner I get corroborating evidence that Charlie's conviction, and death, were criminally motivated, the sooner GGPD can straighten itself out. And if we're lucky, we'll catch the big one."

He didn't have to ask her what she meant by "the big one." His gut took a nosedive at the stark truth of the danger she'd put herself in. How many journalists were willing to go after criminal mastermind Pablo Jimenez? And why did it have to be Dominique?

Most important, why did he still care too damn much?

DOMINIQUE'S HEAD POUNDED and her neck was beyond sore from the roughing up Jimenez's hit man had imparted earlier, but nothing compared to her fury at the way Stanton so easily slipped back into his condescending tone. She knew he didn't mean to sound so dismissive; when it came to security details, he was top in his field, without question. What was easy to see as complete arrogance was in fact his confidence. No one would want anything less from their bodyguard. But as the Michigan countryside whipped by and day turned to twilight, she couldn't stop the sense of complete powerlessness that at once left her despondent and outraged. Not wanting Soledad to worry about her, she texted her, gave her a brief overview of her day. When her sister replied with "hang in there," she wished she was with her now instead of facing her past with Stanton and worrying if she'd live to have a future. Since she didn't do self-pity as a rule, she had to channel her energy into being "ticked off."

There's another way you used to work off your frustration with Stanton.

Heat hit her cheeks as quickly as it pooled in her midsection, then between her legs. A giggle bubbled up and she forced it back, unwilling to share any of her inner thoughts with him. It was ridiculous. She was being immature at best. Stanton was right: she could have died today, before she found justice for Charlie. The story might have been squashed right there. She kept backup, hard-copy files at the *Grave Gulch Gazette*, but it wouldn't be the same if something happened to her. The reporter who dug up all the evidence and connected the pieces was always the best one to file the story. It was hard enough keeping her enthusiasm up for a story when it was her piece, her passion. Another reporter couldn't be expected to carry the baton for her. Not when the *Gazette* was swamped with countless leads relating to Pablo Jimenez's ring here in Grave Gulch. Charlie's death was just one of too many tragic stories surrounding Jimenez's Michigan operation.

The silence between them grated on her.

"This isn't like us." The words shot out of her mouth and she fidgeted with her seat belt. "One thing we've always been able to do is talk. It doesn't feel right, always trying to cut each other off." Her voice still shook, and it sounded like her voice box had been replaced by a toad's, but the quiet had grown too heavy. They still had another twenty minutes to the Colton lakefront estate, and she didn't want to see his parents for the first time in so long while she and Stanton were at each other's throats.

Italia Colton's intensity was going to be tough enough to cope with. Dominique had no doubt that the family matriarch would question her motives about spending time with Stanton again.

"No, it doesn't feel right. I agree." He shifted in his seat and she realized he might be tired. Where was her compassion? *With Charlie Hamm.*

"It's been a long day for you, too, Stanton."

He shot her a quick, wry glance. "Every day is a long one at Colton Protection. You know that. Your hours are as nuts as mine."

"Yeah. Although I've been thinking about forcing myself to take two full days off each week." She'd committed to one, but then Charlie's death had launched her back into workaholic mode.

His grunt should have been a typical male response, but to her, it was so achingly familiar that tears flooded her vision. Her mind may have let go of Stanton and their connection, but her body, her heart, certainly hadn't.

He chuckled. "The day you take a decent amount of time off to take care of yourself will be—"

He cut himself off, focused on the road. Fear sliced through her. "What is it?" Had he spotted the Porsche again in the rearview mirror? Or another follower?

"Relax. We're safe. Give me a minute." His profile was unreadable in the dusk, no matter that they were driving toward the setting sun. Stanton exited the highway, slowing at the bottom of the ramp to turn right, and followed a local road for a mile or so. Into the entrance of a park where they'd once spent a lot of time hiking, camping and exploring.

"It'll be closed, Stanton." Her voice hitched on his name and she silently cursed. No need to sound as if she was excited to be alone with him, even if she were willing to admit it to herself.

"I know a back way in. We won't be long." He took a side road, and within a few hundred yards they were on gravel, rocks dinging off the bottom of the chassis.

"This isn't the best car for these dirt roads. Aren't you worried you'll damage it?" She raised her voice over the noise.

"It's more than a typical vehicle, remember?"

Sure enough, the car acted more like a four-wheel drive than a fine-tuned sports car. "I'm impressed."

The dash lights reflected off his white teeth as he smiled. "Here we go." He pulled into what looked like a camping site, except it had one special feature. It was up on a hill and overlooked Lake Michigan, still several miles distant. A full moon rose against the inky blue sky and Dominique didn't think she'd witnessed anything so beautiful in a long while. She had been working too much. And, truth be told, seemed to have lost her desire to seek out the beauty in everything. Since their breakup, her world had turned from an assortment of flavors to vanilla.

Stanton cut the engine and rested his hand on the steering wheel's twelve o'clock position as he stared straight ahead. His body language was clear. This was to be a conversation, pure and simple. She bit her lower lip, chastised herself for wishing they could both let down their guard, be who they used to be.

No. That woman was gone. In her place was a hardened professional who knew how to get a story down. The Charlie Hamm story could very well give the *Grave Gulch Gazette*, and her, national attention. Nowhere in the mix was getting involved with an ex.

The ex who irrevocably broke your heart.

She waited in the silence, unwilling to guess at his motive for stopping at the romantic spot.

"We need to talk, Dominique, and I didn't want to do it with the distraction of driving. The last thing we deserve, in the middle of all of this, is for my parents to add stress to the situation. I'm still taking you to their home, because I do believe it's the safest place for now, but we should have some ground rules established. The first is always remembering that your life is in danger."

So was her heart.

Chapter Six

"What are your other rules?" Dominique didn't try to hide her sharp tone.

"My parents, especially my mother, are eternal optimists. The minute they see you, they're going to jump to the wrong conclusion." He sighed, looked over his right shoulder at her. "Mom may be a bit, um, overprotective of me. As you know."

"I do." She didn't want to dredge up those first few family dinners that Stanton had brought her to. When Italia asked question after question about her background, her desire for a family, how many children she planned to have. Dominique had never felt good enough for Stanton in those early days. But after several months she'd been accepted as part of the family. So much so that she'd grieved the loss of the Coltons nearly as much as losing Stanton.

It was your choice.

It had ultimately been her choice to leave, to walk away, in that heated moment two years ago. Stanton had blindsided her with his proposal. And he'd been so stubborn, insisting they be married or nothing. Over-whelmed and gobsmacked by his uncharacteristic un-yielding streak, she'd had to walk, hadn't she? Pinpricks of doubt needled her heart as possibilities ran through her mind. If she'd taken just one of Stanton's texts or calls after their hasty breakup, might things have turned out differently? Would he have seen her side, that though she loved him and was willing to commit to him, she hadn't been ready for the white picket fence yet?

"I know my parents are a bit overwhelming, that much hasn't changed."

"So what's your plan, Stanton? I don't want to dis-cuss my story with your parents. I can't, for their safety as well as keeping it under the radar until I have all the facts and witnesses interviewed."

"If they realize I'm working for your dad, and why, they will. Freak. Out." His emphasis caught her atten-tion.

"Why will they freak?"

"They'll try to fix it and want to send both of us over-seas or something similar. We don't have time for the distraction, and I don't want to worry them."

"But look at it from their point of view. Why else would you bring me home, though? Except for a job. They know we're through. I think honesty is the best policy, always." She really didn't see what choice they had but to somewhat level with his parents. Her father knew she was working on a dangerous story. There wasn't a reason to completely hide the truth from the Coltons, but maybe they could soften reality for them a bit. "Why don't we explain that we're working together on a case? Tell them we need to be away from any distractions, and from anyone who might not like what we're researching? You could be providing the security aspect of a story for the *Gazette*, and you picked their place for me to interview you for a couple of hours."

"Hours? First off, we're going to be out here longer than dinner or an overnight."

"What? I thought we were laying low until tonight, when we could go back into the city under the cover of darkness. GGPD is open twenty-four seven." She wanted to continue to protest, but he held up his hand.

"Let me finish. You have got to absolutely be out of sight for the next several days, Dominique. That means no runs into your office, no visiting witnesses for interviews, no moving until I say it's okay. The most we'll do is go into the station tomorrow, but that's it. You can do whatever you need to from the lake house. I'll get your computer equipment brought in, along with clothing and other essentials. But I'm being paid to keep you alive. Are we clear on this part?"

"Do I have a choice? If not you, my father will send out an entire squad of protectors next."

"I'd do the same if I had a daughter. Are we in agreement on my role in your life right now?"

"Yes."

"Back to my parents… This idea I have is going to sound outlandish. I think we should tell them we are exploring a reconciliation, but don't want anyone to see us together. We can say we're only telling them because we trust them—my mother will eat this up—and they will be expected to keep our secret. If we don't reconcile, which we both know we won't, no harm no foul. We'll make it clear that it's not working out, when it's safe for you to move about on your own again."

"We'll be able to have them keep their dignity while ensuring their safety." She interrupted him, warming to the insane idea. And she couldn't ignore the respect she had for him for the sweet gesture. Stanton cared about his parents, his family. He knew what mattered. How many successful entrepreneurs kept their priorities as rock-solid as he had? If she were honest, though, all of Stanton's siblings had their priorities straight. She'd kept tabs on Stanton and his family since the breakup more than she cared to admit. Oldest brother Clarke had fallen in love with Everleigh, even while she was accused—falsely—of being a murderer. Travis had started a family with Tatiana Davison, daughter of none other than serial killer Len Davison. Travis hadn't allowed the sins of Tatiana's father to stop him from seeing Tatiana as her own person, and the woman he wanted to spend the rest of his life with. Melissa and Antonio Ruiz were engaged, planning to start a family soon. A chief of police, under all of the current crime chaos in Grave Gulch, still putting family first.

No wonder Stanton had been eager to settle down into marriage and family. It was what the Coltons did when they found the one.

It'd be best if she just forgot the latter. She wasn't Stanton's "one" and hadn't been since he'd broken her heart. And now she realized, she'd broken his in return. It was paramount that she kept her own priorities straight for this story. Which meant leveling with his parents as much as possible.

Still, she had misgivings. "There's one thing I'm not happy about." To put it mildly.

"Shoot."

"Wouldn't they expect us to be affectionate in front of them? I'm not up for that, Stanton. I don't have the energy to pretend that much." Her hands shook and she shoved them under her thighs. It wasn't from the cold, and it wasn't from shock any longer. It was 100 percent awareness of his nearness, and how even though the plan was just that, a plan, it reminded her too acutely of the passion they'd once shared. And she was lying, about the pretend part.

"You don't have to pretend. We will make it clear we're simply looking for a place to talk things out, like two adults, without any other distractions. We'll be in separate rooms, so that will be their first clue that we're serious about doing things right."

"What do you mean by that? They never disapproved of us sharing a room before. Did they? Not that I want to share a room now. That's not what I meant." Heat warmed her cheeks for the umpteenth time since he'd walked—no, run—back into her life this morning.

"No, they're open-minded about such things, you know that. Look, I know this is highly unusual, and I'm asking for more than I deserve here. I get it, trust me. This is for my parents, Dominique. By doing things the 'right' way, I meant differently from how we handled our breakup."

"Oh, you mean the part where you gave me an ultimatum and I had no choice but to leave?" Tears scalded her eyes but she kept her gaze even with his. Let him see the pain. It was about time.

"No, I mean the part where you didn't give me a second chance after you walked out. You didn't answer any of my calls or texts. You blocked me."

"I had a story—"

"Oh, here we go again. It was about the story. I can't help but think your excuse was a convenient way to get away from me. I was too fast, too eager to make us into something we weren't." His voice wasn't bitter, didn't hold the condescending tone. His eyes sparked with something dangerous, and she saw the moonlight reflect in their depths. "Do you ever wonder how things would be now if I hadn't proposed, Dominique? At least not then. If I'd waited. Or agreed to your suggestion on the spot and we'd stayed together, saw how it worked out over time? I never told you this, but what really made me end it was when you first said you weren't ready to commit to marriage, I freaked out. I thought that if I wasn't your husband, I wouldn't be able to ask you to curtail your more dangerous work as needed. The thought of losing you to a story... I could never face that. Do you ever reconsider leaving so abruptly?" His anguish was laid bare. So much in his soft tone, the sensuous way the words rolled off his tongue.

Her body lit with arousal at the soft query, the genuine wonder reflected in his words. "No. I mean, yes, I can imagine but I can't let myself go there." He turned toward her and reached up to stroke her cheek with a finger. Tingles sparked across her skin and down her throat. They were a whisper apart.

"Why not?" He traced her lips with his finger, then leaned in and grazed her mouth with his. She closed her eyes, unable to contain the shots of lust that pooled in all the right places. "Tell me, Dom. Why can't you go there?"

"I can't risk what it could cost me." As she spoke, her body swayed closer, arced toward him. It might be the events of the day, the prospect of pretending to be trying to get back together, or perhaps it was no more than being near Stanton again. No matter the reason, Dominique was done fighting what had ignited in that decrepit building as she stared into Stanton's eyes.

When she saw his lids lower, she reached for him, needing to get to his lips before he did hers again. He had to know she wanted this, no matter what she said. Her arms wrapped around his neck, her fingers digging into his nape. His curls, curls that she knew so well, wound around her fingers as she pulled him in. He cupped her face with exquisite gentleness as he moved in. Their lips met with zero curiosity, as they were already intimately acquainted. The brief kiss in his apartment had confirmed that.

It was the force of her emotions that took her by surprise. All in a simple touch.

Nothing is simple with Stanton.

All of today's pain, yesterday's regrets and tomorrow's worries blew away. Nothing was stronger than this—the bond she shared with Stanton. His hands left her face and his arms went around her waist, his chest surged across the bucket seats and pressed against hers, the friction against her breasts the sexiest sensation she recalled in her thirty years, ever. Stanton's tongue didn't barge into her mouth, or make tentative strokes on her lips, but seemed to join with hers as if they'd never parted, as if being joined together in any way possible was the sole purpose of their existence.

The kiss went on and on, and their hands roamed and roamed. Each caress raised her arousal, and when he gently squeezed her breast she moaned against his lips. How had she survived the last two years without this?

"Dom." His breath, hot against her throat, healing what had been so broken just minutes before, further stoked her need.

"I know." She forced her hands off his neck, allowed them to grasp his shoulders, wander down across his chest. His arms held her, cradled her, and she knew she was safe, secure. Stanton had always been her safe harbor. "I want it, too, Stanton."

His body stilled and she fought to not cry in protest as he lifted his head, his gaze locked on hers.

What had she done?

DOMINIQUE HAD SAID she wanted it. Not him, not Stanton, not them as a couple, but *it*.

Dang it all to Hades and back. He couldn't break

their eye contact, needing the connection, the reassurance that his attraction, his need, wasn't one-way. Desire made her pupils wide and he felt the strength of her arousal under his fingers as he caressed her collarbone, the way her blood pounded under his fingertips at her pulse points.

"This is what we can't risk, Dominique." He moved away, careful to go slow enough to not hurt her or touch her bruises. He'd been so caught up in the kiss, in her, that he'd forgotten her injuries. He sucked in air, lots of air. "We can't fall back into our physical attraction in front of my parents. It'll get their hopes up too high."

"Is that why you kissed me, to test it out? To see if I still gave you the same thrill?"

Her words drove through him as hard as his lust had, and he rubbed his forehead. "No. I kissed you because, well, it was important we cleared the air." Had he just said that? Did he sound like the biggest jerk to her, too?

"That's fair enough." Her lack of reaction stilled something deep inside him. She straightened her clothing, readjusted her position in the passenger seat. Darkness had fallen and he couldn't see anything through the fogged windows. He started the engine.

At her quick glance he shrugged. "It's getting chilly." It was. Spring was evident in the buds on the trees during the day, but winter held on tight to the night.

"Whatever you need me to do, to keep all of us safe, I'll do it. Maybe we need to look at this, this kiss, like a bad experiment. We tried it—it's only a path to certain disaster between us, and we won't go there again.

I'll go along with your story for your parents. I always liked them, you know." Her countenance was so matter-of-fact it grated on him as he struggled to contain his emotions.

"As they did you." He replied before his grudging admission would stir up more memories. "I'm glad we're in agreement, then."

"Wait, there's one more thing." She put her hand on his forearm, stopped him from shifting into gear. "If we're really clearing the air, let me say this. I didn't thank you for today. Thank you, Stanton. You saved my life. I admit I thought it was only an attempt to scare me, to warn me. But after getting shot at in the parking garage, I realize you're right. Pablo Jimenez has to be behind it all, and he wants me dead. Thank you for seeing what I couldn't. And for saving me a second time."

Her eyes, pools of sincerity, tugged at that same spot in his chest that he was doing his best to keep under wraps, far from the reach of any silly dreams about the two of them. He glanced away before he did something stupid like kiss her again. "It's my job, Dominique. One your father is paying me handsomely for."

If only he could remember this. Before he let his guard down and Dominique got hurt, or worse.

THE LAKE HOUSE came into view only on the last turn of the driveway, emerging from the tall maples and pines as if from a dream. Her stomach flipped. She'd missed this so much, what had once become her retreat from the often harsh pace of her career. Had she been naive to think it could last forever? Or had she confused her feelings for Stanton with convenience?

Her severe self-examination would have to wait. As she got out of the car and joined Stanton for the short walk to the front door, she breathed in the lake air, let it soothe her agitation. The scent of wet grass and early spring filled her with a sense of peace, if only for a millisecond.

His tall form was a comfort no matter that they'd agreed to keep the careful physical boundaries between them. It was always like this around him. She felt at once safe and threatened. Secure in his larger-than-life warmth, afraid of what her feelings for him could do to her carefully constructed peace of mind. She focused on her surroundings, the lake air laden with the scent of whatever was cooking for dinner inside the house. Gravel and seashells—the tiny kind unique to the Great Lakes—crunched under her feet. It was as satisfying as hearing pine cones crush under her hiking boots.

"Do they know we're coming?" She hadn't heard him call his parents all day. He could have sent a text, though.

"No. You know my family. There's bound to be at least one of us kids showing up at any time. They'll be thrilled to see us." He hadn't spoken for the rest of the drive, after the park. After that kiss—

"Are you ready for this, Dominique?" He stopped under the porch light and the soft glow made his dark curls almost blue in the night, which made her think of his eyes, how they could devour her as good as his hands, his lips.

Stop.

"Yes, of course." She had a story to finish and this was another step toward it. Staying alive, getting the statements she needed from all sides, compiling all the information. Whatever it took.

Are you willing to risk your heart?

"Okay, then. Let's do it." He rang the doorbell, punched in a code as he did. He motioned for her to step in first and she walked into the foyer. The video doorbell had at least revealed it was Stanton, and probably her, as well.

"We're back in here!" Italia's musical voice reached them from the spot Dominique always thought of her in, when she allowed herself to dwell on her memories of Stanton's family. They walked forward, across the polished floors, into the large, colorful kitchen. Italia rose from the island, her short brown bob the perfect foil for her bright green eyes. Frank's motions mirrored his wife of forty years as he stood to greet his son. Half-empty wineglasses, water goblets and plates of broiled salmon and rice signaled they'd interrupted the couple's dinner.

"Mom, Dad." Stanton kissed his mother on both cheeks, in true Italian fashion. Italia had immigrated to the States after falling in love with a certain Michiganian, Frank, forty-one years ago. Dominique had the numbers and dates memorized. She couldn't help it; her mind had a yen for numbers. And they'd celebrated an anniversary with his parents years before.

As Italia kissed Stanton back, her gaze strayed to his guest, and her eyes widened when they met Dominique's. "Dominique, *bella*, how wonderful!" Italia didn't miss a beat as she walked over to Dominique and gave her an equally warm welcome. Frank Colton followed with his usual bear hug, and Dominique tried to ignore the guilt that dug its claws into her conscience. She'd never asked Stanton how his parents had taken the breakup, never reached out to them to say goodbye. Belatedly she realized that at least a handwritten note would have been a nice gesture. Grave Gulch wasn't that big a place, and anything to ease otherwise awkward run-ins couldn't hurt. Fortunately she'd only seen them from afar at large charity or sporting events.

"Italia, Frank, it's wonderful to see you both again." The warmth in her voice wasn't forced. In fact, it came from a deep well of longing she'd been unaware of until she walked back into this kitchen, smelled the fresh rosemary that Italia grew, along with other pots of herbs on the massive marble countertop. Frank, a shipping executive, had personally seen to the shipment of Carrara marble from Italy for his wife.

"What brings you here? Both of you? Have you eaten?" Italia fired the questions as she pulled Ravello ceramic plates from the deep drawers under the counter, placed them on the island next to hers and Frank's. "I've got more salmon, and oh, Stanton, your favorite dessert is in the cupboard."

"That sounds great, Mom."

"Can I take your coat?" Frank stood in front of her and she shrugged out of her coat as smoothly as she could without making herself wince. Her discomfort was as much from her bruises as the reality that no matter how nice and cozy this seemed, she was now a guest in the Colton family home. When she and Stanton had been together, she'd hung her coat in the front closet, next to Frank's and Italia's.

"Thank you."

"Here, come sit." Italia patted the seat next to her and gave Dominique her classic "you wouldn't dare mess with an Italian mother" look. Dominique complied, and Stanton slid into the seat on her other side. Was that a smile he was keeping to a minimum? "So tell me, Dominique. What have you been up to?"

Italia may as well have asked how many lovers she'd taken since walking away from her beloved son. Dominique sat up straight and forged ahead. "Nothing any different. I'm wrapped up in several stories but one has taken all of my time as of late."

"Dominique's going to get a Pulitzer for the story she's working on now, if it all goes well." Stanton's praise made her start, and she twisted around to him.

"That's not true, and, well…" She gave him a look that his parents couldn't see. *What are you doing?* He grinned.

"You've always been modest." Italia didn't miss a beat. "Stanton, tell us why you haven't been out here for over three weeks."

It was Dominique's turn to stifle a laugh.

"What your mother means is that we've missed you, and we're certain that Colton Protection has been busy with all of the recent local activity. I imagine the drug issue will keep you busy for a long while, unfortunately." Frank's smooth baritone was familiar—Stanton had his father's voice.

"Not to mention the movie premiere." Italia laughed. "I'm happy to say that I've scored an invite to the Italian movie they're streaming at the theater next weekend." Italia loved any reason to dress up, and she wore evening wear well. Which reminded her of how well Stanton wore a tux. She stifled a groan. *Focus on dinner.*

"That's great, Mom." Stanton helped himself to creamed spinach, homemade dinner rolls and salmon. Dominique did the same, suddenly hungry, no matter that she'd already had salmon at lunch today. The Coltons enjoyed their fish and seafood. It felt good to not be so anxious that food turned her stomach.

"I bet you'll have a blast at the party, Italia."

"I'm sure I will. I was invited to provide artwork for the social beforehand, and it'll be on display at the charity silent auction, too, which is always nice for my business. It might not be the big-time, but it's close enough for me." Italia sipped her wine. "Did you know I saw Sophia Loren once, when I was a girl? My mother took me to Napoli, to the Teatro San Carlo. It was the opening of *Carmen*. Sophia and Carlo Ponti were in the box closest to the stage. They waved right at us." Italia's verve was invigorating, and with longing Dominique realized how much she'd missed her, and Stanton's family. Italia was one of a kind, an artist. Frank's success in steel had paralleled hers. Italia had a larger-than-life personality and charmed everyone she met.

"I'm sure they waved right at you, Ma." Stanton spoke around a large mouthful of food.

"Manners, Stanton." Italia reached around the back of Dominique and playfully swatted at her son's nape. Frank's chuckle resonated through the large room.

Italia clicked her tongue. "Don't be such a slob around your *fidanzata*, son." Her casual use of the Italian word for *girlfriend* or *fiancée* sliced through the easygoing mood.

Dominique's hand froze midway between her plate and mouth, the creamed spinach suspended in unison with her shock. *Here we go.*

"Um…" Stanton chewed, wiped his mouth with the crisp white napkin that Italia seemed to have an endless supply of and sucked down half of his water goblet. "We're, ah… Dominique and I are not back together. We, we've decided to see if we can work on being good friends again." Stanton's voice shook the tiniest bit, but Dominique didn't miss it. Judging by Italia's sharp intake of breath, neither did she. Frank remained silent, always the steady rudder for Italia's enthusiasm and at times, over-the-top emotions.

"I'm so sorry we barged in on your dinner. It's delicious." A change of subject was in order.

"We're just happy that you joined us, Dominique." Frank rose from his end of the island and took his plate to the sink. "You two were awfully close for a while there. I understand that things don't always work out as we hope, and I'm glad you've got a chance to salvage a friendship from your time together."

Dominique blinked. Frank wasn't one for false praise, or overt sentiment. He took things in stride, like when Travis decided to start his own business with Colton Plastics, breaking from the other siblings in their law enforcement or security fields. Italia overflowed with enough emotion for the entire town of Grave Gulch, not to mention her family.

"Thanks, Dad." Stanton had recovered his composure and she looked at him. He met her gaze with a warm smile, made to look as though they were really seeking to become good friends again. His eyes told her the truth. They'd managed to get through dinner, and his parents appeared to have accepted their explanation at face value. But not for one minute should she forget why she was here. She was hiding from potential assassins, and in the midst of a story that did, in fact, have Pulitzer Prize potential.

Funny how the possibility of global attention mattered little since this morning's events. It had to be the shock of the assault, and the shooting in the garage. It couldn't be because she was painfully aware of all she'd lost and left behind. How ironic to figure out what really mattered to her when Pablo Jimenez would do all he could to kill her.

Chapter Seven

The next morning, Dominique lay wide-awake in the guest bedroom from dawn onward. The lake's view was just out the window, but she wasn't interested in looking at the sunrise, or reminiscing over how she and Stanton had made good use of his parents' dock, swimming naked on more than one occasion.

She'd brought Jimenez's wrath to the Colton home, and she had to get out of here. It was one thing to put herself on the line for a story, and Stanton had willingly agreed to protect her. But Frank and Italia didn't deserve this. They had to leave before the cartel found her again.

She left the bedroom to find Stanton and tell him they had to leave ASAP. The clothes his mother had loaned her, a loose sweatshirt and yoga pants that belonged to his younger sister, fit fine and were, in fact, far more comfortable than her usual work clothes. But she had only her high-heeled boots or her sneakers, no slippers, so she padded to the kitchen in stockinged feet. Her feet were still sore from running in her trouser socks on the street yesterday.

Stanton sat at the island, his laptop open, steaming mug of coffee in hand. His hair was sleep-rumpled and he hadn't shaved yet. An old college sweatshirt was stretched across his torso, the logo long faded. He didn't look up at first as her steps were silent on the polished wood floor. She paused. It couldn't hurt to soak in this glimpse of what she'd turned down, could it? Not that she had regrets. They'd made the right decision. Hadn't they?

It was being back here, all the time together yesterday, not to mention the life-and-death situation of her almost strangulation, that was making nostalgia tug on her heartstrings.

"Good morning." She walked in as he looked up, helped herself to coffee from the half-full carafe.

"Morning. How did you sleep?"

"Okay. How long have you been up?"

He grunted. "Since four. I had paperwork to catch up on so it was a good time to do it."

"Are your parents out walking?"

"No. In fact, they're gone."

"What do you mean, 'gone'?"

"They left a note. Apparently they left late last night, after we'd crashed. They're flying out to San Francisco together for one of Dad's business meetings. Said they didn't want us to have to worry about anyone intruding on our 'reconciliation.'" He made air quotes with lanky fingers. "But I think the real deal is that Dad had the business commitment and Mom decided to join him at the last minute. She can't help her matchmaking tendencies."

"Oh."

"You look like the wind's gone out of your sails."

"I was just about to tell you that we needed to leave. I can't live with the fact I've put a target on this house."

"You haven't done anything. Jimenez is the bad guy. If he finds you here, you're not alone. I'm here and I'll protect you. No one's getting to you. Trust me."

"I do trust you. You're the top in your business."

"But?" He was picking up on her worry.

"You said yourself that the cartel has limitless resources. How are you going to protect us against an arsenal that's likely to arrive with his hired criminals?"

"We have backup, Dominique. It's called the Grave Gulch Police Department. Add in the FBI as the cartel operates across state lines, and the Drug Enforcement Administration. Not to mention the state troopers."

She watched his expression become more animated as he spoke. Stanton's passion stemmed from his childhood obsession with law enforcement. He'd often spoken at length about it to her. Two of his three siblings had gone into law enforcement, too, no doubt inspired by the tragic unsolved murder of their Aunt Amanda. It provided the impetus for what Dominique suspected was a Colton genetic trait: to serve and protect. Stanton had picked personal security and protection instead of police work after college, when he'd discovered his real talent was working one-on-one with clients and security systems.

"What?" He paused, tilted his head.

"You are so into your job. It's a good thing, don't worry. I forgot how much you deal with on a daily basis."

"No reason for you to remember any of that." He sipped his coffee and stood up. "Are you hungry?"

She decided to stop fighting him, fighting her every instinct to disagree with him on each issue that came up. "I am. But you made lunch yesterday. My turn to cook."

He shook his head. "Naw. Why don't you tell me about Charlie Hamm, and your story, who you need to still interview? The sooner we get your piece filed, the better."

OKAY. YOU'RE ABSOLUTELY RIGHT." Dominique took one of the stools and watched him as he made them bacon cheese omelets. Bacon had always been irresistible to her. But Stanton was cooking it because it was in the Colton refrigerator, not for a personal reason like the fact that it was her kryptonite.

He did a mock grab at his heart. "Whoa—you're admitting I'm right?" His grin was playful and she smiled back.

"Where to start? First, I already told you, Charlie was my student in the county jail. His poetry was exceptional. I have copies of his poems you can read if you want. They're incredible. Working with him led me to listen to him and I wrote down all of it. How he believed fake evidence had been planted in the form of one of his fingerprints on a suitcase that held drugs. How all of the witnesses that could have testified that he wasn't a pusher, that he was helping local addicts and dealers get off the stuff, somehow disappeared when it came time for the trial. And of course, Johnny Blanchard, whose testimony put Charlie behind bars. Charlie believed that Blanchard was paid off and/or threatened by the cartel. As for the fingerprint on the case with over one hundred thousand dollars in opioids, I can't help but think Randall Bowe had everything to do with that. We don't even know that it was Charlie's fingerprint, as all we had, all the court accepted as evidence, was a statement from Randall that the print was Charlie's. It's as if the entire system let him down. But I think it was more a chain of bad guys who turned at Jimenez's pressure."

He whipped the eggs while the bacon sizzled in his mother's extra-large cast-iron frying pan. "The fingerprint report should be easy enough to dispute. If Randall doesn't have a digital scan of the actual print saved, it boils down to his word. And right now, his word isn't holding a lot of water."

"But he's still on the police force!" Anger made her cheeks red and her eyes flash.

"Actually, Melissa told me he's been furloughed until the investigation is complete. There's a possibility of another corrupt cop, too. But you didn't hear that from me."

"I'm sorry, Stanton. That's awful for Melissa, and the entire department. But it's about time some progress was made on the internal investigation. I hope for GGPD's sake it's resolved quickly." It would be a win to have the evidence against Charlie stricken, too. One step closer to justice for him.

"I don't disagree. By the way, how are your feet doing? I noticed yesterday that your toes were swollen."

She grinned. "I did make a mess of them when we were in the East Side. They're fine, thank you. Wearing socks and sneakers for a while will help."

"You like to wear dress shoes for work, though."

"Since we won't be going into town much, I'll be happy to stay in socks, maybe hiking boots when I can get into the woods. Speaking of which, can we go to my apartment to get some of my clothing, my cosmetics?"

"I'm working on it. Our first priority is to get you into the station."

For the rest of their breakfast she made notes on her phone of all she hoped to accomplish today with the story. And ignored as much as possible how very comfortable it was to be with Stanton in the morning.

It was as dangerous to her well-being as being hunted by a criminal.

THEY WERE BOTH introspective on the drive back into Grave Gulch. Stanton tried to think of something he could talk to her about, but his head was wrapped around keeping her under the cartel's radar. He'd gotten intel via Troy that GGPD had determined that the local heroin kingpin was indeed Pablo Jimenez. He passed the information to Dominique.

"Thanks for letting me know." Appreciation, rather

than the sarcasm he'd expected—and she'd be entirely in her rights to express—laced her words.

"You already had it figured out."

"I was almost certain, but having law enforcement validation is always welcome. Despite what you might think, I always value official information."

"I don't think that at all. I know you, or knew you, pretty well. And you me. I know that you respect law enforcement. That's why it's been so hard to hear you throw accusations at GGPD, warranted or not. Plus, my family has so many connections to GGPD."

"I get it, Stanton, I do. You help the local police by protecting civilians, taking the onus off them. I shouldn't have been so harsh with Troy yesterday. Or you. We all want the same thing—justice."

"I appreciate that, and Troy didn't take anything you said personally. You were there—it was smoothed out before he left. And another thing. Please understand that I respect your work, Dominique. I always have." Even when he resented the time it cost them, how many nights had been lost to her being buried in research or hunting down leads. He'd had the same issue with committing time to their relationship, as protecting people was almost always a twenty-four-seven gig. He sighed. It had been easy to blame Dominique's stubbornness for their breakup, but he had to cast equal blame on his own workaholic tendencies, too.

"I know that I have your respect, deep down. It's easy to ignore it, though, when I'm looking for ammunition when we disagree on an issue." Her brows were raised and the frank assessment was another thing he missed so much. Only she could be brutally honest with him.

He laughed, and after a heartbeat, Dominique joined in.

"You've always been honest with me. So let me be frank about my concerns over the cartel that's taken over Grave Gulch." He hated to douse the warmth of their shared humor so quickly, but they were nearing town. "I've come face-to-face with Jimenez's guys while protecting a client. It kills me to say this, but they're close to invincible. They have unlimited resources—by that I mean money they spend on everything from private investigators to weapons to assassins. They don't limit their assignments to cartel members, or drug dealers, only."

He'd guarded a celebrity earlier this year who'd drawn the ire of the cartel. Stanton had had to use everything at his disposal, all of the resources of Colton Protection and his law enforcement contacts, to keep the star safe until she was able to finish her testimony to the court. Three members of the cartel had been convicted, but Jimenez remained at large, unscathed. He was an expert at keeping his hands clean.

"Right, I've figured out pretty much the same about their business dealings. They hire out the jobs that they can without tipping off law enforcement. I've had to read up on cartel activity ever since I became a reporter. It's constantly changing, and fentanyl has really turned what we thought we knew about the drug trade on its head." Exasperation edged her sigh. "I shouldn't have posted that challenge on social media. I knew better. It's brought the danger too close to those I care most about."

"You wanted a timely resolution to something that's plagued this town for too long." He surprised himself with his response, surprised how easy it was to see Dominique's point of view. It'd always been like this with her, with *them*. They fit each other like a favorite winter sweater. "I'm glad I can be here for you now, even if you wouldn't have chosen me as your body-guard."

"I'm glad you're here, too." She didn't look at him but he risked a glance to see her profile was set in reso-lute determination. Poised to get to the truth, no matter the personal cost.

"Is there anything more you want me to get from your place?" She'd finally agreed to let him be the one to go to her apartment and had already texted him a list of essentials. He was inexplicably relieved that he'd been able to convince her that she needed to stay away from her usual haunts. There was no fighting the ties that still bound him to her. She wasn't just another cli-ent. He was thankful for her business at GGPD—he knew she'd be safe there while he ran over to her place.

"I can't think of anything else. I appreciate you doing this, Stanton. If you feel weird about it at all, I can ask Soledad to meet you there, and she can pack up my stuff." Her tone was so professional, her ability to de-tach from their previous relationship so surgical, he wanted to stop the car and remind her of the depth of what they shared, by kissing her.

That would be the stupidest thing he'd done since giving in last night. *Giving in? Or instigating?*

"There's nothing weird about facilitating a client's safety." Two could play at emotional detachment. No matter that for him, it was an impossible feat.

"I suppose not. You do whatever you have to for your clients, always have. No matter how it ended between us, I've always respected your sense of duty. And I know I'm giving you a hard time now because I want the freedom to research this piece without the shackles of caution. But that's not an option with this cartel after me, is it?"

"No." They entered the downtown area and he stopped at a light. "Speaking of which, now that we're definite about Pablo Jimenez, do you know more about him you haven't told me?"

Her profile was classic, with high cheekbones and long lashes, her curtain of silky hair caught up in a low ponytail. He lov—*appreciated*—her beauty no matter what she wore, whether or not she had makeup on. This morning she'd gone barefaced. It was hard to keep from reaching out, touching her cheek, her throat. His fingers knew every inch of her skin by heart. She'd dressed in the same clothes as yesterday but somehow still appeared fresh.

She shook her head. "I'd like more information on Jimenez for my story, but my priority has been getting to the witnesses who can verify Charlie's wrongful imprisonment, along with others whose lives have been ruined by similar tactics. It's finally official, then. Jimenez is the one who sent the strangler to find me."

"Jimenez must be reading your social media, Dominique. I noticed you didn't tag your location but we're dealing with smart crooks. I hate to admit it, since it's my job to keep you safe, but given enough time, they'll find you wherever you are. You can't provoke him anymore, not while I'm in charge of your safety. It's as reckless as showing up to a gunfight without a weapon."

"Good thing I agree with you on this point. Otherwise we'd get into another argument, Stanton. Remember our old motto that we each do our respective jobs and stay out of the other's?"

"The problem with that is that you're my job right now."

Her eyes narrowed but he couldn't engage in a staredown as the light changed. He thought he caught a low growl and hid his smile. No matter what, he got Dominique. They were exceptional at pushing each other's buttons.

He pulled into the station and parked in the only empty spot on the modest lot.

"They're always busy," she murmured to herself.

"Grave Gulch is a decent-sized place."

"With big problems." She reached for the door handle and he leaned over and placed his hand on her arm.

"Wait. Always wait for me to open the door."

She turned to him. "I'm sorry. I forgot." Her breath hitched, lips parted, her tongue flashing behind her white teeth. He breathed in her scent, free from her designer perfume; he had the gift of smelling her unique scent of sultry sweetness that he associated with waking up in bed together. Her eyes shone with a question he wasn't willing to answer, and she sure as heck wasn't verbalizing. They were too close. The space between them was several inches but it was as if she were pressed up against him again, and he was about to kiss her full lips.

"I'll be right there." He turned and let himself out of the car before he did something catastrophic. The worst part was that for those intense seconds he'd been thinking nothing about her security and only about what they'd lost. Thrown away.

But regrets weren't part of this security detail. Only keeping her alive was.

DOMINIQUE COULDN'T RECALL a time she'd seen GGPD so busy. It wasn't as if it was ever quiet here. It took longer than usual to find an officer who could take her report. After she'd gotten past reception, Stanton had left for her apartment. It should feel freeing to be away from his constant scrutiny. Next to him she always had the sense that while he was alert to any threats, he didn't miss the smallest reaction on her part. Yet instead of relief, all that was left in his absence was a forlorn emptiness. How could this be? She'd done just fine without him for two years, and after only twenty-four hours, she was dependent on him?

It's because your life has been upended. First getting jumped, then shot at. It'll pass.

She was asked to wait in the break area, where she helped herself to a cup of tea and scanned her emails and texts. A quick search in databases subscribed to by the *Gazette* confirmed what Stanton already told her about Pablo Jimenez and the cartel. They'd been poisoning Grave Gulch for months, leading up to the current onslaught of opioid-related crimes and circumstances in her beloved town. Stanton's DEA source also verified that her social media posts about GGPD corruption, her declaration to seek justice for Charlie's death, had triggered a reaction. Pablo Jimenez prided himself on having ironclad control over illicit drug flow into Michigan and remaining anonymous locally—until now. Dominique's overt inquests into the cartel and its connections had hit a sore spot. Jimenez must have slipped up with his communications or whereabouts. The report she read indicated that his sloppiness had allowed DEA agents to ascertain his identity.

But Jimenez was still at large. Drugs remained on the street, and citizens of Grave Gulch were dying from fentanyl overdoses. There weren't enough police or EMTs to get to every OD in time, with Narcan.

As further fuel in an already combustible scenario, separate social media accounts were calling for an inquest into GGPD activity pertaining to forensic evidence. No wonder Stanton was protective of his sister.

"Dominique. Long time no see." As if conjured by her thoughts, GGPD Chief Melissa Colton spoke from a few feet away. Dominique put her phone in her coat pocket and stood. She quelled her nerves with a deep breath. Melissa wasn't about to engage in girl talk with her.

"Chief Colton. I'm here to see an officer, file a report."

Melissa nodded. "I know why you're here. You can file it in a bit. Come with me first." She turned and led the way to her office, a modest space with enough room for her desk and two chairs. "Have a seat."

Sharp blue eyes the same color as Stanton's focused on her. "You always go for the tough stories, don't you?" Melissa's slight grin eased the accusation, but not by much.

"It's my job. People deserve to know the truth. You still haven't released any information about the other cases Randall Bowe tampered with. Drew Orr almost got away with murder before you shot him dead in self-defense. Fritz Emerson's death was first blamed on Everleigh, who could have spent years in jail if no one pursued it. Don't you think the very citizens you protect deserve to know how they were ripped off? How innocent people went to jail and criminals got off? Some may still remain behind bars for all we know."

Melissa leaned forward in her chair, her hands folded on the desk. "You know me well enough, Dominique. Better than any reporter at the *Gazette*, in fact. We're conducting our own internal investigation and you have to trust me that any officer or employee of my department will face the appropriate consequences if we uncover wrongdoing."

"Stop with the formal talk you give all the media outlets. We're talking about lives, Melissa."

"My department works at *saving* lives each and every day." Melissa wasn't budging and Dominique didn't expect or want her to. What she wanted was answers.

"You weren't there for Charlie Hamm."

"Since when is grilling my sister part of your story?" Stanton entered the room and sat in the chair next to her.

"She's just doing her job. And who invited you in here, brother?" Melissa's eyes didn't hold scorn or contempt for Dominique or her profession, as she'd faced with the rare cop over the years. Instead, Grave Gulch's chief of police looked flat-out exhausted. Compassion welled for Melissa, not as Stanton's sister, nor as the police chief, but as a woman trying to do the right thing against what looked like impossible odds. Dominique knew how draining tracking a serial killer and a kingpin must be, in addition to investigating Randall Bowe. No one was immune to the taxing fight against the tsunami of a crime wave, including Melissa.

"As long as I'm assigned to guard Dominique, you get me, too. We're a package deal until we catch Jimenez."

"Mom seems to think you two are reconciling." Curiosity lit sparks in Melissa's eyes.

"Hey, please don't tell them that I'm actually protecting her. I told them that we needed space to figure things out, to repair our friendship. I don't want them worrying. You know Dad. He'll have us on a plane to Europe in no time if he finds out."

"Dominique's become a target, and it won't be private for long. I can't keep our parents from finding out, Stanton. Neither can you."

"They might not see the papers for a few days. They were gone this morning when we got up. Mom went with Dad on a business trip to California."

Melissa nodded. "They like to escape from it all a few times a year. So you're staying out at the lake house for the duration?" She cast her speculative glance on Dominique, who nodded.

"I don't have a choice. Stanton thinks it's the safest place for now, and since your parents left I feel better about being there. The last thing I want to do is attract the cartel to them or any other innocent bystander. This makes my desire to wrap this up all the more urgent, Melissa. I'm sure you feel the same. Which is why I need your help here. With each passing day I'm not getting any closer to proving how Charlie was wrongfully imprisoned. All I'm asking from you is for a chance to look at Bowe's records. Or at least Charlie's evidence file." Dominique knew it was futile but she had to ask. It was her job.

"I'm sorry, but until our internal review is complete, I don't have anything to tell you. Now let's get on with why I sat you down." Melissa's expression was full of concern. "Your social media posts triggered a hit being put out on you."

"We know."

"We figured that out."

Both she and Stanton replied in unison.

Melissa's brows arched. "Well done, you two. Stanton, you read the DEA report?"

"I did. And no, I didn't tell Dominique everything." He turned to her, a question in his eyes.

"I have my sources." She laughed. "The Associated Press published the news this morning."

Melissa grinned. "There's the woman I know."

Dominique smiled back, until she remembered how and when Melissa knew her. Back when she and Stanton were together. As much as her reporting duties brought her over to GGPD to track down stories, she rarely ran into Melissa. But when she'd been with Stanton, she and Melissa had hit it off and gone out for a couple of girls' nights. Their budding friendship had wilted after the breakup, mostly because Dominique had avoided not only Stanton but his entire family. Another regret she'd ignored until now.

"I just want the truth to come out, Melissa. *Chief.*" She smiled, wanting the chief to have no doubt that she respected her position.

Melissa nodded. "I get that. And I also get that Pablo Jimenez isn't going to rest until he thinks you're no longer a threat. To someone like him, that'll be when you're dead."

"I've already figured that out. Yesterday was a game changer." Did she have to spell it out again? Melissa knew she was here to file the incident reports with Stanton for both of the attempted killings.

"It's important that we're all on the same page here. That includes you, Stanton. Neither of you are to go rogue on this story. I want to know exactly who you're going to interview and when. I need to know your whereabouts at all times, Dominique. I'm not interested in curtailing your story. In fact, I relish your eventual publication of the truth. I need your help to break these bastards wide open. I also don't want you dead."

"I appreciate that."

"Don't you agree that it would be better for Dominique to lay low, ease up on the story, until after Jimenez is caught? DEA is closing in." Stanton's interjection made Dominique's teeth grind.

Melissa shook her head. "DEA's not getting the critical intel fast enough. None of us are. Figuring out the kingpin's identity is one thing, a break for us. He messed up, but he'll know that he did. He'll assume there's a good chance we're on to him. That'll only drive him further underground, make him more determined to strike out and prove his power." Melissa looked at her clasped hands, then at her brother. "Let me ask you something, Stanton. If Dominique was a male reporter, would you expect her to ease off?"

Dominique remembered why she and Melissa had become easy friends in the first place. They were both driven women who knew how to do whatever it took to get a job done. And Melissa never balked at dishing out guff to her brother, which frankly delighted Dominique.

"If I were assigned to protect him, yes, I'd ask him to stop whatever was causing the greatest risk." Stanton's quick reply was expected, but Dominique heard the slight tone of defensiveness and looked at him. He was staring at his sister, his jaw stubbornly set.

Melissa's soft smirk revealed that she didn't believe her brother's lame reply, either.

"He's right, Melissa. It's his job to keep me alive, so of course he had to try to convince me to stop agitating Jimenez. Which of course I'm not going to do. But Stanton's actually listened to me pore over the story details I have so far, helped me sift through them." Dominique's unexpected defense of Stanton came from somewhere deep inside. For some reason, she wanted Stanton to know that she appreciated his concern not just for her, but for her story, as well.

"Did he?" Melissa's brow arched but she didn't say anything further as she stood and nodded at them. "I can see Officer Colton headed this way. Give Jillian your report, and then you're free to go. Go ahead and press forward with your interviews, Dominique, but stop back in here after each one if at all possible. I don't want to risk passing information over cell phone lines that can be intercepted by the cartel. We'll combine your information with ours. Please, both of you, be extra careful. This is the most dangerous criminal we've seen in Grave Gulch for a long time. Maybe ever."

As they left the chief's office, Dominique allowed the gravity of Melissa's assessment to settle over her. So far she'd lost two battles: finding the truth about Charlie, and having to spend each waking second next to the one man she'd ever loved. And not let him back inside her heart.

Dangerous times, indeed.

Chapter Eight

"You'll let me do the talking, right?" Dominique waited to get out of the car after he'd turned the engine off. They sat on a residential street on the outskirts of Grave Gulch, in front of the house where the family of another one of Randall Bowe's wrongly imprisoned suspects lived.

"Of course. I'm nothing more than your shadow." Unless circumstances dictated otherwise, but he wasn't going into it again with her.

"Okay. Thanks again for getting my clothes." She'd changed into a caramel turtleneck and dressy dark jeans. He noticed that she kept the sneakers instead of fancier shoes and knew that her feet were giving her more trouble than she admitted. Just as the bruises on her throat were. They'd appeared dark and angry against her skin when he glimpsed them this morning in his parents' kitchen. She tugged at the high collar. "I thought it'd be best to not scare my interview subject."

He smiled. "Good call."

They walked up the narrow walkway that split the

tiny front yard and climbed steep concrete steps to a stoop where Dominique rang the doorbell. It buzzed inside, immediately followed by the ferocious barking of several dogs.

"Stand back." He tugged on her wrist and didn't stop until she was even with him in the middle of the steps.

"I love dogs." She grumbled under her breath just as the door opened. A petite young woman with bright fuchsia hair that matched her fuzzy sweater greeted them. Two large rottweilers sat on either side of her, snarls matching their laser-focused eyes.

"I'm Dominique de la Vega from the *Grave Gulch Gazette*. I'm here to see Beverly Lubinski."

"I know. We're waiting for you. Are you afraid of dogs?" The girl moved, motioned to the animals.

"Not at—"

"It's best if the dogs are restrained for the duration of the interview." Stanton's statement immediately drew Dominique's wrath-of-the-goddess glance but her aggravation was the least of his worries. He couldn't focus on keeping her safe with two burly canine bodyguards in the same room. Dogs were great; he wished he had time in his life to have one. But he'd learned early on in the security business to always eliminate whatever distractions possible.

"Okay, no problem." The girl took each dog by its spiked collar. "Come on, boys. To your crates. Mom! That reporter is here." They watched through the screen door as she disappeared into the house with the "boys," until an older woman with short, spiky silver hair appeared in the threshold.

"Dominique?"

"Yes. You must be Beverly?"

"I am. Sorry about that. Our boys are sweet but loud. Come on in."

Stanton was tempted to enter first, to protect Dominique in case the "boys" escaped their crates, but then she'd be vulnerable to any danger from the street. He kept his hand on the small of her back, let her know he was right there.

They settled in a shabby but clean living room. The younger woman returned and sat next to her mother and held her hand. Stanton noticed their matching dragonfly tattoos on the top of each hand.

"I'll get right to the point, Beverly, and..."

"Trina. I'm the daughter. Daniel Lubinski is my father and he's in jail because of a scumbag cop at GGPD."

"That's enough, Trina." Beverly shot them both an apologetic glance. "She has every right to be angry and she's not wrong about the police department, but I don't like her being so disrespectful to law enforcement."

Stanton clenched his teeth and struggled to stay silent. It wasn't his place to interject. He wanted to right their misconceptions, tell them he knew firsthand how hard GGPD worked, including its chief, his sister.

"I understand your concerns, Trina. To be frank, I have them, too. It's why I'm here. I hope I'm able to help uncover what's going on in the department." Dominique handled them so professionally that Stanton took note. "I also want to reassure you that most of GGPD is top-notch. They're working 'round the clock on the cartel issue and will get to the bottom of any mishandled cases. If there's a bad cop or employee, they will be unearthed and face justice. Why don't we start with you telling me about Daniel and how he ended up in police custody?"

Beverly took a deep breath before she began. "My husband, Daniel, was working on the East Side, doing whatever work he could find. He's a contractor, electrician and plumber. One of the places he was helping renovate for public housing seemed to have a lot of drug deals going on from all appearances."

"By 'place,' what do you mean, exactly?"

"It was an apartment building, next to that center. Now, let me tell you something. My Daniel has never, ever done drugs. He had a problem with booze years ago, but he's been a chip-carrying member of AA ever since, sober for twenty years."

"Since I was born," Trina added.

Dominique took notes on her laptop, her fingers flying. Stanton was mesmerized by how she appeared so relaxed while he knew her mind was racing with the facts of this story.

"Go on."

"I got a call at work—I'm a school nurse—saying that he'd been arrested for drug possession and dealing. I thought it was a joke. I mean, no one believed it. All his AA friends that we've met are certain he was framed, too."

"Why do you think he was framed?"

"He came home one day and confided that he'd seen a man, dressed in fancy clothes, different than the other shady characters there. He didn't get the impression the man was a user, but maybe some higher up with the folks he'd seen selling stuff. The dealers all acted scared around him, and he always traveled with five or six bodyguard types."

"Did Daniel ever tell you what he meant by 'stuff'?"

"Yes. Packets of white powder. Sometimes several to the same person. The day he witnessed what he thinks landed him in jail, to keep him quiet, the woman selling the drugs got knocked around by the man in charge. He hit her hard in the face, made her bleed. Daniel was installing lights in the hallway and shouted so that they'd leave her be. By the time he got down from his ladder, everyone had left the scene. Except…" Beverly shuddered and Trina's grip on her mother's hand visibly tightened.

"Except?" Dominique's prompts were soft yet firm, just the right tone to convey her confidence in her interviewee.

"When he got to the end of the hallway by the back door, where the deal was going down and the woman got beaten, they were all gone…except one of the bodyguards, who looked at Daniel and made a slit-throat gesture." Beverly demonstrated by using her finger like she was drawing a knife across her neck. "He thought he was going to be killed right then and there. He was so shook-up."

"Why didn't he call the police?"

"That's just it. He did. An officer came out here and took a report. But he didn't leave us with a copy of the report, so we doubt it was ever filed."

"What was his name?"

"I think it was Bixman or something like that. He was in civilian clothes and Daniel said he flashed his badge so fast he never caught the number or name exactly." Beverly shook her head. "It doesn't matter. The next day Daniel was arrested in the middle of wiring an apartment."

"And he was charged with possession?"

"And dealing." Beverly took a tissue from a purple print box on the coffee table. "They found enough heroin cut with fentanyl in his toolbox and jacket pockets to charge him with the intent to deal."

"But if your husband wasn't really using, or dealing, then he never touched the packets."

"No, he didn't. But GGPD said his prints were all over the plastic bags."

Dominique's gaze met Stanton's and he knew her thoughts. *Randall Bowe.* He had to be at the bottom of this. Had he been paid off by the drug cartel to plant the evidence? And who was the mystery cop who'd interviewed Daniel Lubinski? It sounded like someone posing as police, which would be a felony.

Dominique shut her laptop and leaned forward, placed her hands on top of Beverly's and Trina's. Stanton felt like an intruder on a girl-power meeting, but he didn't at all feel excluded. Dominique had a way of making others always feel part of the team. He'd missed being on her team.

"I can't thank you enough for being so honest with me. And I promise that I'm going to use the power of my pen to write a story that will help bring down the cartel. As I said earlier, please know that GGPD is not made of all bad players. They're working hard on this."

Beverly nodded. "I know. But understand that I had to take care of my family. Daniel told me that he and Charlie Hamm had become friends in prison due to the fact they both wanted to stay sober. Plus, Charlie had some of the same issues as Daniel." Her gaze sparked with regret, sorrow. "They both strayed from their marriages. Charlie's wife left him for cheating, and I decided to stay with Daniel, to work it out. It's part of the reality of being in the midst of the addiction and disease." She offered a brave smile. "They also figured out that they were both victims of the same bad players, whoever they were. I've retained an excellent attorney, who's close to getting Daniel out. Turns out the evidence was highly circumstantial, because he'd left his jacket in the building overnight, and the toolbox, too. Someone broke into the locked building and planted the drugs. And his fingerprints could have been planted, according to our lawyer."

Stanton knew about Charlie's wife leaving, as it was in the file Dominique had on him and had allowed him to read.

"Did Daniel ever say if he and Charlie thought there

were more people in the county jail who were wrongfully imprisoned?"

"No. He only told me about Charlie after we found
out about his death. Daniel doesn't like to talk about any
of it. Says it's for the best, that as long as we're safe—"
she cast a glance at Trina "—that's all that matters."

Dominique nodded, then stood, her gaze seeking
Stanton's. Was it his imagination, or was she looking
at him as though he was not only on her team, but a
full-fledged partner?

BACK AT THE STATION, Dominique shared a small table
in the break room with Stanton and was grateful for
his ear.

"Now do you get my reasons for being so upset with
how slowly things are going with the internal investigation?"

The muscle on the side of his jaw jumped and he
took a swig of his coffee. She noted that he had his own
mug with the Colton Protection logo on it. In fact, there
was an entire shelf of the mugs in the cabinet above the
counter. "I do. And do you 'get' how concerned I am
about my family, especially my sister? She's got the
weight of all of this on her shoulders. Besides, it's not
your place to delve into an internal GGPD investigation. I don't have to tell you this."

"I know. But I'm not letting up."

"Hey, you two. Want to follow me?" Troy nodded toward his tiny office just off the break area. Once in his
office, she and Stanton sank onto a cracked faux leather

sofa and faced Troy across his desk. Stacks of files, two computers and a printer crowded the room. Yet Troy seemed in charge, confident, if a bit tired.

With a start she realized that every single officer appeared to need at least a nap if not a long rest. Like her, they'd been fighting against time. The longer the corrupt cop and/or employee went unidentified, the greater chance of misfortune falling upon Daniel and any other wrongfully imprisoned people.

"I won't take any more of your time than I need to, but Melissa told us, told me, to report back after every interview."

"Shoot." Troy leaned back as she began to share. She relayed what they'd learned, with emphasis on the description of the man "dressed in fancy clothes" and the possibility of wrongful evidence. As professional a setting as it was, as rapt as Troy's attention was, it was impossible for her to shake how Stanton's nearness affected her. He radiated complete confidence in her abilities, which she was certain helped with Troy's attentiveness.

"What do you think, Troy?" She waited for him to answer instead of prodding him with her opinion and requests for Daniel Lubinski's case evidence file.

"Thank you for telling me all of this. Even though Chief asked you to come back after each interview, you didn't have to provide all of the details. I, and the entire department, appreciate it. We'll add all the facts you collected to our data board in the ops room. Have you by any chance been able to get in touch with the witness in Charlie's case? The one you were going to meet yesterday, Johnny Blanchard?"

She shook her head. "No. I've tried to text and call, with no luck. He's not answering. I'm actually surprised he hasn't blocked me yet."

"You didn't mention that to me," Stanton cut in, and she heard his irritation.

"I can't weigh you down with every tiny aspect of my work. It's difficult enough that you've been roped into this case as deeply as you have." She spoke before she thought about Troy sitting there, watching their interaction. And was that light in Stanton's eyes not disapproval for her work, but...pride?

"You can work that out between the two of you later, but Dominique, I'm with Stanton as far as safety goes. The more you tell him, the more he can anticipate Jimenez's next moves. We all have to be hypervigilant."

"I know." Now to see if Troy would be as stubborn as Melissa. "Do you have anything new on Randall Bowe? I'm not looking for confidential information, Troy, but I need you to throw me a bone here."

He shook his head and she felt Stanton stiffen beside her.

"I can't talk about internal ops, Dominique."

"Come on, Troy," Stanton wheedled. "What would it hurt you to at least confirm that Randall committed wrongdoing or that you suspect he did? At least let Dominique look at Charlie's evidence file." Stanton's support made her insides warm. If she wasn't careful, she'd believe they were more than just a professional team.

"I'm sorry, but I can't comment on an active investigation. Both of you know the rules." Troy's expression was as grim as his reply. Her heart sank but she held on to her purpose—to clear Charlie. There were other avenues she hadn't been down yet, such as talking to Charlie's lawyer. The attorney had refused to see her when she'd reached out last week, but perhaps when she explained what had happened to her, how they'd identified the man responsible for Charlie's incarceration and in all probability his death, he'd do the right thing.

"You know she's right, Troy." Stanton stood up, but not before Dominique grasped his forearm.

"It's okay, Stanton. I get it. We have to play by the rules."

Troy's phone buzzed and his face turned to stone as he read a text. He looked up at first Dominique, then Stanton. "I've got to go, folks. Do you mind going to the ops room and giving the officer on duty the information you've told me?"

"Not at all." But Troy was already out the door, leaving her alone with Stanton. The door shut behind him and the room felt incredibly small. Especially since there were no windows, and mere inches between her and Stanton.

"Since when did you decide I'm on the winning side?"

Stanton's brow rose. "I never said you weren't. My request is that you ask yourself if this story is worth your life. Because that's what's at stake, Dominique. Your life. You're uncovering insects with each rock you turn over and they're getting uglier as you get closer to the truth."

"You're here to make sure I keep my life. Unless my dad told you to try to talk me out of following this lead?"

Stanton's mouth lifted in a one-sided grin. "No, he didn't suggest that."

Heat made its way from her center to her cheeks, then rushed back to her sensitive parts. "Do not tell me that he said you should try to distract me in other ways."

"It's no secret that he was upset at our breakup."

"How do you know that?" She'd never discussed the end of their relationship in detail with anyone but Soledad, and even her twin didn't know the depths of her sorrow and grief over the end of her time with Stanton.

"He called me right after you told your sister we'd split."

"Did he?" She tried to feel angry, betrayed, but it was impossible with her father. Rigo de la Vega loved his family and was incredibly protective. For all the right reasons. "Of course he did. He never questioned me on it, and this explains why. What on earth did he say to you?"

Stanton's expression shut down. "That's between Rigo and me."

"You never mentioned it."

"When could I have? You shut me out of your life the minute you walked out my apartment door."

"I did, didn't I?" What had she been thinking? Her mind raced for one solid reason she should have left him, his heart in his hands, that spring day. Remorse swirled in her gut, self-recrimination close on its heels. "I was rash in the moment. I thought about coming back to talk things over, but we'd said so much." Too much.

"We'd only cracked the tip of the iceberg, Dom." At the pet name her gaze collided with his and the latent heat between them flared. Her nipples tightened under the cashmere turtleneck and she grasped the edge of Troy's desk. It was wrong to indulge in her attraction to Stanton in the very police department she'd complained about. Yet she couldn't look away, nor turn away from the pull of his nearness. When his lids flickered, and she knew he saw her arousal, she did some exploration of her own and saw that he was rock-hard under his dress trousers.

"*Stanton.*" Funny how a name, whispered in the right octave, could betray her deepest longings.

Stanton's reply wasn't verbal. He reached for her and hauled her up against him, and she met him halfway. She was beyond ready for his kiss and didn't hold back. They both knew this was a stolen moment, that Troy could walk back through that door at any moment.

It only made the kiss all the more delicious.

STANTON LET HIS mouth plunder hers, and thrilled as she explored his. He felt every stroke of her tongue, wished to Hades and back that they were anywhere but here in his cousin's office.

Troy's office.

He pulled back, his lips throbbing from the sudden lack of contact with hers. As if they were one whenever they were together, kissing or not.

She stared at her hands as they rested on his chest, both of them breathing audibly. "Wow."

"Yeah. 'Wow.'" He placed his forehead on hers. "It's not wrong, but it's not right in this place." He lifted her chin with his finger and waited for her to look at him. A man could live forever in her gaze.

"This has got to stop. We're adults." She offered a small smile.

"I can agree to waiting until we're alone and in a safer space to take this any further."

She pushed against him, took a step back. Ran her fingers through her hair. His own itched to follow suit. "You're right. No, we can't do this, not here." And if she were smart, not anywhere. "Let's get to the operations center and give them a copy of my interview." Along with taking notes, she'd recorded it, with signed permission from Mrs. Lubinski.

"Right." He opened the office door and checked the corridor before he stepped out. GGPD or no, he couldn't trust anyone else to have her safety as a priority. He felt like he was coming out of his skin at the thought of a cop-gone-bad on the force. The forensics expert was one thing, and more than enough to put him on edge. "Okay, let's go."

They walked next to one another down the corridor. Voices reached them from a room to the left, and Dominique put her arm in front of him, forcing both of them to stop. Her eyes widened as she comprehended what he was hearing, too.

"What's so important that you're this upset, Chief?" Troy's whisper carried into the hallway.

"Desiree called me and she's positive she just saw Randall Bowe lurking in Grave Gulch Park." Melissa wasn't whispering but Stanton had to strain to hear her lowered voice.

"In broad daylight?" Troy's disbelief was evident. "No way."

"Yes, 'way.' He was in a blue ski cap, tight to his head, which hid his hair, and he had a fake mustache on. She said it was definitely Randall. She's a sketch artist. If anyone can ID someone in disguise, it's Desiree." Melissa was convinced.

"I'll get someone out to the park ASAP."

Dominique looked at Stanton, her eyes wide. They had to get out of here before Melissa or Troy knew they'd overheard their exchange.

"What are you two doing out here?" Too late. Troy stared at them.

"We overheard everything, Troy. I'm going to Grave Gulch Park with you." Dominique spoke with her usual gutsy determination.

"You had no business snooping on police business, either of you." Troy's voice shook. Stanton hadn't seen him this angry since he'd lost in a family game of Thanksgiving Day football. Which, to be fair, some of the cousins had cheated at to win. "I wouldn't expect this from you." His anger was all for Stanton.

"Hey, the door was wide-open. We all know that Randall Bowe is on the loose. You've got WANTED posters up all over Grave Gulch. You can't tell us anything about your internal investigation, and yet you expect innocent citizens to report if they've seen him. That's putting civilians at risk, Troy. And the longer you keep us from the truth, you keep Dominique at risk, too."

Troy had the integrity to admit the truth. "I'm sorry. We're as worried as you are about the cartel's next move. Who they'll target next."

"You think Bowe was paid off by the cartel, by Jimenez, don't you?" Dominique never missed a chance to get an answer. But he didn't agree with her on this. In fact, he doubted Bowe had any tie-in with the cartel. Whatever Randall Bowe was up to was his own insanity. The cartel didn't need someone in GGPD to help out their cases, anyhow. They preferred to handle everything with threats and death.

"What I think is immaterial. My objective is to capture Bowe and you're both in my way." Troy looked at the floor, in deep thought. When he glanced up again he looked at Dominique. "You can have the news scoop that Bowe's been spotted in the park. Go ahead and release the description of his disguise—blue ski cap, mustache. We've already got a sketch coming in from Desiree within minutes. Feel free to publish it. Now, let's both get some work done." Troy strode off, and

Dominique quickly punched in a number on her phone. He listened as she reported what she knew to her editor. When she disconnected, she smiled.

"What's so funny?"

"Not funny. Happy. We're this much closer to getting to the bottom of all this."

"Okay."

She playfully punched his upper arm. "Come on, you're excited. I can tell. Your first big scoop."

He grunted, unwilling to give her the broad smile that tugged at his lips. This was dangerous territory for him. If he allowed himself to let go and enjoy the sunshine that was Dominique, he faced certain extinction when she again disappeared from his life.

Stanton didn't have another heart to shatter.

Chapter Nine

It took no more than ten minutes to make certain the operations team had all the pertinent details from her interview with the Lubinskis. Dominique was relieved to leave the station because she wanted to get to the *Gazette* and finish filing her article, as well as brief her editor on what she'd found out to date. Stanton was waiting for her in the break room and she walked toward it, eager to be near him. Or the sense of safety he gave her.

Stop hiding from it. You're loving spending time with him again.

She was, but had to constantly remind herself that they weren't a couple, there was no chance of a reconciliation and Stanton would be gone from her life as quickly as she could say, "Pablo Jimenez is under arrest."

"Dominique." Melissa called to her from inside her office and dread filled her stomach. *Here it comes.* First Troy had chewed her out for eavesdropping earlier; now Melissa was going to have her turn.

"Chief Colton." She entered the room.

"Stop it. I'm always Melissa to you. Where's my brother?"

"He's waiting for me in the break room."

Melissa nodded. "Please don't feel you need to call me 'chief' when we're alone. In front of the officers, sure, but you'll always be family to me, Dominique."

"I appreciate that. I've missed our girl talks."

"As have I. Any chance that you and Stanton are going to make a go of it again?"

"Absolutely not. This is all business. My father hired him to protect me."

Melissa laughed. "I'll bet you were thrilled by that."

Dominique felt a knot of tension in her shoulders go. "Yes, it was a surprise. Let's leave it at that."

"I trust that Troy steered you clear of going to Grave Gulch Park with him. It's too dangerous."

"He did, but he was generous enough to give me the scoop on Bowe's sighting."

Melissa nodded. "I've no problem with that. While I still can't give you any information about our internal investigation, I want you to know that it's perfectly okay for you to interview one of Bowe's lab assistants who still works here. I can't let you interview Bonnie Stadler, yet." Dominique knew that Stadler was fired during the Everleigh Emerson case, and now wondered if she'd been let go over the wrongdoings of Bowe. "Also, one of our rookies, CSI Jillian Colton, wants to talk to you about her misgivings over Bowe."

"I thought GGPD can't tell me anything about the investigation?"

"We can't, but an individual cop can tell you about their personal experiences. Is that clear?" Melissa wasn't going to spoon-feed her any further. Dominique got it.

"Gotcha. I'll find both of them before I leave the station, if that's all right."

"Absolutely. Jillian's down in the bullpen. Her desk is smack-dab in the middle. You'll find the lab assistant in Forensics, probably at his desk this time of day as he's got reports to file."

"Thank you."

Finally, a chance to get some answers.

BOWE'S MOST JUNIOR lab assistant expressed concern about his boss's erratic behavior over the past several months. But he couldn't give Dominique any more information yet, not until the GGPD's internal investigation was finished. Plus it was clear that Bonnie Stadler, the assistant who'd been fired, would know more. This assistant was barely a step above intern. It was as if Melissa had sent her on a wild-goose chase to keep her busy, to prevent her from digging too deeply into GGPD workings. Frustrated, she trudged over to Jillian's desk.

Jillian's demeanor was professional and she seemed eager to talk to Dominique, but again, her loyalty was to GGPD.

"I don't have a ton of information to give you, because as I'm sure Chief Colton told you, we can't talk specifics about the internal investigation. But suffice it to say that I was gaslighted by Randall Bowe on several occasions, with more than one case. As a rookie it's important that I don't mess up the most basic parts of any case, and yet Bowe gave me the wrong information and in one case lost all of the evidence I'd collected during a drug bust."

"Didn't you have a forensics team with you?"

Jillian shook her head, her bright eyes cloudy with anger. "No. It was a short-notice incident. I was on foot patrol on the East Side, on Main Street. If we need to go on side streets, we have to either be in a cruiser or call for backup. Anyway, I received a call about an OD. I rushed to the scene, in front of an old building, and was able to revive the addict with Narcan. She gave me several packets of heroin—I tested it with the kit the backup unit brought—and I was careful to bag it all as evidence. I'd hoped we'd get the dealer's prints on it. But Bowe said the bags didn't have prints, which I found odd as the victim wasn't wearing gloves and at least her prints would have been on the bags."

"Anything else?"

Jillian shrugged. "To be honest, it's all a mess right now. There's the cartel that you're looking at, and we have a serial killer on the loose. We've had three women go missing from Grave Gulch over the past five years, as I'm sure you know. With Len Davison out there still, these disappearances could be linked to him. Our forensics lab is the backbone of many of our cases, and to have it swamped with a backlog, without a senior scientist and with our best assistant fired, is not help-ing matters."

Dominique did know about the missing, but the opi-oid epidemic had "disappeared" many, many people nationwide.

"About how Bowe 'gaslighted' you—"

"Jillian, I need you with me now." Troy stood at Jil-lian's desk and he gave a cursory nod to Dominique. In that one gesture he also expressed that police business trumped journalism.

Jillian shot her an apologetic glance. "Sorry, Domi-nique."

Disappointment roiled in her gut but she offered a smile. "I get it. Can I call you later?"

"Yes. I'm happy to finish this later."

"Jillian." Troy was already at the other side of the bullpen.

"Coming!"

Dominique tapped a reminder into her phone so that she'd remember to call Jillian later this evening, or early tomorrow morning. So many developments were snow-balling into one complicated, layered story.

She found Stanton in the break room, an empty mug next to his open laptop. Engrossed in his work, he didn't stir as she approached.

"I'm done for now. I would like to go to the *Gazette* offices before we head back to the lake house."

He looked up and she thought she'd braced herself for eye contact, but there was no use pretending. It was impossible to prepare herself for the immediate flood of warmth that rocked her every dang time he looked at her.

"Sure thing. Did you get everything you wanted?" He must have seen the shadow of disappointment in her eyes.

"No, not by a long shot. Cop business takes precedence over my story, though." She watched him pack up his computer, rinse out his mug and place it on the drying board next to the break room sink. He turned and faced her.

"You'll have all night to work if you need to, in a safer spot than downtown Grave Gulch." His bodyguard expression was back: lips pressed together in determination, eyes scanning the room as they left.

"I admit I'm looking forward to chilling out at your folks' place again."

"We're going to do more than relax, babe." His words, low and spoken next to her ear, sent tiny thrills of arousal across her skin. If she were sane she'd insist they go back to her apartment, or his, instead of the remote lake house.

Like it would make a difference.

"Mmm." She signed out at the reception desk and pushed through the exit door, sensing his nearness as they walked out into the pale golden sunshine. This time of day was her favorite, as was the season. Nothing like a late spring afternoon—

The sound of gunfire erupted in her ears.

"Get down!" Stanton's command was her only warning before she was thrown to the ground, her body squashed by a solid heavy weight. *Stanton*. They'd been shot at.

A scream echoed and she realized it was hers.

"It's okay, Dom. I've got you. Stay down." He shifted, a knee on either side of her. "Three uniforms are in pursuit."

Footsteps running, more gunfire. An engine's roar and wheels screeching filled the air.

"Stay here." She did as he ordered, completely trusting him. It was difficult trying to catch her breath while face down on the graveled lot, but she was still here, alive. As was Stanton.

"Okay." His hands were on her, helping her up. As soon as she was on her feet she turned to find comfort against his broad chest. Until she saw the bright red stain on his suit's upper sleeve.

"Oh no, Stanton, you've been shot!"

"Have I?" His brows drew together and he looked where she stared, held his arm up. "It's a graze. Never felt it, trust me."

"How can you be so sure? Stanton, you're bleeding! That is more than a graze."

"She's right, Stanton. You need to let her drive you to the ER, or one of our officers will take you." Melissa stood next to them.

"Did you catch the shooter?" Dominique was at a disadvantage; she'd not seen the attacker or the police officers who'd come immediately to her defense and Stanton's. She sent up a silent prayer that they'd be safe as they chased down the shooter.

"No, but we've got a unit in pursuit. We'll get to the bottom of it soon enough, but I think we all know who's in all probability responsible." Melissa's blue eyes sparked with anger. "We're getting too close for Jimenez's comfort."

Dominique found no sense of accomplishment in the pronouncement. Not when Stanton had just taken a bullet in all likelihood intended for her. She swore she could feel her bones rattling at the thought of how close she'd come to losing him. Again. And it wasn't his job that was to blame, but a story she'd insisted on pursuing. Charlie Hamm's justice was a priority, but maybe Soledad was right. Was it worth putting the one man she'd ever loved at risk?

"I'm driving to the hospital, no arguments." She held out her hand and Stanton reluctantly dropped his keys in her palm.

"Only to keep you happy, and because the hospital is nearby." He accepted a large gauze pad from the receptionist who'd brought out a first aid kit, and pressed it to his upper arm. "Let's get this over with. All they're going to do is wash out the graze, trust me."

"You need to go for our insurance purposes, since you were shot on police property." Melissa's displeasure at the fact was evident in her stern reply.

"Roger. On our way."

"Thank you, Chief. And please thank the officers who responded." Gratitude engulfed Dominique and she blinked back sudden tears.

"It's our job."

As she made sure Stanton got into the passenger side and buckled, then took the driver's seat, Melissa's words echoed in her mind. Protection and apprehension were GGPD's job. Getting the dirt on Jimenez and his cartel, whatever it took to clear Charlie Hamm, was hers.

"Don't make any funny moves," Stanton chided her as she drove out of the lot and proceeded to the ER, also downtown. "I'm a little sore."

"You mean like the ones you taught me?" When they were together he'd taken her out to a defensive driving school and taught her some very basic maneuvers.

"Good to know that you remember something useful from our time together."

She bit her tongue from retorting that she remembered more than he'd imagined, including how he'd always made her feel so important, so special. The issue wasn't her memory, but how she'd ever forgotten how good it felt to be next to Stanton.

STANTON WAS GLAD to be home earlier than normal from work. Correction, he was happy to be at his parents' estate with Dominique safely inside, away from the targets that Jimenez's men kept placing on her. He thanked the stars above that he'd been standing where he had and that the thug had been a poor shot. His injury was a bit more than a graze, and he'd been sent home without any stitches, but just a simple bandage that he was instructed to change twice a day for the next few days. The doc's instructions to take it easy were easily swatted away in the ER, when the adrenaline still surged through his system.

Now that he was back at the lake house, he was becoming more aware of the soreness that he knew from experience might bother him for the next several days. He had to ignore it, because he had a job to finish: to keep Dominique alive. No matter how much he repeated it to himself, he couldn't erase the kiss they'd shared in his cousin's office this afternoon. His body thirsted for her touch. That had never eased no matter how much time grew between when they'd been together and now.

"Can I get you anything?" Dominique spoke from the kitchen, where she was putting away the groceries they'd picked up for the weekend. He'd tried to help but she insisted he sit down for a bit.

"You."

He heard a pause in her movements and smiled to himself. There was nothing like the thrill of catching her off guard. It wasn't often when the woman you cared about broke her reserve, not if she was as intelligent and focused as Dominique.

Had he just admitted to himself that he still cared for her?

"What?" She stood at the end of the sofa he was stretched out on, contemplating him with wariness.

He laughed. "I meant I want you to take a break, too. Have a seat." He pointed to the large white easy chair with the woven throw tossed over the back. It was usually Italia's spot when she and Frank spent their nights inside during the cold months.

She perched on the edge of the cushion and looked over her shoulder out the window to the lake below. The house was perched on a high bluff but protected from Lake Michigan's worst gales by the surrounding trees. "It's still as beautiful as I remember. It must be hard for your parents to leave when they travel."

He pushed himself up and leaned against the back of the sofa, his feet on the coffee table. "They certainly love it here, but I know they also cherish the freedom to travel. Dad's business has been successful and they've raised all four of us. It's their time to enjoy life."

"They know how to live, don't they? They could have chosen to leave the area like many do, heading south to warmer weather, or back to Italy, to be with your mother's family. But they've picked Michigan."

"Yes, I'd have to say they've found their paradise." He didn't want to talk about his parents or his siblings. It was a rare gift to be alone with Dominique and he wasn't a fool. He knew that this might be the last time they'd be so close, without interruption. As long as Jimenez's thugs didn't find them here, they were safe for tonight. And they had the entire night in front of them.

"When do you think you'll want dinner?" She looked at the clock that hung over the kitchen's back counter. "It's almost six."

"Any time that works for you." He really wanted to eat yesterday and skip straight to where he hoped they'd spend the night. In his bed. Well, in what was now the guest bedroom, formerly his childhood bedroom. He'd left home for college at eighteen and when he'd returned to Grave Gulch he'd been eager to start his own life downtown, with his security protection business. It had been the right move for him but he still had nostalgia for this house. It meant a lot to him to have Dominique here, whether forever or just tonight.

Stick to thinking it's only tonight, bud. Far safer.

"I'll get it going in about twenty minutes. It won't take long." She stood and stretched. "I'd love a walk on the deck and yard, down to the steps. Do I have your permission to go?"

She stood with the glittering lake as a backdrop, the trees on either side budding, the small new leaves appearing like little golden green birds on the branches. Dominique faced him, her skin flushed over her cheeks, making the sparkles in her obsidian eyes look like diamonds. Her persimmon-red lips were slightly parted, revealing a glimpse of her white teeth. Unable to keep his gaze on her face alone, he took in her full breasts, her small waist, the enticing flare of her hips.

When he looked back up into her eyes, they'd narrowed. But not in displeasure or disgust. Dominique knew what he wanted, and she wanted it, too. But one thing about her he'd never forgotten was how she had a love-hate relationship with seduction. So often she'd stop their flirting, the tug and release of tension, by kissing him deeply, her tongue communicating their mutual need in a most effective manner.

If he was going to follow through with his desire and leave here with his heart intact, he had to remember to keep his cool. Take it slow. To remember that what drove them apart two years ago hadn't changed. Dominique was all about her career, and he couldn't be married to someone he had to worry about each and every second of every day. It was what kept him from succumbing to his baser desire, which would have already found him hauling her over his shoulder and taking her back to his bedroom, sore arm be damned.

"Stanton? Can I go outside?"

"Sorry. I'm a little tired after all the shootout drama." He made it a point to shrug as if he hadn't just made love to her with his eyes. "Sure, you're safe out here. The security cameras are all working and I'll see you the whole time. Stay up here, though—no wandering down to the beach. The tide's high and a storm is brewing."

"There isn't time for that. We still need to eat. I won't be long." She grabbed the blanket off the chair and wrapped it around her shoulders. At the door, he saw her face reflected in the glass right before she slid open the door and stepped into the night. The confusion and, if he were lucky, disappointment on her expression allowed him to hold back and not follow her, warm her with his kisses in the chilly spring evening.

THE NIGHT SKY was visible through the trees and above the lake. Dominique shivered against the cold and wrapped the blanket tighter. Disappointment swam in her gut, but it wasn't because Stanton hadn't followed her, or asked her to stay inside longer. Or to sit next to him. Or to kiss him again.

Face it. The words he'd murmured in her ear in Troy's GGPD office had been nothing more than whispers in the heat of the moment. Even if he'd meant them, that was before he'd been shot. He'd had plenty of time to remember why they were spending so much time together, that it had nothing to do with intention on either of their parts. It was a job for him, and a means to an end for her.

In truth they'd never wanted the same thing, had they? Stanton wanted a woman to spend his life with, one without such a risky job. Not all of her stories involved dangerous situations, but enough of them did. Too many for Stanton. And even if she'd rethought her desire to put off having children, it wouldn't be enough for Stanton. She'd always know he was worried about her, and she'd be frightened every time the phone rang at odd hours when he was out on a protection contract.

She looked up at the stars, remembering again how much she loved this vantage point. Frank and Italia had left the back patio lanterns as motion detectors, timed only for after they retired for the evening, so that they could come out here and see the stars with minimal light pollution. Stanton's parents had lived a dream romance, staying together for over forty years, raising four incredible children, and contributing to the community in a real way. Both donated their time and talents often. Italia's art was a familiar sight at local charity auctions, and Frank's shipping company, at which he was an executive, provided scholarship funds to Grave Gulch High School graduates. Italia's charity work had inspired Dominique to volunteer at the Grave Gulch prison, teaching her creative writing class, right after the breakup.

Dominique knew Frank and Italia's relationship had had its ups and downs; Italia had been quick to tell her that during one of the many weekends she'd spent out here with Stanton. As if Stanton's mother wanted to convey that Dominique shouldn't expect life with her son to always be perfect.

A stab of regret melded with realization. Had she been so focused on perfection—in her job, her relationship with Stanton—that she'd missed out on what mattered? Had she overlooked what Italia had tried to tell her? Soledad had warned her to not throw out the baby with the bathwater, but she'd thought her twin was more concerned about her settling down than anything else. And she'd thought she'd find someone else who wouldn't pressure her into marriage so soon. Stanton's proposal had seemed impetuous and innocent enough, but she knew him, knew his family. Children and a lot of sacrifices she wasn't willing to make were part of the deal. Weren't they?

She shook her head and closed her eyes, gave herself a moment to soak in the trees, the lake, the star-splattered sky. Nature had always given her peace and she didn't think the term "forest bathing" was so far-fetched. As if the trees heard her, a softer breeze swept down, and she heard the gentle scrape of branches against each other. It was the closest thing to lighting a candle and sending up a prayer, and right now, her spirit needed it.

Because when it involved Stanton, she couldn't trust her instinct. There were too many layers of emotion, so much complicated history between them. Yet as she stood in the quiet night, the one thought that kept circling her brain seemed to slip down to her heart.

Maybe it's okay to enjoy the moment, whatever it brings.

Chapter Ten

Stanton made certain Dominique was back inside before he went to his room. He took his time, needing things to be perfect for her. He'd bought some of his own supplies and had them rung up while Dominique was still picking out produce. The candles were her favorite scent—jasmine.

He knew he was a hopeless romantic. His family never ceased teasing him about how he'd wooed women through college, always insisting on bringing flowers to a date. But his father had set a good example. Frank Colton never took his wife for granted, not that Italia would let him. Not for the first time Stanton thought about how much he and Dominique seemed to parrot his parents' relationship; they both were two strong-willed people with their own lives and careers, finding common ground.

But it had blown apart all because he'd let his emotions drive the boat that day he'd ridiculously proposed to her. Her refusal, his pain, followed by her hasty departure, had left a hole in his heart, and from what she'd admitted and how she'd reacted these past few days, Dominique had experienced her share of heartache and regret, too.

Tonight could be a way for them to leave one another with a lasting, loving memory. He wasn't the same foolish man he'd been two years ago. He knew this wasn't the start of anything with Dominique. But he did want a better ending with the one woman who'd ever stolen his heart. He only hoped she'd accept this last gift from him.

"I'M NOT USED to someone else cooking for me."

Dominique tried to keep her cool as she made their meal. With Stanton sitting at his parents' kitchen island, his enigmatic charisma sucked her in deeper with each moment they spent together. He'd been correct about his bullet wound; it was nothing more than a graze. It didn't matter to Dominique because as far as she was concerned, he'd taken a bullet for her. Had he not reacted as quickly as he had, getting her to the ground, she might not be here. A shiver ran through her at the thought, and she focused on mixing roasted garlic into butter.

"I'm waving the BS flag on that one. Your mother cooks for you whenever you visit."

"Which, if you heard her giving me grief last night, hasn't been in a while."

She smeared a baguette cut crosswise with the mixture. "Your parents understand that their kids have their own lives."

"Yours don't?"

"Please." She raised her brow. "You're living proof that my father can't stay out of my life." Satisfied with the garlic bread, she turned the state-of-the-art oven's broiler on, slid the bread onto a sheet and then under the blue flames. "I love my father, he's the best. And in this case, he was right to trust his fatherly instincts. It's unfortunate that I've worried him, yet again. This isn't the first time he's worried about a story I'm working on." And reason number one she'd thought she didn't want her own family, at least not children. She never wanted them to feel stifled by her overprotectiveness, or to not go after their dreams because of what they thought were her wishes.

"I think once you become a parent, that's it. There's no longer a way of ever turning the spigot off. A parent's love is unconditional." He sounded wistful and she took a long look at him. He sat with his uninjured arm on the granite top, his gaze flitting from the basketball game on the elevated, muted television in the far corner of the kitchen, to her, to the meal she prepared. In this moment it was impossible to remember all the reasons she'd convinced herself they'd split. Before she said something stupid, she grabbed the salad greens and began chopping. A buzzer sounded and she pulled the bread out, its top perfectly browned.

"That smells incredible."

"At least I didn't burn it this time." The time she'd charred garlic bread in her apartment had been one for the record books.

"Yeah, we don't want the Grave Gulch FD showing up out here tonight."

"I was mortified, in case I never admitted it back then."

"It was the first time you made dinner for me."

"I'm surprised you ever let me cook for you again." She placed the salad aside and tended to the shellfish she had steaming on the stove top. "We're just about ready here."

"Bring it." Cioppino, an Italian seafood dish of broth over mussels, clams, octopus and scallops, was their main course. When they'd stopped at the small grocery on the way here, there had been a plethora of fresh shellfish and she'd impulsively decided to prepare the recipe she remembered as Stanton's favorite. They'd both agreed that they were together for only as long as it took her to get her story, or GGPD to arrest Pablo Jimenez, eliminating the threat to her life. What would it matter to make the same meal they'd enjoyed several times when they'd dated?

"I've set the table." She'd helped herself to Italia's bounty of cheerily printed table linens while Stanton had showered.

"We could have eaten at the island."

"Are you that into the basketball game?"

"No, not at all. I didn't want you to go to all of this trouble. But I do appreciate it."

She set the food on the table along with a carafe of sparkling water. "I thought you might pass on the wine if your wound is bothering you."

"You'd be correct. I'm pretty sure I won't need any anti-inflammatories, unless this scrape surprises me and starts aching in the middle of the night. Besides, you know I don't drink on duty. Don't let it stop you, though."

"I'm good." She wanted to remain alert, too. "I honestly don't know what was scarier—being directly attacked by that thug or the gunshots. The bullets came from nowhere."

"Only one made contact, and barely at that. This looks amazing, Dominique. You've outdone yourself. Thank you." They sat across from one another.

"You're welcome. It's the least I can do, now that you took a bullet for me."

He grimaced. "Please. Your storytelling abilities are evident."

She laughed. "I don't write fiction, only the truth, backed up with facts. You definitely took the fire today and saved both of our lives."

"Why don't we declare the dinner table a cartel-free zone for now? We both deserve a quiet meal to regroup."

"Works for me."

They dug in. Dominique was grateful for the meal to focus on, instead of her resolve against allowing her attraction to Stanton to overtake her common sense. He'd promised more when he'd kissed her in Troy's office earlier, but since he'd been shot between then and now, she figured he'd forgotten. It was for the best; neither of them needed anything to take them away from their main missions. His to protect her and hers to finish the story.

No matter the keen stabs of disappointment that peppered an otherwise enjoyable meal with her bodyguard ex.

STANTON HAD LIED. His arm hurt like hell, and it was a combination of the minor bullet wound and how he'd landed on it when he'd covered Dominique from the gunfire. He'd had to convince her to stay out of the exam with the ER doctor and thank goodness he had. The doc had told him to take it easy and use ibuprofen regularly for the next several days. As a former collegiate athlete, Stanton was familiar with muscle pain. What wasn't familiar was having to hide it from someone else. He didn't want Dominique worried. She'd been through more in the last two days than probably her entire life, no matter her tough reporter facade.

The last thing he wanted was for her to think they shouldn't finish what they'd started in Troy's office earlier. He didn't give a fig's tree about his arm and needed to make sure Dominique didn't think it precluded him from being able to make good on his promise.

Not a good idea, man. Not if you want to keep yourself together after she's gone again.

"You're awfully quiet. Is the cioppino that bad?"

He grinned. "Not at all—it's beyond compare. Don't tell my mother, but yours is my favorite."

"Really?" Her tone suggested total disbelief and he waited until she looked at him.

"Really. After you left, the one thing I regretted most was that you hadn't written your recipe down for me." He maintained a straight face until her nonplussed expression yielded to narrowed eyes and a smirk.

"You are still such a jerk." She laughed and tossed her napkin at him.

"Whoa!" He feinted a dodge and inadvertently slammed his injured arm on the solid maple table's edge. *Ouch.*

"You okay? Oh, Stanton, did you hit your wound?" Her mirth changed to concern tinged with a healthy dose of annoyance.

"Stop saying 'wound' like I have a life-threatening injury."

She let out a sigh and reached over to retrieve her napkin. He took the opportunity to grasp her hand.

"Stanton…" She said his name like a prayer. Tugged her hand, but he held tight as he stood up and leaned across the table.

"How do you want this, Dominique? Messy and full of crushed shellfish, or in my bed?"

She gasped, and he let the fullness of his arousal hit him at the sight of her pupils dilating under the chandelier that hung over the table. He pulled her hand to his face, keeping their faces inches apart, and stroked the inside of her wrist, her palm, with his tongue.

"No, wait." Breathless, she tugged her hand from his grasp and this time he let go. The seconds it took her to walk around the end of the table and stop next to him felt like eternity. She didn't touch him, didn't move, but stared up at him. "If we do this, it will change everything." Her eyes beseeched him but he didn't know what she was asking. What had he missed?

"It doesn't have to. It can make things better." He balled his hands into fists to keep from reaching for her before she was ready. This had to be entirely her choice.

"How?" She kept staring at him, and he saw her eyes move as if she was absorbing every inch of his face. Her skin, smooth as silk, highlighted the dark curtain of hair that flowed over her shoulders like inky black liquid. He'd never met anyone more beautiful.

"We can make a new ending for ourselves." He thought it was the most brilliant thing he'd ever thought of. Except for the pit in his gut that told him he didn't want anything to do with "ending" what he and Dominique shared.

Her lips lifted into a small smile. "I'd like that. A different last memory."

"So you're in?" Waiting for her to answer took all his strength.

"Yes, Stanton. I'm in." Only when her hands touched his shoulders, her arms wound around his neck, did he let go.

"This first time isn't going to take very long." He sounded like a Neanderthal and felt more primal as all he could think of was joining together with this woman in the most fundamental way possible. Their lips met without preamble and they progressed to tongues, touching each other's most erotic places and loud groans. When she grasped his length and stroked him through his suit pants, he tore his mouth from hers.

"My bedroom. Now."

"No, here. I can't wait." She hooked a leg over his hip, using the table edge for balance as she moved her pelvis against his. When she nipped at his lower lip, he had no choice but to acquiesce. He'd promised himself to let her do whatever she wanted, however she wanted, to him. Stanton was a man of his word.

DOMINIQUE'S RATIONAL THOUGHT fled the minute Stanton challenged her over the dining room table. It wasn't a choice to go to him, to begin what had been brewing not for the past two days as she'd told herself, but for the last two years. Her entire life, it seemed.

Now she was balanced over him, totally trusting that this was the next right thing to do. Make love to Stanton.

His hands grasped her buttocks and pulled her more snugly against him as he leaned against the table, taking both their weight. The table didn't budge and she sent up a silent thanks for the furniture, heavy and strong. Like Stanton. His erection pressed into her softest place and she thought she'd go insane if she didn't find release with this man, in his arms.

"Kiss me." He compelled her to lower her mouth on his, her hands helping her balance by grasping his shoulders. She lost herself in the kiss, and the sensations rocking her body. It was as if they were teens, she was so close to climaxing…and they were both still dressed.

"Stanton. *Please.*"

Smoky blue eyes, half-lidded, looked at her. "What do you want, babe?"

"You. All of you."

He bucked against her, his breath as short and gasping as hers. "You've got it."

"I mean...not here, in the dining room."

"Tell me where." He eased them both back onto solid ground, and when her soles hit the floor she still clung to him, afraid her legs would give out. She wanted him but not here.

"The sofa. Is that okay?"

"You've got thirty seconds to undress." His growl made her laugh and she shimmied out of her slacks, her cashmere turtleneck. The cool air in the living room was no match for the heat that he'd started with one simmering glance. "Wait."

She paused, her hands on the sides of her red thong. He stood fully nude at the end of the sofa and it was all she could do to not lie back on the cushions and beg him to take her. But she knew he'd always appreciated watching her take off her underwear, and more than anything she wanted to pleasure him the way he did her. Without reservation and with a level of generosity she hadn't known before.

"You're stunning." His fingers traced the line of her red bra covered in black lace, burning a line along her breasts. When he slid the straps off, she reached for him, but he stopped her hands and placed them on his waist. "If you touch me now, this will be over faster than either of us want."

"I need you, Stanton."

"I know, babe. It's a two-way street with us." He unclasped her bra and dropped it to the side, allowing her breasts to spring free and brush his chest. The thick mat of hair scratched against her nipples, already hard, and would have made the heat between her legs almost unbearable, if it wasn't so delightful.

"Only you know how to make me this hot, babe." She admitted the secret she'd kept for too long.

"No one can possibly enjoy you as much as I do." His teeth grazed her sensitive skin along her throat, down the curve to her shoulder. "Just wait." But she didn't have to wait as he reached between them, down to her apex, and slipped one, two fingers into her.

"Stanton, I can't hold...on..." Her sudden climax rocked her against him, her body refusing to do anything but accept pure pleasure from the man her heart had never let go.

"That's it." He waited for her to come down from the ride before easing them both onto the sofa, where she spread her legs and watched him don a condom. When he looked at her, he wore an expression she wanted to never forget. Of a man who'd searched forever for the right partner, and finally found her.

"Come here, Stanton. It's your turn."

"No 'turns,' babe. Just us."

He entered her in one sure thrust, and she told herself she'd hang on to meet him, to make sure they both orgasmed at the same time. But after only two strokes she was breaking apart again, screaming his name. Stanton kept thrusting and as she again peaked, he yelled out.

Dominique relished his full weight as he collapsed against her, the sensation of him inside her and their joining the only thing that made perfect sense in the midst of the danger they'd found.

DOMINIQUE SLEPT THE deepest and longest she had since starting on Charlie's story. As she became aware of her surroundings, she saw that it was dark outside, dawn's first fingers of soft peach light at least an hour away. Lying on her side, facing the wide, paned windows of the guest room that overlooked the lake, she was aware of Stanton's breath fanning her neck, his arm resting around her waist. It was the arm he'd injured by protecting her outside of GGPD. First the bullet had nicked him, and then he'd jammed his shoulder when he'd forced them both down. He'd finally admitted just how sore it was after their third round of lovemaking. His wince as she'd dried him off after their second shower spoke volumes. His waterproof bandage had survived the night, much to her delight, but the bruising and swelling clued her in as to how much pain he must be in. He'd agreed to ibuprofen and an ice pack, hence his ability to sleep soundly. His snores were comforting, and a tear spilled down her cheek. It was insane but true: she'd missed Stanton's snores.

Don't get used to it.

She allowed herself to mentally replay the last eight hours. After they'd had mind-blowing sex in the living room, they'd almost made it to the bedroom before they detoured to the bathroom and the tiled shower. Then later, much later, they'd taken their time in his bed, savoring each and every stroke, kiss and whispered plea.

Well, at least *she* knew she'd savored it all. It seemed Stanton did, too, but she couldn't go there. If she did, it'd be too easy to think they'd be able to pick up where they'd left off, or maybe a few moments before he'd proposed and she'd freaked out. Why hadn't she at least told him all she needed was a break, instead of ending it like that?

Fear, pure and simple. She'd been afraid of the strength of their connection. Since that first time they'd met and he'd convinced her to go for coffee with him, she'd known that Stanton was going to change her life. It had been during an early spring snowstorm and she'd been at GGPD to research a story. Stanton had stopped in to check on Melissa, who'd had a particularly rough time with a case that required her to fire her weapon. Dominique had noticed his physique first—it was impossible to pass up the way his body filled his custom-tailored suits—but once she looked into those brilliant baby blues, the ground under her boots had moved. She remembered the outfit she'd worn, too—short black wool skirt, ribbed tights, her favorite red Hunter rubber boots. It had bothered her that she was in the more practical boots instead of her killer heeled leather ones—that was how badly she'd wanted to impress him. Because he'd impressed the heck out of her. Their romance was storybook. Until long work hours on both their parts, complicated by both of their driven natures, had turned the romance part sour.

The sex, though—that had never been anything but sweet. And hot.

His arm moved, his hand reaching for hers, intertwining their fingers. "Why aren't you sleeping?"

"Neither are you."

"Are you okay?" he asked.

"I'm good."

"Stop."

"Stop what?"

"You're overthinking this. Just enjoy it. We can both use the rest, and—" he shifted and rose up, swearing as he put weight on his bad arm "—it's still dark out. Let's try for another hour."

She turned onto her back and looked at him. "Do you need more ibuprofen? You could piggyback it with Tylenol if the pain's worse."

"I'll live. It didn't wake me up."

"I'm sorry that I did. I suppose it's the strange bed. But I slept like a log until now."

"Your brain never shuts down," he said.

"Neither does yours."

"Shhh." He settled on his back and indicated she should rest her head on his shoulder.

"No, not this side. You're bruised. Here." She got up and quickly rounded the bed, slid under the covers next to him, on his uninjured side. "Your shoulder is a hard pillow."

"Then come here." He helped her snuggle down onto

his chest, and she forced her thoughts to a back burner. Stanton was correct. This wasn't the time to rethink anything. As her cheek lay against his bare chest, his hair tickling her skin but in the best way, her body relaxed against him. Her lids grew heavy and the last thing she heard before drifting back to sleep was the sound of his heartbeat under her ear. Slow and steady. Dependable.

For a precious moment, she forgot she was in the crosshairs of a killer.

Chapter Eleven

Stanton woke later that morning to an empty bed. He looked around the room and saw no signs that Dominique had ever been in here, save for her scent in the sheets. His arm complained as he rolled to sit on the side of his bed. The doc was right; he'd need more meds to keep it from becoming a distraction. But there wasn't anything he could take, or do, to keep him from his main distraction: Dominique.

She'd rocked his world last night. Judging from her reactions to their lovemaking, she was feeling the same. Except she hadn't stayed, even though she'd drifted back to sleep after waking him up with her restlessness before dawn. The sound of the guest shower door closing and running water told him where she was. But it gave no clue as to what she was thinking or feeling. Did she already regret their actions?

His phone buzzed with calendar alerts related to Colton Protection and he allowed a wave of relief to calm him down. At least he had his business to take care of while he waited for Dominique to conduct more police interviews and probably stop at the *Gazette* today. He'd been able to put her off going into her office long enough. Security training told him she didn't need to be anywhere near an obvious place she normally went. It would make her an easier target for the cartel to hit. Yet he also knew that Jimenez shied away from highly visible sites for shootouts. He preferred dark alleys, far from the glare of public opinion. To try to take out Dominique at the local media outlet was plain stupid. Of course, Stanton thought firing outside of the police station wasn't a brilliant move, either. Yet it had happened, and from the texts he had from Troy, it was a confirmed cartel hit.

He called Melissa to see if there was any other news on Jimenez or cartel-related crime.

"Chief Colton."

"It's me. Your brother Stanton." Usually she answered with a warmer greeting. Her curt identification underscored how stressed she was.

"I know. I'm sorry. It's all hands on deck, as I'm sure you caught a whiff of yesterday."

"Anything I need to know for my current assignment?"

"Other than keep Dominique in hiding until this is all over, which she's not going to agree to? No, nothing I can really talk about yet."

"I'm not asking you to tell me any details, but give me a break, Melissa. If there's more threats against Dominique I have the right to know."

"It doesn't get worse than being in a kingpin's crosshairs, does it?"

Tension practically crackled over their connection, unusual for the Colton siblings. Recrimination flooded his gut. "Hey, sis, I'm sorry. You're in a crappy mess right now and the last thing you need is any pressure from me. I'm sure I'll be in there with you later in the day. Dominique's far from finished with her long line of interview subjects."

"Look, Stanton. I'm trying to get Dominique another interview with the lab assistant who was fired as the other one didn't give her anything, thanks to Internal Affairs. I know why they're not willing to budge, but I'm hoping to get approval for Bonnie to open up to her."

"Let me guess, you have some leverage?" He knew Dominique was stymied by the lack of transparency and he saw her point, and also felt for his sister's position.

Melissa's pained grunt told him all he needed to know. "I'm trying, Stanton, believe me. And I meant what I said to you both yesterday. The sooner we get to the bottom of this the better for all of Grave Gulch, but especially Dominique. I'm open to anything she needs, anyone she wants to interview, to complete her story."

"I know." He wished Melissa would just throw down a gauntlet and say that Dominique couldn't come back to GGPD or interview any officers or employees until they had Jimenez in custody. But he couldn't ask her to do that, and she wouldn't. Melissa's remonstration over his trying to convince Dominique this story wasn't worth her life proved it.

"I'll see you both later, then? How's it going by the way, out at the lake house?"

"Ah, fine. It's nice to have the place to ourselves."

"How 'nice' are we talking?" Uh-oh. The elder sister that he was never able to get anything past was on the line.

"We'll see you later, Melissa." Before he hit the red "end call" button, he heard his sister's laughter. At least he'd managed to lighten her mood.

DOMINIQUE WAS HAPPY to let Stanton drive them back to town as it allowed her time on her laptop to summarize what she'd learned yesterday and highlight the answers she still sought. The real bonus was not having to look Stanton in the eye. The things they'd done last night!

No. She made herself sit taller in the passenger seat. She was not going to be embarrassed about expressing her sexuality with Stanton or any other man. Not that there'd been another since him. She'd tried to date here and there but had never gotten past the first meetup. Her heart had never let go of Stanton.

"Thanks for agreeing to take me to my office first." She owed him that much.

"I don't want to, and as your expert guard I'd advise against it. But I know you well enough to understand your need to get into the *Gazette* and see your colleagues face-to-face."

"It's more than that. I need to verify some of my sources, and it's best to do it on-site, with all of the tools we have." She also needed to back up the files she'd accumulated so far. It didn't do to trust the cloud when such a powerful cartel was the subject of an exposé. "You can work on Colton Protection stuff in the lounge. You always enjoyed it there before." As soon as she referred to their time together, she wanted to bite her tongue. Stanton had been the perfect gentleman this morning, not teasing her at all about last night. It wasn't like him. He used to love to make her blush, and she was an easy target for his gentle flirting, no matter how much she enjoyed their sex life.

"As long as I have you in my line of sight, I'm cool with it."

"You can't have a straight view of me if I'm in my office." Why did he have to be so unreasonable? Her spaces were safe.

"Then either I work in your office with you, or you enjoy the lounge with me."

The answer was made up for her because immediately upon passing through the building and then the *Gazette*'s second layer of security, Dominique was thronged by her colleagues. High fives, congratulatory greetings and smiles contributed to a festive atmosphere. All were excited over the scoop she'd obtained regarding the Randall Bowe sighting in the park. Stanton took a seat at a small workstation and fired up his laptop.

When the exuberance died down and the other journalists went back to work, Stanton was still on his laptop, looking up to ascertain her presence on a regular basis. Warmth and regret mingled in her center, her affection for him making the reality that they could never be a couple again all the more poignant. He must have sensed her consideration as he looked up from his screen and his brows rose in query.

"I'll work out here with you. Most of the people I need to talk to will be stopping by to grab a cup of coffee, anyway." She plopped down in the workstation across from his, careful to give him lots of space. Thankfully he'd taken a single spot without an extra chair, so it didn't seem odd that she sat at a different table. The last thing she needed was an accidental brush of her thigh against his, or any other body contact. She squeezed her eyes shut, willing the mental images of last night away. They were a treasure she could unlock and examine again when she was alone, after Jimenez was caught. When she no longer required a bodyguard, and Stanton was once again out of her life.

The thought was so sad that she opened her eyes and got right to work. Whatever it took to keep from wondering why it was so painful, when she'd been the one to walk away in the first place.

STANTON'S PHONE LIT up with a text from Melissa.

Have Dominique stop by GGPD. I've cleared the interview with the lab assistant.

His first impulse was to fire back, *Why don't you tell her yourself?* Melissa had Dominique's contact information and he saw this for what it was. His sister wanted him to give Dominique the good news, make him appear as the good guy. Melissa was too busy to be playing matchmaker but he'd learned long ago that some things weren't worth arguing over. Especially when Melissa had her hands full with bad cops and beating back a powerful surge of crime.

"You look...bemused." Dominique placed a mug of coffee next to him.

"Thanks. Actually, I have some good news." His sister might be annoying but he had to admit, it felt good to see Dominique's eyes light up as she continued to look at him. She'd been avoiding him all morning. To be fair, he'd done the same. Mornings after were never easy.

"Oh yeah?"

"Yeah. Melissa said you should stop by GGPD as soon as you can. Internal Affairs has completed the Randall Bowe portion of the internal investigation and the lab assistant is free to discuss everything with you."

"That's great! Not that it shouldn't have happened sooner, of course." He bit back a grin. Typical Dominique, always making certain that he knew she hadn't missed or forgotten an iota of the situation.

"I thought you'd be pleased."

"Melissa had you be the messenger, eh?" She regarded him. "Is she afraid to talk to me directly, or was she trying to give you a friendly shove toward me?"

Surprise gave him pause. "You miss nothing."

"It's my job. Observation." Her cheeks flushed, reminding him of her nipples, dark and hard under his fingers, his tongue. He broke eye contact, needing to mentally regroup. Before he convinced himself that there was a way he could persuade himself and Dominique that they belonged together and could work it all out.

It hadn't worked before, and nothing had changed from what he'd witnessed this morning at the *Grave Gulch Gazette*. Dominique's goal was to win a Pulitzer, and commitment in terms of family and kids wasn't in her wheelhouse. Why couldn't he just accept that?

Nope. Not something he was going to think about. Been there, done that, got the broken heart.

"I WANT YOU at the table with me and Bonnie Stadler. And not just because you're my bodyguard." At GGPD again, Melissa had given Dominique the former lab assistant Bonnie Stadler's information. Dominique had scored a meeting at the coffee shop with her and was in no mood to deal with Stanton's suddenly hands-off approach. Since they'd walked into GGPD, he'd expressed his desire to sit in the break room and work.

"You didn't want me with you at the *Gazette*, yet now you do?" His blue eyes were laced with Arctic ice.

"If I wasn't already certain you're such a badass tough guy, I'd swear you're goading me to a fight." She sank into the chair opposite him and looked around to make sure they were alone. It seemed the police station was as overwhelmed as the newspaper, with the constant stream of events thanks to the cartel, the ongoing corruption scandal at GGPD and Randall Bowe's recent sighting. "The interviews go smoother if you're there. Your presence adds—"

"Stability?" Only after she felt her face grow hot did he allow a slow grin to crease his face. Her gaze lingered on his lips, unable to look away. He was a maestro with that mouth. And his hands…

She blinked, shook her head. It didn't matter if he knew that he'd thrown her off balance. Her hormones had been doing their own thing since he'd saved her life. "Call it whatever you want. But there's something else." She looked away, back at him again. "Until they are certain they've caught the corrupt cops, how do we know the lab assistant isn't one of the bad guys? I mean, Randall Bowe's already a definite, so why not his colleague? If I were working against GGPD, being paid off by the cartel, I'd make it look like my boss was all to blame, too."

"Why don't you just bat your eyelashes at me while you're at it, Dominique?" He ground out the words and she allowed herself a chuckle at his expense.

"Since you're in charge of my safety, I figured you'd want to know all the angles."

He gathered his laptop and bag without comment and they proceeded to the exit. Stanton checked the street before motioning for Dominique to walk next to him. They headed for the coffee shop, a few blocks away.

"Are you certain you have an interview?"

"You're the one who told me Melissa arranged it." Doubt crept in, though, her hopes sinking as she acknowledged the possibility that the woman might not show.

"If you wanted to get me alone, all you had to do was ask." His jest calmed her. This was preferable to the awful quiet in the car this morning, when she'd wondered if he was regretting all they'd done last night. She'd figured out that while it might not have been her smartest move, or moves as it were, she would never regret the time with Stanton. The past couple of days had taught her the hard way just how short life was.

"Stanton, I want to come clean with you on something. About last night—"

"Nope, no talking about personal stuff during working hours."

Dominique took his interruption for what it was. Last night was supposed to be a final, better farewell for each other. Not something to rehash. Fine.

They arrived at the café and he held the door for her. When she entered, she spied a woman sitting alone at the counter and walked up to her.

"Excuse me, are you—"

"Bonnie Stadler, the former GGPD lab assistant? Yes. You must be Dominique." The woman had silver hair and bright green eyes that assessed both she and Stanton. Her features matched the photo the *Gazette* had used when her termination was announced.

"Yes, I'm Dominique de la Vega, with the *Grave Gulch Gazette*. This is Stanton Colton, my personal security advisor." She didn't look at Stanton as she was certain he was trying not to laugh. But "bodyguard" sounded overdone inside a friendly cafe.

"Stanton and I met at the GGPD Christmas party last year." Bonnie smiled at him.

Stanton nodded. "We did."

"Let's get our drinks and sit down." Stanton placed their order before walking with them to a table. Dominique and Stanton took stools across from Bonnie, who leaned back against a wall. She looked Dominique in the eyes, her expression grim. "I'm glad I finally have the opportunity to talk to you about everything. I'm sorry I couldn't see you sooner but until the internal investigation committee gave me the okay, my hands were tied."

"I understand." And she did. But now she wanted answers. "Why don't we begin with what you feel Randall did wrong, if you would?"

"Sure. As long as this is off the record? I want to help you get the story but I don't want my name in the paper."

"That's fine." Dominique's patience was wearing thin but she felt Stanton's calm presence and did her best to soak it in.

Bonnie crossed her arms in front of her chest. "My work here was ideal up until about a year ago. I enjoyed working for Randall. He was a generous boss and mentor, and I learned so much from him. As you can see, I'm no spring chicken. I went back to college in my late fifties and got my degree. I wasn't sure I'd ever be able to land such a plum job. It's very satisfying, when we match up evidence to crimes and help nail the bad guys and gals." She paused. "Randall began doing more and more work on his own. At first he said it was because he was having marital problems and needed the extra time away from home. But then I noticed that I wasn't seeing anything that had to do with the more serious crimes. Randall had processed the evidence and filed his report before I ever set eyes on it. We worked on Drew Orr's case, and Everleigh Emerson's, but I wasn't allowed to so much as read the evidence reports. I thought that was odd, for a man who'd so strongly mentored me previously."

"What kind of evidence are we talking about?"

"The usual. Fingerprints, bullet casings, blood stains, DNA. Mostly we test for fingerprints, the breakdowns of batches of heroin—how much fentanyl it's been cut with, if any—and occasional blood types when there's an assault or worse. Anything with DNA or more complicated lab work gets sent out. Still, we could accomplish an impressive amount of work at GGPD, to enable our officers to get their jobs done. And, of course, our work aided the DA when it's time to prosecute the criminal."

"What specifically do you know Randall Bowe did or didn't do?"

"Several things. First, he was a witness in several court cases against drug dealers for this local cartel. In each case, he testified, under oath, that there was no evidence he'd consider valid for use against the dealers. It took me a while to put it together, but one night I worked late and needed the file for a heroin OD. I wanted to verify the officer's report that the user who'd died was also a dealer. The officer bagged dozens of bags of heroin. When I opened the file, there was no mention of the drugs. Nothing. As if the officer never filed the evidence. I questioned Randall about it the next morning and he said he'd tested the powder, only to discover it was all baking soda."

"Has that ever happened before?"

"Never. We've had one or two times with fake drugs, but that doesn't happen with *this* cartel. They're slick and here to do one thing—make money. How I finally proved that Randall was lying to me was that I found the evidence the officer had brought in, stuffed in a tea tin, you know the kind you find at specialty stores? Randall's a big tea drinker. I'd had other cases that he'd taken over go bad, in my opinion. So I took it upon myself to search his office when he was out."

"Did you confront him with what you found?"

"No. I was terrified, frankly. I'm not sure if you know, but he'd recently purchased a Lamborghini. Really stupid, if you ask me, because it's a red flag when a government employee all of a sudden affords luxury anything. I figured there was a good chance that he was being paid by the cartel to stifle evidence, make it disappear. I wanted to talk to the officers who brought the evidence in, but I didn't know who to trust anymore. Once someone you've trusted, who has made a good difference in your life, goes bad, it's very upsetting."

"So you reported it."

"I did. I went to Lansing, took a personal day, and reported it. I felt awful, going over Chief Colton's head, even though I was fired." Her eyes darted to where Stanton sat, taking it all in. She knew Melissa was his sister. "Randall disappeared days after I reported him, from what I understand. And it looks as though there could be one or two bad cops who've been helping him, too, from what I've read in the paper. It makes me sick to think I was working next to someone who let a serial killer go free. None of us are safe until Len Davison is caught." Bonnie shook her head. "Tough times for Grave Gulch."

"Can you tell me, Bonnie, if you know anything about Charlie Hamm, about his case?"

"The convict who died in the prison fight a while back?"

"Yes."

"We've had so many cases. But I remember his in particular because one day there wasn't a lot of evidence in his file and the next, a suitcase was there. Randall wouldn't answer my questions about it." As Bonnie spoke, Dominique snuck a look at Stanton. His blue gaze steadied her, and he gave her a slight nod. He thought she was handling this well, on the right track.

"I haven't been able to confirm that Charlie's fingerprint wasn't on the suitcase. He swore it couldn't have been his."

Bonnie nodded. "I agree. Randall Bowe made up what he wanted to for the witness stand. Charlie's wasn't the only case. But I got fired before I could do anything more to help."

Dominique looked at Stanton again, and saw her satisfaction at finding the truth reflected in his gaze.

They really made a good team.

It's only temporary.
Best she remember that.

THE DE LA VEGA home was lit up as Dominique and Stanton walked up to the front door. He'd insisted on coming because he was her bodyguard, yes, but he'd always enjoyed her family.

"You can wait outside if it's going to be too awkward. You know my sister is going to assume we're an item again."

He wanted to remind her that for one blissful night they had been an item again, and a hot one at that. But her stilted mannerisms communicated her insecurity over the situation. Dominique's family was from Colombia originally, and she and her twin, Soledad, were first-generation Americans. Rigo had married an American woman he met when he was serving in the US Navy as an exchange officer, in Jacksonville, Florida. She was from Grave Gulch and he'd promised to bring her back to her hometown as soon as his military stint was over. That had been before Dominique and her twin were born, over thirty years ago. Their mother had passed five years ago, leaving Rigo heartbroken.

"I wouldn't dream of it, and not just because I can't let you out of my sight. I love your family and your dad's great."

"He's paying you."

"Handsomely, I might add." Stanton couldn't help teasing her.

"Okay. Well, I gave you an out."

"You did." And she might not believe it, but he was looking forward to the party.

They walked into the amber glow of family, friends and the most enticing aromas of the meal, catered by a local favorite restaurant if the logo on a delivery van in the driveway was an indication. Rigo's pair of boxer dogs trotted over to greet them.

"Hi, girls." Dominique squatted to pet them, accepting sloppy kisses from Rosa and Rita. Another reason he'd fallen for her way back when. She didn't care about what mattered, like the mess a dog's affection could make. As much attention to detail as she paid to her outfits, and as expertly as she applied her makeup, Dominique was grounded.

Dangerous territory.

"Dominique!" Aunt Gloria walked over, her dark hair worn long like her niece's but with strands of silver that reflected the overhead lighting. Her eyes widened as she recognized him standing behind Dominique. "And Stanton—wonderful to see you again." Gloria hugged him and he hugged her back, feeling as though he was some kind of prodigal son. Which was ridiculous, as he hadn't been the one to walk away. And Aunt Gloria wasn't even Dominique's, or his, mother.

You pushed Dominique away. You let her go.

He mentally bristled. Hadn't he been the one who'd reached out with texts, phone calls? And Dominique had let them all go without one single response. Her silence had given ghosting a whole new meaning for him that included pain, shame and regret. He felt a wet tongue on his hand and looked down at Rosa, whose soft brown eyes were beseeching him, as if to say, "Why did you stop coming 'round?" Rita sat patiently and waited for him to pet Rosa, then accepted his attention.

"Where's Dad?" Dominique scanned the spacious great room where friends and family mingled in several groups.

"Back in the kitchen with your uncles."

Dominique looked at Stanton. "Come on. Let's get it over with." Her grin relieved him. At least she wasn't harboring a grudge about her father any longer, for hiring him without her permission. Maybe Dominique would actually enjoy this time with her family.

They walked around a wall to the kitchen, which overlooked part of the great room and the roaring fireplace. So typical for a de la Vega function, the men and women chatting and enjoying themselves.

"*Mija*. Come here." Rigo held open his arms for Dominique, and Stanton waited while they embraced, nodding at the other men who were mostly Rigo's brothers and close family friends.

"Happy Birthday, Daddy."

"Thank you, but let's not talk about birthdays. I'm too old for this." His grin belied his words and the low rumble of male laughter surrounded them. Rigo's dark eyes sparkled. "Who's this handsome man you've brought to our fiesta?"

"Funny, Dad." Dominique turned and greeted the

other men before she returned her attention to Stanton. "I'm going to find my sister. Are you okay with me not staying in here with you?"

"Yes. As long as I can see you." The house was spacious but small enough that he'd be able to keep her in sight range, as long as she stayed on the same floor, as she caught up with Soledad.

"Great." She poured sparkling water into two large red plastic cups and gave him one. "We're both on duty, aren't we?"

"Cheers." He tipped his and as their cups touched he looked into her eyes. There was a light in them that he'd normally attribute to appreciation, but what was she grateful for? It couldn't be him, specifically. That he'd agreed to them coming to the family party, much closer to the center of Grave Gulch?

"Cheers." She smiled and before he realized her intention, leaned up on her tiptoe and smacked his cheek with a very loud, definite kiss. "Don't ever change."

Stunned, he watched her sway as she left the room and walked over to where Soledad stood in front of the fireplace.

A hard grasp on his shoulder by her *tío* Héctor reminded him he wasn't alone. "She sure is a beauty, my niece. What are your intentions, *amigo*?" The group of men again erupted in laughter, but Stanton didn't miss Rigo's more measured look. Like him, the older man seemed to wonder what indeed his plans were for his and Dominique's relationship.

Aw, man, he was so screwed. He'd begun thinking of them as having a relationship again. Not the best place mentally, when she had a big bullseye on her back and a cartel kingpin who wouldn't stop until she was dead.

Chapter Twelve

"You look tired, sis." Dominique motioned for Soledad to join her on the ledge of the stone-front fireplace. The heat warmed her back, still sore from the attack and then Stanton's heroic save in front of the police station.

Soledad laughed. "I'm always tired by six o'clock. You would be, too, if you got up at two a.m. to bake bread Monday through Saturday. I'm usually getting ready for bed about now."

"I suppose you're right." She didn't want to scare her sister, but her curiosity won out. "Have you noticed anything unusual around our apartment building?" They rented at the same address, their apartments across the hall from one another.

"Like what?" Deep lines appeared between Soledad's brows. "Drug deals?" She knew Dominique was digging up information on the local cartel; Dominique had told her twin all about Charlie Hamm and his poetry.

"No. Strange people, probably men, lurking about?" Soledad tilted her head slightly, her gaze on their mother's colorful silk rug. "No, not at all. Are you thinking that the kingpin has a stakeout on you?"

"You know I am. I know you told Dad about my story, Soledad. And he hired Stanton to protect me. I meant to call sooner but, well, it's been chaotic."

"I figured you'd be upset that I told Dad, but can you blame me? I'm worried about you. When he told me he'd hired Stanton, I knew you'd be really ticked off. I thought you weren't calling me until you cooled down. I only told him because I care, sis."

"I appreciate that, but I wish you'd talked to me first."

"Like that would have convinced you to let this story go, or to at least stop instigating a cartel leader to place a target on your back?"

"This isn't all about me, Soledad. There are lives at stake, not to mention the justice I'm seeking for Charlie. This cartel is particularly nasty. They'll go after my family if they think it'll make a difference in whether I keep digging. Please be aware of your surroundings until these bad players are caught. I don't want you to take your personal security for granted."

"Trust me, I don't. I'm not the fearless soul between us, remember?" Soledad's query made Dominique smile.

"Of course I do."

"I'm not sure you do. I'm the one who likes to bake cookies and bread, who made a living out of producing comfort food. You've always been about the adrenaline rush, getting to the truth. Remember when you stuck up for both of us to those three bullies in middle school?"

"Hey, if I hadn't known you were behind me, ready with your baton from drill team, I might not have been so bold." She'd told off all three boys, who'd kept following her and Soledad home from school, to the bus stop, around the school corridors if they stayed after for one of the various clubs they'd enjoyed at the time. Soledad was in the gourmet bakers' club and Dominique found her twelve-year-old kindred spirits in the school paper's office. The memories brought back the scents of that room, from the dusty reams of computer paper stacked against the brick walls, to the dry eraser ink as she'd written on the large whiteboard at one end of the classroom-turned-newsroom. She'd known in her bones that journalism was her calling. No amount of encouragement from well-meaning English teachers who'd insisted her talents might be better used in fiction and its myriad genres mattered. Dominique had answered her soul's calling to find the truth and write about it.

"You're thinking about the school paper, aren't you?" Soledad prompted.

"Of course. Telling those boys to leave us alone was one thing. We scared them for a bit. But what kept them away was the editorial." Dominique had snuck in the bullies' full names, totally against school policy. It had cost her detention for a week straight. "It was all worth it. They never bothered anyone again."

"They didn't." Soledad eyed her. "I get that you're always going to be chasing down justice. It's in your blood. But don't you want more out of life?"

"More?" She tried to keep a cool countenance as her sister seemed intent on her emotional jugular.

"Don't stare at me like a hungry goldfish." Soledad's command sent them both into a fit of giggles, remembering the poor sad creatures they'd won one year at their local parish picnic. They'd come home with the fish swimming in dyed water, pink and green, in fishbowls that fit in their hands. Mom had immediately purchased a large bowl complete with filter, much to Rigo's chagrin.

"They lived for three years. A record."

"Mine lived a day longer." Soledad made Dominique's giggles start all over again. "Back to the subject, sister of mine. I don't know about you, but I've been having serious baby pangs lately."

"What?" Dominique wasn't surprised that Soledad was thinking about starting her own family, but she wasn't in a serious relationship at the moment. "As in, you want a baby no matter what?"

Soledad waved her hand in dismissal. "No, not yet. I mean, I hope I find someone to start a family with. You already have found your soul mate, Dominique. Why aren't you jumping on it?"

Usually they'd have a good laugh over Soledad's choice of wording, as it was a perfect euphemism for sex. Dominique couldn't speak past what felt like a sucker punch to her gut, the snarl of emotion in her throat.

"We—we're—we're not together, Soledad." She

hissed her response, not wanting any of their father's guests to hear.

"Come on, Dominique. You two were making eyes at each other in the kitchen over your water, for heaven's sake." Soledad placed her hand on her wrist. "Hey, I'm sorry. You've been through an awful lot these past few days, and I know you haven't told me all of it. Don't think I haven't noticed the bruises still on your throat."

"I told you I ran into trouble. Stanton was there. He saved my life, I realize now. And has again since then, too. Twice."

"That's why I told Dad, sis. If anything ever happened to you…" Soledad's matching dark eyes filled with tears. Dominique shared her sister's concern, because she felt the exact same way about her twin.

"I know. And I'm sorry that I haven't kept you up on all of the story's developments."

"I don't care about the story, this one or any other, as much as I care about you. I want to know what you're thinking, and what you're feeling." Soledad poked her in the chest for emphasis. Right over her heart, a heart that raced at the emotions this conversation had set free. As if unbridled by Stanton last night while they made love, her hormones raced around, and it wasn't solely about sex anymore.

Was this deep longing in her soul, the one she'd ignored for the last two years, not only due to her breakup with Stanton, but in fact an unrecognized-by-her biological clock's incessant ticking? More likely, it was her extreme regret that she hadn't given Stanton another chance. Heard him out, and allowed him to hear her out, after things had settled. Because if she had, they might be at a point now where having kids wouldn't feel so strange. Where they both accepted each other's jobs, and the inherent risks with them. Wasn't that what two mature, loving partners did?

"You look like you've seen a ghost."

"Maybe I have. Of my past, present and future."

Soledad rolled her eyes. "Stop making it so dramatic. It doesn't have to be a twisted Dickens plot. There's nothing more natural than wanting to settle down, have a home, build a family, if that's what is right for you."

"Maybe." She'd focused on her career so much and had thought she'd found the perfect partner in Stanton, before. Before he'd decided that the only relationship they could have would be if she'd quit her job, or at least switched to "safer" stories, and have his babies. But had he ever asked her to quit? Or demanded that he wanted kids? As she reviewed that painful day, all he'd been asking her, and insisting upon, was that they marry. And that yes, he wanted children as soon as possible. But could she have convinced him to wait?

"What? Tell me, sister."

"I know it's not like me, but these past days with Stanton have got me thinking. Maybe it isn't such an awful idea to think we could have made a go of it. And you know how you're always saying you can feel your eggs screaming for a baby daddy?" They both giggled. "You know what I mean. I think mine are, too, but I ignored it before. Shoved it down."

"So you, Dominique de la Vega, are admitting that— *gasp*—your biological clock is ticking?"

"I suppose I am." But it wasn't a purely biological event. It had everything to do with the sexy man standing in her dad's kitchen, laughing and talking with her relatives as though he were part of the family, too.

"What does Stanton think?"

"I haven't mentioned any of this to him, how could I?" At Soledad's mind-meld stare, she relented. "Oh. My. Goodness. I think I may have made a huge mistake with one of the people who meant the most to me." Recrimination reared its nasty head and pried at her peace of mind, what little she had left. "What a mess I've made of things."

"Well, duh. He was stupid to give you an ultimatum about marriage two years ago, and you were equally idiotic to not answer his texts and calls. We've already determined this. That doesn't matter now. My point is, what are you going to do about it today?"

"I, I'm—"

Her phone buzzed and she pulled it out of her red leather cross-body bag. It was from her senior editor.

Hamm witness wants to talk to you on landline in office. Come in ASAP.

She looked at Soledad, who stared at her with expectation. "Spill it, Dominique. What are you going to do about Stanton now?"

"I'm not doing anything but getting to the *Grave Gulch Gazette*. I've got a break in my story."

"We haven't even sung *'Feliz Cumpleaños'* yet. Dad has to blow out his candles. All fifty-nine of them."

"More like put them out with a fire extinguisher." At Soledad's shocked gasp she laughed. "I'm teasing. He's the one who said he's too old for birthdays."

"Fifty-nine isn't old." Soledad stood with her and held out her hand. "Give me your cup. You go and do whatever you have to."

"Thanks, sweetie." She kissed Soledad on the cheek, gave her a big hug and relished the resounding hug back. There was no one who knew her better than her sister.

Except perhaps one man, who stared at her from the kitchen with unmistakable admiration. And maybe something more that flickered in those indigo depths.

STANTON RECOGNIZED DOMINIQUE'S straight-spined posture, her purposeful strides toward the kitchen as confirmation that the text he watched her read was important.

Her perfume reached him a split second before she did and his nostrils soaked it up. As if being separated for the last half hour was a lifetime. He stifled a groan, the urge to get out of the house, away from her. Away from a second broken heart. He had a job to complete, and he would. Then they'd be out of each other's lives again.

"What is it?"

"I have to go into the *Gazette* offices." She held up her phone so that he could read the text. His stomach clenched as he realized what this might mean. Besides giving Dominique her story, the witness who lied on the stand and sent Charlie to prison might very well know who attacked her.

"What are you talking about, going into work?" Rigo's rich tenor flowed across the kitchen and he watched the interaction between father and daughter. Dominique blushed under her father's scrutiny. Stanton felt sorry for Rigo; he was about to find out what came first for his daughter and it wasn't going to be a birthday party.

"I do have to go in tonight, briefly." She shot a look at Stanton to see if he was going to rat her out. He stayed quiet, wondering how she could justify blowing off her father's celebration. "But not until later. I'm here until the cake is served, Daddy." She walked over to Rigo and gave him a hug. "Nothing's more important than family."

Stanton watched in dumbfounded silence. Where was the Dominique who'd stormed out of his apartment after he'd begged her to stay and start a family with him? Realization dawned and it wasn't welcome. One thing being in security taught him was that denial never kept anybody safe, including him. It was time he admitted the real reason he and Dominique hadn't worked out, despite their incredible chemistry and solid friendship.

It wasn't that Dominique didn't want to settle down; she just didn't want to do it with *him*.

"YOU DIDN'T HAVE any cake." Dominique chided him as they left the house. The cold sting of the early spring night cut through his coat and he shoved black leather driving gloves on.

"Sugar messes with my senses." Not unlike Dominique, but he wasn't having sweet thoughts about her at the moment. And he was telling the truth. He had a terrific sweet tooth and didn't know when to stop when he started. So he mostly didn't start.

"Fair enough. I have to say, though, that it was the best chocolate cake Soledad's ever made. She's finally gotten the cocoa proportions down to a science. It took her since she opened the bakery, and she wouldn't sell chocolate cake there until she got it right." Her admiration for her twin was evident. Like a hot knife searing his gut, right through to his heart.

She didn't want a family with you. Why hadn't he figured this out, seen this, before?

"Stanton, what's wrong? You don't agree with me going into the *Gazette* this late?"

"You're going to do whatever you have to for your story. You always have."

"Ouch. That sounds personal."

"Nothing personal going on here. I'm protecting you and you're choosing to engage in risky behavior."

She stopped in front of the passenger door and faced him. Their breath hung in heavy clouds between them, and he saw her shiver. Dang his arms for wanting to hug her to him, warm her up. His job was to keep her alive, not make her comfortable.

"Something's been bothering you since before Dad blew out his birthday candles. What is it?"

"It's occurred to me that I've read you wrong all along." He couldn't stop his harsh words if he wanted to. "It wasn't that you didn't want to settle down or have a family. It was me. I wasn't the one for you."

Her eyes widened and her mouth gaped open. He'd struck an honest chord, apparently.

"Stanton, that's not true in the least. But this isn't where we're going to have this conversation. And not now, when we're both under a lot of pressure."

"You act as if we'll have things to talk about after the kingpin is captured, after the threat against you is neutralized."

"You never know, we might." Her chin jutted out and her arms were folded across her chest, the way she always held them when he'd angered her.

"I don't know a lot, but one thing I do know, Dominique. When my contract is up with you, so is our time together." The momentary relief he felt at jabbing out at her, inflicting her with the hellish pain he was in, was short-lived. The flicker of confusion across her expression morphed into hurt, and then her icy mask was firmly in place.

"Whatever. Let's go. The sooner I get answers, the more quickly you'll be free from having to spend your time with me." She reached for the door handle.

Explosions rent the night air and he acted on instinct, grabbing her and throwing them both to the ground. A sharp pain ran through his shoulder, his arm, but it was muffled by the adrenaline that immediately began pumping through his blood.

"Stay down."

"Stanton, it's not—"

"We need to get out of here." Fear sliced his heart. He'd been so wrapped up in his hurt, feeling her loss over again, that he'd not been paying attention to their surroundings as he should. He eased off her, onto his knees, and reached for her hand to help her.

"Stanton, no." She sat on the ground, looking up at him. Her hand grasped his. "It's fireworks. My family always shoots them off for birthdays, remember?"

He stared at her, dumbfounded. Laughter and whoops from the back of the house reached them and mortification rushed over him. An uncomfortable heat crawled up his neck.

"I, ah, yeah, I forgot." He shouldn't keep holding her hand, but it was his anchor to reality. He'd allowed himself to be caught in between his feelings for Dominique and the valid fear that she might get hit by Jimenez no matter how well he did his job.

"You okay, Stanton? I'm usually the one who's wound tight." They stood up together, and he couldn't help thinking this was more like her protecting him.

"I'm good. Let's get you to your office."

"I'M GOING TO be stuck here for at least the next few hours. The security guard is on duty, so why don't you rest in the lounge? There's a sofa in there."

"Only if you'll come in with your laptop and work there." Did she really think he'd let his guard down? He might have made a fool of himself with her family's fireworks display, but he wasn't abdicating his duty. Whether Rigo had paid him or not, this was where he belonged.

Protecting Dominique.

"Fine." Her sigh let him know she was as tired as he was of the constant tension between them. Making love the other night had eased it for a bit, but there would always be a level of give-and-take between them.

Once settled in the lounge area, he watched her call numerous people, sometimes by texting first.

"Still no answer from the witness?"

She shook her head. "No. My boss was right to have me come in, as the witness is only going to talk on our office landline. I get it. But he's not been easy to connect with, that's for certain. It took me months to track him down and then convince him to meet with me this week. And you know how that turned out." She pointed at her throat as if he'd need a reminder at how close that jerk had come to strangling her.

"Who else do you want to talk to?"

She pursed her lips in concentration, scrolled on her laptop. "This is becoming so much bigger than Charlie Hamm's story, isn't it? There's Len Davison, serial killer, who targets older men as they walk their dogs. Bowe destroyed evidence against him and blamed Bonnie, his assistant at the time, firing her. The drug cartel wanted to frame Charlie, to keep the heat off of them. Now they're after me. The other person I need to verify statements with, besides Johnny Blanchard, is Charlie's lawyer. His lawyer was less than helpful, frankly, and

I blame his incompetence for Charlie's conviction as much as the false evidence and lying witness."

"Has his attorney ever answered any of your calls?"

"No, but maybe I'll get lucky tonight. Catch him off guard with an evening call." She dialed the phone and put it on speaker. They were alone in the lounge area, the few other reporters working the night shift at their desks, coming in sporadically for hot beverages or to heat up food in the microwave.

"Hello?" A wary greeting.

"Mr. Chambers? This is Dominique de la Vega, from the *Grave Gulch Gazette*."

"I know who you are. I only picked up to tell you in person to stop harassing me. I've got nothing for you."

"I'm sorry, but I have some questions about Charlie's case."

"Don't we all? But the truth, Ms. de la Vega? There are no questions as far as I'm concerned. Charlie was the target of the Jimenez cartel. Yeah, I know all about them, does that surprise you? I've had to protect my family from the cartel, trust me. I suggest you keep yourself safe, because they're ruthless."

"Are you saying you might not have given Charlie's case all of the required efforts because of pressure from the cartel?"

"Heck no. I did what I could for Charlie. But the GGPD lab's director, that Randall Bowe character they just sighted in Grave Gulch Park, he's responsible for Charlie's imprisonment. Him and that darn witness, Blanchard. They made sure Charlie got put away for a long time. And when that wasn't enough, when it was clear Charlie's case was going to be reopened, they had him killed."

Dominique's face paled, then red rushed into her cheeks. "Why do you think that, Mr. Chambers?"

"I don't think it, I know it. Do I have evidence? No. Darn cartel knows the law as well as I do, leaves no crumbs, no traces that would link them to any of the myriad crimes they've committed in this town. Murder's the least of it, if you ask me."

Stanton heard the attorney's frustration, but also wished the man would understand he was speaking to an ally in Dominique.

"All I'm asking, Mr. Chambers, is that we meet and I interview you for the story I'm working on. You of all people will understand that I'm seeking justice for Char—"

"Justice was not served and it won't be until they arrest and prosecute Randall Bowe! Add in the cartel and its entire group of thugs, especially its kingpin. I'm out. I did what I could do for Charlie. He's dead, may he rest in peace. I've accepted that and I'm working on cases where I can still make a difference. I suggest you do the same with the stories you choose to pursue." He ended the connection. Dominique grimaced, but not before Stanton saw the frustrated disappointment in her eyes. His chest ached for her.

"Want a cup of tea? I'm buying." He rose and went to the beverage counter, turned on the coffee maker that took pods of tea, too.

"Sure. Earl Grey." She typed on her laptop with aplomb, as if a nasty, embittered defense attorney hadn't just cussed her out and slammed the phone in her ear.

"What are you writing?"

"He may not be on the record, and I can't use any quotes, but I always keep notes about my conversations and interactions with possible interviewees. You'd be surprised how many of them come around once the bad guys are behind bars and they know they're safe."

"He didn't sound like he was going to change his mind."

"Maybe not, but he has a family to protect. I can't blame him." She paused. "I've been thinking."

Oh boy. Here it came. She was going to lay it on him about their lovemaking, which neither had addressed. He mentally scrambled for an emotionally detached response. Still stinging from overreacting to the fireworks, he needed to demonstrate he had it together.

"Oh?" He pressed the button and waited for her mug to fill.

"I was stupid to show up at my dad's tonight. Family is very important to me, and it would have hurt to miss his party, but honestly, the cartel could have tracked me there and innocent people could have been hurt, or worse."

"I took all precautions to ensure you were not followed."

"I know, but it's a matter of time. I don't think I should go back to the lake house, either. If anything happened to your parents, I'd never forgive myself."

"They're out of town."

"Still…" She blew her hair out of her eyes as she stared at her screen. Was she using it as a shield to keep from looking directly at him? He wouldn't blame her. Whenever their gazes locked, it usually led to either quarreling or being in bed. Neither of which served them at present.

Not that he wouldn't enjoy making love to her again. Dang it, this was going to hurt when it was over. Losing her all over again.

The portable phone unit that was connected to the paper's landline lit up and she hit the speaker function again. "Dominique de la Vega."

"It's Johnny Blanchard." The witness Dominique had sought, had been attacked for, whom he'd taken a bullet graze for.

"Mr. Blanchard, thank you for getting back to me. I'm sorry we haven't been able to connect." Dominique's voice reflected none of the excitement he saw in her alert posture, the way her fingers reached for her cell phone to record the interchange and then flew across her keyboard as she took notes.

"You have no idea. You almost got me killed over this. I want to help you out, but I can't risk coming into the paper, or even into Grave Gulch." His voice was muffled, almost a whisper, and Stanton's hackles were up. If he were alone, wouldn't he be able to speak more clearly?

"Can you tell me where you are?"

"I'm working under an alias at an event place up north. I used to do this before, before…"

"You don't have to explain. Can you tell me where, exactly, and I'll meet you?"

"It's not going to be that simple, Ms. de la Vega. How do I know you won't be followed by them, and bring them to me? I'm safe up here."

"I'm working with the top in the business regarding security. My bodyguard takes all precautions to ensure we're not followed. You can trust me on this."

The static of the connection echoed in the lounge area as Blanchard vacillated.

"You can't bring the cops, whatever you do. Or any kind of personal protection. It'll be a tip-off, if I'm being watched by my former boss. I can't risk it."

"I understand. When were you looking at meeting?"

"I have to work an event on Saturday. It's actually two weddings, one in the morning and one in the afternoon. I think we'll have a better chance of not being targeted, if they're watching us, at such a big public venue." Blanchard gave the information as easily as someone discussing the weather.

"That makes sense to me, but can you give me the address? I have a lot going on with this story and will have to rearrange my schedule." Stanton admired Dominique's ability to sound equally casual, yet continue to pressure him for some answers.

"I'll give you the address at midnight, Friday." He saw her suck in a breath. That would give them only an hour or two of leeway, if this event site was as far "north" as he suspected.

"If you change your mind—"

"I won't. And call me Johnny. We both have too much riding on this to be so formal, Dominique." Before Stanton could let himself get riled by the man's flippant tone with her, he disconnected. Dominique sat still, as if processing what Blanchard had said.

"It's a setup, Dominique."

"Maybe. But maybe not. We can ask GGPD to help us out here, can't we? I don't want to alert the local authorities, wherever this resort is. Besides, there wouldn't be enough time to inform them, and then have the kind of backup we're going to need."

He shook his head. "I don't like this." He hesitated before dropping another information bomb on her. "I heard you on not wanting to involve either of our families in this anymore than needed. Before you suggest it, we can't go to either of our apartments. The cartel's already been checking on both, I'm certain." He set the hot mug of tea next to her laptop, careful to avoid any situation where they'd have skin-to-skin contact. The air was filled with the electricity of the danger they faced. The lethal situation that Dominique was contemplating putting them both in.

"Why don't we go to a hotel? Two adjoining rooms, of course." She blushed and he had a shock of satisfaction for a few seconds, realizing that she was as affected as he was by their being together again.

"I can't trust that. There could be a lookout in every

hotel between here and wherever Blanchard is, especially if it's a setup." He saw the realization soak in as the lines between her brows deepened and her skin paled. The reach of the cartel seemed indomitable. "I do know of a place that's safe, further north."

Chapter Thirteen

"We can go to my parents' cabin."

"The cabin, as in almost five hours away?" Dominique stared at him. "How do you expect me to work there? Do they even have Wi-Fi?"

"Yes, *that* cabin. It's most likely an hour, two at most, from where Blanchard claims to be working. The wedding venues he's talking about are clustered along the lakeshore. I'll surveil it before you can go anywhere near it, Dominique. I'm almost certain this is a setup, but I know you won't let go of it unless we give it a try. We're going to have to have backup from local police, and it'll take time to coordinate it. We'll head up there tonight, and then have all day tomorrow before you meet with him on Saturday."

She contemplated her options as she looked into his vivid eyes. No games, no harsh walls, just Stanton being real with her.

"You're certain the cabin is wired? That it's not a dial-up connection?" She watched the insistence in his eyes meld into laughter.

"Yes, positive. And if it fails, you can use my phone as your hot spot. On my dime."

Stanton and the words "hot spot" were a dangerous combination, so she shifted her attention to the newsfeed exclusive to the *Gazette*. It scrolled on a large monitor mounted in the corner of the lounge room, next to two other monitors that displayed various news outlets and the local police scanner's audio feed. A name caught her attention.

"Stanton, there's been a Len Davison sighting on the outskirts of town." She heard the catch in her voice. It was in the same area they had departed earlier—where her family lived. "I'm calling Troy. Or should I call Melissa?"

"Try Troy first. Melissa's going to be swamped if this is a legit report." His attention was on the monitors, too. As much as she loathed a threat to her family, she experienced some relief to have Stanton's focus elsewhere. Because whenever he looked at her for more than a blink, she internally combusted amid all the conflicting emotions she had for him. For them. For a future with him.

Troy answered on the first try, and she wasted no time getting to the point.

"Is my family safe, Troy?"

"No one's safe if this guy's around. His pattern is to hit next month, though, so there's that. But he's shown a definite preference to kill fifty-something men. Does that match anyone close to you? Your dad?"

"Yes. My father just turned fifty-nine tonight, as a

matter of fact. He walks his two boxer dogs in Grave Gulch Park regularly, morning and evening, unless there's horrible weather." Rigo, Rosa and Rita were practically fixtures there, so consistent was her dad.

"I'd suggest you tell him to knock off the walks, especially to Grave Gulch Park, for a bit. If we're lucky we'll apprehend Davison before he strikes again, but it's not worth the risk." Troy was convincing.

"Will do. Thank you, Troy. Also, Troy? Stanton's going to be calling you soon. We're going to need some backup from the local police up north for a witness I need to interview. Can you handle the liaison?" Troy's audible groan sounded over the speaker.

"I'll give you a call sometime tonight," Stanton interjected, looking at Dominique with chagrin. "I'm not in favor of it, cuz, trust me. But I'm not going to stop this intrepid journalist from doing her job."

"Copy that. Both of you stay safe. Good luck talking to your father, Dominique."

"Thanks."

They disconnected and she began to gather her things.

"Are you through here?" Stanton's disbelief reflected in the pitch of his voice.

"Not in the least, but if we're going to stop at my father's, and make it up to your family cabin before we both collapse from exhaustion, we need to get a move on it, don't we?" She couldn't look at him, or he'd read what she had to hide from him. Her absolute need for him, and the fact that she'd never gotten over him. It was more than the hot sex, the stolen kisses over the past several days.

What she had with Stanton was meant to last a lifetime. Before she could analyze it, she had to make sure they survived the next forty-eight hours.

"I KNOW YOU'RE not keen on me doing the interview, but I find it hard to believe that Johnny's setting me up at this point. We haven't been targeted since the shooting outside of GGPD. I think the increased presence of the officers on the streets and around Grave Gulch has made a difference, don't you?"

Stanton's teeth ground together and he fought to keep from shouting that he wasn't willing to risk losing her, no matter what. If he wasn't driving them to the cabin, and they didn't have a solid three more hours ahead of them on the dark, slick roads, he'd pull over and do whatever it took to convince her to change her mind.

"It's foolish to assume you're not being set up. And let me be clear—Johnny isn't the one doing the planning, the scheming. It's Jimenez. He was able to scare Johnny off your original interview, remember?"

"Your sarcasm isn't going to help us." She turned from him and he peripherally saw the glow of her phone screen as she checked for messages. "My father's agreed to lay low until Davison is caught. Thank you for stopping by there again. It's added a lot of time to your driving. Any chance you'd let me spell you?"

"Nope." Her safety was his main, his only, mission.

It had been since the day they'd met. Since he'd fallen for her. And now, fallen again.

You never fell out of love with her.

No, he hadn't.

"What's so serious that you're sighing and moping over there?"

"What's not serious, Dominique? You're the target of a major kingpin who kills as easily as he sips his morning coffee. Your family's from Colombia. Didn't your father ever talk about why he left in the first place?"

"When did he tell *you*?"

"We've had our conversations over the past couple of years." Rigo had confessed to getting out of his native country to seek a more stable, safer life in the US. When Rigo and his family left Colombia, it had been torn apart by vying cartels. As he'd described it to Stanton, it had been a literal war zone.

"I'm glad he trusts you, he should. He's always tried to protect Soledad and me from the harsh truth of his childhood. I suppose it's like a family who has a war veteran. We didn't talk about it unless Dad brought it up. Did he tell you that's how he lost his father and brother? Only he, my three uncles and his mother made it out."

"Your father's a man of integrity and he'll do anything for his family. Proof is how much he's paying me."

"That's not even funny."

"Humor's not intended. I'm serious. He promised to pay me double the usual amount." A hefty sum, as Colton Protection's reputation and stalwart record allowed for the high price tags. Stanton received the most of any of the agents not because it was his business but because he had the most experience.

"Dad's always respected you."

"And I him." This was getting uncomfortably close to an intimate conversation. They were going to have a hard enough time keeping themselves detached from each other while in the small but modern cabin for the next two nights.

"I honestly thought he wasn't going to agree to stop walking the dogs in the park. If you hadn't backed me up, I think he'd be there now."

"Rigo's proud, and tough, but he's not stupid." The description gave him pause. Was he proud, tough and not stupid? Had Dominique been attracted to him because he was just like her father?

Dominique laughed. "No, Dad's definitely not unintelligent. You're a lot like him, in fact."

He groaned. "Stop."

"No, not in a bad way. I don't have some kind of daddy issue, if that's what you're thinking. You're not, are you? After all we've been through?"

"I think it's best to not think about anything that involves us, especially now. We've got to come up with how we're going to safely have you interview Johnny, and it has to be timed with law enforcement's takedown of the cartel and Jimenez. Otherwise none of this, your hard work, your wish to get justice for Charlie Hamm, absolutely nothing will have mattered."

"Because I'll be dead."

Over his dead body.

STANTON WAS QUIET for much of the drive, and she kept telling herself it was because he was intent on making certain they hadn't been followed. They were in a car that an agent had brought to her father's when they'd gone to warn him off walking the dogs in public for the foreseeable future. Stanton had insisted that all precautions be taken, including assuming that his vehicle had been made and there was a GPS device hidden on it.

Dominique hadn't admitted it to him yet, but she was a little embarrassed that she hadn't thought of all the ways the cartel could track them. She wasn't a cop, and she appreciated being able to leave those concerns to the experts. But still, she should have had more awareness.

Distraction had warred with her sense of purpose. Her focus on the story was paramount, but ever since her discussion with Soledad at Dad's party, she couldn't shake her sense of failure. She'd neglected to realize what mattered to her most until it was too late. Her career still mattered and writing the truth was definitely her calling. But so was being with the one man who made her heart open, who helped her be the best she could be, even when he was scared witless about her activities.

You blew it.

She had indeed blown it to smithereens, hadn't she? Running from her deepest emotions, and the one man safe enough to share them with.

"We're almost there." His calm countenance usually soothed her but in light of her epiphany all it elicited was sadness. It was too easy to imagine he'd always be here, at her side. Looking out for her.

"Great." He had to be exhausted with five hours of driving behind him. It was past midnight and now less than twenty-four hours until Johnny would tell them where he was. Stanton had called Troy on the drive, and Troy verified he spoke to several local law enforcement agencies in the north part of the state, and all were on standby until Johnny identified the resort. FBI, DEA and the state troopers were being informed and in turn releasing all information pertaining to the cartel as it occurred.

She couldn't ask for more. But her heart wanted it all.

The last hour they'd passed zero other vehicles as Stanton had exited the highway and taken them through back roads to the secluded family cabin. The road had become barely wide enough for their car, with tree trunks on either side, giving the impression that the forest was swallowing them up.

"Here we are." The cabin seemed to come out of nowhere, and she let out her breath. It had been a while since she'd been here with him. That last time, it had felt like a honeymoon as they'd spent a long autumn weekend alone in the rustic retreat. He shut off the engine and they both turned on the flashlight function of their phones to get out and gather their few bags. Not for the first time, Dominique was grateful for the go bag she kept in her locker at the paper. She'd replenished it a few weeks ago, her sixth sense telling her that she was going to get very busy with the Charlie Hamm story.

Of course, she'd had no idea how busy, or how much her life could change in a matter of less than a week.

They trudged through damp leaves to the porch, where Stanton waved for her to put her bags down. "I'll bring them all in." He unlocked the door and let them in, flicked on the lights. The cedar scent of the building instantly brought memories rushing back, including the long nights in front of the now-cold woodburning stove.

"I'll start a fire." She relished having a task that had nothing to do with the danger that shrouded them.

"Go ahead. Do you remember how to use this?" It was a wood pellet stove and besides being a cleaner burn, was simple to operate.

"I do." Just as she remembered how he'd taught her, and then once satisfied the heat level was where he wanted it, he'd turned to her and taught her about heat levels she'd never experienced with another man.

Stop it.

She filled the stove with the pre-sized briquettes and used the long matches to ignite them. Blue flames licked up the insides of the piping hot walls and she swung the door closed, latched the hinge. The window on the door allowed her to watch the flames take hold of the pellets, and heat began to emanate. Sounds of bags being dropped on the floor, Stanton's steps, the wind through the trees, all melded into background noise as she stared at the flames and tried to be anywhere but in the middle of a life-threatening investigation, having only now figured out that she'd let the one who mattered most get away.

STANTON TOLD HIMSELF that he wasn't going to go anywhere near Dominique. They were both exhausted and had no idea what the next two days would have in store. Although he had a sinking feeling that the entire pursuit of her story could go very, very badly if he didn't do his job right.

She sat in front of the fire, cross-legged, as he'd watched her do before. Dominique was good at meditating, at allowing herself to zone out when she needed to. He had a pang of envy as he watched her. Quickly replaced by the burning need to touch her. Hold her.

To make love to her, if only one more time.

He kicked off his shoes and walked toward her, the warmth from the stove already significant. She didn't move as he sat down on the floor beside her.

This is a bad idea.

He was tired of listening to his mind, to that place that still had some integrity left. All he wanted was to be able to show the woman that mattered most to him what it was like to be made love to by the one man who loved her most. No matter the cost, because in truth, tonight was all they had.

She turned to face him and watched him. He was lost in her gaze, their eyes locked together as they'd been since he could remember.

"You know what's funny?" His voice caught, and he didn't think he'd ever felt as vulnerable.

Dominique reached out and ran her fingers on his cheek, smoothed back the hair that had fallen on his forehead. "That we're still awake?" Her tender smile tugged on their connection, the thread that ran through him, right to his center. Her hands grasped his and they intertwined their fingers, all the while never breaking eye contact.

"That, yeah." He cleared his throat. "I was about to say something a little more profound."

Her laughter was pure, without the weight of the past days. "It's just like me to stomp on your seriousness, isn't it? Or to jump in, thinking I already know it all? Go ahead, tell me."

But now he was…nervous? It wasn't a usual feeling for him. "I've been thinking that I can't remember a time when we weren't together."

"Um, what about the last two years?"

"Have we really been apart, though? Sure, we didn't see one another and you avoided me at every event we ran into each other at, but it hasn't broken this." He carried their hands to his heart, and then hers. Her pupils dilated in the amber glow of the woodstove, her lips parted as if she needed more air. If she was like him, her heart was pounding in her ears, too.

"No, it hasn't. We definitely have a connection. But…" She kept looking at him, blinking, her eyes reflecting tears. "What are we going to do about it? What can we do about it? We're not compatible."

"I'd say we've done exceptionally well through… let's see, an attack—" he hated bringing that up again, worried that the memory triggered the pain she'd already survived "—being shot at twice, and the worst thing of all."

Her brows rose and she leaned in. "What?"

"Fireworks."

Her gasp of surprise turned into a laugh, until the air between them electrified. They were no more than a whisper apart.

"We have done very well." She agreed. But did that mean she'd been having some of the same thoughts he had? "But we've also been under a lot of pressure. I don't know, Stanton. We're a good team, and we work together like lifelong partners. I mean, career-wise."

"And I mean *all*-wise. I made a big mistake when I pushed you on a solid commitment. Love is an action, and you were right there, every night, no matter how far my jobs took me. Those two weeks I was in Syria—"

"Protecting a hellcat actor on the movie shoot from Hades." She grinned. Her voice on the other end of the line after every day, while he'd been guarding the inconsolable diva who'd insisted on partying each night after her shoot, wearing the entire crew out, had been his saving grace.

"I'm sorry I tried to make you agree to something you're not cut out for." He'd been an ass, plain and simple.

"Oh, Stanton, I was awful to you. It's not that I'm not cut out for family. All during my father's party, all I kept seeing was how it would be if we had a child, who would they look like. Would you be holding him or her or would I?"

The last of his restraint broke. "Dominique, I can't promise you anything, not before you get this story. Not until we know all the cartel players are behind bars."

She placed her finger on his lips. "You're not the one who needs to be apologizing, and we're going to get this story and help GGPD get the bad guys."

"I'm glad we had this talk." He grinned, the elation in his chest almost too much to bear. "We both need rest now."

"Not on your life." She placed her hands on his shoulders. "How's your arm?"

"My arm? It's fine. Why?"

"Because we're going to be up for a while, and the way I want you, you're going to need your arm." She closed the inches between their mouths and when her lips touched his, he let himself be the man he was always meant to be. With Dominique.

RELIEF BUOYED THE constant desire she had for Stanton as the kiss deepened from a physical seal of their mutual regrets and hopes for the future, to an expression of the searing passion they'd never been able to let go of. His lips molded to hers as his hands held her face like a precious piece of glass art, his fingers reaching to her nape and his thumbs stroking her jawline. Heat rained over her skin, each caress heightened by the warmth from the woodstove. She ran her fingers through his hair, pulled him closer, unable to get close enough.

It'll never be enough.

With Stanton, it was true. She could never get enough. But there was an awful lot of satisfaction between her need and how she knew she'd always want him.

"Babe." He broke from her lips, dragged his mouth down the side of her throat. When his hands slipped under her top, she reached down and lifted it over her head. Stanton unfastened her bra and her breasts were free for his appreciation and her pleasure as he cupped one in each hand, played with her nipples.

"Please, Stanton." She nipped his earlobe, clung to his shoulders as the waves of her desire increased.

"Lie down." He helped her onto her back on the fluffy rug, and she shimmied out of her pants. She went to remove her panties but he beat her to it, slowly taking off the silky pair with excruciating deliberation.

"Babe, now, I can't take this." She sat back up and helped him out of his button-down shirt, eased the sleeves from his arms. Kissing his bandaged upper arm, she noticed bruising that wasn't there yesterday. "Your arm, Stanton…this has to hurt."

"Not as much as I'm going to if we don't make love." He stood and quickly chucked his pants, giving her a beautiful view of his glorious nudity, before he rejoined her on the floor. "We can use the sofa or go to the bedroom."

"This is way more fun. Unless your arm—"

"The heck with my arm." His mouth was on hers again, and the kiss was one she'd always remembered.

She savored each and every kiss, tongue stroke, the scent of Stanton as he drove her to the place she only visited with him. Pure freedom from all that ever worried her, freedom to enjoy the delight of being with the one man she loved more than any other. Even his pause to retrieve a condom seemed part of the dance of their sexual reunion, the few seconds just enough for her to position herself to welcome him fully into her.

They joined like the seasoned partners they were, his thrusts met by her hips with vigor and timing that bespoke of how well they knew one another. Just as she thought she'd never be able to relieve the insistent heat and tension that he caused, she broke apart and he shuddered with a force she could only attribute to love. Nothing less. No one else, only Stanton.

Chapter Fourteen

Dominique woke in the cabin's main bedroom under piles of quilts the next morning. The warmth that had allowed her to slumber so peacefully was gone. She reached her hand across the bed, under the sheets, to confirm what she knew—Stanton had left. The numbers on her phone told her it was almost seven. Two hours later than she usually rose. Sitting up, she stretched and yawned before padding to the window. The first glow of sunrise hit the surrounding woods, and she thought it would be nice to allow this image to stoke the hope in her heart.

Her body was pleasantly sore, and she grabbed her clothes, neatly folded on the nightstand, conveniently next to a small handgun that she knew wasn't there by accident. Stanton's work. She never worried about how she stored her clothes when she was camping or here in the cabin, and weapons weren't something she bothered with. Except Stanton had insisted she learn how to fire a weapon and they'd gone to a firing range when they'd dated. The last time they'd been out here in these woods, they'd done target practice with his family's shotguns. She acknowledged for the millionth time that Stanton never stopped doing his job. He was protecting her, even as he folded and neatly stacked the outfit she'd pulled out of her overnight bag and flung over the wooden rocker at the foot of the bed last night. The room had touches of Italia Colton everywhere, from the brightly hued quilts and bedding, to the fluffy towels in the comfortable bathroom, larger than normal for a cabin. Even though it had been years, this log house felt like a familiar pair of socks to her. Warm, supportive, secure.

A gunshot sounded and fear threw cold reality over her post-sex reverie.

"Stanton?" She shouted for him as she grabbed the weapon and scrambled to throw on her clothes. The shower would wait. Her hands shook as she pulled on her underwear and pants.

"Get down!" His voice thundered from the outer room and she complied, making certain she was out of view from the two windows in the room. "Stay away from the windows and take the revolver from the night-stand."

"I am!" Didn't he realize he'd taught her well? Her shirt on, she shoved into a thick sweater and pulled jeans over her leggings. If she had to run outside, she'd have to do it without her coat, still in the car.

More shots sounded, followed by deep voices. She froze in place, wondering if this was about to be her last minutes on earth. When she heard the front door open, she cried out and crawled forward. No way was she going to allow Stanton to launch himself into a gun-fight against the cartel without her help.

Once at the bedroom's threshold, she stood and ran into the living room. The sight of Stanton in the cabin's front doorframe gave her momentary relief. He was still alive. But he wouldn't be for long if he stayed where he was, so vulnerable to any shot.

She trembled in place as he spoke to their killers.

"Yeah, we're here for a quick getaway. My girlfriend and I needed out of the city, ya know?" His voice was remarkably steady.

"Sorry to bother you, man. We were tracking a buck but scared him off." A deeper, gruff voice. It sounded sincere, but how could they know who this was?

"There's no hunting on private property. This stretches all the way down to the public grounds."

"Yeah, we didn't see the signs until we were up on your cabin. It won't happen again."

"Thanks."

She allowed herself to catch her breath, all the while poised to step up and fire at anyone who threatened Stanton. But it sounded like hunters who'd gotten lost. It could be a ruse by the cartel, but she immediately dismissed it. If they were found here, criminals would shoot first, come up with excuses later.

The searing pain in her chest took a bit to figure out. It was her heart, anticipating how she'd feel if anything ever happened to Stanton. Hoping against hope that he'd not get killed while standing out there, guarding her.

How had she ever thought she could be with a man who faced life and death every day?

After what felt like hours, Stanton came back into the cabin.

His face, drawn and pale, made her already racing pulse stop in its tracks, before ramping up again. Maybe she'd been wrong to assume the interlopers weren't dangerous.

"What?"

"It was a man and his teenage daughter, hunting. He's teaching her how to track prey."

"Do you believe them?" She didn't think a father-and-daughter pair fit the description of cartel hit men, but anything was possible.

He closed his eyes, his way of giving himself space to think. When he opened them, their brightness was startling against the backdrop of the log walls. "Yes. I told them that they needed to keep their hunting to public lands. Our property backs up to state grounds, so it's an innocent enough mistake. They're not the first hunters or hikers to make it."

"But usually you don't have the worry of assassins stalking you." She went to him and wrapped her arms around his waist. "I'm so sorry you've been drawn into this."

"I haven't been drawn into anything. This was my choice, to take this particular job, remember?" He hugged her back, but then gently let go. She followed suit, unable to figure out where his heart was at. "We need to figure out our plan of attack. The midnight phone call is going to leave us with enough time to get in place, but only if we have several ways we want to work it lined up."

So that was that. Stanton wanted to focus on why they were here in the first place, and it was a harsh reminder that he wasn't here to work on their relationship.

Neither are you.

No, she was here to get the story. Clear Charlie's name. Maybe help out Johnny Blanchard if she could, if he was able to help law enforcement pinpoint Jimenez's location. It was the absolute pits that she'd figured out, too late, that she and Stanton might have been able to make a go of it. She'd had her chance to tell him how she really felt, her regrets included. The heat of their passion last night wasn't the right time, and it appeared that he thought she'd been clearing the air for them to have another round of lovemaking. It was time to accept that she'd messed up, and let it go. Before the distraction got them both killed.

"Look, Stanton, I'm sending Troy up there along with two other officers, and I think I can get the DEA to cough up one or two agents. But there aren't any guarantees. Isn't there some way you can convince Dominique that she's got as much as she's going to get for her story? She's got the solid facts now about Bowe's involvement and how the evidence against Charlie was planted. I can't overlook that this Johnny Blanchard meetup appears to be a big setup." Stanton listened to his sister via wireless earbuds as he paced the cabin's front porch, using his binoculars to continually scan the woods for any suspicious movement. Dominique remained inside, working on the information she'd already collected, culling it into salient prose. She never mentioned it, but he had to wonder how much of the pressure she put on herself was from her editor at the *Gazette*. It angered him that her boss might encourage her to risk her life for an article, no matter how important.

What really upset him, though, was that he'd not been able to figure out a way to convince her that she needed to call off the meetup with Johnny Blanchard. He'd already lied under oath on a witness stand. Why would she ever trust a perjurer?

"You know her, Melissa. I hate to say it, but she's just like you. Once she's made her mind up, she's going to follow through. And she actually had a good point, about whether the meeting with Blanchard is for real or not. This is an awfully complicated ruse for a setup. The cartels like to keep it simple. A more straightforward manner would have been to threaten Dominique's family if she didn't lay off the Charlie Hamm lead."

"Well, they did threaten her, and tried to kill her, three times. But you're right—this cartel in particular is noted for its brutality. Luring a reporter who's writing a story about an already dead prisoner and reformed drug dealer isn't something I'd expect from Jimenez."

"So you admit there's at least a chance it's not a setup?" He rested his binoculars on his chest, where his heart remained steady only because of years of training and surveillance experience.

"The chance that it's legit isn't great enough to keep me from sending backup." Her frustration plucked at his conscience. His sister worked harder now than he ever had, and she wore the town's safety around her neck without complaint. "There's always the long shot that Jimenez will show, and we'll nab him. That would solve a lot of problems for Grave Gulch. I found the clothing items you asked for, by the way, and I'll have an officer drop them before you and Dominique leave the cabin for wherever the meetup ends up being. Once we know where and which resort, the logistics will be a little easier."

"Thanks for doing this for me." The depth of his gratitude surprised him, until he remembered his true motive. He knew he couldn't live without Dominique. The last two years had been filled with an awful lot of desolation without her. Three near misses in as many days had brought him to his mental and emotional knees. He surrendered. The only way out of this was to keep them both alive to hopefully work things out after Dominique got her story.

"It's not for you, Stanton, even though I don't like the idea of you being involved in this one bit. It's for our native city, and for future generations. If we don't care enough to clean it up, then who?"

Melissa disconnected and he was left alone in the warming air with what he'd been trying to ignore all day. There wasn't going to be a reprieve; the meeting with Blanchard was going down, and whether or not it was a setup, he had to prepare as if it was.

He'd done some research of his own on all of the event venues in the area and narrowed it to two possibilities. Both were hosting weddings this weekend, two per day. It was unlikely Blanchard would use his real name when he was supposedly on the run from the cartel, but Stanton had inquired, to be thorough. No Blanchard on either resort's payroll. But he'd gained some intel that would reassure him that Dominique was being as safe as she could be, in case the cartel had found her. No doubt the cartel had both her and Stanton's profiles memorized, was on the lookout for them. They'd be identified the minute they stepped out of their vehicle at whichever resort.

Unless he and Dominique didn't look like themselves. He had a solid idea, and Melissa seemed to support it. First he had to convince her of his plan.

JOHNNY BLANCHARD'S HAND shook as he dialed the number on his cell phone. His nerves were shot. Maybe with the extra bucks he'd get for helping the cartel land the reporter chick he'd get himself a small place up here, far away from Jimenez.

The connection happened faster than he expected and he almost dropped his cigarette.

"Why didn't you call sooner? Did they take the bait?" It wasn't Leo, the thug Johnny usually dealt with. It was Jimenez himself on the line, his voice reaching through the phone, as if by sheer force of will he could crush Johnny with his words.

"Yes, yes, jefe, no worries. Hook, line and sinker,

I'm telling you." He puffed on his cigarette as he stood on the concrete platform outside the resort's kitchen. "They'll be here exactly when I tell them to. And your niece's wedding will go off without a hitch later this afternoon, too." He knew it had better or he'd be fish bait at the bottom of the lake that the resort so magnificently overlooked.

"I want them at the bottom of the lake before my niece ever says 'I do.'"

"No problem. I'm telling them to show up in the middle of the first wedding, to give the cover of the crowd. Three hundred people will be admiring the grounds and the wedding couple. The last people they'll notice are me and the reporter."

"Don't forget her bodyguard."

"You said Leo will take him out first."

"Leo's not coming. He ran into a snag."

Johnny's blood ran cold and he fought to keep from hyperventilating. *Snag* was Pablo Jimenez's pet word for *dead*. As in, he'd had Leo killed. Or offed him on his own. *Oh, crap.* Not Leo. Leo was Jimenez's longest-running employee. If he'd been killed by the kingpin, no one was safe. Including a weasel who'd lied on the stand. Maybe he could run now, get away before the darn reporter and her bodyguard showed up.

"Don't think about it, Blanchard. I've got eyes on you twenty-four seven. You'll never survive if you try to run. After we take care of the reporter and her boy toy, there's a big promotion for you." Jimenez was practically psychic, with the resources he had. Johnny looked around at where the building's roof began, searching for security cameras.

"Yes, sir. I'm your man."

"You'd better be. Or you'll be nobody's anything."

After Jimenez disconnected, Johnny couldn't stop his mind from racing, his pulse from hammering, his breath from getting so shallow he sank down on his haunches and began to tug at his hair.

He saw Jimenez's plan so clearly now. He wasn't only going to have de la Vega and her bodyguard killed, he was going to make a three-for-one deal. Johnny knew he was in Jimenez's crosshairs, too.

"YOU HAVE GOT to be kidding. I think the lack of sleep is getting to you." Dominique stood up from the kitchen table where she'd been working on her laptop and began pacing in the small kitchen. It was past one in the morning. Blanchard had called and unwittingly verified one of the two resorts Stanton had already figured it was. And now he was asking her to think of going to the interview in some kind of disguise, just in case it was a setup. "I've never had to pretend I'm anyone but me. It's bordering on unethical, since I already have the interview set and Johnny Blanchard's counting on me to show up, at whatever time he gives me."

"He's not going to dictate our arrival time. That would be insanity." Stanton was at his breaking point with her, she could tell from the hard glint in his eyes. He'd agreed to support her through the end, to get the story, but he wasn't going to budge on any of his safety precautions.

"I know you're right, but let me get my head wrapped around this. I suppose it would be okay to try to not look like my usual self. Are you thinking wigs, different kinds of clothing? Or maybe we can look like we're hikers who wander in to use the facilities? That's not so uncommon." She'd used various restrooms as needed when she'd hiked along the lake's edge.

"I'm thinking we should fit in with the kind of event they're staging. A wedding."

"Oh, so you're saying show up as if we're guests of the bride and groom. Crash either, or both, of the weddings." She nodded. "Yeah, I can do that. That makes sense."

"Not guests."

"Not guests?" Puzzlement and the late hour reflected in her impatient tone.

A knock at the door had them both freeze in place, until Stanton remembered Melissa's promise. "It's okay. It's an officer Melissa sent." He went to the door, and after verifying who it was, opened it. A man in civilian clothes with silvering temples walked in, and looked at them one at a time. "Ms. de la Vega, I'm Brett Shea. My K-9 partner, Ember, is in my vehicle. You may remember me from that story you did on the opioid crisis a couple of years back."

"Of course I remember you. Please call me Dominique, Detective Shea."

"And call me Brett." He nodded at her before he turned back to Stanton. "Here's what you asked for."

He handed a large, hanging garment bag to Stanton, and an even larger hanging bag to Dominique. She grasped the bag and gasped.

"What kind of clothing weighs this much?" She looked at Stanton, then Brett.

"A wedding dress," Stanton answered. "It's the best way for us to go in without question, without drawing attention to you."

"That makes no sense. The bride always gets all of the attention at a wedding."

"Yes, but it's not what Jimenez will be expecting. They'll assume we're coming either dressed as guests or waitstaff. We found out the timing of the two weddings and if we arrive just ahead of the second wedding party, it'll be assumed we're the next couple getting hitched." His gaze was unwavering and she'd no doubt he'd gone over all of the different scenarios in his head, and had picked what he thought was best. She trusted Stanton's security instincts, as she knew he trusted her reporter's hunches.

But a wedding gown?

Dominique's gut twisted, but it wasn't over dressing as a make-believe bride to get to the last yet most important interview for her story. It was from the painful stab of disappointment that it wasn't a real dress—her dress, for pledging to love for the rest of her life the man looking at her with complete confidence.

DOMINIQUE SAT NEXT to Stanton in the back seat of Colton Protection's largest SUV as they rode to the wedding venue. Detective Brett Shea was dressed in a black suit and drove, to give a more realistic impression that they were a genuine bride and groom, driven by a professional chauffeur. Brett's K-9 partner Ember sat in the cargo area of the vehicle, her black Lab features appearing calm and sweet, but Dominique knew the dog would help take down any criminal she was instructed to. She was so grateful for Melissa's support and made a mental note to take the GGPD chief out for a nice dinner when this all settled down.

Please, let it settle down. Because the alternative was unthinkable. But also too real, too close, to ignore. She and Stanton might not come out of today alive.

She couldn't look at Stanton, because all it did was send her stomach into flips, ratcheting the anxiety that she was already working overtime to tamp down. Stanton wore a tuxedo as well as he wore his custom suits; he swore they helped him do his job better because they allowed for more physical movement as needed. It was as if she'd conjured this event in some twisted way, when she'd admitted to Soledad that she'd been thinking more about what it would be like to be with Stanton forever. To marry him, be his wife. Have their babies, little mini Stantons.

Wearing the frothy white dress, which fit her remarkably well for a borrowed item out of one of the GGPD officer's closets, must have triggered some kind of subconscious thought stream of ridiculousness. Thinking about being with Stanton forever was one thing, but to picture that their children would be exactly like him, or her, was beyond a dream. It was a certain definition of insanity.

His hand covered hers and he squeezed. "It's going to work out, Dom. Trust me."

Unable to not look at him any longer, she took him in. He was still outrageously handsome, the crisp white shirt and black tie complementing his skin and the purposeful scruff at his jaw. His eyes sparkled with focus.

"I do trust you. It's myself I'm worried about. What if we can't find Blanchard?" The plan was to corner the lying witness while he worked this afternoon, during the preparations for the second ceremony. Blanchard had insisted they arrive at four o'clock, in between the two weddings and a full two hours before the second ceremony was scheduled. He'd told them to meet him near the pier that stretched out into Lake Michigan. Because the resort was in a cove of sorts, it didn't have the concerns of rough waters that other buildings that hugged the shoreline did. Instead, they were going to corner him in the resort's commercial kitchen.

"You'll do what you need to. And don't hesitate to use your weapon." His reminder of the handgun holstered to her thigh in lieu of the traditional garter made her smile.

"We've never done anything the easy way, have we?" She couldn't help but grin and was delighted when he smiled back.

"No. No, we don't." He squeezed her hand again and then let go, turning his gaze to his window. "How far out are we, Brett?"

"Another ten minutes."

It was time for them to focus on their plan of action.

THE FIRST WEDDING party was nowhere in sight when they pulled in front of the employee entrance. The DEA agent working with them today was already inside the venue, posing as a photographer, taking pre-event shots. The same agent had ascertained that a man matching the description of Johnny Blanchard was indeed working as a dishwasher in the large commercial kitchen. As of now, there was no hint of other cartel members on the premises. No dark figures skulking about, no whisper of drugs available for a good price.

"We can wait here as long as you need us to, Stanton." Brett turned to look at each of them. "Dominique, I hope like heck you get the truth out of this lying scumbag. We've all been following your reports back at GGPD, and while I have to say I wasn't thrilled when you first exposed the corruption going on in our lab with Randall Bowe, I'm positive we're on the same side. Whatever you two need, I'm here."

"Thank you. That means a lot." Dominique fought back tears. It was one thing for Melissa, who knew her well, to support her efforts, but for a seasoned veteran like Brett to back her spoke volumes.

"Now, go get him."

Chapter Fifteen

Only after they were certain no one would see them entering this back way did they leave the safety of the SUV. They walked into the resort's back entrance holding hands, each rolling a small suitcase provided by GGPD to help with their disguise. It was all about appearing like the about-to-be-married couple that they weren't. Stanton was humbled by the grasp of Dominique's hand in his. *"I trust you."* It weighed heavy, the gift of her complete confidence. And he vowed to meet it, to get them out of here alive.

Stanton had gone over every inch of the plan that Melissa gave him to follow, including the intel they were being fed from the DEA as their assigned agent, David Gonzalez, uncovered more about Johnny Blanchard and Pablo Jimenez. There were zero indications that any of the cartel were present at the resort yet, with the only guests confirmed present with the first wedding party. The second wedding's party and guests would begin arriving in an hour, as per usual resort protocol.

He hadn't worked as long as he had in the security industry to ignore the one thing his most influential trainer had told him. *Always trust your gut, and don't give up until you figure out the source of your unease.* Something was bothering him and it began with Blanchard's insistence on speaking to Dominique on the resort's pier. He'd checked out photos of the long wooden structure and it didn't look like an obvious choice for what was supposed to be a private meeting.

Go over your checklist.

His professional routine tried to take over but he couldn't stop staring at Dominique in the wedding gown. It was nothing like her taste. He'd always imagined she'd wear a very simple dress, if they ever took vows. Her figure was all the decoration any outfit worn by her needed. And though this wasn't her style, the over-the-top, celebratory design showcased her beauty. And his secret desire that one day, she'd really be his bride. Or maybe it wasn't such a secret, after all he'd revealed it to her last night. The dress belonged to one of the officers who'd married in the last year; she'd gotten divorced six months ago and told Melissa that she was happy to see it used for a "better cause." He'd grinned when Melissa texted him that tidbit, and passed it on to Dominique in an effort to lighten the energy flowing between them in the cabin as they worked and prepared. Dominique hadn't done more than offer a shadow of her usual smile, preoccupied by their plans.

"Stop looking at me." She hissed out of the side of her mouth as they made their way down a corridor, past employee locker rooms, and wound up in front of the catering kitchen. Thank goodness for the DEA agent who'd emailed and texted the resort's floor plan, complete with all of the employee offices. He'd tracked Blanchard to the kitchen, and the plan was to walk through the large space together, acting as if they wanted to see their cake early. It was confirmed that cakes had already been delivered for both weddings, so it wouldn't seem that unusual.

"I can't help it. You're so…foamy." He swallowed a chuckle.

She tugged the yards of a veil to the side, showing her annoyance with the overdone dress, and frowned. "The word is *frothy*, and dang it, I just got my lipstick on the veil." A large smear of crimson stood out among the sea of pearl white netting.

"Good thing it's a loaner, and the previous wearer doesn't care what happens to it." Warmth struck in his chest, and if it wouldn't be a risk to her life, he'd suggest they disappear into an empty space and enjoy a bridal kiss or two.

"Stanton, there's so much I want to say." Tears reflected in her eyes, and the heat in his chest bloomed into all-on protective mode.

"We'll talk later, after you get the rest of your story." He tugged on her hands, willing her to stay steady, focused on the plan. He used his finger to catch the tear running down her cheek. Keeping her alive was all that mattered. They could sort anything else out later, couldn't they?

She nodded, sniffed, swiped at her eyes. "Of course." Her chin jutted out and she let go of his hands. "Yes, let's get on with it."

"Do you have your phone on its record setting?"

"Yes, and—" she pressed the screen "—we're connected, right?"

His phone vibrated with her call and he answered it, leaving the line open. "Yes."

"Are your earbuds in?" She was teasing because he hadn't suited up his audio yet. He retrieved them from his trouser pocket, also checking to see that his weapon was holstered. He set the tiny speakers in place.

"They are now. Ready?"

"Ready."

She began to turn toward the kitchen entry but he couldn't let her go in yet. His arms reached out and he looked up and down the corridor to verify they were safe before he planted a searing kiss on her lips. If anyone did see them, they'd assume it was wedding-day magic.

Her lips were so soft, her tongue, her body willing as she clung to him. He forced himself to pull away before they got lost in the moment, lost in each other, lost in the bond they'd have no matter what the future held for them.

"You've got this, Dom."

"Thanks."

A quick wink was her parting gesture before she disappeared into the kitchen and he began the hardest part of the entire plan: the waiting.

THE KITCHEN'S HIGH noise level startled Dominique after the quiet of the corridor. The doors she'd entered through must have some kind of noise buffering. Pots and pans clanged and voices rose over the cacophony as a woman she assumed was the head chef issued rapid-fire directions to her sous-chef and other workers. They were at the far end of the large space, underneath a humongous rack of cookware, and hadn't noticed her yet. Scents of sautéing vegetables and butter hung heavy, and like the decibels, the temperature of the room was higher than in the corridor, making her perspire as if it was a summer day and not early spring in Northern Michigan.

Several other workers were scattered at various workstations, including two women who were fussing over the wedding cake, adding last-minute decorations. Blanchard was reportedly the dishwasher, and she saw one man working at the large stainless steel machine, pulling out clean dishes and stacking them on serving carts, then pushing the carts into a precise line closer to the long, spotless island where all manners of chopping, tossing and mixing were going on.

She sucked in a deep breath and headed for him. Her phone felt heavy in the pocket she'd cut a hole in and wired the microphone through. The device was taped inside the dress's bodice. Since it was white, it was practically invisible against the padded fabric. As she approached the dishwasher, the man she hoped was Blanchard, the noise quieted a bit, urging her to move faster. The last thing she wanted was the full attention of everyone present—Blanchard would never talk to her then.

"Excuse me, are you Johnny Blanchard?"

The man twisted so quickly to face her that he dropped the stack of white porcelain plates he'd been holding. As the sounds of ceramic crashing against the hard, tiled floor echoed around them, he stared at Dominique with eyes widened in shock. His skin visibly paled as his lips trembled.

"Who are you?" His voice shook.

"Mr. Blanchard?" She needed him to verify before she continued.

He looked away toward the chef's table, and gave a quick wave. "Sorry, I'll get it cleaned up. No worries, we have lots more dishes."

"Johnny?" She was sure this was her man, as his unique voice matched the phone calls.

"Yes, it's me. Johnny Blanchard. Who are you?"

"Dominique de la Vega. *Grave Gulch Gazette.*" She added the last in case she'd scared his memory away.

She shrugged, looking down at the wedding dress. "I'm sorry for the surprise but I had to make sure this wasn't a setup."

"Sure, I get it, but I can't break away right now." He walked over to where a broom and dustpan hung on a far wall and brought it back. "And now I have this mess to clean up."

She wasn't going to apologize for his skittishness. "We can do the interview right here as you work, if that's okay with you. Everyone here will think I'm the bride, checking in on things, right? Why don't you take me over to the cake after you're done sweeping? Pretend to help me get a peek at it."

"I think it's best we don't talk right here." He was so shaky as he swept up the broken dishes that her hackles went up.

"Why is that?"

"I'm due for a break now, anyway. We can go for a smoke and I'll tell you all you want to know."

"Mind if I wait here with you?"

"I guess not." His frown contradicted the words but she knew that she had to keep pressing him. She'd lost interviews before because of nervous sources who'd changed their minds at the last minute. The stakes were too high to lose Johnny Blanchard, now that they had him. "You're welcome to go wait for me on the loading platform. Door's over there. But I can't tell you anything, not anymore. If you're smart, you'll get out of here." He pointed to the exit.

"You can tell me everything I need to know now. Did you lie on the witness stand for the Jimenez cartel? Did Pablo Jimenez pay you to perjure yourself?"

He stared at her with wild-looking eyes for a solid second before his gaze scuttled away.

"Not here. Outside."

She and Stanton had anticipated this, and she knew she'd be safe on the platform as the DEA agent was nearby. Troy and the other officers had also surrounded the resort at critical points. Stanton would hear this exchange and have everyone move to the best vantage. But he'd told her to always give it five minutes whenever she could, to ensure the agents and officers were in place.

"Okay, I'll go out there, but since I don't have a coat, please hurry. We'll have to make the interview a quick one." Hopefully this would encourage him to spill it all. Less time to consider his words.

"Go ahead, I'll be right there." He nodded at the door as he carried a dustpan full of porcelain pieces to a large trash receptacle.

She stepped around the remaining mess and smiled at the gawking cooks and cake decorators as she made her best attempt at being the happy, about-to-be-married bride. It was surprisingly easy, acting the part.

Because you know it's not all an act.

Yeah, she wished it was really happening for her. With Stanton. And as soon as this was behind them, they'd talk. He'd said it, and she wanted to.

As she stepped outside, the early spring wind hit her skin first, followed by the scent of Lake Michigan. The pale blue sky made the water appear like a sapphire, broken only by white caps frothed up by the high winds. Her voluminous skirt felt like a scrap of fabric for all the protection it offered against the weather. She ignored her shivers and spoke aloud, knowing Stanton could hear her and would relay all to the others.

"I'm on the loading dock platform. The dishwasher confirmed he's Johnny Blanchard and he looks just like the witness sketches the newspaper printed during Charlie Hamm's trial and he has the same voice as the man I've spoken to in numerous phone calls. I believe it's him. I identified myself to Blanchard. He has a smoke break coming up and agreed to speak to me then. All that banging and crashing you may have heard—I surprised the heck out of him and he dropped several dishes that he was moving. So far no one's questioned me as to my identity." She scanned the surrounding grounds, from the parking area to the rocky beach to the water, but saw no agents or officers. It wasn't a reason for concern; they were all trained to blend in. Still, it would have been nice to see a familiar face.

And then she did. She spotted Stanton's unmistakable profile near a grove of trees to the right of the resort. It gave him a perfect line of sight to her. Confidence buoyed her and she turned when she heard the door swing open, ready to get this last crucial interview over. To get what she'd fought for over the last year. Justice for Charlie Hamm.

Johnny Blanchard walked out but wouldn't make eye contact with her. Her nape hairs rose, and the shudder that racked her body had zero to do with the outside temperature. Following behind Blanchard was a shorter man in a tuxedo. She wanted to believe it was a legit member of the wedding party, but the man's face was stamped with determination and…satisfaction.

Charlie stepped to one side and the man approached her, closing the distance in three steps. But not before she saw the knife blade in his hand.

"Finally we meet, Dominique de la Vega. Allow me to introduce myself. I'm Pablo Jimenez. I believe you've been upset with how I conduct my business?" He smiled broadly, his teeth accentuating his dark looks, but the smile wasn't jovial. It was the leer of imminent death.

Never had Dominique regretted not telling Stanton she still loved him more.

STANTON KNEW THE figure on the cement platform with Dominique and Blanchard a split second before he spoke, because he matched the physical descriptions of the kingpin. He saw the flash of metal, knew that the bastard had chosen now, this resort so far removed from Grave Gulch, to make his appearance. To prove his point that no one was out of his reach.

"The man identifies himself as Pablo Jimenez, and he is holding a weapon to her midsection, a knife blade approximately six inches long." As he fed the other agents the information, he fought to stay in the moment, to ignore the existential, psychic pain ripping through him. He'd made a huge mistake by not staying in the corridor, but he'd wanted to be in place as soon as he'd heard she was going outside. If he'd come through the kitchen he would have seen Jimenez and stopped him before he ever stepped on that platform.

"I can't get a clear shot of him or Blanchard, not without risking hitting Dominique." Troy's grim assessment enraged Stanton. "Neither can David." Troy was working closely with the DEA agent, too.

"Someone has to be able to take them down. This guy's unstable. He could drive that blade in at any point."

"If Jimenez wanted her dead, he'd have already

stabbed her." David's voice was calm, controlled. Because *he* wasn't in love with the woman dressed in a bridal gown. "Let it play out. He's making sure there aren't any law enforcement agents in the area. He thinks we'll react right away."

David was right: Stanton knew it in his bones. But as he watched Dominique, clearly agitated, arguing with Jimenez, he couldn't help but see everything that ever mattered to him being snatched away.

Dominique.

Why hadn't he told Dominique that he still loved her, that he wasn't going to take no for an answer this time? That he'd live with her, they didn't have to get married, it could be on her terms? Why had he been so obtuse?

Steady is as steady does. He had to rein in his emotions or he'd lose her…forever.

"If you try to make a move or give me any reason to think that you're here with anyone but that stupid bodyguard who I see is near that tree over there, I'm going to slice out your heart and hand it to your father. Wrapped in a copy of the *Grave Gulch Gazette*, of course."

Dominique stared at the man whose criminal machinations had cost so many lives, and the one she was here to avenge, Charlie Hamm's. Johnny Blanchard was standing next to her in silence like the spineless, lying jerk that he was. And she knew Blanchard wasn't her threat. Jimenez held all the power, total control, over whether she lived or died.

"You're a backstabbing, evil little snake." She spat

at Johnny Blanchard, who remained in place in such a resolute manner she was certain it was to block any attempt at a shot to his or Jimenez's head.

"You're like all the rest. You don't understand who's running the show." Blanchard snarled at her, his rotting teeth revealing he wasn't only a lying witness but probably one of Jimenez's users. Johnny's newfound confidence sickened her.

"Do you understand what he's telling you, Dominique? I have all the power. Whether you live or die. Understand?" Jimenez said her name as if they'd known each other for a lifetime. She hated it, hated all he stood for.

"I do." Teeth clenched against her shudders, she refused to engage him further.

"You must understand that it's hard for me to trust people at their word these days. If you are lying, or do anything I don't tell you to, I'm going to have your bodyguard's head blown off. I have dozens of my men surrounding this hotel. There's no way out. You must come with me."

She mentally heard Stanton's voice screaming at her to not go anywhere, not with Blanchard or Jimenez or anyone. But Jimenez threatened Stanton's life, leaving her no choice. Plus, the tip of his knife was pressing against her ribs through the bodice. The way Jimenez was leaning into her, she'd be surprised if her skin hadn't been pierced. At least she wasn't feeling anything deeper.

"Where are we going?" She spoke for the mic. Stanton and the others would be able to at least follow them. Maybe, if they were lucky, someone would get there ahead of them.

"Oh, I can't say, sweetheart. How do I know you're not wired?" He viciously pulled at her bodice, yanking her up onto her tiptoes as peered down inside at her bare skin, her breasts. She held her breath. If he saw the mic on the underside—

"Nice view, *querida*, but better for you that you're not mic'ed up." He pressed her bodice back against her chest, hard, knocking her backward a few steps before Jimenez grabbed her and pulled her back to standing. She glared at him as the imprint of his hand made her want to scream, to kick, to rage. Amazing how a small piece of stainless steel aimed at her liver could keep her from acting.

"I'm the one you want. Leave the rest out." She didn't want to draw attention to Stanton, not knowing how much Jimenez knew.

The slap came hard, across her mouth. She tasted blood.

"No one tells me what to do." He motioned at Blanchard. "Frisk her. Now!"

She endured the humiliation of being felt up her front by the slimy man.

"Not her top, you fool. Her legs. Make sure she doesn't have a weapon." Jimenez's forehead shone with perspiration, his tone impatient. Great. Not only was she facing a psychopathic drug kingpin, but he was getting annoyed by his minion. Blanchard's calloused, dirty fingers scaled her legs under the billowing skirt, and she held her breath as he found the holster and retrieved the handgun with a satisfied smirk. She fought to not give one back to both of them, as Blanchard hadn't noticed the phone in the concealed pocket. Probably didn't realize such a fancy dress could have pockets.

A car moved in her peripheral vision and Jimenez turned her around to face forward. A black SUV with blacked-out windows stopped at the bottom of the platform's stairs.

"Get in the car." He pressed the knife into the crucial space above the small of her back, right over her kidneys. The man had a thing for vital organs.

Every instinct warred with what she had to do if she was to have a chance to keep Stanton alive. Getting in the vehicle was all but a warrant for her death, but she couldn't risk Stanton's life, too. Getting into Jimenez's SUV was her only choice. She had complete faith that Stanton would use every available resource to save her.

As she was stuffed into the back of the SUV's hatchback, she felt the weight of the phone on her thigh and risked a look back to where Stanton had been. One last connection to help her through.

He was gone.

STANTON WAS ON his last shred of sanity. His only reprieve was the fact that both Troy and David had vehicles and were following Jimenez's. The DEA agent was lagging behind because he'd been positioned inside, and Stanton had to wait for Troy to run out of where he'd hidden and get his car. The other officers were scrambling to follow, and they all relied on Dominique's phone's information. The SUV she'd been taken in was out of sight, through the copse of trees that lined portions of the property. It felt like years when Troy pulled up to where Stanton had concealed himself. He jumped into the passenger seat. Troy floored it before Stanton got the door closed.

"We can't lose her." He watched the map on his phone. He and Dominique had synced GPS systems. She was a blinking dot about a mile away on the drive that circumvented the resort. "Stay on this road. He's a mile ahead of us, driving around the grounds on the access road. What the hell is he doing?"

"We're good. You've still got comms with her, right?" Troy expertly drove at top speed along the graveled path.

"She still has her phone but can't talk or they'll know. Wait…she's texting!" He stared at the jumping dots, willing words to form.

Locked in back of car. Blacked out back here. Impossible to see where I'm going or what they're doing. Partition between me and them. Heard gunshot. Think he killed Blanchard.

Exultation urged him to not give up, to keep the belief they'd get through this. That somehow he'd help her, because he sure hadn't done her any favors by not being in the kitchen when she'd needed him.

Are you okay? He'd seen the blade dip into her dress and prayed it hadn't broken her skin or worse.

I'm good. I lo—

Her text cut off and he switched to the map. "They've stopped. They're at the resort's beach—here, turn right—and the location looks like, like…" His heart stopped for several beats, and he struggled to breathe. He didn't want any of his organs to work, not if what he was seeing was true. The pulsing red dot indicated that Jimenez had driven onto the resort's infamous pier, used for romantic wedding shots.

"What is it?" Troy's professional edge cut through Stanton's fear.

"It looks like she's in the middle of the lake. In the water." Alone with Pablo Jimenez. The man who'd put a hit out on her was going to make good on the threat himself.

DOMINIQUE FELT THE car stop. She prepared for the back hatch to open. She was on her back, her legs poised. When it lifted, she waited for Jimenez to move. When his hands reached forward under the hatch she reared into a back arch and kicked at him with all her might. One of her feet landed in his face but his surprised grunt of pain held no satisfaction for her, not as long as she had to fight for her life. She hadn't been able to finish the text to Stanton, because the car had stopped and she wasn't about to let Jimenez haul her out like a sack of potatoes.

Using his momentary confusion, she slid out and righted herself, and ran for her life. One step, two, three—

She came to a dead halt as something stopped her midstride, so violently she fell flat down, her hands catching her. Splinters dug into her palms as she realized he'd stepped on the long skirt, trapping her. The dock was under her hands, her knees, water surging around in the bay that the venue used for photo ops. Was this how it was going to end for her? Gutted and tossed off the pier?

Two boots were on either side of her as the kingpin crouched over her. She was on her stomach, on her elbows. She could buck up, try to hit him in the privates with her head—

"Turn. Over." The cold steel of a different weapon— a gun—at her temple. And he still had that knife, because he flashed it in front of her eyes. "Now!" he growled and she slowly, methodically, got to all fours, trying to figure out how to get on her feet. She could dive off the pier, hope his aim was awful and that she'd be pulled out of the icy depths in time. The sounds of slamming doors reached her and she knew that at least she wasn't alone. But she never wanted Stanton to witness her death at the hands of this cruel, sick man. As she attempted to stand, though, her hair was painfully pulled as Jimenez flipped her over onto her back. She was vulnerable, staring up at him.

Astride her, Jimenez leaned in and she felt his breath on her face. He had a weapon pointed between her eyes and a knife at her rib cage, and in a moment of horrifying clarity she understood what he was doing. If Stanton or the other officers shot at him, he'd collapse atop her, stabbing her to death, even if he didn't fire a bullet in her brain before he gasped his last.

"If you're going to kill me, at least tell me why you did it."

"Why does anyone do anything? Grave Gulch is mine, my area. Charlie Hamm was like all the other dealers who got a case of the guilts over what they'd done. So he tried to turn my best dealers around. That was his first mistake. He should have shut up and been glad he'd only gotten years."

"So you paid Blanchard to lie on the stand about Hamm?"

"Of course I did."

"Where's Blanchard now?"

"I didn't find him useful any longer. Much like you." The barrel pressed deeper in her skull and she knew he wouldn't be able to crouch like this forever.

"You'll never get away with it. You're going to be caught."

"No, *querida*. You can't see it, but there's a skimmer craft awaiting me at the end of this pier. I'll be in Canada sipping on cerveza for lunch, before your body is cold. Before the fish finish you off."

She let him talk, and in the one instant he glanced up and looked down the pier, presumably at his escape boat, she made the move of her life as she lifted her leg up and kicked him as hard as she could in his privates. At the same time, she pushed at his arm, moving the knife blade the precious inches that allowed her to twist to the side without getting stabbed.

Caught by surprise, he teetered on one foot, still holding the gun and knife, one in each hand. Dominique shoved against his chest with all her might, prepared to be dragged into the lake with him. But a gunshot rang out, and she saw his shoulder jerk. The knife blade was so sharp it cut through her skirt in a perfect arc, and took yards of fabric with Jimenez as he plunged into the lake. She scrambled to her feet and ran back toward the beach, toward the man at the end of the pier who ran toward her, gun in hand.

Stanton.

"GET DOWN!" STANTON YELLED, his relief that Jimenez had been hit and that Dominique had broken free short-lived as the man surfaced and leveled his weapon on her. Stanton stopped, fired his second bullet for the day.

Gunfire rent the air, throwing chunks of the wooden pier airborne. Stanton ran. There was no way to be certain that the fire was friendly, and there was nothing he could do if they were surrounded by cartel shooters. He had to get to Dominique.

Dominique wasn't going to stop for anything, either, as she barreled toward him.

More gunfire, but this time he saw Jimenez fall backward, clutching the hand that had held the gun. Pounding steps behind him, the other officers moving in to apprehend the kingpin. The splash when Jimenez hit the water, the same water he'd planned to dump Dominique's body in.

Dominique.

He stopped in his tracks, allowed it to sink in that she wasn't dead. She'd made it.

No thanks to you.

He'd put her life at risk.

"Stanton!" His name, spoken by her, the sweetest gift. He held up his hands to stop her; he didn't deserve to hold her ever again. But when she wrapped her arms around him, his own mirrored hers and he held as tight as he could without crushing her.

"Dom."

"Oh my heavens, I thought I'd never get to see you again." She sobbed against his chest and he sank his face into her tangled locks, breathed in the scent of her. He wasn't worthy of her but he couldn't stop from surrendering to the embrace.

"You made it, babe."

She pulled back. "No, Stanton, *we* made it."

STANTON'S EYES SHUTTERED the moment she said *we*. His body tensed, and the warmth she'd clung to disappeared when he took a step back. He shrugged out of his jacket and helped her into it. Good thing, as she was shaking all over. A combination of cold, shock and relief. It was impossible to pinpoint any one emotion. Except the one singular feeling she had for Stanton.

"Stanton, I tried to text you." Maybe he hadn't seen it. She had to tell him.

He held up his hand. "Don't. You've been through so much. You're a hero, Dominique. You helped bring down someone who's been Grave Gulch's scourge. And you rescued yourself."

"Now wait one minute, Stanton Colton. I wouldn't have known how to do any of those defensive moves without the training you gave me. And if I hadn't had you to fight for, to come back to, I don't know…" She couldn't finish as sobs broke through again, tears spilled, whipped away by the lake wind.

Flashing lights caught her glance and she saw two EMT units arriving, along with several police cruisers. "Holy cannoli, I had no idea so many LEA were here." She looked at him. "Did you know?"

"No. They weren't part of the original plan, but Troy and the DEA agent called them in two hours ago when intel revealed Jimenez might be here. But no one has a recent photo of him and didn't know who to look for."

"Wait—so Troy knew Jimenez was here? Did he tell you?"

"No. He couldn't."

"So I didn't have to throw my back out? There were snipers all around?"

"No sharpshooter was going to risk the shot while Jimenez had both the gun and knife on you." His face contorted in pain and she knew it wasn't physical. Her heart, their heart—because it was one, she didn't doubt it any longer—hurt.

"Stanton, I'm okay, we're okay. Look." She held up her arms, turned around, her one leg bare where Jimenez's knife had cut through the skirt. But he wasn't looking, he was letting go of her hands, making way for the EMTs jogging up to them. "Stanton, wait!" Desperation clawed through her shock, through the adrenaline coursing into her body. "We are not ending it this way."

Stanton stepped one foot closer, held a hand up to halt the EMT. "Give us a minute, will you?"

"Ah, sir, we've got to tend to her."

He turned back to her. "You made it out okay, and that's all I was assigned to do."

"But—but we aren't done, Stanton. Your job may be over, sure. Hasn't this taught us about what's most important?"

"What's most important is that you're safe and alive. And my job here is finished."

Pain wracked her and it wasn't from the assault by Jimenez. This was one-hundred percent heartbreak. "Is there nothing I can say to change your mind?"

He didn't answer, instead stepping back and nodding to the EMTs to move in. Tears streamed down her cheeks, their warmth zero comfort as she was forced to see reality. Nothing had changed between her and Stanton. Not as far as he was concerned.

"Ma'am, come with us. Are you able to walk?" The young woman in an EMT uniform placed a space blanket around her and Dominique realized how very, very cold she was. Her heart felt as if it was freezing inside her chest, which seemed empty as the one thing that had kept her going walked away, toward the blue flashing lights. It shouldn't have surprised her. He'd said that when the assignment was over, he'd walk away. For once she wished Stanton wasn't a man of his word, so damn stoic. That he'd have realized he, too, was still in love with her. Which clearly he wasn't, because a man in love fought for his soul mate.

"Ma'am, you okay?" Dominique blinked, looked at the EMT, whose face was stamped with concern. "It's warm in the truck."

"Okay." She let the EMT walk her to the emergency vehicle, too numb to do anything but comply. She'd used up her defiance against Jimenez, and it had saved her life. But she'd lost her heart, the one man she'd ever loved.

As the EMTs took her vitals and hooked her up to a saline drip "as a precaution against shock," she watched Jimenez as he was wheeled by on a stretcher, his shoulder and arms wrapped in bandages and an oxygen mask on his ugly face. Her mind tried to connect the dots; she'd gotten him to confess, had proven Charlie Hamm's innocence. He'd go away for life with the almost certain conviction the DA would obtain with the evidence she'd been instrumental in uncovering. The *Gazette* might get that Pulitzer after all. But no matter what her thoughts revealed, nothing mattered to her heart. Broken, shattered, hollow, lost.

Without Stanton at her side, her joy was extinguished.

Chapter Sixteen

Two weeks passed with no word from Stanton. After the shock at all that had happened wore off, Dominique had thrown herself into the story. The initial overview had made headlines but now she was writing the deeper parts, including how she'd gone undercover to sneak into the resort. Of course that hadn't gone so well, but at least it had worked out in the end. She'd been interviewed by several television news outlets, and her reporting skills had garnered accolades she'd only ever dreamed of.

Just as stubborn was her belief, deep down, that somehow, someday, Stanton would get over his pride over how the takedown hadn't gone quite the way he'd planned. She acknowledged that it had to have been difficult to see her in such a vulnerable position, but she'd survived. They'd survived. Why couldn't he see that?

"I'm so impressed with all you've accomplished here, Dominique." Melissa sat back in her desk chair. They'd spent the last two hours going over statements and checking facts. "And I appreciate that you agree we're on the same team."

"Of course we are. Have you had any luck figuring out if there are more corrupt people at GGPD?"

Melissa shook her head. "I have my suspicions but it's slow going. Nothing worse than a corrupt cop, I'll tell you."

"I'm sorry you're dealing with this."

"You sound like Stanton." Melissa must have seen the shadow pass over her face. "Speaking of my brother, what's going on with you two? He's tight-lipped with me."

"Nothing's going on. He was so upset with himself that I was ever in danger with Jimenez. I haven't been able to break through his wall, and he hasn't spoken to me since the resort takedown."

Melissa sighed. "My brother can be an ass. This is all his pride. He'll come around, Dominique. I've no doubt you're the love of his life. My only question is, is he yours?"

"I'm sorry, but I can't comment on an ongoing investigation." She winked and Melissa laughed. They promised to get together for lunch soon and Dominique left the station. It was a perfect spring day with bright blue skies and a hint of warmth in the breeze that came off the lake. She couldn't help smiling to herself at Melissa's observations.

The tables had turned on her communications with Stanton. Unlike when she'd walked away from him two years ago, this time she was the one texting and calling him, leaving messages that went unanswered. Her one consolation was that he hadn't blocked her.

Soledad had cared for her the first few days she'd been back in her apartment, and she appreciated it but they all knew the only person she wanted at her side was unable to be there, away licking his emotional wounds. Her father had promised to continue to avoid walking his boxer dogs in Grave Gulch Park, to her relief. Her twin had been a huge support and texted her frequently to keep her chin up and have faith that Stanton would be back.

All of these thoughts whirled in her mind as she left GGPD and walked to meet Desiree Colton to get the sketch artist's story on spotting Randall Bowe. The colorful playground equipment caught her eye and she headed toward a bench where she saw the woman with a tiny tot, her son, Danny. Dominique's heart constricted as she recalled Desiree's son had been kidnapped back in January.

"Desiree, hey!" Dominique stood in front of the mother and child, smiling at Danny's cherubic smile. The boy's tiny hands clutched a plastic dinosaur to his chest as he leaned against his mom, his gaze looking up at Dominique in question. If she ever had a child, she'd never want them to go through what he had. Desiree's eyes were bright and hopeful but the lines around them highlighted the hell she'd lived through.

"Hi, Dominique. Here, have a seat."

"Mommy, I want swing."

"Honey, play with your dinosaur here on the ground

for a bit, then I promise I'll push you." Desiree hugged her son and guided him to a spot next to her feet.

The toddler plopped down and began to push the plastic beast through the wood chips, making growling noises.

"Godzilla has nothing on that dinosaur."

Desiree smiled. "He loves it. Ever since… January, he hasn't let go of it."

"I'm so sorry for all you've been through, and I promise this won't take long. Thank you so much for agreeing to meet with me."

"I would have sooner, but I had to have Chief's go-ahead." Desiree's expression was apologetic.

"I understand." She pulled out her notebook and re-read her notes.

Desiree's phone sounded and she fumbled in a large combo tote/diaper bag. "I can never find my phone when I want to."

"I get it." Dominique wrote down a couple of quick questions she wanted answered, but was interrupted by a high-pitched scream.

"Mooooommmmyyy!" Danny was halfway across the playground, tucked under the arm of a woman in a straw hat, yelling for Desiree. His chubby hands reached toward them on the bench.

"Danny!" Desiree yelled as she shot like a rocket from the bench and ran to him. The woman carrying Danny looked over her shoulder, spotted Desiree coming after them, and dropped the child as if he were nothing more than a pillow. The woman took off and disappeared through the trees at the end of the park. Shock and panic pulsated through Dominique as the unbelievable scene played out. Her hands shook and she remembered she had her phone, she could get help.

Dominique verified that Desiree had Danny in her arms before she pulled out her phone and dialed Melissa's number. She reported the attempted kidnapping to Melissa, and when Desiree and Danny returned, handed the phone to Desiree. "It's Chief Colton."

Desiree's hand shook and she wasn't letting go of Danny. Dominique guided her to the bench and helped her sit down.

"Chief. It was this same woman I've seen before. I've actually seen her, in that hat and sunglasses, at this playground the last few days. It could have been Hannah." Dominique knew Everleigh's grandmother Hannah had kidnapped Danny once before. "I can't deal with this. Do you think Danny's being—" She cut herself off, obviously aware of Danny's innocent ears. Desiree was clearly concerned that Danny was being targeted, that this attempt wasn't random.

Dominique seethed with frustration and anger that Danny had been almost taken again. Desiree and he had been through enough. As soon as the call ended, Desiree's eyes filled with tears.

"You're okay? Danny's okay, aren't you, buddy?" Dominique did what she'd want Soledad to do if she was in the same situation. "Are they sending out a unit?"

Desiree nodded. "They'll be here any second. Thank

God." She hugged her son to her, her grief at almost losing him a second time palpable.

"I'll stay here until an officer arrives. And we'll do the interview another time."

"Oh no, we won't. These awful people have had enough hold over all of us for too long." Desiree looked at her with steely determination. "What do you want to know about Randall Bowe?"

STANTON WENT OVER his intended words, the phrases he'd memorized, again as he drove out to the de la Vega house. Thankfully, Rigo had agreed to his plan. He didn't risk telling Soledad every detail as she'd tell Dominique in a Michigan minute, and this was one time he wanted to truly surprise her. It was the least he could do after all he'd put her through.

It'd be easy to back out, to hide behind the truth that he'd let her down and was too protective to ever be comfortable with what she did for a living. But she, and he—*they*—deserved more. Their love deserved every iota of effort and work, no matter how difficult. Because love like this came about once in a lifetime, and he was tired of living his life without her.

He hoped she would still have him. She'd kept up a constant stream of encouraging texts and voice mails over the past fourteen days. It was difficult to not respond, but he wanted—no, needed—for her to see that he'd changed, too. He would have her any way she agreed to be with him.

Nerves made his palms slick on the steering wheel,

so unlike him. Yet it was nothing compared to how he'd perspired in abject fear as Dominique had lain vulnerable on that pier, under the threat of vile Jimenez.

Let. It. Go. If he allowed the memories of that day to rule his actions, he'd never forgive himself.

Pulling into the de la Vegas' driveway felt like coming home. They were as much his family as his own and had been since he had first dated Dominique. Her car was already in the driveway, but if their plans were on track, she had no idea that anyone was here.

The hands that waved at him and gave him a thumbs-up through the garage windows made him smile. The family was all hiding, waiting for his signal to burst back into their own home.

He walked to the porch and rang the bell.

Running behind. Be there within the hour.

Dominique stared at Soledad's text, annoyance at her twin flaring. She fired back her own.

What do you mean you're running late? Where is everyone else?

She thought that it was going to be family pizza night, but when she'd arrived at her father's home, no one else was here. Even Rosa and Rita were nowhere to be found.

The doorbell rang and she paused. It was past delivery time, and it was a Saturday night, so it wasn't the postal service. Maybe her dad had ordered the pizza since everyone seemed to be late, and hoped someone would be here to get it.

When she looked through the door's side windowpanes, she paused. The profile was one she'd memorized, one every inch of her being recognized.

Stanton.

Opening the door, she looked him over from head to toe.

"Where's the pizza?"

"No pizza. But I have these." He brought out from behind his back the largest bouquet of red roses that she'd ever seen and handed them to her. "Can I come in?"

"I don't know. Is this going to be an easy conversation, or a difficult one?"

"It all depends on you, Dom." His eyes were brighter than usual and her breath caught.

"Stanton, please don't get upset."

"I'm not upset, babe. I'm in love. And I'm lost. I'm nothing without you."

She moved aside. "Come in, then." The roses were heavy in her arms, arms that only wanted to hold Stanton, and never let him go. But they gave her shaking hands something to grasp as she watched him enter the house and close the door, walk the few steps to where she stood in the foyer.

"Did you get my texts? My voice mails?"

He nodded, his gaze never leaving her face. As if he was memorizing every millimeter of it. Hope blossomed under her rib cage but she stood still, wanting him to have his chance to say what he wanted to say, to know she wasn't going anywhere. Never again.

"I did. And I read them, and listened to them, at least a hundred times each."

"Why didn't you reply?" She sounded like the breathless woman in love that she was.

"I had to get things right in my head. It was my fault that you were alone with Jimenez and Blanchard at the resort. I know what you're going to say, and you know what? It doesn't matter. I still got to you in time, because I helped you learn all those spectacular defensive maneuvers. See? I listen to you, I do. Always. Between you knowing how to handle yourself and me shooting, along with everyone that was there that day, we got through it. We make a great team, Dominique. I'm in love with you, always have been, always will be. And I'll be next to you in any way, shape or form that you'll take me. It's your call, Dom. No more wedding bell pressure from me."

"What if I *want* to marry you?"

His head did that tiny tilt that melted her heart. "Do you?"

She nodded. "I do. If I'd been more mature the first time you asked, I would have stayed, worked things out with you back then. But you're right, I was so into my job that I was missing everything. My family, a life outside of work, and most important, you. Being with you, working together these past weeks, has taught me that I can have both. I can be with you and be me. In fact, I'm the best me when I'm with you. I'm in love with you, too, Stanton. I love you and I'm here, whenever you want to marry me. If you still do."

He took the few steps needed to be face-to-face, and leaning over the roses, kissed her with such reverence that her stomach quaked as her heart blossomed. When he lifted his mouth from hers, he grinned.

"What is it, Stanton?"

"Give me the roses first." He opened his arms and she handed him back the humongous bouquet, which he placed on the living room sofa. But instead of walking back to her, he turned toward the kitchen.

"Okay, everyone, come on out!"

The garage door opened and Dominique watched in delight as her sister and dad, aunts and uncles, along with the dogs, poured through the door, filling the kitchen and living room. Frank and Italia Colton followed, as did Melissa and her fiancé Antonio, Clarke and Everleigh, and Travis and Tatiana, plus the rest of the Colton family. Stanton smiled at everyone. "Now remember the plan, everyone."

He turned back toward her and walked to where she still stood in the foyer, as surprised as she was awestruck at what she knew he had taken planning. And thinking. And most of all, love.

Stanton's eyes glittered and he took her hands in his. "I was hoping you'd say what you did about marrying me." He pulled something out of his trouser pocket and sank to his knee. "Will you marry me, Dominique de la Vega?"

"Yes, Stanton Colton. Yes!"

He placed a stunning white diamond on her left ring finger in one swift move, and before she could admire it he was on his feet, pulling her into his arms. Where she belonged.

The family cheered and clapped, wiped joyful tears from their cheeks as Dominique and Stanton sealed their commitment with a kiss.

Dominique knew this was what mattered most. Family, love and Stanton.

* * * * *

COMING SOON!

We really hope you enjoyed reading this book.
If you're looking for more romance, be sure to
head to the shops when new books are
available on

Thursday 29th April

To see which titles are coming soon, please visit
millsandboon.co.uk/nextmonth

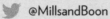
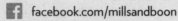

MILLS & BOON

THE HEART OF ROMANCE

A ROMANCE FOR EVERY READER

ODERN

Prepare to be swept off your feet by sophisticated, sexy and seductive heroes, in some of the world's most glamourous and romantic locations, where power and passion collide.

STORICAL

Escape with historical heroes from time gone by. Whether your passion is for wicked Regency Rakes, muscled Vikings or rugged Highlanders, awaken the romance of the past.

EDICAL

Set your pulse racing with dedicated, delectable doctors in the high-pressure world of medicine, where emotions run high and passion, comfort and love are the best medicine.

rue Love

Celebrate true love with tender stories of heartfelt romance, from the rush of falling in love to the joy a new baby can bring, and a focus on the emotional heart of a relationship.

Desire

Indulge in secrets and scandal, intense drama and plenty of sizzling hot action with powerful and passionate heroes who have it all: wealth, status, good looks…everything but the right woman.

EROES

Experience all the excitement of a gripping thriller, with an intense romance at its heart. Resourceful, true-to-life women and strong, fearless men face danger and desire - a killer combination!

To see which titles are coming soon, please visit

millsandboon.co.uk/nextmonth

JOIN US ON SOCIAL MEDIA!

Stay up to date with our latest releases, author news and gossip, special offers and discounts, and all the behind-the-scenes action from Mills & Boon...

 millsandboon

 millsandboonuk

 millsandboon

It might just be true love...

MILLS & BOON
MEDICAL
Pulse-Racing Passion

Set your pulse racing with dedicated, delectable doctors in the high-pressure world of medicine, where emotions run high and passion, comfort and love are the best medicine.